On the Road . . .

"Sit down there." Augur pointed to the neat little bench behind the truck driver's seat. "I'll ride up front."

Cecilia folded down like a rag doll being dumped.

Augur looked across at the old black driver. The truck roared into gear and the man tabbed the radio on to an urgent voice.

". . . as soon as the criminals are apprehended, we are assured that our streets will be returned to normal . . ."

He glanced at the driver, who went on with his work, his movements smooth and automatic.

The announcer read off about as perfect a description of the two of them as you could get. Damn. Augur looked at the driver again. Nothing. Did he hear?

Augur cleared his throat, his mind already buzzing with lies. "You might be wondering—"

"Ain't no one in the cab," the driver cut in, looking straight ahead, his voice old and raspy. "So nobuddy to talk wi'd."

Augur shut up.

GENE RODDENBERRY'S EARTH: FINAL CONFLICT
Novels from Tor Books

The Arrival
by Fred Saberhagen

The First Protector
by James White

Requiem for Boone
by Debra Doyle and James D. Macdonald

Augur's Teacher
by Sherwood Smith

*Heritage**
by Doranna Durgin

*Legacy**
by Glenn R. Sixbury

*forthcoming

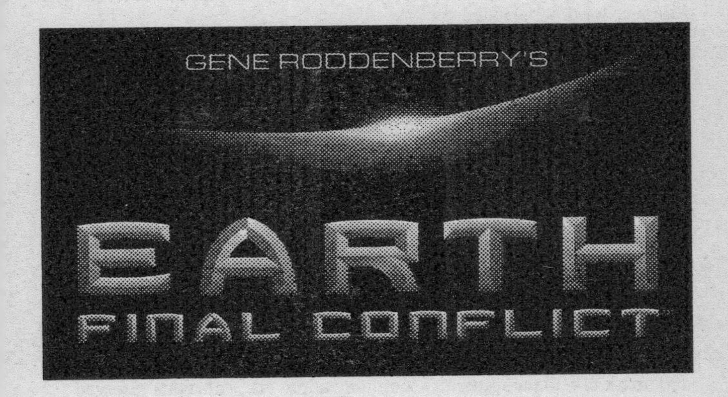

AUGUR'S TEACHER

SHERWOOD SMITH

A TOM DOHERTY ASSOCIATES BOOK
NEW YORK

This is a work of fiction. All the characters and events portrayed in these stories are either fictitious or are used fictitiously.

GENE RODDENBERRY'S EARTH: FINAL CONFLICT—
AUGUR'S TEACHER

Edited by James Frenkel

A Tor Book
Published by Tom Doherty Associates, LLC
175 Fifth Avenue
New York, NY 10010

www.tor.com

ISBN: 0-812-55734-4
Library of Congress Catalog Card Number : 2001027699

First Edition: August 2001
First mass market edition: December 2003

Printed in the United States of America

0 9 8 7 6 5 4 3 2 1

To the teachers of the world.
Overworked, underpraised,
busy shaping the future. . . .

ACKNOWLEDGMENTS

I have a lot of people to thank: first and foremost Dave Trowbridge, my tech wizard extraordinaire; Amtrak, for a fascinating journey from Los Angeles to Boston and back again; Joe J. Rodriguez, an investigator I met on a train (though not that one) who gave me some tips for my P.I.s.; my agent, Valerie Smith, who let me sit in her house and watch a zillion hours of videotapes; Gregory Feeley, Pamela Miller, and their lovely children for graciously hosting me in New Haven and then tirelessly answering a bombardment of phone calls and E-mail about Yale. And, finally, my thanks to the anonymous Bonesman who left the back gate open one pretty day in August 2000, so that I could help myself to a little tour.

—SHERWOOD SMITH
January 1, 2001
Orange County, California

P.S.—The Senegalese monks of Keur Moussa are real, and their music is exquisite. Check it out.

ONE

The fourth graders of Miss Robin's class groaned along with the rest of the school when the bell rang for lineup, but it was a groan without conviction, the groan of solidarity with the rest of the student body.

The fourth grade loved Miss Robin's class, enough to be kinda sorta sorry to see the school year drawing to an end, though of course it wouldn't do to come right out and admit it.

Cecilia Robin had worked very hard to make it that way.

They filed from the bright Southern California sun into the shadowy room and found Miss Robin waiting for them. It always took a few seconds for your eyes to adjust, so at first she was just a short, round grown-up lady shape, but as the kids stashed lunch pails and backpacks and dropped into their chairs, the shadows in the room melted away and there were all the bulletin boards they'd made together this year—the California Mission over by the blackboards, the math tangram puzzles opposite, the creative writing corner by the cupboards—and Miss Robin was writing on the board, her brown hair as usual almost falling out of its bun, her glasses slipping down her nose.

Hers was a plain face, but a kind one, full of smiles, her light eyes steady as they looked at you. Really, really looked, not just glared, or frowned, or glanced down and then away, like most adults.

The children gradually stopped whispering and nudging one another as they turned their attention to the blackboard.

As for Miss Robin, fifteen years of experience had

honed her sense of timing. She didn't turn around until the room was silent, the little restless noises stopped.

When she did turn, she still did not speak. Instead she watched the kids shift their attention from her to the board, where they saw written in big letters,

WHY VOTE?

The fourth graders looked from the board back to her again.

Then she said, "Remember in January, when we discussed the California Convention and the debates on who could become a citizen and who could vote? I promised you a demonstration after we finished our text?"

The children all nodded.

She said, "All right, then. So. Who remembers? In 1849, could women vote?"

Hands waved wildly.

"Jamal?"

"No, Miss Robin." Jamal wriggled and added, "Neither could Chinese people, or—"

Miss Robin nodded. "And several other groups, each of whom were granted their rights over the years afterward. I'm glad you remembered. But right now, I want to skip to the present. Who can't vote now?"

Six or seven voices yelled out, "Children!"

Miss Robin waited, acting as if she'd heard nothing.

Hands waved this time. Some of their owners rose half off their chairs, and a couple of kids grunted "Oh! Oh! Oh!" in their efforts to be noticed.

Those kids still kept forgetting that grunters and wigglers *never* got called on.

"Aisling?"

A soft, quiet voice almost whispered, "Children and people who aren't citizens yet."

"Like my grandma!" Wu cried out, and then he clapped his hands over his mouth.

Miss Robin gave him a stern look over her glasses, but her mouth smiled, just a little, and Wu grinned back.

"Why should they want to vote?" Miss Robin asked.

"Why was it so important to those groups who were denied their rights—"

Just then the door opened, and there entered a tall, distinguished-looking woman with gray hair and ebony skin. The principal! The wrigglers stopped wriggling, the whisperers clammed up, and everyone sat up straight.

Miss Robin nodded to the class, and the children rose and chorused, "Good morning, Mrs. Pinochet."

"Good morning, children," the principal said in her quiet, softly accented tones that somehow never failed to get instant obedience.

Louise Pinochet opened the door wider and watched the impact on students and teacher as her guest glided into the room. Utter silence met the tall Taelon who faced them with equal quietness.

Miss Robin blinked, for a moment looking just as blank as the kids.

A Taelon? *Here?* Taelons were the business of governments and television news, and maybe occasional flyovers in their oddly pretty bug-shaped vessels. Even those flyovers, rare as they were, caused comment. No one in this classroom, child or adult, had ever expected to see a Taelon in person—and here was one, standing right there next to the lunch cubby!

Miss Robin thought, Why?

"We have a surprise visitor today," the principal said in her cordial voice, the one she used when a parent showed up on the warpath for some reason. Mrs. Pinochet used just that voice when she begged a few moments of time for a "conference." It signaled to Miss Robin, at least, that this visit was neither expected nor sought. "This is Companion Sector Adviser on Education Za'el, who has come here to observe the classes at our school. Please, carry on with your lesson," she added.

Another signal, Miss Robin thought. *Could* this being be here just for her vote demo?

No, that kind of thinking was just egotistical.

Cecilia Robin firmly turned her eyes away from that tall,

slender figure, the smooth hairless head, the large light blue eyes. Really, the Taelons in person—if this one were any example—were far more . . . what, imposing? No. The Taelon stood there at the wall, not moving, not speaking, hands loosely folded together in a pose of peace. Imposing wasn't the word, for there was no overt threat, no attempt to take over the class. Compelling? Yes. But how much of that effect was the knowledge that these aliens had in effect conquered Earth, however peacefully?

She cleared her throat, jammed her glasses back up her nose, and forced her attention back onto the children, who were all facing her in unnaturally obedient postures, but she felt their attention pinioned somewhere between the principal—a known authority—and the Taelon, who represented the unknown.

"Why is it important to vote?" Cece asked.

No hands, of course. Instead the children sat amazingly straight and wiggle-free. Before visitors they would answer only a question they were confident about. Speculation did not happen before strangers.

Cece looked around at the children—consciously avoiding the figure next to the lunch cubby—and though she had been doing this demo for years, she felt her usual fire about the subject of freedom and choice damping before the implied danger in this unannounced and unexpected visit.

"Let's try an experiment," she said, forcing her tone to stay upbeat and cheery, though she knew she sounded as fake as the children's unnaturally alert posture looked. "Let's pretend it's September and we have to decorate the classroom for the rest of the year. But what color is going to be our main choice?" She looked around. Ordinarily the children would be waving their hands and grunting in their efforts to name their favorite colors, but now they just sat quietly, sometimes stealing covert looks at that still figure in the slightly glittering peachy-blue "skin," standing over there by the bulletin board.

So she picked up her packet of paper squares she'd cut

up earlier and bustled round the classroom, placing a paper on each desk, which gave her another minute or so to get her thoughts in order.

"Since everyone has a different favorite color, how can we be fair if we can pick only one for our decorations? The only fair method is to vote, and whatever color the majority selects will be our choice. Of course some won't like it, but if most do, then it's as fair as we can get—and next year, in fifth grade, the ones who didn't get their choice will have another chance."

As she spoke the words she'd spoken before so many classes over the past several years, her mind dashed away between question and possible answer. Why did this surprise visit have to happen today? Why now? Why not yesterday morning, when they were reviewing the delegates to the California Convention, or tomorrow morning, when they'd review the Treaty of Guadalupe Hidalgo? Why not after recess, when they'd be busy with dividing fractions, or after lunch, when they reviewed adverbs and How Bees Make Honey?

Because it's no surprise, not for them. Only for me. Is that because the Taelons object to my little demonstration? Inner conviction resolved into a little ball of anger, which she resolutely did not show.

And, as she plunked down the last bit of paper, she said in her chirpiest Parent Night voice, "Now, remember. You are all citizens of this classroom and have the right to vote. So write down your favorite color in the rainbow. Fold the papers—no talking—and pass them forward. Tomas, you collect them, please, and hand them to ShaNissa, who is going to help me tally them."

Ordinarily there would have been nudges, exchanges of looks, and covert whisperings, as rival cliques of girls—as long as there are classrooms there will be rival cliques of girls—ascertained almost by semaphore what color the leader of their clique liked, so they could vote in solidarity. And the inevitable riff of gross whispers from some of the boys, "What color are guts?" or "Yeah, puke green! Co-ool!" meant to challenge the girls and to get attention.

Now there was no sound, except for Tomas's new shoes squeaking on the old linoleum and then ShaNissa's assured voice as she called the colors out.

Cece wrote them all on the board—green, black, purple, pink, red, lavender being the most popular—and put tick marks under the corresponding color. Some—brown, polka dot, orange, blood, barf yellow—got only a single vote and no tick marks underneath.

At the end she turned around and gave the class another fake smile. Now their attention was divided between the visitor, who really did stand silently, she had to give him—*it*—that much credit, and the numbers on the board. Anything that directly concerned them was the strongest attraction, even over a passive Taelon intruder.

Finally the last vote was read out, and ShaNissa put the papers in the recycle bin. From her spot behind the teacher, she watched gravely not just her classmates but also the Taelon and her teacher and the principal as well. The adults seemed as still and stiff as the kids.

"There," Cece said. "Looks like we have a winner: Twelve of you like green best, five like purple, lavender got three votes, and black, red, and pink two each. So we could say that green is the class's favorite color, couldn't we?"

Nods—with sidelong looks to see what the visitor thought. Meanwhile, a shadow flickered in the window; Cece, the only one facing it, saw a tall man walk slowly by. The Companion's human Protector? She thought of those CVI things—Cyber-Viral Implants, didn't they call them? All she knew was that those interfaces between Taelon and human communication technology were implanted in one's neck, near the spine, and she repressed an inward shiver.

"Now, supposing this. Who voted for green?"

Fourteen hands went up, almost all girls. A fast look telegraphed between two girls, and a fifteenth rose. The girls had won, as usual, for they'd already learned the effect of social suasion; the boys had splintered their possibility of winning by trying to outgross one another.

Cece did not count those fifteen hands out loud. Instead, she said in her blandest voice, "You, Ashley, don't vote in the next election. Why? You always win. So this time you won't even bother. Taylor, you and Kayla decide you're going to go shopping instead." Covert giggles. "Merritt, you have a little cold and don't want to go out in the horrid weather." She pointed to the sunshine outside and got a louder giggle. And she went down the line, giving each of the fifteen an excuse; as she called the names, most of them bridled self-consciously, and at least half sneaked looks at the visitors for a reaction, which they did not get.

"Now, who voted for purple?"

Four hands went up, the one girl who'd changed her mind about green looking around guiltily as though her name had been on the piece of paper.

Cece assigned excuses to each of the four, and then she passed out papers again. As she moved around the room, she said, "I want those of you who were given excuses to draw a picture on your paper, or keep it, or make a fortune-teller with it, but don't vote. The rest of you, write down your colors again."

When the votes had been gathered, Cece switched colors of chalk and began a new column. This time, lavender had the most votes—the original three.

"There," Cece said, standing back. "The class favorite is now lavender!"

She paused for the usual *Eeuw!* from the boys at a color that had been deemed a "girl" color, but this time the reaction did not come. A few feet shuffled; the compelling presence over by the story board sustained the silence.

"Don't think it's fair?" Cece said, looking around. "Only three votes decided for the entire class, after all. And so all the rest of the year, our room will be decorated in lavender, and we'll make a lavender banner for our class at the

School Olympics next-to-last day, and we'll wear lavender name tags when we go on our field trip Monday. Does that make you happy?"

A few shaken heads—followed by quick looks to the Taelon for a reaction. There was none.

"Since the rest of you didn't bother to vote, you have no real grounds to complain, have you?"

Taylor Throckmorton-Ockleberry, who desperately wanted to be a leader, glanced at the two alpha girls in the class for cues and then shot her hand into the air. The kids were beginning to revert from wooden effigies into themselves. And Taylor would be the first one to try to get the Taelon's attention.

Cece said, "Yes, Taylor?"

Taylor sneaked a look over at the Taelon standing peacefully at the wall and then said in her prissiest voice, "But you told us winners not to vote, Miss Robin."

"I was just making a point," Cece responded. "Remember our talk about analogies?"

Taylor bridled in her chair, again glancing at the other girls for approval. She nodded when she saw the two class alpha girls nodding and then sat back with a self-important air. The real point for Taylor and friends had not been the observation about analogies, it had been the word *winner*. Girls scoring social points with one another. Did the Taelon understand that? Did he—*it*—even care?

"So," Cece said, "think about our analogy. You all represent adults over eighteen. For various reasons you could have voted but chose not to, and your excuses were the ones I assigned. The important thing is what happened. Who can define it for me?"

Taylor's hand shot up, followed by some more tentative ones. The Taelon hadn't done or said anything nasty, so now the urge to get his attention was slowly altering into daring.

"Jarrod?"

Jarrod did not look at the Taelon, but his unnaturally stiff shoulders revealed how self-conscious he felt under that alien scrutiny. "We got stuck with an ugly color," he said.

"True—from your point of view. Can anyone rephrase that? Maguire?"

Maguire Billiger-Ledundas shook back her curls, said in an airy voice—glancing at the Taelon no more than four times—"The people who voted got their choice, even though everyone else really wanted green. But the green people didn't vote the second time, so now we have to have lavender."

Now would have been the time for Cece to start her carefully worded talk about how everyone might have thought that lavender was going to win anyway, since it was the most popular color in the school, and so why bother going against it, but she hesitated when she perceived a slight movement from the Taelon.

Mrs. Pinochet's chin lifted a little. Cece knew it for a signal and waited, smiling her Parent Night Smile. Meanwhile the humanoid creature who wasn't even remotely human, but wearing a "skin," looked on impassively.

"Thank you, Miss Robin," Mrs. Pinochet said in her principal's version of the Parent Night voice. "I am sorry to interrupt, but our time is limited. Companion Za'el is willing to answer a few questions, if you have any, children?"

The kids exchanged looks, and Cece could have predicted the hands that shot up, just as she could have predicted the questions.

The Taelon nodded at the closest child. "Please."

The voice was mellow, soft, almost toneless, more pleasing to listen to than not. Hard to remember that this being was pure energy, cold fire.

"Is it true you don't have children?"

"It is true. Please?"

Now the nod to Taylor, who wriggled in her chair, checked the girls around her, then cooed, "And you don't get married either?"

Repressed giggles.

"We do not," said the even voice, the hands gesturing with slow, almost mesmerizing grace.

What are you learning from these questions? Cece thought, forcing her attention away from those hands.

The Taelon moved on, responding in that inhumanly emotionless voice to the kid versions of the same banal questions that had been asked of Taelons ever since their appearance: No, they did not eat fast food, yes, they did observe television but had no favorite shows, yes they knew what rock music was but no favorites.

After about a dozen of these nonanswers to silly questions, all in that same patient, mellow-toned voice, Mrs. Pinochet saw just as Cece did that the children's interest had switched from the getting the Taelon's attention on themselves to daring to provoke a reaction. The rude questions were imminent; from the looks of the crimson faces and smothered giggles over there in the far corner, Jeffrey Beeson, the class daredevil, was being covertly nudged by seatmates into asking about Taelon toilet habits.

Mrs. Pinochet cut in smoothly, "I'm afraid we have run out of time. I believe our visitor would like to see the other classrooms now."

A nod from Cece, and the children rose. "Good morning, Mrs. Pinochet."

The principal opened the door and led the way out.

As soon as it shut, whispers whooshed through the room like a forest fire, and the hands shot up.

Cece used her firmest voice to put out the fire. "Yes, that really was a Taelon, and no, I didn't know that there was to be a visit today." She glanced out the window, saw the two visitors enter Mr. Salazar's class. "Probably this visitor is touring all the local schools. Now, shall we return to our subject?"

Tomas said, "My dad said that's why he doesn't vote." His voice vibrated with repressed passion. "My dad says that the Taelons control everything, even the government, so why bother?"

Another forest fire of whispers, as Cece saw the visitors

open Mr. Salazar's far door and pass on to Mrs. Moore's room.

"*My* mother says that the Taelons brought us peace and prosperity," Taylor pronounced importantly. "And wonderful new technology."

"Many feel both ways," Cece said in her blandest voice, evoking Teacher Rule #47: *Never say anything that can be construed as criticism of any parent, even by kids' garbled versions of their day*. "Tomas, each adult has to make his or her own decision, of course. Your dad makes the decision that is right for him. But when you are eighteen, I want you to remember this day, and whether the Taelons are still here or not, think about whether you really want lavender chosen for the entire country, even if lavender seems to have all the pow—all the popularity. If you think green or purple is the right color you should never fail to go vote on it. Meanwhile the Taelon is learning about us, it seems. They just went to visit Mrs. Moore. Please take out your language books and have a pencil and your vocabularly journals ready to hand."

And she watched the children's sour faces and reluctant movements as they opened their desks. They would have liked to have been special, the only class chosen. Speculation would have been rife then—and would have been rife at home tonight, Cece thought, watching the kids lose interest in the Taelon in favor of vying with one another about the kinds of questions they would have *liked* to ask.

Luckily, none of them thought of watching through the windows, so they didn't see Mrs. Pinochet and the Taelon come out of Mrs. Moore's room after a forty-second tour.

And Cece made sure they didn't get time to look, or to do the mental math. "Now, open your textbooks to chapter seven. We'll begin reading the next segment. Everyone gets three sentences, but if you aren't following, you lose your turn. . . ."

TWO

The faculty lounge smelled like coffee and hot copy machine, smells that had come to mean comfort to the staff of George Washington Elementary School. Or if not comfort, at least a retreat from the endless energy of the kids and of prowling parents.

"Za'el? Who za hell is Za'el?" Jon Salazar was saying when Cece slipped in through the door.

When the appreciative chuckle died down, Trisha Liu went on, "And how do we know that he's Za'el?"

"Or a 'he'?" Marcia Cohen put in, wiggling her brows Groucho-style. "Why do we say 'he'?" she added, chin in one hand, the other stirring her coffee with a pen. "From what I hear, their testosterone count is not exactly measurable."

Jon sat back in his chair. "It's too damn hot to get into a sexism debate about Taelon pronouns! I think 'he' is a default."

"I won't argue with that," Marcia said, still stirring her coffee. "It's true they don't look like men, but they look even less like women."

A laugh from one or two of the others. Cece got a fresh bottle of water from the ancient fridge some parent had donated and leaned against the counter. Here it comes, she thought, noting the angular body language and remembering the speculative looks sent her way when she walked in.

Marcia added wryly, "If they were short and shaped like puffer pigeons, with high birdie voices, I'd say 'she.' "

Trisha shook her head. "What I want to know is if that really was Za'el. For all we know it could have been that horrible Zo'or—the Big Kahuna himself. I mean, until today I've never heard of any Companion Adviser on Education, and you'd think that might have been mentioned in the reams of garbage the district floods our boxes with."

"Pinochet say anything before school?" Old Mrs. Moore poured out her third cup of coffee.

"Zipperino." Trisha drew a forefinger through the air. "And I was in the office dealing with a parent over the phone. Saw her, and she said absolute zip."

"Ah." Mrs. Moore, who sat in the corner, snorted. Many didn't like her, for she was short-tempered and a heavy smoker, so sitting next to her at faculty meetings was no pleasure. The standing joke about Mrs. Moore was that she hadn't changed her classroom curriculum in thirty years, despite all the spectacular changes in government, technology, and district administration. Cece suspected that the woman had worked hard to perfect her basic curriculum forty years ago, when she was a young woman, and she knew sixth graders—and sixth grade—with the kind of distilled, effortless knowledge that old karate masters displayed in performing katas.

"Didn't any of you check your in-boxes?" Brad Poindexter was the most sarcastic teacher on campus—and also (the single female twentysomethings among the staff had decided) the cutest. He tapped a blue flyer lying on the table before him, drawing attention to his well-manicured hands. "You'll be relieved to know that the visit was made in the name of peace and goodwill, yada yada importance of education—"

"Bedee bedee bedee," Candace Lipsky said, rolling her eyes. "The higher they pile the hyperbole, the deeper the real reason."

"Politics," Brad said, his well-shaped mouth now sneering. "That is, if you'll pardon me, one smell you cannot wipe off your shoe."

Jon waved a sheaf of spelling papers at Cece. "Noticed they stayed longest in your class."

"Of course," Brad said, a little of that sneer remaining in

the lift of his handsome brows. "But didn't we expect that? Isn't Cecilia our local dancing bear?" He smiled his even white smile.

Cece smiled back, without showing just how much she loathed Brad Poindexter. She found his wit cruel, especially when he exercised it on kids.

"It's true," Candace said, her round brown gaze earnest. "I was watching as they blipped along the quad. Came in my room, ogled the bulletin boards for about five seconds apiece, gave one of those nods at the first graders, and then out again. In and out of the rest of the rooms faster than a fire drill."

"Well then, maybe Teacher of the Year is being scouted for Taelon Training?" Brad's joking tone and his big smile were not at all friendly.

Cece repressed a sigh. She'd been at this school four years now, and each of those four years she'd been awarded Teacher of the Year. She knew what that meant—nothing, really. She was already in the administrative eye for having won similar awards at the tough high school where she'd started her career. The rep, and the awards, seemed to transfer with her from school to school, which made her suspect the perpetuated attention was for funding purposes, if nothing else.

But even if Teacher of the Year meant little more than administrative gamesmanship, other teachers were still human beings, and behind some of those smiles here in the teachers' lounge were the same hurt or envious feelings that the most popular kid in class elections got from classmates. Which was why Cece never had kids elect one another, only colors.

Cece had long ago made herself a promise: Never participate in politics, either internal or external. And that had come to include speaking her feelings about the Taelons.

So she shrugged and smiled, jammed her glasses back up her nose, and got to her feet. "Too bad. I don't speak the language," she said to Brad, being as oblique as she could. "Well, back to grading math tests," she added to the room at large, and left, knowing that her smile was fake and feeling that nasty inward sensation that you get when you know that others are hungry for gossip flambé, and you're the one about to be dished—with relish.

"I hope," Brad said as soon as the door clicked shut, "our brilliant Miss Robin is not going to be disappointed."

Mrs. Moore thumped her mug down. "That girl wins what she does because she eats, sleeps, and dreams teaching."

Trish shrugged. "I suppose that's another way of saying she's a getalife, but whatever it is she does that I don't do netted me the funding for a brand-new art lab last year, instead of the same old bargain basement budget, and so I say, let the dancing bear keep on doin' her jig."

"And more power to her," Marcia added, jabbing a glance Brad's way.

"Ah, you gotta love women's solidarity," Brad commented, his gaze skimming the ugly plaster ceiling.

By which they all knew that he meant that the current district administration, being mostly female, picked one of their own for Teacher of the Year.

Was it really that way? Some of the younger female teachers, who liked Brad's looks as well as his jokes, and knew he was popular with his class, wondered why he hadn't gotten the award.

Mrs. Moore could have told them that administrators who had done time in the trenches would spot Brad in a New York minute for the type of teacher who favors the popular kids in class, reserving the best jokes for them, and the best classroom jobs, if not grades. A common enough error, overlooked because he was a superlative math teacher, and his science labs were inspired; and besides, rare enough is the perfect teacher, just as it is rare to find the perfect human, and the most we can hope for is some enlightenment, occasional inspiration, and no harm to the students from year to year.

The administrators who had worked for years in classrooms would also know at a glance that Cecilia Robin considered herself an ordinary woman, but she was an extraordinary teacher. Mrs. Moore, long-time vet, suspected that district files were full of testimonials from parents and past students proving it.

Files that Taelons, in their quest to understand the psychology of the humans they governed, appeared to have found.

The question now was, What did they intend to do with it? So far their control had extended pretty much to government and military—the channels of authority, of force. Civilian life had been relatively free. Was education the next realm to be brought under the blue crown?

A week later Cece got to school right at seven, hoping she could get to the copy machine before a line formed—and before the dry weather started the inevitable jams. The surprise visit from the Taelon had receded to the back of her mind, to be replaced by the more urgent demands of report cards and the inevitable beforehand parent-teacher conferences. The many hours of tabulating grades and writing comments had to be fitted in and around the regular flow of papers to be corrected and lessons to be planned that went home nightly in her mail-carrier-sized schoolbag.

The office was open, for Mrs. Pinochet arrived every day at six-thirty. Cece sailed in, glad of the air-conditioning. Already the outside air was hot.

She bumped the door open with her hip, both arms loaded with bags and books. "Good morning," Cece said to the principal, who was standing in her doorway; Cece's glasses had slid down her nose, which was of course sweaty, so all she saw was a dark blur.

"Good morning, Cecilia," Mrs. Pinochet murmured. "Do you have a moment?"

Cece nodded, surprised. "Of course! Um, I'd just hoped to get these history tests copied, for the machine was down again yesterday—"

Mrs. Pinochet nodded cordially to her secretary, who was watching them both as he typed at his computer. "Frank, would you see that Miss Robin's tests get copied?"

Cece rummaged through the top layer of her load, found the test master, handed it to the silent young man with a word of thanks, then followed the principal into the cool office, thinking, Parent problem? Child problem? Staff problem?

Louise Pinochet watched the teacher's face, interpreting correctly the rapid mental assessment, the balance of concern and tension caused by a surprise interruption in a carefully planned morning.

She shut the door, gestured to the chair, and then said, "I believe you are currently doing a Civil War unit with your fourth graders?"

Cece plopped down, dumped her load into her lap, and then pushed her glasses back up her nose. "Yes," she said, making it a question.

Louise nodded. She respected Cecilia Robin, having recognized on their first meeting a kindred spirit. Louise Pinochet was not a forthcoming principal; she was known for fairness and for the endless hard work that rendered the decision-making portion of her job almost unnoticed. In the world of schools, to be unnoticed was to be a success; most parents took smooth running for granted and complained bitterly when events did not go smoothly.

"I wished to know," she said slowly, "if you teach the children about primary sources."

"Always," Cece said. "I bring in primary source material whenever I can."

She looked, and was, surprised. Mrs. Pinochet had never inquired into the details of her curriculum before! Had there been a parent complaint? Sometimes steering between truth and the beliefs and backgrounds the children brought to the classroom required very careful planning indeed, and even more careful speech.

"Do you offer contrasting viewpoints for the children?"

Louise asked. "For example, the writings of, say, John Burgess, or James Ford Rhodes?"

Cece stared up at the dark eyes that regarded her steadily, giving nothing away.

She was about to say, But the garbage written by those nineteenth-century bigots isn't appropriate for nine-year-olds. Which Mrs. Pinochet would know, wouldn't she!

So . . . was there something else behind the question?

Like another conversation, one that might be overheard?

A shift in perspective almost made Cece dizzy. Another conversation going on underneath meant that this room might not be secure, despite the closed door.

And who might have the room bugged, if it was bugged?

Taelons?

Astonishment, worry, speculation caused her mind to dither. "I believe that the writers with that view were once regarded as authorities, because they were the ones in power," she said with care and paused to push her glasses up her nose again. "But I don't." Her heart thumped in her ears. Was she right? Did the principal understand what she was saying?

Mrs. Pinochet's chin lifted, just slightly. "No, I don't either. But many respected officials do feel that they ought to be included in curriculum planning," she said, "even if they have no classroom experience."

Cece was right! This strange conversation *was* about the Taelons!

Cece licked lips that had suddenly gone dry and said, "I leave that subject to high school and college, where the students are prepared for debate. In fourth grade, the important lessons to be learned are the basics, such as the Declaration of Independence and the Constitution."

Louise nodded once. She had, until the SI War took the life of her husband, valued two things: teaching and her beloved. Now her life was dedicated to her school and its integrity.

"I quite agree," she said, trying not to show more approval than the odd conversation warranted. And she saw by the telltale flush in Cecilia Robin's cheeks, and the unwavering wide gaze behind those smeared glasses, that she'd figured out what was going on.

Louise went on, "I think, perhaps—"

The buzzer on the principal's phone set bleeped. Louise frowned and pressed a button. Cece always felt a spurt of inward amusement when she saw that old-fashioned handset—she kept one at home as well. She glanced at the ID numerals, which meant nothing to her, but Louise obviously recognized them. "Will you excuse me a moment?"

"Do you want me to wait outside?"

A shake of the head as Louise picked up the handset. The conversation was brief, the principal's voice polite and bland. "Yes . . . yes . . . thank you. If the teacher agrees, I'll arrange for a substitute. Good-bye."

She looked up, pressed her lips together, then said, "I was going to say that it's always a good idea to be clear on staf lessons plans."

A quick look. Cece said, "I always write them out in detail a week in advance, just in case an emergency comes up. Beyond that are the weekly notes."

"Excellent strategy," Louise said blandly, opening the door. "Perhaps you might share your curriculum-planning method at our year-end faculty meeting."

Cece got up, jerking up her watch. Only 7:10. Whew! Why did it seem an hour had passed? She clutched her load of bags and books to her and walked out.

Frank, the secretary, stood outside the door. "Here are your tests, Miss Robin," he said.

"Thanks," Cece said, reaching to take them.

Of course one of her bags began to slip.

Louise was beside her in a moment. Although Cece, with years of practice, had caught the slipping bag with the crook of her elbow, the principal firmly gripped it and lifted it away. "Permit me," she said. "You look as if you're carrying a full field kit for a hundred-mile march."

"That's what it feels like, in this heat," Cece said breathlessly, balancing the sheaf of tests on top of her diminished pile. "Thanks!"

Together they walked out into the worn school corridor with its sun-cracked blacktop and industrial-green paint, so familiar by now it was invisible.

Neither spoke until they had rounded the corner, and then Louise said abruptly, "Did you once have a student named Scooby?"

Cece had thought she was beyond surprise. "Well, yes! Karen—Scooby was her nickname—was one of my American history students, when I taught at Alta Vista High."

Louise said with a slightly sardonic smile, "And how often do you answer your E-mail?"

"During the school year, once a week or so—on weekends," Cece said. She felt her face burn. "I know it makes me sound like a Luddite, but there's, well, a reason that I have the cheapest possible global, one without E-mail capabilities."

Ordinarily she would not have said even that much, but after that surprising conversation in the office, followed by the mysterious phone call, instinct prompted her to be a little more forthcoming.

Louise nodded once. "You would find, I think, a copy of the message I found this morning, mirrored through a couple of sites, so there is no tracing it. But it said for me to warn you that the Taelons are 'after' you—and it was signed 'Scooby.' "

Cece said voicelessly, "Taelons? 'After me'? After, as in sending out a posse, or investigating, or just scouting me for another meaningless administrative back pat?"

"I don't know, but I suspect you are shortly to find out. That phone call was from the district supervisor, who said that you are being honored with an interview with Companion Da'an—"

"Da'an. Not . . . Za'el, I believe it was?"

"Da'an."

"As in the North American Companion? Head honcho for this continent?"

"That appears to be the one."

"Wants to see *me*? Can they *do* that?"

"Cecilia," Louise Pinochet said gently, "they can do anything they want. Who is to stop them?"

Silence prevailed for several seconds, then Cece said plaintively, "Why? Why me?"

"You will apparently soon find out, as they are sending a car to pick you up at nine."

"Nine?" Cece repeated numbly.

A nod. And grim smile. "Today."

THREE

"If I agree? Then there really isn't a choice?" Cece asked.

Louise said sardonically, "They tried hard to make it sound like you had one, but then they are always polite. What do you want to do?"

Cece wiped her sweaty nose against her shoulder, jarring her glasses sideways. She scarcely noticed her skewed vision; her mind seemed to have been knocked ajar as well. "I hardly know. What will happen if I refuse?"

Louise glanced across the campus. The glare of the morning sun was fierce off the cars in the visitor parking lot adjacent to the office. "Understand this. No one has threatened me—overtly. The oblique message, not from Za'el's flunky but from the district secretary, implied I could lose my job, maybe my pension, if I don't cooperate and send you."

Cece thought back. "How false is their pose of peace?

I'm thinking of that one Taelon who murdered that military fellow with just his fingertips. You know, the one on the televised trial. We all saw that."

"Ah yes. Rho-ha." Louise gave Cece a thin, sour smile. "Supposedly he was . . . tainted . . . by human DNA."

Cece shook her head. "So they said. But what I remember is how easy it was for that Taelon to murder a trained soldier." She drew in a deep breath. "I don't trust them. I don't believe in this threat about a mysterious race called Jaridians who want to destroy the Taelons. Taelon weapons haven't been used against any Jaridians. We've never seen any Jaridians—at least, that I have ever heard. But their fantastic weapons *have* been used to threaten *us*. And it's worked. It's why I have an old phone at home and avoid using my global. And why I have old-fashioned E-mail. I don't trust Taelon technology, impressive as it is."

"I don't either," Louise said.

Cece frowned as they started down the hallway to Cece's classroom. "Mine is a general mistrust. Do you have specific information?"

"Remember when the Interdimensional Travel Ports first opened up?"

Cece shook her head. "Vaguely. It's nothing I would ever use."

"Well, one of my late husband's fellow officers started out as a fighter pilot, and he always felt he ought to support new tech. He and his wife decided to go to New York to see the ballet and return that night. They stepped through the New York I.D. portal together. She arrived here promptly, but he inexplicably arrived an hour later."

"An *hour* later?"

"No explanation, nothing. Time went on, and he had this problem with his neck. Went to the doctor. The lab tech frowned over the X ray, said something about an anomaly, left the room, and he never saw her again. The doctor came in, said everything was fine, normal. Went to another specialist. Normal, perfectly normal. But he's always wondered about that. Questions."

Cece felt sweat trickle down her armpit, and not from the heat. It was the cold sweat of fear.

Louise gazed out at the parking lot and then turned to face her. She said, "You decide what you want to do, and I'll back you up." She glanced sideways. "But if I'm right, the decision can't be made in an hour, it has to be made right now, because if I'm not mistaken they are in a bit of a hurry."

Cece turned around and saw what Louise had just spotted. A late-model rental car drove up slowly into the lot. As the two women watched, the car stopped in the green zone before the office. Two people got out, one a dapper black man, the other a tall, broad-shouldered white man. They vanished inside the office.

"Neither is one of our parents, nor do they resemble our local district officials. They look," Louise said in her soft drawl, "mighty like hired muscle, don't they? Rather eager, wouldn't you say?"

Cece jammed her key in the door of her classroom. Her hand shook so hard she almost couldn't control the lock. *Why me?* her mind keened. *Why me? It can't happen to me!*

"I can't do it," she said, dropping her things onto her desk.

Louise smiled. "Then you'd better get going, had you not?"

Cece swallowed. "I—I don't want you to get into trouble."

"Oh, I won't. I'm going to toddle back to my office and smile and smile, and smother them with officialese about children, substitutes, tours, and goodwill, before I offer them the tour of the school ending with your classroom. And with any luck I can talk so fast they won't remember their globals for at least half an hour."

"Thanks."

"Good luck."

Louise did not wait for an answer but started back along the hall, pausing to greet two teachers and a handful of kids who, unmindful of the heat, were racing back and forth along the halls.

When Frank came looking for her, she was in the middle of reminding the culprits about school rules and the dangers of running up and down the hallways, and she left him standing there while she finished her lecture. A very long lecture, with a mental apology to the bewildered children who had suddenly netted this super-long rant for breaking a minor rule.

She gave no outward hint—long practice at keeping a stern face enabled her to maintain the proper note of awe-inspiring authority—but Louise Pinochet was enjoying, very much, her covert act of resistance. Only why the hell did Frank have to stand facing just that way? She tried turning, but he stayed planted.

Cece glanced through her window. The glass was tinted to diminish the sun's glare, and as long as her light wasn't on, no one could see in. She saw the little tableau: Mrs. Pinochet gesturing, the children standing, unwontedly subdued, and the impatient secretary. Frank faced her way, so she stayed put.

Was he some kind of, well, spy for the Taelons? The very word seemed absurd, especially in this setting. Somehow spies and governmental shenanigans didn't really seem to fit a run-down grammar school in the full glare of the Southern California sun.

But he wouldn't have to be a *spy,* he only had to be a sincere believer in the Taelon superiority and good intentions, and if so, then reporting what he heard among the faculty would seem duty, wouldn't it? Especially if someone asked?

Louise waved the children off and gestured to Frank. His back turned to Cece's room now, and he began talking, gesturing toward the office with one hand.

Cece gripped her handbag, slid her car keys into her hand, and crossed to the back door. Open, close, and she was soon in the faculty parking area, which hitherto everyone had cursed for being out behind the buildings, but now that was a blessing.

No one was about. She unlocked and slid into her car. She fired up the engine, put the car into gear, and drove out, not realizing until she got to the end of the block that she'd been holding her breath almost since she left her classroom.

Left turn, and the horrible sense that someone might be watching her faded. All right, she was away. Now what?

Home. Time to think, to plan.

She edged onto the main boulevard, feeling safely anonymous in the commuter traffic. Two streets, three. Red light! She stopped, feeling paranoid. Scorn. It's just a stupid red light, not a world conspiracy—

Flashing red lights! Thumping heart—*it can't be!*—and the police car rolled on past, turned down a side street, siren screaming.

Green light. Feeling like she was stuck in a sweatbath, Cece turned on the AC. The cool blast was oddly reassuring, as if it could restore sanity to a world suddenly gone nuts.

It was right then that she heard the *tweet-tweet* of her global.

Her global? It was a family joke how much she loathed this technology. She'd bought one only in case her parents, living in a retirement center down near San Diego, might need to contact her in an emergency. And it was the cheapest possible model, really no more than a cell phone, without Net capabilities.

She pulled into a fast-food parking lot and left the engine running as she pulled the global from the depths of her schoolbag. Snapping it open, she stared at the bland, totally unfamiliar face of a young Asian woman. The ID below it said *Ellie Siu*.

No one Cece knew. Should she take it?

The coincidences were scary, but it was scarier not to know. She pressed Accept. Immediately the ID rippled, changing to a garble of letters and numbers that were either a code or just garbage. The young Asian face was replaced by that of a handsome older woman.

"Cecilia Robin?" this woman asked. "I'm Julianne. Look, we need to meet in person. Right away."

"I don't know you," Cece stated.

Once again the ID rippled, this time showing the name *Josipa Coriescu.*

"No," was the response, "which is why I'm going to suggest a neutral place, so that you can decide if you can trust me. But the information I have is urgent, and I do not trust this link for long."

Cece thought rapidly. "Did you fake a message to my principal this morning, in the name of one of my former students?"

"No," the woman said, frowning. "We haven't time for explanations over this link. But I promise them as soon as we meet. Please go to—"

Cece felt a spurt of anger. "No," she declared, "I won't go anywhere, and I won't be ordered by a stranger."

"But you must understand—"

"I can take care of myself," Cece said. "Thank you for your concern."

She deactivated the device and flung the global back into her bag, ignoring the *tweet-tweet* of another call. Slammed the gear into reverse and drove out of the parking lot. Not burning rubber, no way. She did not want to call the least attention to herself. She drove out slowly, choosing the middle lane, and when the next red light stopped her, with trembling fingers she nipped off her specs and put her sunglasses on. And then, no longer feeling any kind of self-mockery, she pulled out her battered sunhat, which she used when she had yard duty, and put it on, yanking the brim low over her eyes.

Home, she thought, impatient for the light to change. But as she started forward, a sickening inner lurch made her wonder if home was really safe? After all, those people had gotten her global number, which she paid extra to have unpublished. Her address would be in all her files.

So home was off-limits.

Where, then? Instead of turning right, she kept on going straight, keeping to the middle lane and checking her mirrors every few seconds or so for the half expected monster van with blackened windows to loom, TV-like, on her bumper.

This crazy morning had apparently begun with an E-mail—

She smacked the steering wheel.

Of course. Scooby!

But how to find her? Cece thought back. Scooby had come to visit her the year before. What had she said? "I'm going to UCLA now, and I'm either going to major in American history or poli sci. . . ."

UCLA. Why not? Even if she wasn't on campus, they had a student directory, didn't they?

Yes.

Now that she had a game plan, her innards stopped acting like a pit of boiling snakes. She turned west and headed for the San Diego Freeway.

FOUR

"Miss Robin!"

How strange it is, Cece thought, when child faces take on the contours of adulthood, and yet I don't feel older. "Scooby! Or do you prefer Kar—"

"No, Scooby's fine," came the quick response, too quick, really, and a furtive narrowing of the eyes. Then another smile, almost as wide as the first and not as unguarded. "Where are you?"

"I'm just off the freeway, heading toward UCLA. I looked up your global ID while sitting at red lights."

"I'm so glad you got my message. Shall I flash you the map?"

"I don't have Net capabilities on this thing," Cece said. "Just give me the address. I'll park and look up the address in my old fashioned but trusty and true Thomas Brothers Map Guide."

Scooby's face creased with silent mirth. "Go back down Sunset, a little past Beverly Glen, you'll find the turnoff. Riding Circle."

"Good heavens, isn't that Beverly Hills?" Cece asked. "Don't tell me they have dorms there?"

"No, I'm rooming with friends," Scooby answered. "The guy at the gate will ask where you're going, and you tell him Thomas Paine."

"Thomas Paine. Is that some kind of code?" Cece started, and then she felt her face burn. Duh. Thomas Paine wasn't a code, it was the name of an estate. Feeling more like she'd somehow fallen through some modern form of the looking glass, Cece said, "See you soon." And they ended the connection.

She eased back into the traffic and was soon on her way to Beverly Hills. The buildings along Sunset abruptly gave way to beautifully manicured lawns and trees, affording occasional tantalizing glimpses of estates twice the size of George Washington Elementary School. And these were only the small, cheap ones, so close to the boulevard.

She found the turnoff, which was narrow, and stopped at a formidable gate. An armed security guard poked his head out of his box. "You're here for . . . ?" he prompted, neither friendly nor unfriendly.

"Thomas Paine." Now she felt slightly foolish.

The man glanced into the car, keyed something into his computer—probably her license plate—and then said, "Go up that road, right, right, left. Top of the circle is four fourteen, which is what you want."

She thanked him and drove slowly up the narrow, winding roads, all of them overshadowed by old, luxuriant trees. How much water did it take to create this verdant oasis in the middle of hot, dry Los Angeles basin? It was at least ten degrees cooler here than Sunset Boulevard had been. She tabbed her windows down and breathed in the scents of expensive gardens. The *ticka-ticka* of sprinklers underscored the breeze-hush of leaves and the occasional chirpings of unseen birds.

Bridle paths wound in and out along the road and once even crossed over it on a charming little brick-and-ivy bridge. No houses were in view at all; the only cars were old-model junkers, which surprised Cece, until she thought, Oh, of course. These on the street belong to cleaning staff and pool maintenance people and tree trimmers and the like.

She drove to the top of a gentle hill. When she reached 414, a video camera swung around to point at her, and before she could wonder what to do next the wrought-iron gate swung open.

Up a very narrow cobblestone driveway, with what looked like fantasyland forest on either side. The drive suddenly opened into a great circle before a spectacular replica of an English mansion. What seemed a hundred diamond-paned windows threw back glitters from the sun; ivy climbed the brick walls. Had to be facade, she thought, slowing down almost to a crawl so she could stare in appreciation. No matter how much one wanted to pretend that this was Pemberly, pride of Derbyshire, the house was actually located in Southern California, land of quakes. Nobody wanted to be inside a brick building during a quake.

Both wings of the house opened onto extensive gardens. Cece heard a waterfall down one end, sloping away into green shadows. What must the gardening bill cost each month? More than I make in a year, of course.

She drove slowly along the front of the house and was about to stop when she saw a discreet driveway off the far wing. She glimpsed several cars beyond it. Pulled up, parked next to an ordinary car much like her own; if there were Rolls-Royces and Daimlers around, they were hidden.

But there were a lot of cars. Either the house had a royal palace–sized staff, or else a party was going on.

Cece got out of her car, smoothed down her dress, hesitated, then hauled out her schoolbag. She didn't carry a handbag; her schoolbag was load enough. She slung it over her shoulder, locked the car, and when she turned around, found three young people standing there.

"Miss Robin!" Scooby ran forward and gave her a hug. The skinny, ardent fifteen-year-old of high school days was now about twenty, beautifully dressed, her thick brown hair so long it brushed against her hips when she pulled away, laughing. "Here! Meet Che and Fitz. You know, for Lord Edward Fitzgerald—the Irish Rising of ninety-eight. You taught us about that," she added, as Cece studied the two young men with Scooby.

They were both tall, smiling. The slim one looked to Cece like D'Artagnan, with his fine mustache and pointed beard and the long curling hair lying on his shoulders. The big one looked like a berserker—huge, muscular, long black beard and hair. But they didn't dress in costume; the big one wore jeans and a black T-shirt, the slim one expensive slacks and an expensive shirt rolled up to the elbows. Since she didn't know which was Che and which Fitz—and since these were obviously false names—she privately named the big one Moose and the slim one D'Artagnan.

Hired muscle. Louise Pinochet's phrase came to mind when Cece glanced again at Moose's big arms and broad chest, his flat, dispassionate gaze.

"Come on inside. Meet the others. It's so good to see you again!" Scooby added, laughing her old, familiar laugh, her wide-set brown eyes crescents of mirth. "I've told them all, *so* many times, how you were my favorite teacher ever. How you got me to love history. In fact, you got me to stop messing around in school and get to work!" She turned to the two young men. "Haven't I!"

Moose nodded. D'Artagnan said, "Yes, you did. We're honored to have you with us, Miss Robin."

"Well," Cece said, feeling her way in this conversation. Ordinarily she did not like dialogues that opened with compliments. Too often the flatter-patter was a prelude to being hit up for something someone wanted, usually for free. "We're all adults here," she said, smiling at Scooby. "Call me Cecilia. Hearing 'Miss Robin' makes me think I'm about to go before the School Board."

She won a tolerant smile back for her tentative joke. D'Artagnan extended his hand to the left, and they started moving toward the house. As she walked, Cece watched the others. Was her paranoia from earlier still lingering, or was there a problem? Though the air was not cold, Scooby gripped her arms just above the elbows, and Moose kept checking out the peaceful scene as if playing hide-and-seek. Only D'Artagnan walked along smiling, his attitude easy.

They crunched up a gravel pathway, passed through a lovely rose garden, and D'Artagnan opened French doors with a proprietary air that solved the mystery of whose house this was.

The doors opened onto a conservatory full of flowers. Sitting on little chairs all over were about twenty young people, all of them sporting very long hair. The scents of expensive shampoos no doubt added to the flowery bouquet of the air.

"Shall we go inside where it's more comfortable?" D'Artagnan asked, with an elegant wave of his hand inside the house.

At once the group got to their feet and filed into a cavernous living room with a sunken tête-à-tête circle. A fountain was built into one wall, trickling quietly, opposite a huge fireplace, quite dark now, of course. Couches upholstered in expensive weaves lined the circle, before exquisite cherrywood coffee tables. There was plenty of space for everyone.

Cece sank down where Scooby pointed, her reactions midway between alarm and laughter at Scooby's proprietary air. The alarm was caused by the way Scooby kept glancing at D'Artagnan and licking her lips.

Was she worried, Cece thought?

Well, yes, Scooby was very worried, but she tried desperately to hide it. Weren't older people supposed to shrink when they got *really* old? How did Miss Robin get so *small*? Scooby remembered her as being this big woman, her glasses flashing with reflected light as she talked about the Declaration of Independence, the Constitution, and the Enlightenment in Europe that had inspired the Founding Fathers—and how Jefferson, and Paine, and Franklin, in their turn, had inspired all those jaded old kings and nobles back in Europe.

But now, look at those little hands and those lines on her forehead. Were those, like, *worry* lines? Was she a little scared of Neville—no, must call him Fitz! Miss Robin isn't supposed to know anyone's name until she joins—

"Welcome, Miss Robin. We are the Students of Liberty," said Neville Carlton IV, great-grandson of one of Teddy Roosevelt's political Rough Riders, who later became one of Los Angeles's toughest robber barons back in the wild 1920s, when Prohibition and land speculation made rich men of those who thought themselves enterprising.

Neville Carlton IV was slim and handsome, resembling more his spectacularly beautiful movie star great-grandmother than his bear of a great-grandfather, but he definitely had the old man's smile.

"You can call me Fitz for now. As Scooby told you, I took as a nickname Lord Edward Fitzgerald, although I trust our cause will be triumphant and not tragic. Lord Edward suffered from unbounded enthusiasm and misguided trust, without careful planning. I do not make such errors."

Cece nodded, her face blank from many years of dull district "workshops" and angry parent conferences and heartrending family tragedies. But her palms, pressed together in her lap, unaccountably began to sweat, and her heart clacketted in her ears. Her antennae—intuition—subliminal senses—call it what you will, it felt like that sickening first moment an earthquake hits, when you know something's wrong but not what.

"Look around. This is merely our local branch," he went on. "We are actively recruiting on all major college campuses, and our membership grows every day. We don't care what anyone's politics, race, gender, background, or tastes are. The one thing that binds us together is our wish to win back the United States of America for Americans. And that means getting rid of the alien overlords who call themselves Taelons."

Silence. To fill it, Scooby said hurriedly, "I know you don't like 'em. We—back in high school, just after they came—we all knew it, even though you never *said*. See, that was the most inspiring part of all, that you trusted us enough to drop those hints. And you kept telling us that we had to act or we'd lose what freedom we had!"

Cece turned her head, looking into that anxious young face. What were the real stakes here? "I encouraged you to vote when you reached eighteen, to exercise your rights as guaranteed by the Constitution," she said.

"Yes." Scooby nodded several times. Then she gave a nervous giggle. "Notice how much we look like hippies? Weren't you part of the hippie generation? Think we'll bring long hair back into fashion? It's also a political statement."

Scooby was talking too fast. Her friend Marina, sitting on her other side, nudged her with an elbow and added in a slower voice, "The Taelons are hairless, and you know those stupid fashions by Taelon lovers. Shaving their heads. Wearing the bodysuits."

"I see," Cece said. She smiled. "Ought I to make my own statement then? My bun seems to be falling down anyway!" Not quite sure why, she put up her shaky fingers and pulled out her remaining pins (how many had she scattered all over Orange County over the past twenty years?), and down straggled her long gray-streaked brown braid to her lap.

The Students of Liberty applauded.

"Hurray for Miss Robin!" Scooby cried, looking around.

The other young people smiled, nodded, laughed. Cece saw that despite the humor, the atmosphere—the postures of those watching—remained tense.

Neville smiled. It was no longer his shark smile, but something less threatening and more smug. We've got her, he was thinking, and it showed in his face.

Cece said, "You are right. I do not trust the Taelons. I don't think that any alien culture, no matter how well intentioned, can rightly know what is best for us. Of course I know we've made terrible mistakes, but I believe that humans can learn from their errors, and in any case, I strongly believe that the best government is that chosen by the people themselves, with everyone contributing. Not one imposed by superior force, no matter how benevolent."

"Exactly," Neville said, taking control again. "The key words here are 'superior force.' You will agree that their weaponry far surpasses ours?"

"Yes," Cece said.

"And that they used the threat of that force to take control of our government?"

Cece said cautiously, "It was implied threat, rather than the use of force—"

"But they effectively control the president. The Congress makes no law without Taelon sanction. And," Neville said, ticking points off his fingers, "they control us by controlling human beings in key places? That's what those Cyber-Viral Implants are, mind control units, by which they get humans to use force against other humans. The very worst of them being the North American Companion Protector, FBI Special Agent Ronald Sandoval."

Cece nodded, licking dry lips. Even she had heard Sandoval's name.

"Use," Neville said again, "of force. They have no problem using it against us. The media finesses it, but we've all heard rumors about mysterious disappearances of important people. About horrible experimentation on humans. You've heard of kryss?"

Cece shook her head.

"A kind of crystal, call it, that the Taelons apparently need to ingest to ward off the effects of our planet. Sounds benign, doesn't it? Until you find out that the quickest and cheapest method of manufacture is inside human digestive systems."

Cece winced.

"The harvest is just as nasty as you can imagine. Oh, supposedly they've stopped . . . here. On the planet. Do we really know what they're doing up there in space? And we all saw what happened after the last election, when they sent implanted humans in with weapons blazing to murder every single Resistance member they could find, during the State of Siege. Not even the media could finesse that. True? You know it's true."

Cece's palms were slick now. She nodded again.

He said slowly, and with utter conviction, "So the only effective way to fight force is to use force. We must first get our fellow citizens to abandon their passive ease, and reclaim our republic, just like the revolutionaries of 1776 created our republic."

"We have to be active, not passive," Scooby exclaimed, looking around for approval. And the other Students of Liberty made signs of assent.

"As revolutionaries, we have to take certain risks," Neville went on, smiling at his flock before he turned again to Cece. "But they are for the common good, as Paul Revere and Washington and Nathan Hale all knew."

"You name military figures," Cece observed. "What about Betsy Ross?"

"No," Neville said, shaking his head, so his fine hair drifted over his shoulders. His voice was gentle, as it would remain so long as he kept control of the conversation's direction. "I name figures who believed enough to take action. Betsy Ross could have sewed flags until she died, but if the talkers and dreamers had had control, we'd still be bowing to England's royal family now."

"There's being active, and then there's violence. You advocate violence, I take it," Cece stated. "I must tell you right away that I do not."

"Against human beings, we do not advocate violence," was the swift answer. "Like you, we support the Constitution. Best in the world. But it seems to have been superseded by the Taelons, hasn't it? If we remove them, why, then Americans can relearn how to govern themselves, and the Constitution will be our guide."

"I am all for effecting change through law-abiding methods." Cece crossed her arms.

To Scooby, she looked like some medieval saint, with her long hair hanging down all around her. Except didn't all those old saints die really nasty deaths? "And so are we—" Scooby began quickly, wanting Miss Robin to understand, to say yes, to be *safe*.

Neville half raised a hand, and Scooby sat back.

Cece looked around. Saw anxious postures, quick exchanges of looks. What were the real stakes here? Instinct insisted that the real business had not yet been gotten to.

Neville strolled down the two steps into the pit, quick and elegant and very much in control. Cece realized he'd stood opposite her, still on the steps. The position of command.

Now he lounged in the center of the circle, his manner assured, his smile an assurance that she was no adversary—in direct contrast to his stance. "Use of force, yes, but not against any citizen. We're not talking about bombing cities, or even burning down crowds, as they did to the Resistance. Let me explain our plan," he said.

"Please."

A movement from Scooby, and Cece felt fingers as sweaty as hers touch her hand and take hold. It disarmed her; just so did small children take her hand, when they were frightened, or happy, or just to express trust when the words wouldn't come. To have a young woman take her hand seemed a gesture of both admiration and desperation.

"We will place a team of people near each Taelon embassy, except here in the States, where Zo'or, the most powerful Taelon—we just found this out—is going to preside at a statue unveiling on the Yale Old Campus. Our people will have a given amount of time to learn the movement patterns of their target. On the Fourth of July, at a given signal, Zo'or at Yale will be assassinated, which will function as signal to our other people at the embassies to follow suit. Taelons only. The very ones who order our people to be shot, to vanish, to be experimented on."

Cece swallowed. Or tried to.

Neville did not wait for a response. "During the resultant chaos, we will step forward and take control of communications networks and publish our goals on the Net, bringing down the Taelon Security Net."

"Can you do that?" Cece asked, surprised.

"We're working on it. I have confidence."

"And you're telling me all this because . . . ?"

"Because you have a part," Neville said gently, smiling and smiling.

Bingo. Here it was, a 9.5 on the cardiac Richter scale.

"I trust in a classroom somewhere," Cece said.

Neville laughed, and some of the others in the group tittered.

"No. But your being a teacher makes you perfect—even better than a student. Scooby has talked about you so much that we all feel we know you, and meeting you, I see that she was right. You're not a sinister assassin or a shady government spook. You're a middle-aged teacher, a popular one, no threat to anybody, and afterward, people will realize that ordinary people can act, and they'll listen to you."

"Afterward. After what?"

Again she got the shark smile, even white teeth, unblinking dark gaze.

"After you take down Zo'or." He put his hand in his pocket and came up gripping a lethal-looking automatic handgun. "With this."

FIVE

It was to be Da'an at the unveiling. He does not have the reputation for evil that Zo'or does, so what could be better for us than this last-moment replacement? But to resume: We will fly you there, as we do not use Taelon portals. We will take care of the logistical planning. You just need to get next to him and rid the country of one oppressor. That will serve as the signal for the other assassinations, which in turn should trigger uprisings all over the world," he continued.

Silence.

Neville turned the weapon over. "We don't know if lighter pistols can bring Taelons down, but this H&K forty-five ought to be heavy enough to do the job, as we want to use American products in this, too, and not Taelon tech."

"We know we can kill 'em. Worked on the former Synod leader," Moose growled. "Quo-on. We know that much. Though they tried to hide it."

"No," Cece said.

"But—"

"No. To make myself clear: I will not shoot anybody, with anything, whether buckshot or energy beam. I do not believe in violence."

Neville dropped the weapon into the pocket of his

slacks. "And if George Washington had said the same?"

"I thought it fairly obvious that I," Cece fought hard to keep her voice from shaking or squeaking, "am not George Washington."

A snicker from one of the watchers caused a quick, unsmiling look from Neville. Instant silence.

He came forward and sat on the edge of the coffee table so they were face to face. "Let me get this straight," he said. "You'll be happy to help out after someone else does the dirty work?"

Cece flushed with anger. "You did not listen to what I said. I will repeat: I do not, under any circumstances, advocate violence, if there is any other possible way. I'm not convinced that violence is our only recourse for getting the Taelons to leave us alone. And who's to say you will be successful? How, after all, did the Taelons know where the Resistance cells were located, in order to blast them? The Taelons might know all about you."

"Then why aren't they here?" Neville spread his hands.

"They could," Cece said in her sharpest you-will-stop-that-now-children! voice, "merely be waiting until you perform a criminal act before they strike."

She did not have to look to see the impact of her words on the listeners. Nor did Neville. They both felt it.

"There is no Resistance anymore," he said, getting to his feet. "Just big talkers. There is no one to help us but us. Even you will admit that one of the oldest American proverbs, dating right back to the Pilgrims, is that if you want something done, you do it yourself. Please, step this way." He opened a hand toward the other side of the living room. "You have had a long day. You can get some rest. Think over what we've said."

"I'd rather go home," she stated.

"You can't. The Taelons are there waiting to pick you up."

"And that is why I came," she said, staying seated, though it hardly constituted safety. "How do you know that? And *why* are they there to pick me up?"

Scooby bit at the side of her thumb.

Neville lifted his head, gave her a long look, and Scooby didn't speak. Nor did anyone else. He said, "I am a graduate student with a teaching assistanceship, and most of my group are students. We stay in contact with teachers' organizations as part of our recruiting. Your name came up in a list of teachers being investigated and then again as a target for one of their summary interviews. Scooby saw it. It was her idea to invite you here. We all voted to invite you into our plans."

Cece remained silent.

"Come along," he said.

"I'd rather go home. I'll take my chances with the Taelons."

"And have them rip from your mind everything we've told you? I don't think so." At least he didn't pull out that weapon. "Che, escort the lady, will you?"

Cece got to her feet. "I believe I can walk on my own."

She'd lost the verbal battle, but she would not lose what remained of her dignity by being hauled along by Moose.

Neville saw it and smiled. "We'll bring along some food in a while. I hope you like grilled halibut and baby carrots with fresh basil."

"Delicious," she responded in her flattest voice.

She and Moose did not speak as they walked through the length of the beautiful house. She walked slowly, forcing him to match her pace, and looked around as if on tour. And the house really was lovely—immaculately kept, full of antique furnishings and art.

Up a curving stairway. They stopped outside a room midway along a hall. Moose said, his voice a deep rumble, "Think about it, like he says. If you aren't with us, then you're against us."

He opened the door. She stepped inside. He shut it and locked it. A Yale lock, activated from the outside.

She turned around and surveyed the room. It was a small bedroom, prettily decorated in rose and peach and cream, the furnishings blond wood. Cece clutched her schoolbag against her side and studied, then dismissed, the quilt-covered bed, the dresser, bare except for a crystal vase full of fresh flowers, the reading table and lamp. Closet? She opened the door, saw that it was absolutely empty.

French windows opened out onto a balcony. At first she'd ignored them, thinking that they'd either be locked or else someone would be outside watching. Now she thought, why not check?

So she tried the latch—laughing at herself for turning it slowly and quietly. Open! She pushed and stepped out onto the balcony and stared out. No one visible in the beautiful garden below. The back of the house was much higher than the front, as it was built on a slope; the drop was at least three stories. Beyond the garden the lawn sloped away, to be swiftly swallowed by great trees.

To either side a balcony opened off French doors. Below those, two stories of smooth wall.

She stepped to the edge and leaned out. Yep. At least three stories. Maybe some of those athletic young women in the other room could successfully negotiate that drop, but Cece Robin couldn't. Either a broken ankle or a broken neck would probably be her reward for her daring escape.

So what about these balconies?

She moved to the edge, looking back again to see if anyone was watching. As far as she could see, no one was about. Yet she still had that awful feeling. Maybe it was just the result of what had been, so far, a spectacularly hellish day.

Balcony, dear. She frowned, estimating the distance from this railing to that one. About four feet? A short distance—until you thought about the drop below.

She looked back inside for something like a rope. Nothing. Bedsheets knotted? Considered that for about five seconds, then dismissed it. Maybe it worked in the movies, but she couldn't see how to get two bedsheets tied together, not without cutting. And if you cut them too thin, would they break? What about knots slipping?

No, it was going to have to be the other balcony. Only what if the door was locked? Well, then she'd climb back.

She paused to finger her long hair into a hasty braid, and when that was done she hefted her schoolbag, swung it out, and let it go. It landed on the other balcony.

Now she was committed.

"What do we do with Scoob's teacher?"

Marina Aguilara stared up at Neville. He stared back at those unwavering black eyes, considering. Marina was his fastest, quickest operative, the most passionately devoted to the cause, so unswervingly honest that everyone in the group trusted her implicitly. But her second passion was women's rights. If he lost Marina, he'd lose the group.

So he smiled and flicked one of her shining dark braids. "She gets an all-expenses-paid vacation up to my house at Lake Arrowhead. Supposedly to think over her decision, but actually to keep her safe from the Taelons. My guess is they'll be coming after Scooby in fairly short order, having traced her well-meant message to the teacher, so we'll reassign her to the New Haven team. And her teacher can watch our success on the TV up in the mountains."

Marina considered, then gave a short nod. "Sounds fair. And after?"

"Well, afterward she won't know anything important, will she? We can put her back in her car and let her go home."

Marina got up and left.

Neville shut the door behind her and put his back against it. "Che."

"Yo."

"The problem with prisoners, as I see it, is that we lose the use of good people. We don't have enough good people to waste watching fools."

Che shrugged.

"Marina and Scooby are too romantic, shall we say, to

be practical. I hold nothing against Miss Robin, but we do have to be practical."

No response.

"Soon as it's dark, put the teacher in the car and take her up to Lake Arrowhead, just like I said. Make sure she doesn't get near any kind of comm gear. Give it a week or so and then pick a nice, cool day, one that will promise a cold night, and take her for a hike in the woods. Nice and pleasant. Miles from civilization. When they find her body, the cause of death will be exposure, not violence. Got it?"

Che nodded once.

Neville smiled. "For now, why don't you see that she gets something to eat? Marina can give orders to the cook herself. But you take it up."

While this millionaire almost young enough to be her son was settling her fate, Cece swung her legs over the railing and clung backward, her skirt bunched uncomfortably behind her, and her sensible slip-ons dangerously slippery. Take them off, idiot, she thought.

So she eased herself back over again, pulled off the shoes and her cotton knee-highs, tossed them onto the other balcony. Reclimbed the railing. Reached, reached, holding tight behind her. Her toes groped a foot or two short.

Knelt down and reached. Still a foot short. So she stood up, drew in a deep breath, let go, lunged over—and her foot landed between the vertical rails, and her sweaty fingers grabbed and clung viselike to the rail. Pulled her second foot up, climbed, pulled on her stockings and shoes, despite trembling fingers, picked up her schoolbag, tried the door—it swung open.

She stepped into a room set up like an office, only there was no phone set. Just a table and a computer that had been shut down. Dare she try it? What if it was on a password?

No, just get out of here, get to her car, and scram.

She opened the door. Hallway was empty. She eased out—

—and almost ran into Moose, who came up a stairway right then, carrying a tray. She let out a squeak. Moose gave her a sardonic look and pointed with his chin.

Back to the rose room, with a supper tray. The door locked. She left the window open—and within a minute or so heard the decided *click* of the French windows on her former escape balcony locking. And a couple minutes after that, the one to the other side.

So she sighed, sat down, looked at the tray of food. Beautiful Havilland porcelain, linen napkin, a meal presented like a four-star restaurant. A silver pot of coffee. She opened her schoolbag and pulled out her current reading, Fanny Burney's *Evelina*.

Nothing is going to happen to me, she thought. Not if they give me a lovely dinner.

Propping the book up on a lampshade, she began her meal. It took three tries to get into the familiar eighteenth-century story, but eventually it worked its usual magic.

She'd just finished the apple compote and was sipping the coffee when she heard a clicking in the lock. A pause, more clicks.

The door swung open.

She stared into a golden-brown male face. A very attractive face, she realized with a sort of vague surprise; quite a debonair face, with a goatee and orangish-tinted glasses, that somehow managed to make the bland cap and overalls of a cleaning service seem quite fashionable.

"Want to escape?" he asked, smiling.

SIX

"Who are you?" Cece asked, backing into the room. Absurd, really, since she was hardly safe there—but nothing bad had happened in the room yet, had it?

The man stepped in, shut the door, set on the table a roll of white cloth that he'd been carrying under his arm, and pulled a slender palm computer from a side pocket. All this he did smoothly, swiftly, with an air of smiling competence.

He held out the palm and keyed a replay. In silence Cece listened to Neville's voice say, with casual confidence, "Soon as it's dark, put the teacher in the car and take her up to Lake Arrowhead. . . . Make sure she doesn't get near any kind of comm gear. Give it a week or so and then pick a nice, cool day. . . . When they find her body . . ."

Cece found it difficult to hear it all past the sudden thumping of her heartbeat in her ears.

"Why?" she whispered. "Why kill me? I can't believe it. All I said was no. I didn't threaten them. Or is it some kind of revenge?"

The man in the cleaner's coverall shook his head once. "A combination of wealthy arrogance and a personnel shortage." He had a warm whiskey voice, as attractive as his face. "So, shall we?"

"All right." Cece's voice trembled. Her fingers trembled. Her knees and wrists felt like someone had taken out the cartilage and replaced it with water. She forced her voice to steady. "What do I do now?"

"Put that on. Over your clothes, fast." He pointed at the roll of white cloth on the table.

Coveralls, she discovered. And a cap, which fell at her feet. While the man held his global to his ear, Cece forced her shaking body into the suit and zipped it up. It was meant for a man twice her size. Luckily. She was not certain she would have gotten it on otherwise.

"My schoolbag?" she asked.

"Inside the suit. Add a few pounds, change your profile." A brief smile.

She hung the strap around her neck, unzipped the coverall, tucked her bag in, zipped it again. The suit was still too big, but it certainly did change her profile.

She retrieved the cap, tucked her braid up into it, and pulled the brim low over her glasses rims.

"Good enough. Now follow me. I'll give you something to carry, which you can use to hide your face. If anyone talks to us, leave the answers to me."

He opened the door, looked. Touched the rim of his glasses, nodded. They moved out and around the corner, where a pile of towels waited. The man indicated for her to lift them. She did.

They progressed in silence down the stairs, the mysterious young man occasionally scanning slowly around, holding the rim of his glasses, and Cece trying to still her drumming heart. But escape, after all, turned out to be blessedly anticlimactic. They passed three or four of the young people, not one of whom gave them a second glance. Cece did not see Scooby, and neither Che nor his leader appeared.

Out through a huge kitchen that smelled strongly of cleaning fluids. Two other people in white coveralls joined them, both carrying various types of cleaning equipment. As they climbed into the back of a big white truck that was parked next to a delivery service truck, more people came out in the cleaning uniforms, put their equipment on the racks above the benches, and sat down, some of them exchanging laughing comments. Someone else passed out covered cups of coffee. Cece was offered one by a woman about her age. She shook her head once, her hands still clutching her pile of towels on her lap. The woman turned away and sat down, falling into conversation with another woman. Cece listened; their subject was Eli Hanson's talk show.

The young man who'd rescued her sat next to her, also without talking. Now he was busy with the palm. Cece heard a couple of faint bleeps and then the engine starting up. She jumped, startled. The people swayed as the truck eased into gear, rounded the drive, and started down the hill to the first gate. Pause. Clash of gears—and the truck had passed through.

Twist, turn, brake. Turn, turn, turn. Wind down, and they stopped again. The back opened. The security guard glanced in, waved a hand, the doors shut. They were through.

Now what?

This was, Cece realized a few minutes later, a legitimate cleaning service, for they stopped at another Beverly Hills mansion, this one on a public street. Just as they parked, the driver up front turned around, holding his global.

"Jones? Gamble?"

"That's us," Cece's rescuer said, glancing at Cece.

"Della says you two have been reassigned. Some rush job in an office over on Olympic. Says a car will be by to pick you up."

"We'll walk down to Sunset and wait for it, then."

A nod at Cece, and they followed the others out of the truck. While the rest of the cleaning staff trooped up the back way to the house, carrying their equipment, Cece and her rescuer walked down the street toward Sunset Boulevard.

Neither spoke. Cece's heart had stopped thumping in her ears, leaving her feeling as if she'd dashed right back through Alice's looking glass.

They'd reached the end of the street and were about to turn when her rescuer looked around, then stepped into the thick shrubbery bordering the corner home. He gestured to Cece, who hesitated, then stepped after.

Slamming heart again. They were now standing in a shady spot, surrounded by carefully manicured flowering shrubs. The young man was already halfway out of his cleaning suit, revealing stylish black skateboarder pants and a black crew neck shirt. His head was smoothly shaved except for a round patch at the back of his head from which dangled a thin braided tail. He lifted a brow—she realized she was staring. No, gaping. Her cheeks burned, but he only gestured a zipping motion, and she wrestled quickly out of hers as well, then hastily straightened out her rumpled school dress.

When she was done he took both suits and caps, rolled them up, stuck them into a bag from Tower Records, then motioned for her to step out.

"You appear to know who I am," Cece said. "Who are you?"

"Augur," he said, smiling. "We'll be at a nice little park in about two minutes. Easy questions first, okay?"

"Is 'How?' easy or hard?" Cece found that her throat had gone dry, but she struggled to match Augur's wryly humorous tone. She liked that tone, because it was the tone of someone who was in control, who was not afraid.

Cece very badly wanted not to be afraid.

"How did I know you were there? We'll get to that. How did I get you out? Easy enough. Cleaning services and the like still largely use old pre-Taelon tech, which has the virtue of being cheap. Got into the system at the cleaners, tapped in a photo and employment file for one Thomas Gamble. The turnover at those places is high, so no one in the truck paid any attention to a new guy. We got in through the gate, the infrared scan showed thirteen bodies inside the truck. When we got to the house, I cracked back into the security system—" He touched the palm in the pocket of his jacket. "A couple changes, one of which was to zap in a photo and employment record for one Donna Jones. Used your photo from your driver's license. Cracked into the security gate grid. Made certain that fourteen bodies were now listed as having been in the truck. Next, find you. We make our way, nice and easy, back to the truck. No one pays us any attention; the estate gate is no problem. The main gate infrared counts fourteen bodies, which matches the entry scan, and that is that."

"Amazing."

"Initiated the little program I'd set up to call in the 'emergency' that got us out of the truck. All traces of which are now gone. No one will remember us."

At that moment they passed a litter basket, and Augur folded up the Tower Records bag with the coveralls in it and tossed it through.

Cece stared at Augur. His wire-rimmed glasses were slightly tinted, but they did not hide a pair of well-shaped, intelligent dark eyes.

"And if it hadn't been cleaning day?" she asked, her sense of unreality increasing.

"Someone would have called in for a delivery of flowers, or a package, or food, or a repair, though those are a little dicier. But the perfect disguise is always the ordinary, the expected."

"So how did you know I was there?"

"Ah." He smiled slightly. "We'll get to that. For now, let's take a stroll, sit down and watch the sun set over Santa Monica."

Cece shook her head, still fighting against that sense of unreality.

They walked down to Sunset Boulevard and kept moving along the tree-shaded sidewalks until they reached a bus stop. Two or three people were there, sitting on the bench, one of them having some sort of argument on her global. Augur made a courtly gesture, inviting Cece to sit down on the one space left. She did, trying not to listen to the argument going on three feet away, and Augur took up a stance next to her. She heard his global beep faintly once. He pulled it out and activated it, said, "Yes?" and after an interval, "Fine."

A bus trundled up, and everyone but Cece and Augur got on. No one gave them a second look. The bus doors slammed shut, and the vehicle moved smoothly back into the traffic.

Augur sat down next to Cece.

"Are we waiting for something? Or someone?" Cece finally asked.

"Yes," Augur said. "Your car."

Cece stared at him blankly.

Augur gave her a brief smile. "Your former host, Neville Carlton IV, ought to have discovered you'd gone missing about the time we reached Sunset. Add on a few minutes for him to figure out the cleaning service was the likely culprit, and to call, just to find himself stymied. His next order will most likely be for his big friend to hot-wire your automobile, drive it nice and quiet to some big supermarket parking lot—somewhere away from Beverly Hills—and leave it there. Somewhere down below Olympic would be my guess. When he leaves it, the signal I planted on it before I went into the house will let me know." He tapped his palm computer.

Cece was both nervous and fascinated. "That's assuming he hasn't all that arcane tech that you've got."

"He hasn't," Augur replied in a mild voice, "or I wouldn't have found it so easy to bust his house system. He's not a professional. He's an amateur who thinks he's a professional, which is far worse than a straight-on amateur, who at least knows he's ignorant." A quick smile.

And you're a professional, Cece thought, waiting for him to say it, but Augur didn't. "You're part of the Resistance," she observed at last.

He did not confirm or deny. Just smiled.

At that moment the palm bleeped. He pulled it out, unfolded it, looked at the screen, tapped a control, pocketed the palm. "Now," he said, "it's time to plan."

"No," she said, the haze starting to clear from her mind. "It's time for me to call the authorities."

Augur shook his head slowly.

Cece turned to face him. "Why not?"

"Do you really want to land yourself in a windowless little room somewhere, you and a Taelon and one of their CVI techs?"

Cece touched her neck and shuddered. Then frowned. "How do you know that was to be my fate?"

"I don't. But I think it likely, based on their MO so far, when dealing with certain types of humans. You came up on their radar, for some reason, so they want to deal with you. Nice and polite and perfectly legal—except you won't have any say in the matter."

"I don't believe it," Cece said. "Oh, I don't trust them, but it's their influence I don't trust, and their oblique threat."

"Then why did you run this morning?"

Good question, Cece thought. She said, "Maybe it was a mistake. But I've committed no crime, and I'm just an ordinary citizen; and so far, the biggest threat I can name has been from a fellow human."

Augur cocked his head to one side.

Cece said, "Speaking of whom: If you don't permit me to call the authorities, then I am as much a prisoner here as I was in that Carlton fellow's house."

Augur sighed. Another bleep sounded. "Your car is around the corner up that way a few blocks," he said. "Our buddy Neville didn't see fit to have it taken very far away, just out of his turf."

He said nothing more as they crossed a major boulevard and then turned down a smaller street. At once Cece spotted her homely old car, looking odd among the expensive late models lining the street. She dug her keys out of her bag and somewhat apprehensively approached, but Augur didn't say anything about ruined wiring or car bombs or anything else.

She unlocked the car, which looked exactly as she'd left it. Her global still lay in the glove compartment; she was surprised to find it there. In silence she retrieved it, looked around at the houses. No one was visible in any of the windows, but she still felt curiously exposed.

All right, then, she'd make her call around the corner, back in the park, away from the windows.

Meantime, how to get this unnerving fellow to go away and leave her alone? She owed him her life, which made a rude "Please go away" impossible. How about ignoring him?

Augur walked beside her in silence as she led the way back to Sunset and to the little grassy park along the street. No one could see them except people in passing cars, but those whizzed by too fast for her to feel spied upon.

She looked at Augur, who said nothing. Somewhat defiantly she tabbed the little red key that automatically dialed 911.

A middle-aged woman in a gray uniform appeared in the screen. She said, "Ms. Robin?"

It jolted Cece to have her name known. But of course her global was registered in her name, and there was the little winking eye of the vid pickup. And caller ID had been a fact of life for many years. Still. All this cloak-and-dagger stuff so far had made her jumpy.

"I would like to report an attempted kidnapping," she stated.

"Thank you," replied the woman, glancing down again. "If you will remain where you are, we will provide an escort, and you may make your report in person and safety." A short burst of static almost blanked the woman, but there she was again.

"Thank you," Cece said, feeling more unsettled by the moment. She didn't really want *anyone* taking her in for "safety." She was about to insist that she stand there on the street and give her information and then continue home—except she remembered that they knew where her home was.

Stop it, she thought irritably.

Either she trusted the authorities, or she didn't.

"I'll wait," she said.

The woman smiled, nodded. Another short burst of static, and the global blanked.

Augur said, "I believe this is my cue to exit—" He frowned, staring down at the global in her hand.

Cece looked down at it, half expecting to see it sprout wings, but she just caught the end of a brief flicker of lights through the screen and then a kind of stylized overlay—like a map, with a light that blinked with a frenzied speed. An urgent speed, somehow.

"Here," Augur said, taking it from her grasp. He hadn't seemed to move fast, but quite suddenly he had it and she didn't, and before she could draw enough breath to protest, he threw it away, hard, onto the grass.

"What the—" she squeaked as Augur thrust her behind the sturdy bole of a California black oak and held her there.

A moment later a perfectly straight bolt of lightning lanced out of the sky. Cece's global—and an eight-foot radius of grass around it—exploded.

SEVEN

They got back around the corner fast. Cece never remembered how, later. In her memory, one moment she was staring at that terrible light, smelling the hot stench of ozone and vaporized soil and then burned grass. Next moment, she stood, panting, across from her car while Augur glanced skyward, took his global from his pocket, snapped it open.

Detect location program initiated on <AUGUR>. Deflection program <MIRROR> initiated. Estimated duration of deflection 1.46 minutes. Do you wish to initiate deflection program <JACKAL>?

He tapped the command sigil for Search on source.

Blocked.

Another tap: Vector?

Encrypted comms, sender: <LIAM KINCAID>.

Well, damn.

Initiate <JACKAL>.

He hit the Enter key, his emotions in a turmoil. Not that he was going to show it.

He looked up. Saw Cece's blanched, staring face and said to her, "There are tracking devices built into most commercial models. Most people don't know about them simply because the Taelons don't bother with the movements of most people."

Cece said numbly, "Don't you have one in yours as well?"

Augur considered his words as he stared down at the new overlay, an outline of the continental United States, with a circle edging slowly outward from somewhere in the east—Washington, D.C., at a guess—though that could be faked, the signal bounced off the same sort of sat that had been activated to zap them. For that matter, the search could even have originated off the Taelon Mothership.

Search sender Liam Kincaid. No, don't think about that now.

Now was for the immediate problem: He had maybe sixty seconds until the searcher's program took down Augur's mirror global sites and located him.

He smiled at the anxious-looking teacher. "I programmed mine to ward the latest snooptech, but you never know what's really recent, do you?"

With that he touched the key pattern for total hard-data wipe, waited until the final bleep, carefully placed his global on the sidewalk, lifted a shoe, brought it down with a crunch. The device flickered and then went dead; he paused, memory forcing its way into his mind. He'd smashed his global once before. Image: Lili Marquette, face pale, body trembling in the grip of the lethally addictive drug bliss. Emotion: regret, tenderness—

Forcing away both emotion and memory he bent to retrieve the smashed device. He kicked it into a thick shrub, dusted his fingertips, and said, "I suggest we move along."

Cece became aware of the noise of people around the corner, exclaiming, wondering, and in the distance fire sirens.

"The grass is probably still smoldering. And I suspect someone—whether Volunteers, police, or someone in plain clothes with a serious lack of a sense of humor—will be by to nose around within a minute or two. When they don't find our charred remains, they will probably look around the corner. We really don't want to be lurking nearby."

"No." Her voice squeaked, but she no longer cared.

Twenty seconds later they slid into her car. No more question of being alone, or safe, or contacting the authorities. The authorities! As she went through the mechanical motions of buckling her seat belt and starting the car, Cece kept seeing that light, and the explosion, over and over in her brain. The rest of her thoughts flickered limply in and out of view, like flies in a fog.

She drove south, a randomly picked direction. Augur said nothing. He took out his palm, and she heard the modem tweet and hiss, then the silence of connection. As she stopped for a red light he began tapping at the keys.

They'd crossed Wilshire Boulevard and were surrounded by traffic, when a stray thought glimmered long enough in her mind to express it. "Someone might be looking for my license plates."

"Yes. We're staying in your car only long enough to get to one of those parking lots I mentioned. Please take a left on Santa Monica."

She did. Four or five blocks later—short blocks, but slow traffic and long red lights—Augur nodded at a huge supermarket on a corner, and in silence Cece drove in and made her way to the back row. She slowed down to a crawl, parking when Augur indicated. She sat, still stunned, while he finished whatever it was he was doing on the palm, then shut it down.

"The car's over here." They got out, and though she knew it was foolish, she locked her car anyway. A gesture of defiance—even though her privacy, and rights, had been violated six ways to Sunday this long, nightmarish day, she was not about to make it easy for them. Let "them"—whoever they were—go to the trouble of picking her lock when they did pounce on her car.

The waiting car was late model, plain, the engine starting up with the hum of the well-cared-for vehicle. This time Augur was behind the wheel.

As he eased onto the boulevard, he said, "How much cash do you have?"

"Not much. I have my cash card—oh."

"Right. Useless, unless we want to let them know you're still alive, and provide a vector on where we're going at the same time."

Cece sighed, leaned her head back, took off her glasses and rubbed her eyes. "Where are we going?" she asked presently.

"For now, I think out of L.A. will do."

While Augur drove and Cecilia Robin stared in numb shock at the lane dividers flashing by in endless rows on the smooth gray tarmac, Da'an opaqued a window in the Taelon Embassy in Washington, D.C., and stared out at the sunset colors washing past the monumental plinth built to honor the young republic's first president.

To Da'an the United States was a very young republic, desperately young, still struggling to define itself despite accelerating technological change. Such instability was usually a lethal recipe, yet somehow—so far—humankind had not quite managed to destroy itself. As had other cultures, alas. Yet they were so very far from stable in any rational sense. Human beings were a danger, to themselves and every other life-form on their planet.

They were also endlessly fascinating. That too was dangerous. Was protracted exposure to the vagaries of human civilization as poisonous on the mental plane as it was on the physical?

And what about the potential of Liam Kincaid, hybrid human and Kimeran, born just a couple of years ago yet gifted with memories from a race more ancient than the Taelons?

Da'an turned away, aware of the need for energy infusion. Yet it would not do to reveal weakness, just as it would not do to reveal even to Liam either the continued need to ingest kryss, or the fact that it was still being manufactured, only not on the planet.

Da'an's attention shifted from contemplation to the specific and immediate: Liam Kincaid had interrupted his own unconscious rhythms in viewing the day's communications on the data stream and now stood with the alert stillness of the deer at bay.

Another human trait, betraying both the youth and the vigor of this species, how fast—how compellingly vivid—were their physical instincts. What had caused Liam to stand so poised for either flight or attack?

Da'an would discover in time, if circumstances required. More important was to maintain the very delicate balance of . . . conditional trust, call it.

The centuries had trained Da'an to be patient and to watch.

So while Da'an stood in the center of a blue-lit chamber and waved on the energy shower, Liam covertly observed. Da'an appeared to be serene, lost in meditation.

Liam watched for a few moments the mesmerizing pattern of the energy shower, visible as multicolored lights, a beautiful but lethal to humans display safely prisoned behind the Taelon virtual glass.

Then he returned to the data stream and flicked his fingers over the control that would shift the rest of the day's E-mail to his terminal.

By the time mail got to this level it was usually something that had to be dealt with. Not always, of course, which was why Da'an had come to rely on Liam to do a preliminary scan.

There was normally a continuous stream of diplomatic CCs that were relayed by courtesy, to be noted and deleted. Liam usually worked fast, sorting communications into various categories by priority. But when he saw a CC from the National Council of Concerned Parents and Teachers, he went on the alert.

At his desk he punched up the E-mail: As per your request we are sending this reminder of the award dinner (five hundred dollars a plate is the requested donation) to be held in Oak Park, Illinois, honoring the newest recipient of the Curriculum Advisement Honorarium, on June 27th, to which the North American Companion Da'an is invited to attend.

Liam deleted the letter. His office deleted hundreds of such requests each day, and no one would ever hunt up the log to check on this one. Liam did not smile or in any way show his inner amusement at Augur's tricks for hiding in plain sight.

Only Augur would send E-mail to Da'an's office, however many layers disguised the real intent. He operated on the age-old principle that the safest place for the criminal to hide was under the sheriff's bed—and so far, at least, it worked.

Liam sorted through the remainder of the mail, forwarded the highest-priority messages back to Da'an's data stream, and then rose to make a circuit of the office. Quiet, peaceful, everyone busy, Da'an motionless in the energy bath, the atmosphere blue-tinged, deceptively peaceful.

He logged on to the Internet, checking various sites, then clicking on links within the sites until he reached a series of links for hobby collectors. Yet another of Augur's many dodges: This site was for collectors of nineteenth-century sheriff badges, and it just listed rows of items and the basic offering price.

All of them legitimate—or almost all.

There—moments old—was a new listing whose code signified Augur's birthday, or at least what he claimed was his birthday.

Liam hit the link, and information about a fictitious badge windowed up, briefly overlaid with ancient Irish runes. He touched one, and the downloaded data decrypted, new text replacing the old.

Found the teacher. She called 911, effecting laser strike on our position. I have 86ed my global. What do you know about this?

Liam touched the rune again, and the overlay as well as the text vanished, one of Augur's embedded worms erasing the letter from the log.

Laser strike?

He turned around, staring across the quiet space at Da'an, who still stood motionless, mind shifted into the Commonality.

It's not what I know, he thought, it's what they know. But Augur's question implied distrust, underscored by the fact that he hadn't added any data on his current position or plans.

Liam faced west, as if he could see across the miles to the California coast. Laser strike, not on a military threat but on a civilian who had no record of any kind, except as an educator of human children. Zo'or? Sandoval? Half an hour ago he would have insisted that they wouldn't do anything like that—but Zo'or, and Sandoval, had surprised him again and again.

EIGHT

Augur slapped his palm shut, sat back, and sighed.

He thought wistfully of his lair seven hundred feet beneath the quiet St. Michael's Church in D.C. His stronghold, where he had all the tech and power he needed.

That is, if his Jackal program did not blow it up first.

With Liam Kincaid inside.

Leave that. For now he was sitting here in this car on a barren cliff overlooking the Interstate 15. Car lights whizzed by below, punching into the otherwise intense darkness. Overhead, the clear-etched stars glittered with alien indifference in the desert sky. The air was warm, as the earth released the day's heat. Far in the west the sky glowed faintly, a vast umbrella of reflected light from L.A.'s millions of gigawatts of electricity.

Silhouetted against it was Cecilia Robin's unprepossessing figure, and Augur sighed again. It wasn't just the total lack of elegance in that silhouette. Augur did like the company of elegant ladies; brains, beauty, and cool competence were surefire attraction magnets. But he didn't require elegance in his female companions. He did, however, prefer to avoid protracted interaction with constituted authority.

He'd distrusted authority ever since he could remember. And it was amazing just how many forms of constituted authority human civilization managed to concoct—some of them contradictory.

That short, round silhouette represented the constituted authority called School. Supposedly the safe haven of learning, School. Hah. They'd been told that, but as young as four Augur had figured out that what adults told you and what really existed were too frequently night and day.

Was School ever a haven of learning? Did Plato, sitting under the olive trees with his students in long-ago and faraway ancient Athens, have rules and regs that forced his students into conformity, thus creating ideal citizens as envisioned by the state? Of course, even if they had perfect freedom, there was only a narrow segment of society that could join: Greek freedmen, leaving out 98 percent of the rest of the ancient world.

Why was he wasting time?

He stashed the palm in his shirt pocket and opened the car door.

"Time for a war council," he suggested.

Cecilia Robin turned around, the faint reflected light not weak enough to hide her puffy eyes and red nose. She'd been standing there silently weeping and made no effort to hide it. But she didn't whine or whimper.

"First some questions," she said. "That you are a member of the Resistance I guess I can assume. But that doesn't tell me how or why."

Augur kept his voice even. "How much do you want to hear?"

"I want to hear the truth."

"I said 'how much,' not 'what.' Of course I'll tell you the truth," he retorted, but mildly. He'd spent most of his life on the run. This appeared to be her first brush with trouble.

She made a helpless gesture, noticed that her fingers were shaking, and clasped them tightly before her. "Why did you come to my rescue? Who sent you?" she asked, fighting to steady her voice.

Augur's head tipped back, and the corners of his mouth quirked sardonically. "Let's regard my initial response as hypertext," he said. "Every use of the word *somebody* is a URL leading to encrypted information. If you choose to hit the tab, you have to take responsibility for what you might hear, just as I will have to take responsibility for how much I tell you."

"Why tell me anything at all?" she hedged. Her glasses flashed with yellow streaks, reflections from headlights passing below, hiding her eyes.

"Because you cleared the first level, you might say. Unknowingly, but still. Someone was traveling in L.A. That someone contacted another someone who routinely monitors Taelon interactions with civilian life and found out that you—among several others, but you headed the list—were slated for an interview with the Taelons for some new television program."

"Television program?" Cece laughed. "That hardly sounds sinister."

"It does when you add in the rumor that the job comes with built-in Taelon tech—such as a Cyber-Viral Implant, commonly called a CVI. By which the Taelons can insure obedience to their will. Now supposedly those are outdated. But the tech is conveniently there."

"Uhn." Cece's shoulders went up, and one hand rose protectively to her neck. "So Lou—someone at school thought, as well."

Augur pretended not to notice the slip. "Anyway, my somebody was not the only one who monitored this information. As you are aware, someone in Neville's group monitored the same data. At about the time that your student friend was sending you warning E-mail, my first somebody—let's call this one Somebody Three—who knew I was out here on the coast taking care of some completely unrelated business, contacted me and asked me to make a quick end run."

Cece drew in a deep breath. "That *was* you, wasn't it? At school—" She had been about to say "yesterday," but in fact it had been that very morning, the start of an impossibly long day.

"Yes. It seems that while I and my Somebody Four, who was a local contact who happened to be free and have wheels, were being jabbered into catatonia by your principal, you were sliding out the back way. Smooth work," he added. "Didn't know teachers always leave open a back-way escape route as part of the school curriculum."

"How else do we avoid troublesome parents?" It was a weak retort, but she was trying, and he responded with the smile she'd hoped to get.

"Well, the reason—" Augur hesitated, thinking again of Liam's name showing up on that search parameter some-one had initiated on his global just after the laser strike. Fake? Or not?

He'd know for certain soon.

"A possible reason," he corrected, "that I was sent, and not a local, is that I happen to be very good at certain kinds of . . . shall we call it electronic information retrieval?"

"Cracking," Cece said, but not accusingly.

"And that as well." Augur saw that she was smiling, and he smiled back. "Anyway, your global being the cheapest possible model, I was able to cut in and retrieve record of your incoming and outgoing calls. Your friend Scooby had listed Neville Carlton's place as her address; it popped up when I ran a search on her number, and so I set a few things up, while traveling up into L.A., arriving not long after you did."

"I wonder if Scooby's group knows that I was rescued rather than that I escaped on my own?"

"No telling," Augur said, grinning. "My guess is that our friend Neville has by now gotten his place lookin' squeaky clean, and they're sitting tight, waiting for the Volunteers to crash through the back windows, because of course he'd expect you to nine-one-one 'em as soon as you could."

She smiled.

"And then there was that laser strike."

That wiped her smile away.

"Carlton probably has just enough contacts to find out that it was triggered on your call. But that's ahead of the game. Let's go back."

"All right."

"Just about the time I got into Carlton's house, with my

electronic ears up, you might say, almost the first thing I overheard was that conversation I played back for you, so I decided you might need a hand, and here I am." He added, "I don't usually do the breaking-and-entering kind of thing. I'm more of a data broker, you might say."

Cece looked down at the dusty ground. His easy tone and mild words made the whole thing sound effortless, but she thought of that cleaning company, the faked phone calls, the uniforms, and realized just how much work had gone into her rescue—and how fast it had been done. Augur had to have had willing help from unknown people, whose motivation seemed to be just a wish to be helpful. Or?

She glanced up, her glasses flashing again. "That first Somebody. Can you tell me his or her motivation? Was it altruism? It does sound like it."

"Yes, I can attest to that," Augur replied. "Altruism indeed. But before we go further with motivations and identities, the first firewall is one you'll have to break yourself. The subject," he added in a quiet voice, "is the Resistance. You're a law-abiding citizen. I'm not."

Cece drew in a shaky breath. "I thought—I didn't know the Resistance as a movement still existed. I assumed they were wiped out. During the State of Siege. After the presidential election."

"Many were. Too many." Augur glanced down at the freeway, the cars whooshing by now fewer in number. "But not all. And they have reorganized."

"I see." Cece rubbed her aching forehead. "I don't believe in the use of violence. Or in actions that make a mockery of our country's laws. With those as a given, tell me what you can."

"Many of our country's laws are a mockery," he replied, "but I realize that my retort could be construed as merely flippant. You mean the spirit and not the letter. I think I can work within your given parameters, if you in turn can promise me that what I tell you will stay behind your own communicational firewall."

Cece hesitated, then her head bobbed, a quick determined gesture, betraying her tension.

"The first Somebody is Dr. Julianne Belman," Augur said. "Out here for a medical conference at UCLA Medical Center, focusing on human-Taelon developments in surgery."

"Julianne." Cece breathed unsteadily, thinking of that call on her global just after she left school. How quickly—one might say how self-righteously—she'd disconnected the call. If she'd listened . . .

If she'd listened, where would she be?

"The second Somebody is the new Orange County cell leader. Only one cell, right now. There used to be a couple more, but they got caught in the State of Emergency dragnet. This is another reason why I was dispatched: They don't have many people left anymore who can down tools, formulate an excuse, and slip out of their real lives to run to the rescue. Too many with hidden lives have learned to keep them hidden, because we all saw what happened to people who trusted too wide a circle with news of their Resistance membership."

Cece winced. "I couldn't watch the news during that time," she admitted. "Once I knew that the president was all right—" She shook her head. "And your Somebody Three?"

"Ah, that one has another firewall," he said. "And perhaps another again. Let's wait on that, shall we? Until I find out some facts myself."

Cece pressed her lips together, against words about violence, trust, betrayal, and outlaw behavior. She might be wrong, and she would certainly sound wrong. "A last question."

"Yes?"

"Do you think Scooby's group somehow got that laser thing to try to fry us?"

"No chance," Augur said. "Neville may think he's got some hot crackers, but they're just script kiddies, probably think their ability to morph music videos with their favorite anime figures means they're hot stuff. No way could they crack the defense systems. No, it's probably all over the news by now, and I suspect they are as scared as you are."

"Script kiddies?"

"Pre-Taelon slang for computer amateurs who think they're hot stuff. Crackers write and put up the real heavy programs. Script kiddies DL 'em and use 'em. Even little kids use various scripts to make their own music vids now, just as teens were passing music back and forth a few years ago."

"Oh." Cece felt a sense of helplessness. "So what do we do now?"

"Well, we're here with a full tank of gas, but not much else. And L.A. is way too hot for us. Unless you have someone to call who might hide us?"

Cece thought of her sibs, and then shook her head. Everything Augur had said about the State of Siege applied to her family. They'd be sick with terror—on their own behalf, on behalf of her nieces and nephews.

In fact, there were probably sinister people knocking on their doors right now, and the best thing she could do was make certain that they were speaking the absolute truth when they denied knowing where she was, or what could have happened.

She sighed, feeling the tug of grief again, but she fought it back.

Augur had hesitated. She looked up, and he said, "I suggest we get ourselves to the City That Makes All Things Possible and equip ourselves appropriately. By then a few more answers might turn up, pointing to our next step."

" 'City That Makes All Things Possible'?"

"If you have enough money." Augur nodded, grinning. "Aka Las Vegas, Nevada."

NINE

Renee Palmer crossed Constitution Avenue and stepped onto the pathway leading into the Mall, Washington, D.C.'s most famous park. Early morning during spring and early summer was the only time to be outside in D.C.; the air was warm and soft as sun-dried silk. Puffy white clouds drifted overhead, lacy against the pale blue sky. Surrounding monuments were obscured by the last pastel cherry blossoms on the trees.

Renee drew in a deep breath, smelling fresh-cut grass, flowers, and the occasional tang of expensive scents on passing joggers. Most likely rain was on the way, probably thunder, and before then the warmth would intensify into sticky heat, but by that time Renee would be ensconced in her climate-controlled office at Doors International, where humidity, lightning, and thunder could rage uselessly against the walls. Control.

She loved her office. It was a bastion of command, of control—except that particular image was deceptive, or she wouldn't be here at all. Tight as she held the leash on ever-changing spytech, she had to admit that the Taelons still held mastery. The horrors of technological mind manipulation that had secretly been built into the great business center at 1 Taelon Avenue was still a painful memory; the living proof Joshua Doors, once her friend, now no more to be trusted than Zo'or. *My tech's bigger than your tech.*

So while she held the leash on Doors International's tech R&D, the Taelons leashed the world. An inescapable truth that fueled her determination to break that leash in such a way that they could never reforge that choke chain.

A good image. She smiled grimly.

The Mall was full of people out to enjoy the mild morning while it lasted. Small children ran about, a few nannies walking more slowly, their faces vigilant as they watched their charges. Joggers stitched their way through the slower crowds, most of them wired into music or the news. A cluster of elderly men encircled a park bench where two of their number played their eternal chess game. In the middle distance, where there was nothing but open grass, she saw the usual soccer game, a scattering of people gathered on the perimeter watching.

Renee noted them all, her eyes rising inevitably to the weird yet compellingly graceful tower of the Taelon Embassy opposite the Washington Monument.

Weird. Compellingly graceful. *Alien.* Commanding the view, which was both symbolic and ironic. If people came out here to forget the existence of the Taelon overlords, they had to keep their eyes lowered.

Renee came here because no Taelons did, and their tech—despite their damn choke chain on the world—was not sophisticated enough for snooping in the open air. Though she never went near the deceptively artistic public ID portal at the far end of the Mall.

She walked on, smiling gently at those whose gazes she encountered, until she saw a familiar tall male form approaching from the other side of the park. Then a row of flowering shrubs blocked Liam Kincaid from view. At the same time two long, lanky teens in slouch pants skateboarded by. One of them, kind of cute in a puppyish way—no older than seventeen—gave Renee a brashly appraising look, and when their eyes met, he grinned.

She knew her effect on men. She always dressed carefully. It was a measure of control as well as a desire to live as artistically as one was capable that made her conscious of her appearance. And of her effect on others.

She did not lose her own smile, but she didn't increase it either. A cool lift of her brows, and the kid sailed past with a challenging flourish of skateboard technique as if to say, See what you're missing?

Yeah, right. Tell it to the Taelons.

Liam emerged from the tree-shadowed pathway and fell in step beside her. Renee looked up into eyes that were sometimes blue, sometimes greenish gray, as changeable as the sea, and felt the customary tug of attraction. But—this had become habit—she squashed it. He looked like a very attractive man somewhere in his early thirties, but she knew that he'd never had a human childhood, had been denied the comfort of a family, much less the emotion-fraught trials and tribulations of adolescence.

"Your news is?" she asked, keeping her tone wry.

"First: Did you watch television news last night or this morning?"

"Neither. I was at the theater last night, and this morning I breakfasted with some investors. Just got away. So color me ignorant."

"Last weekend Augur went to the West Coast for more of his obscure business affairs."

"Okay." Renee repressed a smile. Business affairs, right, she thought to herself.

"Yesterday Julianne contacted me, and I contacted Augur. Orange County was one of the hardest hit among the Resistance groups during Sandoval's bloodbath after the election. Right now it's difficult to find anyone who can run errands at a moment's notice, and Augur was there, so I asked him to make what looked like a fairly routine, but last-minute, Resistance rescue on a civilian who has no ties to either the Taelons or the Resistance."

"Not a military person, then?"

Liam shook his head. "A schoolteacher."

"A schoolteacher?" Renee frowned. "Well that's got to be a first. I wonder—no. Go on. So Augur didn't get this person?"

"Oh, he did, all right, and they were almost shot by a air-to-ground laser strike, triggered by her global call to nine-one-one."

"You did say a *schoolteacher*?"

"Yes."

Renee heard the echo of the laughing schoolkids. "I take it this was not a legally constituted military operation."

Liam gave her a brief smile. "Someone broke through the firewalls and raided the sat command codes. The entire upper levels of the various services are snarling like wolves, Sandoval being the chief snapper, as you can imagine. I'm surprised you didn't hear."

"There might be something waiting in my message queue, but as yet this isn't exactly private sector news. No one in the Resistance contacted me, either, which I realize is more puzzling."

"That's because it's a mystery to them as well. None of them could get those codes, though many have tried."

"So we don't know who. How about why?"

Liam sighed. "Well, that's what I have to find out. Now, what was it you were about to say?"

"I just wondered if this teacher business could somehow be related to this prospective education program that keeps popping up on my radar at Doors International."

"What is that about?"

"I don't know. I have to confess, I really didn't think I needed to know. I leave the purely PR nonsense to the staff, and that includes visiting schools and talking about the Taelons' greatness to the kiddies, which is what I assumed was going on there."

Liam thought rapidly. "Curious."

"You do know something!"

"Well, it might not be related, as you said. Except that this particular PR dog-and-pony show is taking place on a college campus."

"Go on," Renee said. Liam looked around, his manner unconcerned, but she felt that inward visceral sense of impending danger.

He said, "You probably already know the superficial details, since Doors International matched the Taelons' education grant providing scholarships for promising future biotechnicians—"

She flicked her fingers up in a quick, butterfly gesture. "Don't tell me. Da'an's scheduled appearance at Yale's Old Campus in New Haven on July Fourth, to unveil the new statue honoring the Companions."

"Except it's not Da'an who's making this appearance."

"What?" Renee looked askance. "He's still the North American Companion, or have I suddenly got lost in a time warp?"

"No."

"Well, then, it's his purview—"

Liam shook his head once.

"You can't be suggesting that Zo'or is going to go instead?"

"Got it in one."

"Why? This is, as near as I could tell, one of those boring political goodwill appearance things whose only real benefit for us is in keeping Sandoval and his minions busy scurrying about providing security."

"A job Sandoval just assigned me," Liam put in, looking sardonic. "That is, as soon as he checks out the territory himself."

Renee frowned. "Something is not computing here. Zo'or has replaced Da'an as the Taelon rep at the Yale unveiling?"

"Correct."

"And you are still Da'an's Protector."

"Correct."

"Just as Sandoval is Zo'or's."

"Correct."

Renee paused as a swarm of giggling school-aged girls ran by.

"So you're telling me that our favorite hands-on, trust-no-one FBI agent is not going to oversee every inch of that very public spot, Yale's Old Campus green, his very own personal self, the entire time?"

"That's what I'm telling you. Though he did say he's going there to check it out before he turns it over to me, which is more in character."

"Meaning he expects it to be so boring, so tedious, that he can't be bothered to be there—"

"Or he's got something else going at the same time. I've been thinking just that," Liam said, his expression and voice serious. "Meanwhile, there could be any number of reasons Zo'or is doing the gig himself. He really could be worried about his public image, which even he knows stinks."

"This is true."

"Look, you could help me here. I need to investigate this business with Augur, which is going to take time and care. But I'd also like to know for certain why Zo'or was substituted for Da'an, because Da'an himself doesn't know. When asked he told me it was Synod business and as such could not be discussed."

Renee nodded; she'd heard that before. The Taelons' controlling body, so to speak, was the Synod. Most of them stayed somewhere in space, communicating with Zo'or—and Da'an—by the psychic link they called the Commonality. Frequently the Taelons gave as reasons for their actions "Synod business"—which wasn't any reason at all.

"That excuse can work two ways," Liam went on. "Zo'or could have been given an order without a reason. Maybe there's a better clue in the Doors data files. Like *when* the substitution was made."

"All right, I'll run a check. So when do we meet again?"

She smiled, watching how the ambiguity in her tone caused a slight flush along Liam's handsome cheekbones.

She knew she ought not to bait him. And she didn't do it often. Not really. She did have her standards, and she was usually careful to keep her distance and use a light tone. He felt more comfortable with wryness, they both knew it.

But now she smiled at him, thinking, You've got a big boy's body, and you're going to have to grow up some time.

"When we have something to share," he said.

Ooh, a zinger! She laughed, waved a hand, and took off down a side pathway, without looking back.

While Liam and Renee returned to the embassy and Doors International's HQ respectively, the miles sped away under Augur's hands. Broken lane markers blurred into white lines stretching forever parallel into the faint smear of dawn on the flat horizon. Cool air whispered from the AC vents, for even at this hour the desert air was as searing as the breath of some vast dragon.

Augur lifted tired eyes, saw a smudge against that horizon, not the sky but on the ground, and blinked. They had split the driving, each taking three hours. The teacher now slumped against the shotgun-seat backrest, snoring faintly in the deep sleep of exhaustion.

A quick glance. Unlovely as she looked right now—mouth half open, glasses askew, her hair untidy around her middle-aged face—Augur smiled in appreciation. She'd gamely offered to take the first driving shift, though from time to time he'd seen the gleam of tears drip down from under her glasses onto her rumpled, sensible beige dress. But complain? Not she. When, during her last hour, she'd said, "Talk to me, please," they'd discoursed on nineteenth-century literature, and her observations were sharp, her tone one of very dry humor.

After the changeover she'd tried gamely to keep talking for his sake, but right in the middle of a comparison of Melville and Twain her considering gaze had gone distant, and then, suddenly, she'd conked off.

Augur blinked, glanced up from the mesmerizing road to the horizon. Ah. The glow of dawn was augmented by the radiance of the ferocious wattage of Vegas, tall rectangles etched against the arid sky.

Good. Just a couple hours more, and this dreary road would stretch behind them. His three hours were up, he supposed, but he'd keep driving. All-nighters came with

Augur's territory, whereas he suspected the times Cecilia Robin made it past midnight were probably countable on one hand.

First things first. Get to the city, find a hotel, a shower, and a phone jack. Not necessarily in that order.

As Augur considered which of his many identities to resurrect, Renee considered her plan of attack. She had done some checking on Liam's errand, finding nothing. She expected that. In fact, the blatant lack of data, she decided, was evidence.

She closed down her system after cleaning the RAM and encrypting her log and then closed her office. A brief stop in her private rest room to check hair, lipstick, and the hang of her exquisitely tailored linen suit, for she would not be stepping out into the 90-degree heat and humidity. Doors International had its own ID portal. Of course the Taelons, ever helpful in providing it, kept a log on who went where—but she knew that. And used the knowledge to strengthen her own cover.

The Volunteer at the ID portal greeted her with a respectful nod, and she stepped through, not without a visceral pang of trepidation. Inward, of course. No sign of how difficult it was to trust the Taelons to shift her from this location to that—even when "that" was the Mothership itself—diminished her poise.

No chance. She was on the warpath.

The hum of energy reverberated through her teeth; she sniffed a faint whiff of ozone and then stepped out into the cool blue interior of the Mothership.

An upper-rank Volunteer greeted her. "Miss Palmer?"

"I have an appointment with Agent Sandoval."

The armed guards stood, impassive, as she passed them by. Her footsteps were soundless on the slightly giving floor; air with a faint exotic scent blew against her face. Despite the Taelons' main biological component being energy, there was no heat here, no killingly dry air, no sense of the withering of living tissues as used to exist in rooms with high EM. The Taelons had evoked the atmosphere of an autumn herb garden.

Sandoval stood, hands behind his back, before a flowing data stream, his dark eyes scanning rapidly. He was dressed, as always, in an elegant dark suit, his tie knotted by a precise hand, his expensive shirt fresh. Renee knew without ever having discussed such a subject that Ronald Sandoval, like her, regarded clothing as armor. That it also was elegant was meant to deflect focus, to deceive.

He saw her. She felt the impact of his gaze through the flashing lights of the data stream, an impact not unlike a jolt of electricity. Was he as aware as she of this unspoken attraction?

Yeah. Had to be. For it was the attraction not just of chemistry but also of danger.

His mouth tightened in a slight smile, one expressive of mockery.

He anticipated the duel just as much as she did.

"Miss Palmer?" he said, waving a hand.

The data stream vanished. Long-time etiquette stated that you don't glance at anyone's terminal unless invited, or step within the sound cone of his global; Sandoval didn't want her to politely avert her eyes. She would have read it if she could. And he knew it. His gesture was the opening move in the duel.

"You asked for this interview," he went on. "What is so important we could not be in contact by global?"

Time to riposte.

"I so detest," she drawled, "those mysterious emergencies, or power surges, or interferences that cause communication to mysteriously shut down just when discussion is at its most interesting."

Was that a suppressed laugh narrowing his eyes?

It was, but his control was just as innate as hers.

"And so?" he prompted, neither confirming nor denying. "Your interesting discussion?"

"Several things." And she launched into her list.

It was a list with worldwide reach, chosen so that he would not know which item was her priority query. He dealt with the first five items, and in exactly the same tone she'd used previously, she said, "Then there's the—shall we say—abrupt substitution of Zo'or for Da'an at the Yale Companion Statue unveiling."

"This is a problem?" he countered.

"My security team insists that it is, because, as you probably know, most of the Doors execs will be present. It is you yourself who has previously refused to cooperate with Doors International on security setups. We've had no such problems with Da'an's embassy staff."

"You mean," Sandoval said, "you have no problems with Liam Kincaid. So we have noted."

Lunge, disengage, riposte.

"Good," she said, smiling. "I like a reputation for cooperation. It's good for business."

Sandoval gave her a sardonic glance.

"So . . . is there a reason for this substitution?"

"Zo'or wishes to improve his public relations," Sandoval said.

It was too ready, too facile, but she hadn't expected any more than that. What she wanted to do was let him know she was interested—and then find out what he did about it after she left.

She nodded, then went on to the next item on her list. She was done within three minutes; the entire interview had scarcely lasted ten. As usual.

She thanked him for his time, and just as dryly he said, "Glad to be of service."

She left, the waiting Volunteer escort falling in behind her, and Sandoval watched her go. Through the archway of artistically drifting leaves representative of a planet far from Sol he saw her: the smooth line of her bright hair, the fit of the blue linen jacket, the flawless curve of hip and long leg.

He was watching, and he knew she was aware of it. Was

there an extra swing to those perfect hips? If it was, she meant it as a challenge.

He turned his back, flicking open his global.

"Tate."

"Boss?"

"I had expected a report by now on who initiated that laser strike in California."

"Still working. Wasn't any of our people. I'm getting some flak from the services. Doesn't seem to be Resistance either." And, in a plaintive tone, "Several have suggested it's got to be the Jaridians. They're the only ones who can manage Taelon tech so quick."

"Must be the Jaridians," Sandoval mimicked. "Over the past four years, that claim has preceded just about every failure of investigation, until I took a personal interest, and suddenly it wasn't the Jaridians after all. Who have not betrayed any sign of being anywhere in our solar system for over a year. I don't want to hear 'must be the Jaridians,' Tate."

"Yes, boss," Tate said—thinking, But every time the Jaridians do show up, we always find out afterward. But you didn't say that to Sandoval.

"I want to know by morning, or I will look into the matter myself."

Sandoval saw subtle signs in the listening techs at the data banks how effective his threat was. They all, even Tate, knew what it meant. Likewise the various spokespersons of the military branches would know.

He frowned at his global. It wasn't quite true that the Jaridians hadn't been around, but only Sandoval knew about the last contact. He was certain, therefore, he'd know if another one showed up.

So who else could it be? And—almost more important—how had they accessed the military codes? Third: Why? The hit, if the report was right, had been aimed at some California schoolteacher who was on the short list for another of Da'an's goodwill public relations stunts.

Sandoval would find out the truth.

He cut the connection, then waved the data stream into existence, enjoying the covert glances of the techs. The spark of chemistry with Renee Palmer had been superseded; the ephemeral pleasure of sex was a mere candle to the sun, the sweet seductive sun, of power.

TEN

Cece emerged from the shower and sat on the nearest bed, staring in bemusement down at her bare feet. She wiggled her toes and watched them flex and scrunch. Yes, she was awake, though her head ached, awake and therefore not dreaming. But the ongoing sense of unreality had become so, well, *real* that all she could really believe for sure anymore was her own physical presence.

Her temples throbbed too hard for any thought beyond that: The idea that she'd slipped somehow from the real world into a some sort of movie world flashed through her mind, except if she were a movie heroine she'd come out of the shower looking fresh and incredibly soignee, ready for the next adventure, and the new clothes would, of course, fit like something custom-made that in reality would have cost two months' teacher pay.

She glanced up at the mirror and saw a pink-nosed middle-aged face, butterball figure, straggling wet hair, and she grinned. Nothing was going to make *her* look soignee, and anyway movie heroines never got sinus headaches from dry desert air.

She looked around the room, trying again to anchor herself to reality. It was a typical hotel room, square, pasteurized artwork with vaguely Southwestern motifs bolted to the walls, freshly vacuumed neutral-toned carpet, smooth bedspreads on each of the queen-sized beds, everything in the bathroom both new and antiseptic clean. She had stood in the shower for a long time with hot water beating down on her neck, which was stiff and sore from the awkward angle her head had rested while she slept in the car; the water smelled faintly of chlorine, much like it did at home. She'd tried to breathe the steam, to ease her poor sinuses, but that chlorine smell had finally made her give up.

She turned her head, surveying the clothes she'd picked out so hastily in the lobby store. Then she looked at her beige dress lying in a huddle on the floor. Hazily she remembered waking up, her mouth dry (except for the horrible dampness of drool at the corner of her mouth, which she'd surreptitiously wiped off on the shoulder of her dress), her head pounding.

"Just sit in the lobby for a minute," Augur had said when they walked from the car into the hotel he'd picked.

Wearily, embarrassed and achey, she'd noticed that except for subtle marks under his eyes *he* looked just as handsome as ever, his dark clothes hiding the possibility of wrinkles and grunge.

She snorted a laugh. No help for it. She was here, a fugitive from—from what? Augur would tell her, no doubt, when he reappeared from wherever he'd gone. So it behooved her to be ready for that.

She got up, forced herself to pick up her dirty clothes. She doused them with shampoo and then washed them in the bathtub, rinsing and rinsing until all the bubbles were gone, then she wrung them out and hung them along the shower curtain. One good thing about desert air: They'd be dry in no time.

Then she padded back out and reached for the plastic bag of her new things. The stores in the lobby didn't seem to close any more than the casino adjacent. As she slowly got dressed, more impressions flooded through her mind.

The pale dawn sky, milky-blue against the east, a vast bowl elsewhere. A whisper of hot desert breeze placketing through the brightly colored flags along the hotel roof.

Inside the lobby, another carload of people arriving, a family of four who'd obviously driven all night, all as soggy and rumpled as she. Cece's eyes had gone to the children, staring around with bewildered faces, fighting yawns. An older woman had emerged from one of the elevators and walked by, and the kids had stared at her stiffly laquered hairdo and enormous false eyelashes and four big turquoise rings on each hand. She'd headed toward the casino carrying what sounded, from the faintly chinging noise, like a bag of quarters. As she passed the small girl, one of those ringed hands had come out and surreptitiously stroked the child's curly head. The girl hadn't moved—she was nearly asleep on her feet—and the woman passed on in silence, vanishing into the casino, the fleeting moment of tenderness vanishing with her.

"Here. Get what you need," Augur had said, reappearing suddenly, taking her heavy schoolbag off her shoulder and handing her four crisp, new fifty-dollar bills. "And here's the hotel room card. Get some shuteye. I'll be back." She was too tired to ask why he carried her bag. Too tired and too relieved.

No answers, no questions. She was too tired to process them anyway.

So she went into the store and bought underthings, a plain cotton summer dress that looked like it would more or less fit, a toothbrush, and toothpaste. They had it all there, as if people often arrived carrying only what they stood in and needing outfitting from the skin out.

Cece had never been to Las Vegas. It, too, seemed unreal, with the lights on so bright even at dawn and the casinos with the cool fresh air and no windows, as if time had ceased to exist. She'd heard a live band playing on the opposite side of the casino when she emerged from the store, had looked in and saw people bent over the blackjack tables, their focus utterly absorbed, as if it wasn't five A.M.

Weird.

Her last purchase had been a bottle of sinus painkillers.

She finished putting on the cotton dress, smoothed it down, and then swallowed a couple of tabs of painkiller, using hotel water. It tasted as flat and nasty as tap water at home.

She stretched out on the bed, making a mental note to get some filtered water. . . .

As Cece slipped into slumber, Liam Kincaid followed yet another labyrinthine trail through intersecting sites on the Internet, but this time he used an ID Augur had once set up for him. This time he found himself wafted through threatening firewalls. No E-mail, though.

Surely Augur can't think I'm connected to that damn laser, he thought, watching data flicker across the screen, splinter into gibberish, and then at some command far distant—for he had not touched his keyboard or activated the vocal command feature—the words swarmed around, rearranging themselves, and now he discovered he was in a chat room for the Kit Kat Klub—Young, Single, and Swinging! So why all this cloak-and-dagger stuff?

At least Augur had set it all up for Liam. All Liam had to do was sit here and wait for contact.

A window popped up: <Welcome, Jackal!>

Jackal?

<Would you like to register under a nickname, or enter as Jackal?>

He hesitated, then typed, <Jackal>

Another window popped up: <Morty requests you meet in Room 17>

Liam grinned. Morty? *Mort*—the root word for death. Coincidence?

Who knew, with Augur?

He scrolled swiftly down the lists of rooms. There was 17, labeled Kiss and Tell. And what did that mean?

More amused than anything, Liam clicked on the Enter

button and discovered that the room had several people already in it.

He paused, reading the exchanges as they scrolled by. Most of them were badly spelled, banal, the usual stuff you see in chat rooms. Liam had once explored chat rooms, early on after his rapid genesis, in his quest to understand the humans whose form he wore; his interest had waned rapidly. Whatever joy people found in chat room exchanges evaded him, leaving him convinced that he would never find enlightenment there.

<MORTY> Jackal?

<JACKAL> Yo.

<MORTY> What's new and cool out your way?

<JACKAL> Zip.

<MORTY> You ought to go to church, man.

Does he mean what I think he means?

<JACKAL> Church?

<MORTY> You meet the coolest chicks there. Last one I saw, this blonde. Very cool.

Liam was in the midst of typing a carefully oblique question when the screen scrolled a line down, stating <Morty has left>.

Liam flicked out his global, entered Renee's code. For a moment it looked as if she would not answer, but then the screen cleared, and there she was. He heard faint voices in the background. Board meeting? "Yes?"

"Meet me at St. Michael's."

She gave a single nod and cut the connection.

Augur shut the palm and turned away. Strange how memory would intrude, casting the shadow of the past over the present—and the future, for didn't one's experience as well as circumstance prompt life's decisions and revisions?

And so Augur sat back, for a brief moment not seeing the quiet library and its little Internet cubicles, but the muddy streets of his village . . . the back streets of Dakar, when he first ran away from school. Waking in pain, not for the first time, having been robbed and beaten nearly to death for the coins he carried, coins probably worth a total of sixty cents.

Life is short and then you die. Isn't that what the unknown assailants said to him before they dumped him in the alley refuse heap, or did he dream it?

Delirium . . . dreams.

Waking up high in the mountains, tended by a gently smiling monk while in the background men's voices rose and fell in song unsurpassed in beauty, the Mass sung in French-accented Latin by the monks of Keur Moussa, their melodies combinations of ancient European chant and Senegalese song. "Life is beauty, but more beautiful is the eternal peace that passeth all understanding." He knew that the monks had said that, but he'd considered it just a dream, and left.

He sighed, his mind returning reluctantly to the present. He knew what he wanted to avoid thinking about: the possibility that Liam Kincaid had betrayed him. He'd acted as though nothing had happened, as though his search program had not divulged Liam having initiated the search on his location. Of course it was possible that Liam had not done any such thing but had been set up by someone very, very sneaky with system control.

Possible? Truth was, Augur wanted to believe it was probable.

Well, time would tell. A very short time, in fact; if he knew Liam, he'd be calling Renee in and starting for Augur's lair before Augur himself got out of the library.

He leaned forward, blocking the old computer from view, and deftly switched the cables from his palm back to the ancient Pentium someone had donated to the library—resale value being nil—and then left.

Withering heat blasted him as soon as he opened the heavy glass door. He narrowed his eyes against the shimmers off the street, the intense glare peculiar to the dry sunlight of this climate, and walked swiftly toward the hotel, debating how much to tell Cecilia Robin.

By the time he got to the hotel, he decided not to go up to the room at all. He'd find out what had happened in his lair first and then make plans from there.

So first thing to do: Find another safe place from which to log on.

And find out if Liam, Renee, and his home had blown into kingdom come.

ELEVEN

"Augur seemed insistent that we come here," Liam said as he and Renee slipped quietly into the elevator, which was set into the back of a small utility closet.

He keyed in the code that Augur had provided, and the elevator began to descend rapidly underground.

"Well, of course," Renee said, as fresh air cooled their faces.

After all, nothing else had worked. They were going to have to access Augur's database link to the Mothership.

"Yes, but why from here?" Liam frowned. "Augur could just as easily have linked us in from wherever he is."

"And that link opens us to one more level of discovery," Renee countered. "May I remind you, O Companion Protector, that Augur's totally illegal backdoor in the Taelon Mothership database is dangerous enough. Every single use puts him closer to discovery. Jacking in from dubious crypto—i.e., anything outside of the room below us—just increases the danger."

Liam made an impatient gesture; of course he knew all

that, but equally true was the fact that Augur could get around those problems if he exerted himself. Or maybe he was limited by distance—and where exactly was he, for that matter? He really hadn't said.

The elevator reached the bottom, and the doors slid open. Liam started out—and paused, startled, when a scanner he'd never noticed before flickered redly.

"Retinal scan?" Liam asked.

"ID Liam Kincaid," a disembodied voice stated. "Corroborated."

A solid, thunking *clank* caused both Liam and Renee to whirl around. Both pulled hidden weapons—then looked at one another as, all around them, Augur's deceptively welcoming lair transformed itself into what it truly was: a steel-exited vault carved from living rock seven hundred feet below ground.

"Computer?" Liam asked.

None of Augur's attractive holo figures flickered playfully into view.

That same disembodied voice stated: "Countdown initiated. Search initiated."

"What are you doing?" Renee demanded.

Silence.

Liam looked around for a CPU to disconnect—anything—except Augur had apparently learned this lesson, too, after he'd smashed his own equipment in the first excesses of grief after Lili Marquette's first disappearance.

Helpless, angry, puzzled, Liam and Renee watched, until somewhere a green light flickered, too quick to identify where.

And the disembodied voice said: "ID of Liam Kincaid does not match location parameters available on source of search program. Jackal program terminated. Countdown terminated. Power restored. Egress restored."

Lights came on then, the steel doors retracted with a whisper of expensive hydraulics, and then a breathy female voice cooed, "What is your command, Liam?"

Renee and Liam saw the tall, curvaceous form of one of Augur's holo playmates. This one had glowing honey-colored skin and silver hair. She smiled coyly, stroking one hand down her clinging evening gown.

"What was that all about?" Renee asked, more amused than disgusted.

"Computer," Liam said, "define Jackal program."

The computer holo smiled and stretched out on a lion skin couch. "Jackal is a defense program we designed in case of attempts on our life."

Renee picked up a smooth ebony carving of a cat, a very Egyptian-looking statue. It probably dated back three thousand years. She was severely tempted to fling it into Augur's exotic raised living room area, with its gaudy pillows and fabulous objets d'art. "He tried to kill us, the weasel!"

"No, he held us here while his program matched us with whoever it was who tried to kill him," Liam said. "Remember the laser strike?"

"If there really was a laser strike." Renee felt her spurt of anger drain away, leaving tiredness. It had been too long a day, with too many interruptions and so far, a noticeable lack of recreation. "Assuming there was one, the target was supposedly this teacher you mentioned," she stated. "But was Augur really there?"

"What makes you think there wasn't one?" Liam frowned.

"We both know that Sandoval is good at manufacturing events that never happened, just as he's good at covering up things he doesn't want known. This one was on the news, but by the time I got home from the park this morning and checked, this news just as suddenly vanished—no mention anywhere."

"Sandoval shut it down, pending investigation." Liam waved a hand. "I ran a scan on SecNet just before I left for this meeting. There definitely was a laser strike in Los Angeles, locked onto the global belonging to a Cecilia Robin."

"But no mention of Augur?"

"Correct."

"So again how do we know that Augur was anywhere near?"

Liam sighed. "We don't. But in turn, Augur was led to believe that I initiated the search on his global, apparently seconds after the strike. As if checking to see if he was still in this universe. And it was I who had sent him to rescue the Robin woman. So it stands to reason Augur is going to think he was the actual target and not that woman. And he has to rule me out as the obvious suspect before he can search for the covert."

"Well, that's sufficiently disquieting."

Liam gave her a sardonic nod. "Augur provided me with a couple of chances to come clean, and when I said nothing about it, he lured us here, knowing that we'd be all right if we really hadn't set him up."

Renee frowned. "Who else knew that you sent him on that mission?"

"No one," Liam said. "But whoever tracked his global could also have gotten at least limited access to his E-mail, including the message from me asking him to look into the problem. I was moving fast that day and used one of the old Resistance mail programs."

"Under what name?"

"Just Liam."

"That would be enough, if someone were trying to get to you through Augur," Renee ventured, thinking rapidly. "Computer."

The holo turned her way, smiling with an allure that tickled Renee's sense of the ridiculous. "Source of the search program on Augur that terminated in the laser strike?"

"Source unable to be determined. Disseminated through multiple mirror sites."

"Then how do you know that Liam Kincaid did not initiate the search?"

"Point of origin and date of original posting do not correlate with Net movements of Liam Kincaid." A graphic flowed onscreen. Liam's eyes tracked the symbols and the stylized map, and he saw that he'd been on his global at the given time—and his exact location was listed. He'd been in London that morning, via the ID portal, on Da'an's business: The retinal scans on the ID portal would match up with the scans just taken by Augur's system.

Renee bit her lip. "I don't like how easy it is to trace your every movement."

Liam said, "It's SecNet's job to provide that data. Knowing that, I have to exert myself to get around it when I choose to be invisible. Luckily I hadn't chosen to be invisible right then."

Renee nodded but privately resolved to get a copy of Jackal for herself and see just how accurate her own defensive firewalls were. How invisible were they, really, when they needed to be? Who was to say that Sandoval wasn't tracking them right now?

They would never know until he chose to let them know.

Unless, of course, Augur really was better at spytech. So far the evidence was on Augur's side.

She glanced around the room, noting the blend of stylish art, outré colors, and sexy tech that characterized Augur's trickster persona. This lair had been designed with a display of humor that quite hid the ferocious intelligence driving it.

Aware that their reactions were probably being recorded for Augur's later edification, she said in her coolest Doors exec drawl, "I keep forgetting just how naughty Augur can be."

Liam snorted a laugh, glanced at his wrist, then said, "It's three A.M. Let's get the link up. The Mothership is in orbit over D.C., which means Sandoval and the prime crew are still on East Coast time. And asleep. The night crew aren't given full access to the data stream."

Renee nodded, repressing the urge to wipe her palms

down her skirt. She knew very well what Liam was implying: The link, while open, was in danger of being detected by anyone on the Mothership.

Liam faced the ghostly hologram, who smiled softly into space. "Computer, connect to the Mothership's data link."

They watched in silence as Augur's program cracked through Sandoval's protections, and then Taelon script flowed.

Liam took over, his movements swift and sure.

He first called up Sandoval's logged orders for the past twenty-four hours, found the one concerning the laser report. Another series of commands brought up a list of known Resistance or other individuals or groups in California that had been, or were being, investigated on Sandoval's command.

"Too long," Renee said, scanning the list in dismay. "It'll take us days to get through all that."

"It's way too long," Liam agreed, eying an occasional code that popped up. "Makes me wonder—"

He didn't say what he wondered. Instead, he frowned, then reentered the command, but this time he narrowed the search by also entering the code he'd seen.

And only half a dozen names appeared.

Liam downloaded these into his global, then looked up at the ceiling. "Augur!"

Renee stared in surprise but habit kept her silent. One of the first lessons she'd learned in her rise to power was that certain emotions were never to be revealed, unless for effect. Surprise was one of them.

And moments later, Augur's voice spoke: "Yes, Liam?"

The voice was tinny and flat. Renee glanced at the expensive, powerful speakers and then gave herself a mental shake. The problem wasn't the speakers, it was the pickup.

"You know now we weren't part of whatever that was."

"Color me relieved." The distortion did not mask Augur's sardonic drawl.

So their queries had doubtlessly been mirrored on Augur's palm—wherever he was. Figures, Renee thought. After all, they were using his system, not Liam's.

"Could Sandoval have caused that laser strike?" Renee ventured.

Liam shook his head. "No. First of all, his MO is the silent knife, not a heavy-duty, very public laser from military sats aimed at a blameless civilian. Second, it can't have been him, not with this size of search as reaction." He scrolled back, showing the list of Resistance cells being investigated the day before. "He wastes that much manpower only when he's seriously pissed."

"And someone stepping on his turf, without his knowledge, is way up high on the list of things that seriously piss him off," Augur's voice stated in corroboration. "All right, I know where to begin—"

Liam's global signaled then. He bit back a curse and pulled it out, then spoke the curse under his breath when he recognized the ID code.

"Sandoval." He looked around.

"Not to worry," Augur said, and even the tinny pickup didn't hide his smugness. "Go ahead and open it, but just keep your back to the wall. As long as you're in my lair, the frequency mirror I set up means your global is protected. He'll think you're at the Smithsonian."

Liam stepped next to the elevator and turned his back so the vid pickup would show only the featureless steel doors. Renee followed, staying out of range of the vid pickup.

Liam snapped open the global, which whirred and bleeped. Renee easily heard Sandoval's voice, tight and impatient as always: "Where are you, Major Kincaid?"

"Doing some research for one of Da'an's goodwill projects," Liam said, with a brief glance at Renee.

"At the Smithsonian Institution?" Sandoval queried, more in bad humor than in real question. "At three A.M.?"

"I have a special pass, and at this time of night, there are fewer interruptions," Liam said, shrugging.

Renee mentally awarded one to Augur.

Sandoval said impatiently, "Well, assign that to a flunky. There must be fifty idiots on the embassy payroll all sitting around on their hands! And get up here at once."

Sandoval, as usual, cut the connection first.

Liam said, "Augur? Back to our original question. Who did you mean by 'those id—' "

Augur's voice cut through with a stream of startling invective.

Renee and Liam saw Augur's big terminal flicker and then load the familiar Taelon Web site.

But instead of the customary bland "We come in friendship" text, they saw printed across the top:

Taelon Enemies sighted in Las Vegas, Nevada.

And below the words, pictures of an unfamiliar woman wearing glasses—and Augur.

TWELVE

ShaNissa Bolt, fourth grader in Miss Robin's class at George Washington Elementary School, usually woke up early. She got her own breakfast, put the dishes into the dishwasher, showered, and got ready for school, all by seven or so. That gave her half an hour to mess around with her computer.

She was proud of that computer, which was her very own. Her parents, both employed in aerospace as design techs, had decided that as soon as ShaNissa started having homework she ought to have a computer to do it on, and as Miss Robin had begun assigning homework right away in September, the computer had been bought and installed.

It was no longer new, as ShaNissa had been using it every day through the entire school year, which was almost over. But that didn't matter, because ShaNissa had discovered what having a computer *meant*. It meant you could look up whatever facts you had a question about, and also you could find kids all over the country—even all over the world—who liked the same books and movies and games and music you liked. Some kids designed Web pages dedicated to special favorites, adding in bulletin boards so kids could exchange views. Others just created characters or stories.

So ShaNissa sat down. She had half an hour before she had to leave for school and cruised through some of her favorite sites. No new talk—just a few of those dumb AMs—anime morphics—based on famous anime characters, bouncing around to the beat of popular songs. The latest fad. Ho-hum.

She knew how they worked. The kids who thought themselves so cool for animating the characters to music didn't even design them. (Jamal Curan, at school, said his hacker big brother called those kids "script-brats," or something like it. It was supposed to be an insult, if you were a hacker.) The real work was done by the ones who designed the AMs and put them up on the Net so others could capture and add movements to them, or put them in their own stories and vids.

ShaNissa shrugged off most fads, which she thought were stupid. She sure didn't see any purpose in wasting time on cartoon stuff. She liked real talk, or at least most of the time she did. It was kind of hard to think about books and shows when something bothered her.

The computer reminded her of school, and school reminded her of that weird business two days ago. Several kids who got dropped off extra early had seen Miss Robin arrive, just like usual, and go into the office, and then come out with the principal, and then she'd just . . . disappeared.

Of course the grown-ups hadn't said anything. A substitute came to class and gave them their test and acted like everything was just as usual. But ShaNissa kept thinking back to the day the Taelon visited, when the adults all had that fake smile and stiff sort of posture that grown-ups got when they were being extra polite.

Were the two things connected? No Taelons had been around the day Miss Robin went away so strangely. Still, the principal had acted just the same way when she brought in the sub, nice and polite, and a fake smile.

ShaNissa glanced back at her closed door. Her parents had never *said* anything, but ShaNissa knew that they did not really like the Taelons. Or they sort of disliked them. When it came to talk about technology, they'd get all excited, and words like *cold fusion* and various equations would fly back and forth like a volleyball game over the dinner table. And that included Taelon biotech. But when it came to politics, or talk about that nasty business a couple years ago—the State of Emergency that had made some teachers cry and all the adults go whispery when kids weren't around, and silent when they were—well, then her parents would get stiff and use that grown-up polite voice that meant kids weren't going to get the truth.

ShaNissa flicked up her favorite search engine and typed in Taelons.

And moments later a pretty blue background painted itself on her terminal, and a lot of nice words about the Companions and peace and how they wished to help Earth.

ShaNissa frowned and almost turned it off. This stuff just looked like the Internet version of adults' polite voices. She scrolled down one last screen—and suddenly she found herself staring at a photo of Miss Robin, just like it was in the yearbook!

ShaNissa sat back. The other picture was of a man, one with a little beard. And below it, a lot of words about last seen in Las Vegas, Nevada and illegal Resistance organization and violence against persons and property.

Miss Robin? Breaking the law? That was just as hard to picture as the idea of her teacher being in Las Vegas, a place that ShaNissa knew had a lot of bright lights and casinos. Casinos, her mom had told her in first grade, was where people go to throw away money. Since then she'd found out a little more about what gambling really was, but she still got this vivid inner picture of grown-ups lining up to toss handfuls of dollar bills into trash bins, while millions of Christmas lights twinkled all around them.

No matter how you pictured it, Miss Robin just did not fit in.

There had to be some mistake. Like, did she have an evil twin sister or something? Except there was her name, right there, Cecilia Robin. Right next to Man identified under many pseudonyms, the most recent of which is Devon Marcuse.

ShaNissa frowned at the screen, trying to understand exactly what it was that they were saying Miss Robin had done. It didn't really seem to say, except that she was consorting with known Resistance criminals, and afterward there was a whole lot of stuff about being good citizens and keeping the peace if people who saw or heard from these individuals contacted the authorities.

ShaNissa opened her mouth to yell for her mom, then closed it again, thinking back to how her parents acted when the subject of the Taelons came up. Would they get mad at her? Think Miss Robin was secretly a bad guy?

What could they *do,* really?

"ShaNissa! Time to go! Got your backpack?"

ShaNissa glanced at the clock. The half hour had gone by already!

She backspaced through the windows and shut down her computer. Then she walked downstairs, trying to think. No, if she asked the grown-ups, she strongly suspected they would just go stiff and polite and not tell the kids a thing—just like when Miss Robin went away.

So she turned her mind to the kids at school. Whom could she talk to? She mentally sorted through the girls and then the boys. There were two kids in class who also had computers, and were smart, and didn't blab all over the place: Aisling Goldstein and Jamal Curan.

In fact, didn't Jamal have a big brother in high school who once got in trouble for hacking systems?

ShaNissa smiled.

Her mother smiled back and kissed her cheek as ShaNissa got into the car. "You look cheerful today," Mom said. "Think your teacher will be back?"

"We'll see," ShaNissa said.

And at the very moment that the car door slammed on ShaNissa, a rapid knock sounded on the door to the room where Augur and Cece sat, each cradling a mug of coffee, fighting against lack of sleep.

Cece jumped, and coffee splashed from her cup onto the bed.

Augur held out his hand, palm down, and moved to the door. He opened it a crack.

A man in a bellhop outfit said, "Mr. Sengal, or Marcuse, or whatever your name is, we do not like trouble in this town. However, many of us like the Taelons even less. So if you are gone in half an hour, this room will have a new guest in it, and this conversation will never have taken place."

He turned around and walked soundlessly down the clean, new carpeting.

Augur shut the door.

"Hear that?"

Cece nodded.

They'd just been talking about what to do first. Not two minutes before the knock, Augur had been telling Cece to relax—they were registered in the hotel as Mark Sengal and Lisa Jones—and that the Devon Marcuse under his picture on the Taelon site was just an old bank account of Augur's, emptied the night before.

Cece said, "They recognized us by those pictures, and they put your old bank account and your new ID together."

Augur smiled but forbore congratulating her on the obvious.

"What we're going to do is disguise ourselves." He

lifted a hand before she could ask how. "Remember what I told you before about disguises?"

Cece nodded again.

"Then you scout the room. Make sure nothing of ours is on the floor or under the bed. Not even a tissue, which can be tested for DNA. While you do that, I'll get the disguises."

"Wait! What did you do with my schoolbag? Everything I had was in it!"

Augur grinned. "Everything incriminating, you mean. It's all gone."

"You destroyed my ID?"

"It can all be replaced when we resolve our problems. Until then, it just gets you into trouble." He held out her dark glasses case. "I did save these. But I'll give them to you only if you promise not to do something stupid like put them on at night, thinking they're a disguise."

"I promise." She knew he was teasing, but she felt her face burn. She probably would have done just that. She winced. "You didn't destroy my copy of *Evelina*?"

"Destroy a book? Especially a classic?" Augur shook his head. "Never. They've got it down in one of their lounges, with a lot of other books. And from the looks of the choices, they badly needed a hint of taste."

She laughed, though she didn't really feel like laughing, and he left.

Fifteen minutes later, with hammering heart, Cece pushed a hotel cleaning cart down the hall past at least two groups of people, none of whom gave her a second glance. Her hotel maid uniform clung to her other clothes, full of static. Twenty feet ahead of her walked Augur, wearing a cook's cap and carrying a tray with covered dishes. They took the service elevator down, and no one bothered them as they made their way through the back part of the hotel to a delivery dock.

"Leave it," Augur said, pointing to the cleaning cart.

Cece left it in front of an elevator and picked up her plastic bag containing her new toothbrush and her old beige teacher dress.

Augur set his tray on the edge of the cart and leaped down onto the cement ground.

Cece followed, squinting against the ferocious glare. It was barely nine A.M. but already the heat made her neck prickle, and sweat trickled down her forehead.

Augur looked around, hands on hips, the cook's hat still perched on his head, hiding his ponytail. His tinted glasses flashed and gleamed.

"Wait there," he said, pointing to the shady area beside several huge wooden flats of boxed paper products.

Cece went over and crouched down between two flats. Augur vanished and reappeared soon, beckoning.

Within a few more minutes they climbed into the back of a refrigerated truck full of frozen pastries.

The air felt cool and delicious. Cece started to pull off the maid's uniform that Augur had gotten from somewhere in the hotel, but he motioned for her to wait. "You're going to need it before long," he said, his breath steaming in the frigid air.

"What's going on?" Cece asked.

Augur said, "The driver will be back in a moment, and he'd better not hear voices. But five stops from now is Kingman, Arizona, followed by some quick sleight-of-hand—you can safely leave that to me—"

"I was hoping you might say that," Cece put in in her most cordial Parent Night voice.

Augur's lips quirked. "—after which we'll have all the time we need to talk."

"May I ask what the significance of Kingman, Arizona, is?"

"You may."

"What," Cece said, matching his grand tone, "is the significance of Kingman, Arizona?"

"Our accessway to the one form of transportation on which no one checks for ID or DNA," Augur said, smiling. "The *Southwest Chief,* on its way to Chicago."

THIRTEEN

When Ronald Sandoval paused to consider such things, he decided that of all the human qualities he distrusted most, forbearance topped the list.

That's what he saw, from time to time, in Major Liam Kincaid's pale gaze: forbearance. In practical terms, it meant that whoever looked on you with forbearance had something on you. Sandoval loathed the idea that anyone had secret knowledge that he might choose when—or if—to use.

And Sandoval had plenty of secrets. If Liam Kincaid had somehow uncovered one, which was it?

The chirping of his global broke into his thoughts.

Good. With less irritation than he might have shown, Sandoval snapped the global open and saw Frank Tate's lugubrious expression.

"No dice on the laser strike, boss," the agent said. "No hints, clues, or traces on the perp."

"Why not?" Sandoval snapped, glancing at the CVI-implanted neck of the driver. He tabbed the sound baffling in the car's backseat and felt the weird cottony sensation closing in around his head. He no longer heard the sound of the tires or engine as the car cruised down Whaley toward New Haven.

"Because according to Garnitz and her hardware gnomes, whoever hacked the Taelon site used Taelon tech and not hybrid. And knows how to use it, I should add."

Tate paused, looking expectant.

Sandoval felt the pang of a headache behind his eyes. How he loathed any slip of control!

"Fine. Leave it for now and get back to hunting down the teacher and that Resistance hacker." He had recognized Augur the moment he saw the renegade window on the Taelon website. 'Augur.' They didn't—as yet—know his name, but he'd been involved in far too many of Sandoval's rare defeats. "As long as this new cryptojockey appears to be working for us, we don't need to know who it is—yet. But with his—or her, or its—help, you ought to be able to nail down those two fugitives quickly."

"Yeah, boss."

"Very quickly, Tate."

Tate heard the threat in the low voice, all right. He tensed. "Yes, sir. But what about the rest of the Resistance list you said you'd check personally?"

Yes. Neville Carlton. "When I finish here."

Sandoval slammed his global shut against his palm and stared moodily out at the pretty white houses lining the street on the outskirts of New Haven. But Sandoval did not see the houses, nor did he see the extravagant early summer greenery growing in profusion over the low Connecticut hills. He saw only order and quiet, with his own Volunteer units in place where he wanted them, at key highway intersections.

The car turned toward the older section of New Haven, slowing in traffic. Sandoval had set himself this task, a sort of reconnaissance. But that didn't make it interesting.

He sat back and continued to brood.

Kincaid. The questions did not concern brains, courage, or even loyalty. Time and again the major had proved his loyalty to Da'an, when he could easily have left the Taelon to danger and covered his own ass.

It was also true that Kincaid was occasionally found in places he had no business being. Sandoval tapped the global against his knee, looking back over some of those incidents. Kincaid's being in places he had no business being did not necessarily bother Sandoval per se—it was not knowing why he was there and what he was doing. Sandoval himself took great care, at times, to make certain that his movements could not be traced. And he was certain that anyone who did manage to follow his actions might be puzzled by anomalies. That was because no one knew his real plans.

Kincaid's inexplicable movements cast no doubts on his loyalty, but they could not be easily explained. Sandoval did not, in fact, know where Kincaid's true loyalties lay—leading him right back to that curious forbearance.

Damn it all.

Anyone else, anyone at all, Sandoval would arrange for a quick and maybe even painless accident. The dead have no ambition. But, with Kincaid . . . *something*—was it his own form of forbearance?—stayed his hand.

Forbearance. Too expensive a commodity.

Sandoval thought of Yale, and the unveiling, and what was going to happen; yes, he'd have to make his visit to Carlton, who had probably white-knuckled long enough.

But that was later. This end of things had to be seen to first.

He dismissed the matter of Kincaid and his loyalties with a mental shrug. Sandoval didn't have to do anything to Kincaid. Within a very few days, events would take care of it for him.

The car rolled on toward Yale. Sandoval shifted his attention to his plans, as overhead in the Mothership, Da'an walked down the ramp to the bridge toward Zo'or in the command pod.

It was interesting how often they both chose to wear their human skins and to communicate in English. Da'an had always done so, in taking another form. It was an intellectual exercise, an effort to use the cultural forms of the given planet.

With Zo'or, Da'an suspected that the context was quite different. Zo'or had become addicted to the intensity of physical experience. Da'an had been grieved, but not at all surprised, to discover that Zo'or had secreted one of the disastrous memory-capturing devices for private use, plus an increasing secret store of human memories. Da'an did not know what form of memory Zo'or preferred, but it was not really necessary to find out. Anguish, horror, grief, satiation, violence, exaltation: Intensity would be the measure, rather than type.

Zo'or sat back on the command pod—a chair they had constructed to accomodate human skin presence—watching the infostream. Zo'or was aware of Da'an's presence. They both knew it. But Da'an had learned patience.

When it was clear that Da'an would not speak first, Zo'or said—in English—"You sought this interview."

"We have been over this matter before. You have superseded me yet again in one of my education programs. North America, I feel obliged to remind you, is my jurisdiction." How limited this language was! And correspondingly how easy it was to hide secrets! Yet to shift to Taelon would, Da'an knew, be perceived as weakness. "Perhaps bringing the matter before the Synod would permit us to examine the best way to serve both Taelon and human interests."

"There is no necessity, Da'an." One reason Zo'or liked English was for the endless possibilities of its sarcasm. "The Synod will concur that Taelon interests are served. Human concerns are secondary."

"Yet why continue to make enemies? Does that truly serve Taelon purposes?"

Da'an's voice was calm; meaning was conveyed through gesture.

Zo'or's eyes appeared to gather light, but the incipient energy blush was controlled; the betraying blue glow diminished. "The possibility of enmity in implementing this plan exists only in your own mind. It grieves me to point out that your thinking is not perhaps as clear as it might be, Da'an. But you are on the planet, feeling the effects of its gravity and its complexities of dimensional form."

Time, in other words. They had little time; this planet was poisoning an already fragile race.

Zo'or sat back. "You may go before the Synod if you wish to present yourself as . . . unnecessarily officious."

"We both know that unforeseen consequences of our interactions with human beings interfere with our plans. One of the foreseen consequences that I question is your insistence on taking my place at Yale."

"Correct." Zo'or's gentle hand gestures denoted harmony, but Da'an sensed underlying tension.

Zo'or knew what was going on. More than that. Zo'or had, if not authored this double-layered plot, certainly maintained control over the events.

Or believed so.

Da'an bowed acquiescence, gestures echoing harmony. Zo'or smiled.

Da'an withdrew to contemplate what must be done.

At a distance behind followed Liam Kincaid, who had in silence witnessed the entire conversation. Da'an, of course, had known he was there. Zo'or probably knew and did not care.

Liam did not speak to Da'an, whose countenance was meditative as they approached the ID chamber and were waved through by the techs on guard.

Below, at the embassy, Liam watched Da'an move straight to his preferred chambers, after which Liam did a fast systems check. When he was satisfied that everything was status quo—and no word from Augur—he waved to the downstairs staff, saying, "Out for dinner."

His security staff took up position outside Da'an's chambers, and Liam stepped out into the soggy wetness of a very humid night. City smells hung in the hot air like a miasma, making one feel instantly gritty all over. Traffic noise seemed unnecessarily loud as he crossed the street and started walking south.

Before he reached the opposite curb, his global chirruped quietly. He cast a look around, then flipped it open. No one paid him any attention; of all the pedestrians in view, probably 70 percent of them were murmuring into their own globals, every one of them looking sweaty and harassed.

Renee's face appeared on the screen. Of course she looked cool and fresh. "You're free?" she asked.

"Just now," he responded.

"Did Da'an get anything out of Zo'or?"

"No." He knew that smile of hers. "But you got something on Da'an, right?"

She gave a mendacious sigh. "Am I that readable? Don't answer that."

He laughed. Then: "What did you find?"

Renee said, "Joke's on us. Everything we needed was in the data net but buried under 'educational programs.' Nobody in spooksville would ever think of searching on anything with the word *education* in it." Renee's even, perfect white teeth showed briefly. "Our future lies in the hands of teachers, yet we consider them to be the dullest, most negligible people possible, barely adults."

"Why is that?" Liam asked. "Is it universal?"

"It's American," Renee said with corrosive cheer. "And my theory is because women were the first ones who took the job when we started schools. We're also a surprisingly anti-intellectual nation, for one so powerful. Once so powerful."

"Oh, we've got some bite yet."

"Preach to the choir, Father Kincaid," she retorted. "Anyway, searching on 'Volunteer' *does* trigger all kinds of alarms, especially in me. Put the two together, and we have contact, Houston."

"Tell me."

"What we seem to have going is a new plan designed by Da'an."

"Hmmm. Who was the leading force behind the original Volunteer program."

"Correct. As I recall, Da'an supposedly meant the Volunteer program to be a kind of rescue effort for youth in jeopardy—vocational training—before Zo'or took it over for his own purposes. Anyway, this new program would call for Volunteers from all college-bound youths."

"Go on."

"Ages eighteen to twenty. Everyone, excepting only the severely handicapped. On their release their college education would be paid for, which seems to be the draw. No more college tuition to be saved for. All funded of course by the Taelons, the state, and other biggies—"

"Including Doors International."

"Of course. And we'd get our pick of the top grads, which was the reason Joshua Doors even considered it."

"Ah. So . . . tie this in with Yale, Zo'or, and the Fourth of July."

"Well, no ties that I see." Renee shrugged. "It's not a done deal yet. Hasn't been announced. Maybe the Yale thing is where they'll unveil it, along with their statue. Make a big positive showing—as a contrast, say, to that college campus mess with the crazy Dr. Creighton that got noised all over the Barry Calvert show and made the Taelons look very ba-a-a-a-d."

"But if it's Da'an's project, why did Zo'or take it over?" Liam stopped, staring at the traffic moving slowly by, the feeling of law and order and ordinariness deceptive. "And why didn't Da'an let me know about this plan of his, if it's so beneficial?"

"You're the Companion Protector, and those two are Companions. The rest, it seems to me," she drawled, "is up to you, sugar."

Just about the time Liam finally got home and sank into his computer chair to review all the files that Da'an made available for him, Sandoval stepped through the portable ID field in New Haven and appeared in Los Angeles.

From warm, humid air to dry heat, the sun just disappearing beyond the Pacific Ocean, which was a glittering rosy silver line from the top of the FBI building. The time was just before midnight in Connecticut, which made it just before nine in Los Angeles. Sandoval turned his head from side to side. He'd been up since five, and his body knew it was midnight. Not that he'd permit himself to exhibit tiredness.

Anyway, adrenaline would get rid of it: He was looking forward to a little face time with Mr. Bonesman Carlton at last. He passed by the waiting ranks of heavily armed Volunteers and out the door to the waiting scoutship.

It had to be a scoutship, not just a police helo. If his plan was to work at all, he had to make a display of power, a hammer with which to threaten a gnat.

Tate waited beside the ship, global in hand.

"Why'd you save this one for last? Anything I should know?"

He was probing, of course, and a spurt of irritation zapped through Sandoval, to be dismissed. He didn't pay Tate to be stupid.

"From what I saw in the records, this one seemed least important. But it pays to be thorough. Bring me up to date."

Tate gave him one of those not-quite-insubordinate shrugs and launched into the data accumulated on Carlton's movements over the past forty-eight hours. Sandoval already knew it all, but it kept Tate busy. Frank Tate could be trusted with a great deal, but not with everything.

No one was trusted with everything.

Sandoval sat back, and the Volunter pilot waved up the controls and raised his hands. The scoutship rose, then flashed over the city. Sandoval did not permit them to drop into ID space; instead they moved over the city at supersonic speed, smashing a concussion over Los Angeles, an ear-slapping reminder of who gripped the controls.

Mentally he projected ahead to tree-shrouded Beverly Hills, imagining what Carlton and his groupies thought as they heard that sonic boom, followed by the roar of force.

The flight did not take long. Sandoval glanced down at the vast panorama of Los Angeles at twilight, a fairlyland lacework of lights, then he shut his eyes and did not open them until the craft set down.

He stepped out on a beautifully tended lawn. Sandoval smiled to himself. How many times had the law invaded this pretty citadel, evidence of money and class—or what passed for class in the United States of America?

Two Volunteers ran on ahead, one standing with his weapon at port arms while the other rapped on the door.

A servant opened it, looked with frightened eyes from one to the other, until she found Sandoval. He was used to that look, and it no longer evoked any reaction, not from the powerless.

"We need to speak with Neville Carlton," he said. "Is he in?"

Of course he was.

They stepped down into a huge living room. Two or three people stood around. Sandoval scanned and then dismissed them all from his attention, all except the skinny one with the long hair and arrogant stance. He knew the bastard instantly, not that he showed it.

"Gentlemen?" Carlton said, coming forward, brows raised.

"Special Agent Sandoval. FBI," Tate said, raising a hand toward Sandoval and then touching his own chest. "I'm Agent Tate."

"May I see some sort of identification?" Carlton asked.

Tate looked over at Sandoval, who gave a nod of permission.

And watched Carlton's eyes sightlessly focus past the ID, sweat beading on that noble brow. Did he really read it? No. Did he think he was establishing his own authority, here in his house, in front of his followers? Let him wonder about that. Stew about it. All night.

As soon as Tate was done, Sandoval said, "The fact that you have no connection with the recent illegal activation of a defense sat has already been established, or we would not be having this conversation here in this fine home but in a far less decorative location."

He paused and watched that sink in—and the reaction of repressed anger in Carlton's face.

"The sat strike was targeted on one Cecilia Robin. Though we have established that you had nothing to do with the override of the nine-one-one automated system, during our investigation we also established that her last communication before the strike was with a global registered at this location."

One of the young women twitched, her face so pale she seemed ill. She opened her mouth, looked to Carlton for cues, encountered a cold glare, and compressed her lips.

Sandoval watched this byplay with no change in his expression.

Carlton said, "Yes. She was here briefly, to visit one of her former students. I take it you do know she's a high school teacher."

"Elementary school, to be precise," Sandoval stated. "So she was here. From when to when?"

Another exchange of looks, and then Carlton said, "I really couldn't tell you. A lot of people stay here. The place is large, and many of my students prefer it to the dorms. They all have visitors from time to time. I don't monitor the students' social lives." A smile; he was recovering his savoir faire. Let's see what we can do about that, Sandoval thought. "All I know is that she was here for a time and then left." He turned his head toward the pale young woman. "Can you add any more details, Karen?"

Karen Geneva, aka Scooby. Sandoval turned his attention to her.

Scooby's pupils were huge, her face whitish-green with fear. She licked her lips, the picture of helpless guilt, and then she said in a trembling voice, "She was only here for an hour. To say hi. Then she left."

"Did she say where she was going?" Sandoval asked.

A look to Carlton for clues. Then, "No. I thought—I thought she'd just go back home."

"Did you think it peculiar that she was here on a school day?" Sandoval asked.

"No. I—I didn't know she was still in school," Scooby said, lying desperately. And it was obvious to them all she was lying. "We're on the quarter system, you see, and for us finals week was just—"

Sandoval cut through the nervous babble. "If she contacts you, I would like you to let the local FBI office know. Just use your global: Your ID will clear you right through to someone on the case. An unknown criminal tried to kill her, and we're concerned. We want to help."

Scooby nodded, relief blotching her face. "All right."

"Thank you." Sandoval turned to Carlton. "You are an instructor at UCLA?"

"A TA—teaching assistant. Yes."

"Is it customary for instructors to have students living with them?"

Carlton shrugged, but the anger was back, all right. "If they have a big enough home, conveniently near campus, why not?"

"All these people study political science with you, correct?" Sandoval asked, waving at the cluster of young people behind Carlton.

"This is illegal?" Carlton countered.

"No," Sandoval replied. "Curious, yes."

He watched that strike—touché!—turned around and walked out, Tate and his armed muscle filing after, the monarch slapping down the unruly baron.

Outside, as they climbed into the scoutcraft, Tate said, "I pulled up files. This guy was dirty with Resistance contacts before the State of Siege, but no one ever pulled him in."

"I'm aware."

Tate grimaced at his global. "No arrests. He seems to have gotten off whenever there was a question."

Sandoval nodded, thinking, And I know why. My instincts were right. This boy is going to be my bomb in that old crypt.

"You want me to put them under surveillance?"

"You have better things to do," Sandoval said, shifting the ground under Tate. "I am waiting to find out how that sat was fired, and by whom."

"Right, boss." Tate sat back, subdued during the short ride to the FBI HQ in downtown L.A. Chewing over his own problems.

Good.

Sandoval IDed back to the East Coast, leaving behind a very angry Carlton.

Very angry. No one spoke in that pretty Beverly Hills house, not for a while, and when they did, it was in the bright tones of people pretending nothing was wrong, punctuated by artificial laughter that did not even remotely resemble the sounds of humor and release. Everyone watched Neville for reactions.

Neville Carlton sat on the couch in the center of his expensive conversation pit, elbows on knees, fingertips together before his face, which could have been carved of marble, so devoid was it of human warmth. He ignored everyone.

Slowly, slowly, normal life began to reassemble around him, for habit is strong. Someone had just laughed—almost a real laugh—when he straightened up.

"Scooby?"

Silence. Scooby looked almost tearful. "I didn't tell them anything! You heard."

Neville made an effort. "No, of course you didn't. Good job, Scooby. You were cool under fire. So cool that I think you can be trusted with a lot more than you have been."

Silence again, exchange of looks. What did that mean?

Neville got to his feet. Smiled. "I considered this option before, but now I'm certain. Pack a bag, Scooby," he said.

"Summer wear, for about a week. You'll like Yale. Very pretty and full of historical import."

Scooby looked around, then spread her hands. "Pack?"

"Now," he suggested, in his most gentle voice.

FOURTEEN

Augur was right.

The refrigerated truck's cold air felt refreshing for a while, and then it got a little cool, and gradually it chilled right down to *cold*. Augur had spent the first few miles working away at his palm, often rubbing and blowing on his fingers. After he closed it he began walking back and forth, between the pallets of insulated goods; Cece's instinct was to crouch over, just as she had in unheated pools as a kid, thinking that that would keep her warm. What she had to do was move about.

So she got up and joined him. At first she shivered, just like those days long ago when she finally got out of the pool, and her joints all creaked and panged, but that didn't last.

Augur gave her a distracted smile but otherwise said nothing. Nor did he need to. She realized that she'd become comfortable with him, somehow. Sharing an adventure, including a hotel room, with someone would either make you friends or enemies, was that it?

The truck growled under them, lurching. They braced themselves against the cold walls of goods and listened as the driver downshifted: They were leaving the freeway again.

"Shall we hide?" That had been their routine so far.

Augur shook his head, his fingers running along the inside door to the cab. This particular truck had two doors, which was probably one of the reasons why he'd chosen it, Cece thought. On the previous stops they'd hidden in the cab-side corners during the brief stops for unloading.

"No," Augur said.

"Are you going to try to get to a phone line?" Cece asked.

"Yes. This stop ought to be Boulder City, which is a fairly big town on the edge of Lake Mead."

Augur looked over, saw Cece looking worried. He did his best to smile reassuringly. "It's large enough, on enough routes, that even if that mystery sniffer picks up my location—and I've built some whopping firewalls to foul the trail—he won't get a vector on us."

Cece nodded. She just looked forward to being warm again.

More growling made them both look up. At the same time they realized that nothing was wrong with the truck. What they were hearing was thunder.

Cece wound her way back to the big doors, stood on her tiptoes, and pressed her forehead just above the rim of the dirty little window someone had installed. Blue-purple lightning flared, revealing a jumble of buildings off to one side of the street. More lightning. Trailer houses sat adjacent to adobe structures, all of them in between the clutter of lit signs—billboards and storefronts—then darkness again, except for the streetlights.

As she watched, the truck lumbered its way down a tight circle and into the parking lot of a fast-food joint. Up behind, she saw the lights of the highway.

"Cece."

She turned away, inching back behind the boxes, in case the driver opened the door. The truck stopped, the cab slammed.

"I think this is a food stop," she murmured.

"We'll know in a moment."

The back doors did not open. Augur did something with a thin metal thing, and the door to the cab snicked. He rolled it open. They peered out through the slanting rain, just in time to see their driver go inside the fast-food place, which sported huge windows and bright lighting. A TV was balanced in a corner. The place obviously catered to truck drivers; all around them, like motorized dinosaurs, trucks hulked. A few had running lights glowing.

"Shall we—"

"Wait." Augur raised a slim finger.

Cece waited.

"Let's see if he's just getting coffee and hitting the can—no. He's ordering a full meal. Good." Augur leaned forward. "I'd say we have half an hour, but let's call it fifteen minutes to be safe. What I need is a phone line, and we need some food. You'll be in charge of that."

"All right," Cece said.

Augur eased open the cab door, glanced at the fast-food place. Cece saw their driver take a tray over to a bright-colored plastic chair-and-table next to the window, where he could see the TV.

"Oh, damn," Augur said.

"What?" Cece hunched her shoulders.

"Look."

She'd been aware that the TV was on, the flickering colors reflecting wetly against the rain-streaming window, but she hadn't glanced at the content. She did now.

A news anchor talked, with something or other in a square at the right. The something was blue. As Cece squinted against the rain, the reflections, and her fogging glasses, the screen blinked and against a blue background she saw the same snapshots of Augur and herself that had appeared on the Taelon Web site. Augur had showed her *that* back in Las Vegas, just before the fellow came to warn them to leave.

"I wish I knew what they were saying," she murmured.

"Oh, it has to be the usual hype about Resistance and 'be a good citizen, report them on sight.' " He frowned. "Still. We have . . . let's call it thirteen minutes. Let's not waste them."

She nodded, swallowing despite her very dry throat.

"Take this cash and hit that diner over there." He pointed across the street to an all-night diner built into an old trailer. Crackling bills pressed into her palm. "I'll explain as we walk. But leave that hotel maid outfit here. We'll need dry clothes when we get back."

With shaking hands she slipped out of the stolen uniform, wearing only the rumpled blue sundress she'd bought in Las Vegas. Augur shed the cook's outfit. Warm rain hit them when they got outside.

"Now get rid of the glasses."

"I can't see without them."

"Take them off after you go in and see where everything is. Don't squint. Also you probably should do something with your hair. Something different. That ought to suffice as a disguise, since no one here is actively searching for you. At this point, we just don't want anyone wanting a reason to study you closer."

"How about braids?"

"Perfect. You'll look like an aging hippie, not like a teacher." Augur grinned, and she grinned back. "Me, I'd stand out in this environment, so what'll happen is this. I see only one waitress in there. Those diners are usually family operations, minimum staff. I'm going to cut round to the office and use their phone while you keep the waitress busy talking."

"About what?"

"Anything. Anything that doesn't raise suspicion. Get *her* talking. They usually like to talk. This is not your high-interest job. . . ."

While he was speaking she swiftly pulled apart her bun, divided her hair, and fingered it into braids, tangles and all. The rain didn't help; she winced, knowing that her next brush-out was going to be a tough one.

They separated at the side of the diner, before the row of windows, Augur vanishing in his black clothing almost immediately, except when lightning flared, briefly outlining his slim silhouette.

Cece continued on, looking in the windows. Tables. A

couple at one table, and at another a man hunched over, staring a thousand miles beyond his coffee mug. Truck driver? Probably. Cece realized there were a lot more trucks in that big lot across the street than there'd been customers in the fast-food place.

She opened the creaky door, scanned fast, then slid her glasses off, and the world went fuzzy. Blinking rain from her eyelashes—working against the urge to squint—she walked in, lifting her feet with care, lest she trip over some flaw in the old linoleum flooring, or a cord, none of which she'd be able to see.

She walked up to the counter.

"Evenin'," the waitress said.

"Nice night for a swim." Did that come out sounding too nervous?

"You got that right."

Okay. Keep it cool, keep it normal. You're nobody interesting, a trucker's girlfriend. Cece took the plastic-covered menu and resisted the urge to pull it up two inches from her eyes. The letters blurred into fuzzy caterpillars across the page; she didn't look at them but mentally invented and discarded random facts about her new life. Keep it boring, she thought. Keep it boring.

"So what'll you have?"

Good question. Cece could not admit that she couldn't read the menu.

Augur's parting words sounded in her head. "Some kind of sandwich, and coffee. Hot."

She put the menu down, trying to think of items that you usually saw in diners. "A couple turkey sandwiches to go," she said and faked a yawn.

"You want the cold or the grilled?"

"Grilled," Cece said, thinking of Augur's "hot." "And two coffees, one with cream and sugar."

"I'll let you do that yourself," the waitress said, her hand making blurry scribbling motions. Then she handed something through some sort of little window and bustled away.

A few moments later the woman set down two cardboard cups of coffee, with plastic lids that would fit over. "Just use the cream 'n' sugar here," the woman added, her hand now blurring against the background. What was she pointing at? Were those white things the coffee stuff? Yes.

Cece managed to doctor her coffee without spilling, though she did squint once or twice. But no one would notice—

"Headache?"

Cece looked up, saw a blur instead of a face. Wishing she could see, her heart hammering, she said, "What?"

"You look like you got a headache," the woman said, her voice sympathetic. What would make mild curiosity change to suspicion?

"Thunderstorm," Cece said. "And these all-nighter drives. Does it every time."

"Yeah, that I can believe." The woman leaned against the counter. A tiny TV was adjacent, Cece realized; she saw the flickering glow. The news again? Then she heard Cary Grant's voice and Doris Day's giggle. Old movie. Relief.

"Hate that run up to Vegas," Cece ventured, carefully fitting the plastic tops over the coffee. She had to do it by feel, without being able to see the edges meet.

"You alone?"

"Nah. My boyfriend and me—" Cece almost stumbled over the bad grammar. Too many years of teaching. "We trade off, four hours behind the wheel, four hours racktime." *Racktime*. She felt a spurt of pride at that one, then pointed over her shoulder toward the fast-food place. "He eats over there. Me, I prefer home cooking, when I can get it."

"You got that right," the waitress said in the most cordial voice she'd used yet. "Regular run? I don't recall seein' you in here before."

"Usually we come in from the north, but we had a special run."

"Uhn. Well, if you come back this way, tell the rest of them suckers over there at that greasy chain dump 'bout us.

They're payin' top dollar for grease. And salt. Not a single decent spice, nothing fresh."

Cece nodded in agreement as the waitress launched into what sounded like a habitual rant about fast food. Meantime she surreptitiously ran her fingers round each coffee top, testing the fit of the lids.

Thump! Swish-swish, crackle. A hefty paper bag pressed into her fingers.

"Here you go. That'll be eleven-forty."

Cece handed her a ten and a five from the thirty dollars that Augur had given her. Or she hoped it was the ten and five, which she'd kept on top. "Here. Rest is yours. Thanks."

"And thanks to you. Come again."

"Oh, I will. Next Vegas run from the south," Cece promised, wondering if her suddenly weird life would actually cause her to keep that promise.

She picked up the warm bag, gripped the coffees, and marched to the door and out, wondering what she would have done if the news had come on, showing her picture, while she was standing right there.

Despite the dryness of her mouth, and her mouse-pittering heart, she almost wished it had.

While the door creaked open, Augur was in the back room of the diner, having wedged the door shut to the kitchen. The cook, half asleep, hadn't even noticed. So far.

Augur crouched over his palm, hoping the glow from the screen didn't reach the windows. He glared at the screen as his search program blinked on hold. Come on . . . Come on . . .

Up in the corner a window popped up. He hit the zoom and cursed fluently under his breath. There was the Taelon site again, and his and Cecilia's pictures, but below it the legend now said: Update: now in Boulder City, Nevada.

He killed the connection, slapped the cord back into the office phone, and was out the door in under a minute.

Back at the truck, he found Cece perched up on the shotgun seat, the food in her lap, her glasses reflecting the light from the fast-food joint as she watched their driver finishing his meal.

"He looks like he's about done," Augur said. "I think we better get out of our wet clothes and back into the uniforms. I also brought these for insulation." He held up a roll of industrial-sized trash bags that he'd found in the office.

Cecilia smiled, and the two of them clambered back into the refrigeration area. After the warm rainy air, this place felt *cold*. Neither spoke as each retreated to a corner and shrugged out of wet clothes and into dry. Cece pulled off three bags, tore a head hole in each as she stuffed them inside one another, then pulled them over her. The plastic crackled with that awful squelchy sound, but she knew she'd be grateful for its heat-trapping qualities before too long. So she ignored the sound, and the feel, and used two more bags to insulate her legs.

Then she wolfed down her food, quickly, before it got cold. It warmed her up, as she'd hoped; she felt her core temperature rise.

Sitting down in a ball in order to conserve that warmth, she finished wrapping her trash up. Just then they heard the cab door open. The truck rocked slightly as the driver resumed his seat. The engine started up, and the truck pulled out.

Under cover of the noise, Cece said, "What did you find out?"

"That my machine isn't strong enough to ward off the damn bloodhound on the Taelon site." Augur held up his fingers; light from the high window in the cab and the door flashed in, outlining them. "That I am effectively cut off from any kind of communication. At least for now." He added that in a voice edgy with suppressed anger. Then he forced a smile, blue-lit by the glare of lightning. It was not a pleasant sight, but it was somehow reassuring. I'm just glad he's on my side, Cece thought, as Augur said, "I also know that this blasted cracker—shall we call him, or her, D.C. for short?—is trying to break through to get at Liam, but at least I foiled that."

"Liam?"

"Liam Kincaid."

"Liam Kincaid," Cece repeated, frowning down at her hands. "I think—have I heard that name before?"

"If you watch the news," Augur said. "Companion Protector to Da'an, the North American Companion."

Cece stared, stunned. "A *Taelon* Protector?"

"Also my Somebody Three. Sent me after you."

"Why?" Cece rubbed her eyes, the plastic bag around her crackling. "Oh. Is he—" Her voice went low and tentative. "Is he really on our side, then?"

"There are more seeming villains than you'd think who are really on our side," Augur said. "The problem here is that we don't know how many people on our side are really on theirs. Anyway. I scrolled back in my log while you were asleep in the hotel. This machine is new, see. Picked it up on the Fringes just before I came west. Took it along thinking that I'd be using it for easy contact over a weekend." He tapped the palm in his inner jacket pocket. "The E-mail ID in the log was from Liam from an old Resistance drop, which I guess was the attraction for D.C. And the E-mail itself won't have made any sense because it was all in a code we'd set up once, a simple one in which certain common nouns substitute for key words. But he'd signed his name—Liam. Easy enough to surmise it might be the same Liam Kincaid whose name comes up when people gossip about the people in power. D.C. obviously decided our connection was good enough to set us up as the goats for the strike and sit back to see what Liam might do."

"That's horrible!"

"One way of putting it. I have to find out who. And why."

Cece winced at the sudden threat in Augur's husky

voice. *People in power*. Well, this Augur seemed to be familiar enough with the major names on the news, didn't he?

Cece felt very, very out of her depth. She tried to unravel meaning not just from his words but from what he was leaving out, then finally gave up with an inner shrug. Augur's high connections and battles over the nets with mystery crackers were none of her concern. What she did understand was that Augur was as cut off from his life as she was from hers.

So she decided it was time to voice what *did* concern her. "What do we do now?" Cece asked. "Are we still going to get on that train?"

"Well, that's what we might as well discuss. I'm going on the train, because I need to go east anyhow."

Cece said, "You know, I've been thinking."

Augur laughed softly.

"Is the idea of my thinking that funny?"

"No. It's my lack of ability to think right now. If you have any ideas, by all means let's hear them."

"I don't know if my idea applies to what you wish to do," Cece said with scrupulous care. "But for what it's worth, it's this. Especially since you seem to be cut off from communicating with your, ah, colleagues." She hesitated.

"Go on."

She shifted. The squick-ripple sound of plastic was barely audible above the growl of the engine and the heavy thunder of the truck's rim noise.

"All right," she said. "I know this will probably make you laugh, but it seems that I—that *we* are the only ones who know what Neville Carlton's plot is. Outside his group, that is. So I'm the only one who can attempt to stop him. Especially since—well, this is all conjecture, but after a certain number of years, you get to know certain personality types. And one thing I've noticed is that, more often than not, the character quirk you see in a fourth grader you see mirrored in at least one parent. Some people grow older, but they don't change a lot in essence."

"Go on."

"Well, that Carlton, I don't think he's been crossed very often in his life. I crossed him that day, in front of his followers."

"Yes," Augur said, "you certainly did."

"And so he's going to want to strike back at me. Even though it's petty, I just know it, as much as I know his fourth grade self probably got back at any teacher who crossed him, however long it took."

"Go on."

"And the best way is to carry right on with his plans, but he'll make Scooby do the actual shooting."

Augur whistled softly. "Yes, I think you may well be right."

"Well, I can't let that happen. I don't really believe she could, or would, do it on her own. Fear might force her to pick up that weapon. If I am there, I believe I can talk her into putting it down again."

Silence.

She said a little desperately, "So that's my plan. I can't go home, so I may as well see this plan of mine through. I mean, in a way it's my fault. Somehow Scooby saw me as encouragement for her joining that group. I really believe I have to stop her and prevent violence, if I can."

Augur let out a long sigh. "You're serious about that."

"Well, yes I am," she said and hated the tremble in her voice.

"Then that's decided." Lightning flared, and she saw him smile. "We're off to Yale."

FIFTEEN

"Your teacher *what*?" Tarek Curan stared at the three kids ranged before him, and then laughed. "Wow! I can't believe it! The Taelons are after a *fourth grade teacher*?" And he laughed again, harder, at the mental image of an old biddy in a flowered polyester dress and dorkmeister teacher shoes with a whistle around her neck, running around in circles and squawking while these laser-eyed blue guys chased after.

"Tarek, you're such a jerk," Jamal yelled, his voice just as shrill as a girl's.

"Your brother really is a jerk," said the girl with all the cornrows. Geez, she was going to be a knockout someday—not that she even knew what sex was.

None of 'em did, Tarek thought, looking at his little brother and chuckling. Amazing what total babies they were. Was *he* ever that stupid? They didn't know anything about *anything*. Imagine getting their shorts in a twist over a teacher!

The urge to snicker ballooned inside Tarek's chest, but he fought it down. His little booger of a brother was obviously ready to go screaming to Mom about being picked on. Tarek did not want to be grounded this weekend, no way, José.

"Look, forget it," he said, and all the kids turned back.

Their faces were so . . . hopeful. Weird, like he could really do something about it.

"Tell me exactly what the hassle is," he said.

Exchange of looks. Little hand signs, like *You go first,*

No, you, that made Tarek want to laugh all over again. What did they think he was, another teacher or some damn thing? He remembered, with a jolt of disgust, his fourth grade teacher, Miss Price ("That's Miss, and *not* Miz, children") and her fat hands and her voice like the whine of a mosquito. The sixth graders had warned them at the beginning of the year that she hated boys, especially ones as tall as she was—the taller you were, the more you got blamed for everything—and while most of the time they'd lied like rugs, about Miss Price they'd been right. What a crappy year that had been!

"Miss Robin is in trouble with the Taelons," Jamal said. "And we don't believe that it's her fault. So we want to help her."

"How?" Tarek asked, not bothering to hide his skepticism. "How are a bunch of nine-year-olds who can't even cross the street without an okay from Mommy and Daddy going to help anybody do anything?"

Exchange of looks.

"On the computer. If. You think you can do it," the girl with the cornrows stated. She was cute, but man, she had merciless eyes. Tarek looked down into ShaNissa's dark gaze and saw a glimpse of the adult to come. Ten years and this kid would be in some kind of high-dollar systems management—if she wasn't leading a regiment somewhere.

"If I can do what?" he asked carelessly, not liking to admit even to himself that he'd looked away first, that he'd lost an eyeball-to-eyeball duel with a nine-year-old kid.

"Find a way for us to help her."

He was on the verge of shaking his head and kicking them out of his room. The words were right there, right behind his lips, but he thought back to sixth grade. Not all teachers were dingbats like Old Lady Price. Mr. Levy, now, *that* was a cool teacher. Could shoot three pointers from over his shoulder, not even breaking a sweat, and he'd actually made them laugh during *math*. That had been a decent year. The year he found out he was actually smart, instead of a total screwup.

Well, maybe this Miss Robin was the same sort, who knows? The thing is, Tarek also loved a challenge. Just as much as he hated authority.

The Taelons, now . . . wouldn't it be cool if he could find some way to finesse those dorks, despite all their heavy tech and the Volunteer spies and CVIs and the totally bogus threat about the Jaridians and all the rest of that crapola?

He lifted his feet off his desk. "I don't promise anything, but I'll give it a shot. How's that?"

Three nodding heads, like a row of puppets.

"And you." He poked his finger into his brother's skinny chest. "You have to cut out the whining to Mom every time you feel like getting my ass in a sling. Got it?"

"Got it," Jamal muttered.

"All right, then. Tell me everything you know."

In Washington, D.C., Da'an sent a summons to Liam.

It was noon. Rain pounded against the translucent blue skin of the embassy, running down in braided patterns of silver, a sight that ordinarily would have caused Liam to pause and watch, at least for a moment. So very much sensory experience was still new to him, riveting his attention with the awe and curiosity of the child he'd never been.

But he had time only to note the effect and then turn away, for he was still wrestling with his data searches. He had a day, maybe two, before he had to get to New Haven and oversee the security setup for the Yale gig. He'd not only be exponentially more busy, but he'd not have a quarter of the tech available. And he had to find out why Sandoval had investigated those suspects himself.

Plus he had to discover, if he could, what Sandoval had found out. Was there some connection between this laser attack and the Yale visit? Superficially only the most ephemeral: Augur's rescuee had been a teacher, and the real purpose behind the Yale visit was to kick off this new plan of Da'an's and Zo'or's.

But instinct yammered a different message, insisting there was some connection. Experience with Sandoval—and Zo'or—so far leaned toward following instinct.

Liam forced it all from his mind when he found Da'an standing in his chamber, head at the angle that Liam knew denoted decision. Da'an's manner was always mild, sometimes deceptively so. Whenever Liam felt he understood Da'an—had nothing to fear—he forced himself to remember that it had been Da'an, and not Zo'or or Sandoval, who had hired an Amoralist to dig up data on him. Threatening Augur with death along the way.

Liam remembered that now as he gazed across the chamber into those cerulean blue eyes.

"Liam," Da'an said, voice mellow and pleasant. "I am disturbed by this unauthorized addition to our Taelon Web site on the Internet. The site's function is to facilitate peace and understanding between our two species. This intrusion is disruptive to that process, and other Companions are lodging protests."

"How about Zo'or?" Liam asked. "Waste of time lodging protests if he's behind it in the first place."

"Zo'or disavows any knowledge of this intrusive data. I might add that Zo'or has never considered our presence on the humans' World Wide Web as a necessity."

"In other words, he could care less."

"Possibly." Da'an's fingers flowed in an intricate pattern. "But I do. And I want you to eradicate this intrusive data from our site. Or if you cannot, I authorize you to hire someone who is capable of so doing."

He wants Augur, Liam thought. Well, that makes two of us.

Liam stared down at his hands, feeling the pressure of all the tasks awaiting him and the diminishing time in which to accomplish them.

He forced himself to mentally set them aside and nodded. "I'll see what I can do."

"The harmony and trust developing between our two species require that you act quickly, Liam."

"Right." Liam walked out, the internal voices taking up their yammer once again.

SIXTEEN

Kingman, Arizona, is regarded by road warriors as the thunderstorm capital of America. Intersecting thunder cells over the mountains made it seem as if one storm followed Cece and Augur's truck right down the freeway.

It was both harrowing and lucky, this spectacular storm raging around them. Harrowing because the frequent lightning strikes reached down from the sky to touch the earth as often as they lit the clouds, and one could never predict where the next strike might be. Lucky because everyone else moved fast, preoccupied with anxious looks up at the sky and not with possible fugitives in their midst.

And so Cece and Augur managed to get away from their inadvertent host while he was dashing and splashing through puddles to the office of his Kingman delivery, and they managed to get to the train station, which was not far, without anyone paying them any attention.

Augur said, "I'll be right back," and vanished into the crowd.

Cece knew what her job was: to look normal but different. She spent some time in the ladies' room trying her best to wash with paper towels and the nasty soap in the dispenser. At least she had her toothbrush in the plastic bag with her beige teacher dress; no one gave her a second look when she brushed her teeth. Not in a train station, with people coming and going at all hours. As she finished, a young woman who seemed to have all her worldly goods in a bulging backpack took up station at the next sink and began brushing her teeth. Cece saw her, smiled inwardly, and repressed the urge to wish the young woman well.

She then turned her attention to her image in the mirror. Her hair still hung in braids, but she hesitated before brushing those out. Would that call attention to her? She remembered the change in her pocket left over from the diner food, left the rest room, and made her way to a little concession stand. There she bought a cheap scarf with a scene of the Grand Canyon printed on it. She retreated to the ladies', got into a toilet stall, and there hastily brushed her hair out (eyes tearing at the damp snarls), pinned it firmly, and then wrapped the scarf round her head. Emerged, glanced into the mirror as she washed her hands for the second time. Hey, it worked! She really did look different!

I think I've got the idea, she thought happily and forayed to the concession stand again, this time in search of a bright lipstick, the brighter the better. She hadn't worn lipstick since she was a teenager, when she'd decided the disgusting taste of it on food outweighed the doubtful enhancement of her looks, but now she applied it with happy abandon. The effect with the scarf was even more startling. She stared triumphantly into the rest room mirror, thinking that she couldn't look more different from the severe teacher photo stuck all over the Internet.

Her last job was to wedge the stolen maid's uniform firmly down in the trash can, wrapped in her trash bag "coats."

When she emerged from the ladies' room, she spotted some benches, but on the way an Amtrak worker intersected with her path. She started to sidestep until she looked up and saw Augur's face above the uniform.

Where had he gotten those clothes? They didn't fit very well, she realized, but no one gave him a second glance.

"Here's your ticket, ma'am." He handed Cece a little folder.

"Thanks," she began, but he'd already turned away.

Okay, well, I guess that means we get on separately, she thought and continued on her way to the waiting area. There, tired-looking people sat, many staring into space, others reading or talking quietly on globals. She found a seat and unfolded the ticket holder to find that he'd bought her a sleeper compartment to Chicago, which was the end of the route for the *Southwest Chief*. Presumably they'd get another train east, then.

Chicago. She'd never thought to see the rest of the country and certainly not like this! She dropped her hand, still holding the ticket, and looked back through the years, the summers of missed opportunities for travel. Somehow it had always been a future possibility, one ever receding behind the necessity for teaching summer school, or using a summer to prepare a new class curriculum. She remembered the summer she'd toyed with the idea of going to Washington, D.C., in order to visit the Smithsonian, after which she'd see the major Civil War sites, but at the last minute a friend had been forced to give up her adult night class teaching ESL and begged Cece to step in. And it had been a wonderful experience.

She thought of those adults, people from all over the world, who had in common only a lack of knowledge of English and a desire to obtain citizenship. She thought of classes filled with children from Central America, and the Pacific Rim, and Russia, and the scattering of Western Europeans and Arabs and Africans, and reflected that for a time it had seemed her place in life was to stay put while the world came to her. But now, here she was, at least seeing her own country, if not the world—

"Passengers to Chicago, please proceed to track one."

The announcement broke into the running stream of her

thoughts, and she joined in the group of people moving out to the platform, while thunder exploded and rain sheeted down all around them.

Augur, standing in the doorway to the baggage room, watched her go, relieved. All on her own she'd found an effective disguise. He'd have to see to another one, but for now she was safe.

Lightning struck the street five hundred yards away. Heads turned, people exclaimed and ran to doorways and windows to see.

Augur stepped back into the baggage room.

When the train pulled out, Cece sat in her little roomette with the curtains drawn and watched with relief, exhaustion, and mild pleasure as the scenery quietly slid by.

She was startled by a knock at the door, but the relief came back when she slid it open to reveal Augur, still in the Amtrak uniform.

He said, offering a tray, "You wanted some coffee?"

Cece heard a door slide shut farther up the narrow passageway, and Augur ducked in and shut their door. "No one's around," he said, setting the coffee on the little pull-up table. The aroma reached into Cece's hindbrain with its cheery message of normalcy.

"Don't the crew all know one another?" she asked, pointing to the uniform. She couldn't quite bring herself to ask if he'd stolen it.

As he was aware. He said in an easy voice, "I helped myself to an extra and named myself as a supernumerary from the New York–Florida route. They're used to workers crossing country via the trains. This persona will vanish at the first stop, and the uniform will be found again."

"Oh."

"So here's my plan. You take this compartment for tonight and sleep in comfort. Morning, say seven, we switch. I have a coach seat up in car fourteen-fourteen. Seat number twenty-three. Whenever we come into a city, the one in the coach seat hides in the rest room until we pull out. That's when it's most likely that local police will walk through on a visual sweep."

"But won't they suspect something?"

Augur shook his head. "We have a paid ticket, and the marker above the seat matches with the tally sheet the car's attendant holds. The worst they'll do is count empty seats and then count occupied rest rooms. Lots of people wait until the trains stop in order to use the rest rooms, because they don't like the swaying and rocking. There don't seem to be any four-alarm manhunts going on, where they stop and check ID and retinal scans, but we don't even want idle questions, since we don't have any ID."

"Okay. That makes sense." Cece nodded. "So you don't think we ought to travel together, is that it?"

Augur snorted a laugh. "In this part of the country a sandwich made of white bread and brown bread is still a curiosity."

Cece's face flushed. "Oh. All right." She looked down, her mouth pained, and Augur repressed the instinct to pat her reassuringly. Bigotry existed: a fact. But she was living evidence of how steadily it was being beaten back into ignorant corners of the country.

He left soon after. The train attendant made up the bed while Cece drank the coffee. Cece stretched out then, and even caffeine could not keep her awake.

SEVENTEEN

Jamal and Sharif Curan almost never paid any attention to the news.

Neither did their big brother Tarek.

Like most kids, nine-year-old Jamal and eight-year-old Sharif considered TV news boring. They had no idea that most adults also considered the news boring these days. Most watched out of habit, or because every once in a while something broke through the benign stranglehold the Companions held on the world—and the media—and genuine news came through, fast as light, contradictory, passionate, unedited—and real. The State of Siege had begun with real news, but as time progressed, the sense of immediacy had slowly altered into the usual filtered news feed, read off by groomed and polished anchorpeople, leaving real events again hidden behind the blue curtain.

Tarek thought the news was for idiots. If you wanted truth, you cruised the Net.

The TV was on in the Curan home, tuned to the news channel, but the boys' mother was talking on her global and their father's mind had shifted from the well-enunciated verbiage of the anchorperson to the current hassle at the clinic, and would they finally fire that incompetent fathead Abrams, or would he pull more political strings, the weasel.

Tarek was in the kitchen banging the dishes into the washer just as loud as he dared, angry because Kayla hadn't called, and ought he to call her, no, then it'd look like he was begging, wouldn't it, and why did girls always seem to call the shots in relationships? *Clank! Clunk!*

So when Jamal came back out of the kitchen with an ice cream bar in hand and glanced at the TV, his sudden squawk startled them all.

"Hey!" He pointed with the ice cream bar, then hastily licked it when he saw a drop forming. "That's my teacher."

They all looked, even Tarek.

On the television, in the corner, was an enlargement of this year's class picture. This was in lieu of the headshot that appeared on the Taelon Web site, the photo on file at the school district office.

This enlargement showed a smiling Cecilia Robin standing there in her sensible cotton beige dress and sensible teacher shoes, glasses glinting, her bun straggling slightly, as the fourth grade inevitably got photographed late in the afternoon, at the tail end of a long, hot day.

The anchorwoman said, "And here is the school where the mysterious Miss Robin taught."

The TV flashed to George Washington Elementary School.

"That's my school," Jamal crowed in delight. Here's fame! *His* school, on national news!

"Mine too," Sharif protested loudly.

Both boys watched, mesmerized, as the anchorwoman led the way along the familiar halls and then introduced their principal.

"Did these accusations about one of your staff members come as a surprise, Mrs. Pinochet?" the anchorwoman asked, sticking a microphone in Mrs. Pinochet's face.

Mrs. Pinochet gave the woman a cool glance, the sort that the kids knew was a warning to stop whispering and wriggling, and even the anchorwoman moved back a step without quite realizing it.

Mrs. Pinochet then said, "I was not surprised, I was shocked, for I have never seen any evidence that Miss Robin had any connection with any illegal organization whatsoever. And—" A very wintry smile. "As for the unnamed 'criminal activities' she participated in, I find those difficult to believe. This is the very end of the school year. Few teachers have, during the school year, enough free time to walk their dogs or get their laundry caught up with, much less lurk around setting off bombs or spying or whatever it is the unnamed accuser thinks she might have done."

"So you believe the accusations on the Taelon site are a hoax, then?"

Mrs. Pinochet's brows lifted faintly. When the staff saw that expression in staff meetings, they stopped whispering and fidgeting. "What portion of what I just said was unclear?" she asked in a pleasant voice.

The anchorwoman grinned. "We can see that Miss

Robin certainly has your support, then, Mrs. Pinochet, and thank you for your time."

And the TV obediently cut away before Mrs. Pinochet could slice and dice the remains.

Huh, Tarek thought. And: Damn.

Jamal was looking at him with that *look*, and Tarek knew what was coming next: Every brat in that damn class would be harassing him with stupid questions, like, What was he doing for them? He promised! Was it too hard? Did he lie?

Truth was, it was hard—sort of. But he hadn't really put time into it. He leaned in the kitchen doorway as both his parents and Jamal watched the anchorwoman tour the classroom ("Look! See? That third one, that's my math test with one hundred percent! See, Mom? See, Dad? Remember it at Open House, huh, huh?") where Miss Robin had taught, and thought hard.

He didn't give a snap of the fingers for this stupid teacher. But—he had to admit it, if only to himself—he didn't really want to look like a dork to his kid brother. And also, it really would be sweet to scam the jerks running the country, wouldn't it?

But how?

". . . and here is one of Miss Robin's colleagues. Brad Poindexter—" Turning to face a youngish, decidedly photogenic man who grinned straight into the camera with the ease of one who knows he's good-looking. "What can you tell us about Miss Robin?"

"Well," said Mr. Poindexter, consciously lowering his voice, "she's been with our little band four years. As an old hand, I offered to show her some techniques for dealing with elementary school children. . . ."

As Brad Poindexter shifted the subject firmly onto himself, Tarek watched with all the skepticism of the young male for an older. He's trying to make himself out to be some superteacher, he thought—

Yeah? Hot damn! He had it!

And vanished in the direction of his room.

Jamal watched, his emotions veering between that nasty, earthquake sense of injustice that kids get when adults are not even remotely being fair—how *could* they talk about Miss Robin as some kind of bad guy?—and delight at all this fame for his school and classroom.

The interviewer finally cut into Brad's flow of self-praise and brought on a succession of three female teachers, all of whom maintained quite firmly that they thought Miss Robin one of the best teachers in the school, dedicated to education, and as for breaking the law, Marcia Cohen declared that she couldn't believe Cecilia Robin would run a stoplight at four A.M. with no one in sight.

The last to speak was a tough-looking old veteran teacher—anyone could see that in a nanosecond—who stared straight into the camera and said with grim portent, "We look forward to seeing this mistake resolved and Miss Robin back in her class in autumn." Implied: Or we'll know the reason why.

There seemed nothing to say to that, though the interviewer dithered and grinned and motioned for the anchorwoman to take over for the sum-up.

Upstairs, Tarek's fingers raced over his keyboard.

He snickered with glee as a figure took shape on his screen. Clipped right off the Taelon site and plugged straight into his own secret weapon, the thing that made him great among his netpals: his AMG, Anime Morphic Generator. He called it AMaging (instead of imaging, a little wordplay there), and only those of his buds in the know knew what it meant.

Miss Robin transformed from a photo to an anime. But that was just the beginning. Tarek remembered what the kids had told him about her, how she lifted her head up when she was talking about something she loved, how she jammed her glasses up her nose every time she looked down. How she bustled along. Quick walk, short legs.

"Oh, this is hot, oh man . . ." Now he wheezed with laughter as his new Superteacher flexed her muscles, shoved her glasses up her nose, and chirped in her anime voice, "I stand for truth, justice, and the American way!" Tarek's hair flopped in his face and his mouth hung open as his fingers labored to keep up with the lightning speed of his mind.

"I am so good," he whimpered and executed the program.

As it propagated swiftly through the Net into the caves where teens mostly congregated with their characters to act and interact in ways they no way could do in face time, he sat back and snickered happily. His greatest one yet. Oh, *wait* till those blue bozos tried messing with Superteacher. Oh, he couldn't stand it, how would he sleep?

Downstairs, the news shifted to sports, and Jamal looked around at his family and said, "Isn't that cool? I bet everyone in class will report that as this week's current event!"

His parents nodded. Smiled.

Dr. Amir Curan thought, What the hell kind of political stinkpile lies behind this teacher hullabaloo?

Adira Curan, mother, looked with hooded worry at her small and still-innocent sons, particularly Sharif, who would be going into the fourth grade next fall, and thought, I don't believe that teacher would intentionally do anything wrong, but was it a good thing to put a nine-year-old in a classroom with someone who had been in trouble with the law?

EIGHTEEN

"Look," said Agent Tate of the FBI. He stood with his back to the door and put his hand on the doorknob. He knew he was just a dumpy, dough-faced guy, would never have the lethal elegance of Ronald Sandoval, but that didn't mean he couldn't make underlings sweat. "Our asses are going to be in the fire big time unless we report some success. You've got the people here, and you've got the tools and the permission to use them."

He opened the door, knowing that the prisoners inside the steel gray waiting room, sitting on the steel gray benches in air chilled to sixty-two degrees, would hear every word. "And do whatever you have to to get information. Lots of information. Fast. I'll be waiting for your report."

He smiled into the gray faces behind him, saw sweat and fear and dry tongues licking lips, and repressed a laugh. God, he loved scaring the crap out of prisoners and minions alike! And why not? The job had to be done, so why not by someone who was good, who loved his work?

Tate slammed the door on them all, stumped across the room to the desk he'd taken over, hooked a haunch over the edge of the desk, and pulled out his global. The owner of the desk had moved to his secretary's desk and was busy typing away, not looking up. Good dog.

For the next forty-five minutes Tate shuffled through the rest of the Las Vegas investigation, screen by screen, then dumped the reports into SecNet archives, using his forefinger like a gun. Blam, blam. The Resistance spook, aka Marcuse, and the schoolteacher had been definitely seen at the Desert Sunset Hotel. That was enough for Tate. Somebody there had to know something.

He looked down at the list of names of these adjunct workers sweating it out in the next room. Smiled. Shifted them to an <ACTION PENDING> directory. Just in case any of those scumwads had the temerity to squawk about being pulled in without a warrant. Like you really needed one anymore! Who on his team was going to complain? Not when Tate was known—and he made certain it was known—to run "special errands" for Sandoval.

As for these hotel lice, well, they lived in *Las Vegas*, for crying out loud. They daren't protest his friendly invitation to visit the HQ for a chat. If they didn't have records themselves, they surely had old connections that were about as clean as week-old kitty litter, right? Tate remembered unfondly his early days in the agency, way before the Taelons came, when the Mafia were the kingpins around here—and how their boys used to smirk at him. No more, baby, no more. Since his rise to the precincts of power he'd taken the time to pay off a couple old scores, as publicly as possible. Called it earning back proper respect for the agency.

He gazed sightlessly out the window at the barren terrain, baking under the harsh desert sun. What was it, one hundred and fourteen out there? He hoped his prisoners enjoyed a little free AC—

The door opened, and McNeil stepped out, her lab coat fresh and wrinkle free as always. She said in her corpsicle voice, "Your targets were there, all right. Until midafternoon, when this one"—she nodded behind her—"Harold Elkins, warned them to take off. He didn't see them leave."

"You made certain of that?"

By now the smell of strong antiseptics had wafted in from the room, bringing also the sound of harsh breathing. *Clink! Tinkle!* McNeil's lab assistant, who was as cold a troll as his boss, was shifting steel thingies around on trays, just for effect, Tate would have been willing to swear.

McNeil's lips widened in what passed for her smile. It reminded Tate of horror movie serial killers. "Oh, I'm certain."

Tate nodded. "Well, go through the rest of 'em. Find out if anyone else saw anything. When they're back in shape, send 'em home."

McNeil nodded.

Tate was about to tab Memory 1 on his global, which would ring through to Sandoval, but he decided to wait. That was good news, but he wanted better. So why now go downstairs and see what his dragnet on Las Vegas public transportation had revealed?

• • •

Just as well Tate didn't try contacting Sandoval just then.

Ronald Sandoval was incommunicado. Completely incommunicado, even more than he was those times he hid behind a number at the arctic-spirited Kobe Club where, if you had enough money and power, you could buy a slice of anonymity behind which you could indulge your secret desires. Not that Sandoval bothered with gluttony, drunkenness, or sex. He could have those anytime he wanted, and no one would blink an eye. What he craved, at times, was the escape of utter oblivion.

But Sandoval wasn't seeking oblivion now. No need, not when he was winning. But you didn't win unless you were constantly on the alert and never got sloppy. Every corner you cut someone else always seemed to find. And use.

So this chore he monitored himself. Of course he had the aid of heavy tech, programmed himself, or it would have been impossible personally to review the ever-running logs of the individuals who—without knowing—functioned as Sandoval's eyes and ears in those few (and ever-diminishing) secret corridors of power to which he otherwise had no access.

Each one of his test subjects had once used an ID portal that Sandoval's assistant, Vasser, had personally rigged. Each one had stepped through and reappeared safely on the other side, not knowing that he or she had taken a fourteen-second sidestep in order to have a listening device planted under the skin at the base of the skull.

It was a program that would have had spectacular promise, and reach, but Vasser had gotten herself killed. And maybe that was just as well, for evidence had come up that she too, so seemingly loyal, had been playing both sides of the fence.

Trust no one, that was the route to success.

Sandoval dismissed the dead Vasser from his mind and turned his attention to the computer.

Each one of the individuals had a separate program sorting through all the drivel human beings spoke each day, with flags keyed on certain words. Rare were his opportunities to monitor real time; human life being what it was, almost inevitably the person and time he chose would reveal nothing but eating, or snoring, or extramarital hijinks, or a long, dull ramble about sports. Sandoval rarely monitored real time.

As it was he had to take time out at least three times a week to scan those flags and listen to conversations that seemed to be important, or the overload became overwhelming. And he'd be tempted to cut corners.

Already once he'd cut a corner and missed what appeared to have been a crucial afternoon.

Check, check. Check.

Down the list. His eyes were gritty, his head ached, but this job had to be done now, because tomorrow's schedule would not permit any unexplained disappearances. Right now Zo'or was in mental communication with the Synod and safely out of reach.

Check.

And now, his new priority: Neville Carlton, whom he had been scanting of late—that corner again—because he'd seemed just another pretty rich boy sent east to Yale for snob polish before being tracked by his rich, influential family into a political career. Yale, because his grandfather had gone there. And, like Grandpa, he'd duly been tapped into Skull and Bones, the most secret of Yale's seven secret societies. Neville Carlton had been waylaid and inserted with a listening device not on his own merit—there wasn't any, in Sandoval's opinion—but because Sandoval had decided that secret organizations were by definition inimical to the Taelons' cause, and so he'd had Vasser rig the ID chamber in New Haven and wait for a Bonesman to come through. Carlton had decided that weekend to go to the Côte d'Azur instead of study for finals. Bad boy.

And so Carlton became Sandoval's ears into the Bonesmen—not that he'd witnessed anything worthwhile in the—what, three? four?—four years since he'd been awarded those ears.

But then came the State of Siege and the usual wild talk. Carlton—a lazy graduate student at best—had splintered off from the main Los Angeles Resistance cell, fulminating about their lack of forward movement. Like anyone could do anything in those glory days.

Sandoval had relegated Carlton to the low-priority list, not even scanning his key words until he checked a week before the laser strike.

Surprise! Flags had popped up all over his files during the recent months. Right around the time Da'an's Yale visit had been put forward, and Carlton found out through connections at Yale.

The substitution of Zo'or—secret, but of course Bonesmen got around that news with ease—and Carlton's subsequent frenzy of planning had provided Sandoval with much-needed amusement in a far too stressful life.

But he hadn't checked often enough. In between checks that teacher managed to show up on Carlton's doorstep. And there was the real lesson in cutting corners. Sandoval had been pissed when he listened to that. It would have been so easy to have her picked up right from that house, and how the hell had an ignorant schoolmarm gotten ahold of Augur to engineer her escape? He decided that he and she were going to have a little talk, when Tate did catch up with her.

Sitting back, he checked the time and frowned. Why hadn't Tate reported in? He set his scanner to pull up Carlton's most recent data, wheeled his chair around so that a matte black wall would be visible behind him, and hit Tate's code.

The man himself came on, wearing his biggest grin. "I was just about to yell for you, boss. We located the hotel where the targets were staying. Staff gave positive IDs."

Glance. Red flags all over. Ah. That was when they must have heard the scoutcraft in the sky over L.A.

"And?"

Tate said quickly, his eyes shifting, "We're doing a sweep right now on public transportation. You yourself said to be thorough, and that does take time. Of course, if you want to release more people to me, especially since my prime team has been on deck for almost sixteen hours—"

"Negative."

He cut the connection rather than listen to Tate whine. Turned his attention to the tape, which he scanned rapidly. Just a lot of invective, nothing to any purpose: orders to his rabble to keep mouths shut, let him talk. Yada yada.

Then he and Tate obviously came in. Sandoval showed up in person from time to time in some of these people's lives, but he rarely bothered with reviewing his own words. This time he indulged himself, cut on the audio, and noted that Carlton's speech revealed far more tension through the recording than he'd displayed in person.

Sandoval smiled and sat back, hands behind his head, to listen to what went on afterward. At first the silence puzzled him, and he skipped through the not-quite-clear whisper of other voices in Carlton's vicinity. So the followers had hovered about, eh, wringing their hands? Typical.

Then Carlton spoke, summoning Scooby.

Sandoval's smile widened when he heard the final order to pack her bags. He flicked the control back to text mode and scanned rapidly through the subsequent series of orders and repetitions to the various followers as he snapped open his global.

"Kincaid."

Liam Kincaid's face showed up, blurred background. Kincaid looked as tired as Sandoval felt. Good. "What are you doing?"

"Da'an has assigned me to oversee the avalanche of E-mail resulting from the breaching of the Taelon site."

"Delegate that. Your orders are superseded. Use Zo'or's name if Da'an objects, though I don't think he will."

No comment or change of expression from Kincaid.

"I've finished overseeing New Haven. Meet with Jordan at noon for a sitrep. He also has files on local troublemakers. Then you'd better be on your way. You'll need two weeks; you've got a week."

Kincaid stared back through the global, his eyes as blue as the Taelons', an unexpected twist of fate, eh?

"Right," he said finally.

They cut the connection at the same time.

NINETEEN

Cece fell asleep with no problem, but despite her exhaustion it was, at least at first, difficult to stay asleep. The rocking of the train took getting used to, especially at first when sudden sways or jolts caused her mind to imagine disaster looming, and each slowdown or stop made her peer wearily at the edge of the curtains for the expected hordes of armed searchers coming to scour through the train

But then she adjusted to the rhythm of the rocking cars, the regular stops, and dropped at last into a deep sleep.

At dawn she woke and discovered to her delight that the sleeper car entitled one to a shower. A shower! Her last shower, in Las Vegas, seemed a century ago.

Coping with the rocking of the train, the snake showerhead, and her blurry vision without glasses was quite a challenge. She longed to tell her brother and sister about it all. She could envision—so well—her sister's laughter, but of course there could be no communication, none whatsoever, until—

Until what?

She leaned against the wall of the shower and wept, short and hard. Then she forced herself to rinse her face and get out, doing her best to towel off in the rocking little space, before she turned her attention to the problem of clothes. That beige teacher dress was the very same one, as luck would have it, that she'd worn on picture day, and so she dared not wear it. In fact, she wondered if she ought to just toss it somewhere, or would that somehow turn up as evidence? How did such things work, anyway?

The blue one was rumpled, but it didn't smell. A night in a freezer was good for that, at least. So she put it on, pinned up her hair, replaced the scarf, used the lipstick, and scanned the result. Very different from Miss Robin's usual.

Then she looked down at her feet. Thank goodness she'd bought another pair of knee highs at the hotel! She washed out her old pair by hand, using shampoo.

In her cabin, she set the stockings out to dry. Then her gnawing stomach made her consider her next move. The dining car was next car down, meals came with the sleeper, and it was now Augur's turn for rest.

The waiters in the dining car, she discovered, put people together at tables. She soon learned that asking personal questions was the way people expressed politeness. During a surprisingly good breakfast she heard all about how her table companions, a couple and their son, were going all the way to Boston, that they did it every other year, and on alternate years the woman's family came out from Boston to stay with them in Flagstaff. To their questions Cece spun a yarn about visiting a cousin in Arizona in order to tour the Grand Canyon, and now she was on her way back to Chicago.

As they all got up to leave, the woman said, "Well, if you like historical sights, be sure to go down to the lounge car when we reach Gallup. They have a Native American person who comes on and talks about the history of the area. We've done it at least a couple times. Isn't that right, Ricky?"

The boy nodded, they exchanged wishes for good journeys, and parted.

Cece headed toward the coach cars. She'd just reached the observation car when the door swooshed open and Augur was before her, now dressed in a colorful caftan. Where'd he get *that*?

He didn't look at her, so she passed by and through the observation car. The lounge was next; she saw people reading on palms, or talking quietly on globals, or just watching the scenery. The only TV she saw was the big one in the lounge, but it was showing movies. No one seemed concerned with the news, or with his or her neighbors. No one seemed to be looking for a fugitive teacher and her mysterious companion.

Cece found car 1414 and seat 23, sat down, and tried to look unobtrusive. Did she dare try the lounge car in Gallup?

While Augur slept, far away Tate slept as well, dreaming of little blue men with very big knives. Sandoval also permitted himself some sleep, but he did it at the Kobe Club, where he could guarantee that sleep would be dreamless.

Last of all Liam Kincaid retired to rest, his dreams a collage of stars and alien images that he found comforting, laced through with the harmonics of the Kimera—a melody that would take a thousand years to sing.

Renee Palmer was up, through her workout, showered, and ready for the day by the time the sun came up. She chose a chic black outfit as armor for a day that promised new depths in executive politicking, but first a good start; she was breakfasting with a girlfriend from her Harvard days.

Morgan always knew the out-of-the-way places that were offbeat yet good, the ones that would be trendy in six months. By then she'd have moved on to some new discovery.

Washington, D.C., was already baking when they sat

down at a tiny table overlooking a traffic-clogged intersection. Hanging plants almost obscured the dismal scene. The walls around them were old, the plaster covered with murals of fantastic willow trees, all gnarled wood and draped leaves in art deco sweeping curves.

"You like?" Morgan asked, brows raised inquisitively. Her hair was red this time, Renee noted.

"The place or your new look?" Renee asked.

Morgan waved a well-manicured hand. "Both."

Renee nodded. "For the place, I reserve judgment until we eat, though I like the forest touch. Ironic, isn't it? Here in the concrete jungle." Morgan snorted at her tone. "As for the hair, I told you ten years ago I thought you were meant to be a redhead."

"You were referring to my temperament."

"Maybe. But the observation still stands."

Morgan grinned and sipped at her latte. She looked across the table at Renee, whom she'd admired since she first saw her, cool and collected, doing a verbal samurai kata on a twit with more wealth than brains who had apparently decided that her three years in a French boarding school made her the dormitory arbiter of taste—and that meant bullying unmercifully all the girls from Nebraska and Oregon and Missouri whose entire families had saved to send them east for college. Wrongo!

She narrowed her eyes, looking at Renee, whose cool, icy-blond beauty had not aged, only matured. "I can't see you as anything but a blonde," she said.

Renee grinned. "I can't either, to tell the truth. Besides, it's so much more fun when people in the business world go into a negotiation basing their strategy on the assumption that blondes are stupid."

Morgan snickered.

They chatted about college pals and recent doings, as the perfectly prepared food came, was eaten, and the remains carted away.

Finally Morgan sat back with her second latte held in

both hands and studied her old friend. Renee had always had the best poker face in their group. "So what is it this time? The pleasure of my company or the pleasure of my connections?"

It had been a guess, but Renee made the fencer's gesture for a hit. "Both," she said, echoing Morgan.

"Some things never change," Morgan observed, intrigued. "I supposed business is never far from your mind—even when."

"Especially when," Renee said, looking sardonic.

Morgan thought of the sorts of guys who'd think Renee a fine trophy to win, and grinned. "You ever want to get away? Have kids, maybe? Not that I can see you dealing with diapers and baby barf and wailing at two A.M., three, four, and five. And snail eating, and reading the same fifty-word book over four thousand times."

"You make it sound worse than a horror film," Renee joked. "And the answer is: I don't know."

"I suppose the Taelons will make it easy for us before long. You know, select your genetic match, pop the baby into a bottle, decant it when it's born. Maybe even decant it when it knows how to eat, sleep, and clean itself."

"Oh, they've already tried," Renee murmured, her voice low.

Morgan whistled and did not ask how she knew. If Renee said they'd tried, then they'd tried.

"And?"

"Zip. They don't seem to understand that all that crawling and snail eating and so forth is a part of the human experience. We live in our bodies. They wear our forms like costumes, adopting personae to match."

"Huh." Morgan frowned. "That means we really don't know their natures, then, any more than they know ours."

"Right." Renee's teeth showed. "They also don't know how our psychology interfaces with biology systems. Or rather, they don't care."

Morgan nodded. The entire subject of the Taelons made

her uneasy. She used their tech every day but hated their hold on the government. And from what Renee had just hinted, there was reason to hate it.

"Well," she said, knowing it was inadequate.

Renee smiled again, that tight sardonic smile. Then she said, "So what interesting news have you heard?"

While Morgan considered all the professional gossip she'd been hearing, Renee watched her consider. Morgan had started college in business law but had ended up in statistics. Oh, people joked about how boring statistics were, but Renee had listened to Morgan outline the subjects of her papers and discovered that what statistics revealed about societal shifts was always enlightening and sometimes surprising.

Morgan's sweetheart of five years was a rising star on Wall Street. Together, they knew an enormous number of people and ways to get info.

Morgan finally shook her head. "Nothing really different. Same old same old. Market recovering after the mess we got in following the election. Cautious optimism, always with an eye to our friends in blue."

"Ah, yes, so good for business, our friends in blue."

"Take away with one hand," Morgan said, making a juggling motion, "and give away with the other. Like my brother. You know he stayed on at the old homestead in Colorado, right?"

Renee nodded. "Even after things went bust out there."

"All the R&D. Computer companies. For a while it was a big joke that our town had the most PhDs outside of aerospace asking if you wanted fries with your order."

Renee winced.

"Well, after a couple years of being afraid they'd end up living in a tent, my brother reported that the Taelons put that Volunteer training camp out nearby, which at least provided some business. And some jobs. And now—just in the past couple weeks—it appears they're expanding in a big way. New jobs all over the place. Things are booming again, he said."

"I like hearing good news," Renee answered. "It's so refreshing a change."

Morgan laughed as they got up and paid.

"Speaking of bad news," Renee added, looking at her watch, "I have my own corporate wrangling starting in about fifteen minutes."

"Go get 'em, girl."

Renee laughed and waved.

TWENTY

The last day of school was a gas for Tarek.

As soon as he got to the high school he lounged over to where his buds usually hung out before the bell. Every palm he saw had a little crowd around it, people laughing. Superteacher had been busy during the night. He'd known that anybody who watched the news and saw that crapola about the teacher being hunted by the law would find Superteacher irresistible. And everyone who DLed her and added on characteristics and dialogue made her a little more real—and helped propagate her further across the Net.

And . . . And . . . the beauty part . . .

He pulled out his own palm and logged on, punching up the Taelon site.

Damn, he was good! Snickering helplessly, he stared at the update on the fugitives, stating that Cecilia Robin had been reported at 4:13 A.M. (Pacific time) to be in Atlanta, Georgia.

So that meant some kid in Atlanta had been on-line at what? 6:13? 7:13? Tarek couldn't remember Atlanta's time zone, but it didn't matter. What did matter was that somebody had cruised through a cave and DLed Superteacher, and the extra zip he'd tagged on almost as an afterthought had worked: Once a day, between four and five A.M. Pacific time, when somebody DLed her to add script, Superteacher's secret weapon would activate once, ghosting a log-on for Cecilia Robin. Just as well the teacher seemed to have been a total dork as far as tech was concerned—her ID had taken half a minute to jack and plug into the program.

He signed off, slapped his palm shut, and ambled off to daydream through the remaining hours of junior year, imagining teenagers all across the country grabbing Superteacher off the caves and scripting her to music, news feeds, chat rooms, and everywhere else people hung out, thumbing her nose at the Taelons and their CVI-brain-dead human spies.

Damn, he was *good*!

As he plunked down into his homeroom seat, he frowned. Jamal just better keep his mouth shut. Oh hell, what little kid ever kept his mouth shut? Why'd *he* have to open his big yap and tell the brat over breakfast what was happening?

Tarek sighed, thinking, If he even breathes a word, he's gonna wish he'd never been born.

At George Washington Elementary School, the harassed teachers divided their time between overseeing wild kids and fending off parents who had come on the wildest pretexts basically to nose out news of Miss Robin and air their views—as if anyone wanted to hear them.

Still, they listened to one another just enough to find their own crowd. Parents who thought the teacher should be fired and put in jail and prosecuted and maybe a class action lawsuit (Anyone here in law? Can we get someone pro bono?) all stood in the baking quad beside the cafeteria, ignoring how unpopular they were with most of the kids, including a surprising majority of their own offspring. There's nobody more self-righteously deaf than he or she who minds your business for your own good.

But Miss Robin was far too popular to make a good scapegoat. And so the other crowd thought, as people assured one another (no one listening, only waiting with barely concealed impatience for their turn to talk) how much their kids loved Miss Robin, how much good she'd done for older siblings, and whatever it took to protect her, why . . .

In the classrooms, the kids were even worse than usual on the last day, which is never any picnic. Until the bell rang kids ran in huge circles, howling, despite the withering sun, and finally lined up, crimson-faced, when Mrs. Pinochet quietly overrode the bell system and rang four long blasts eight minutes early.

Adults jerked watches up to faces—of course school bells would be the One True Time—and moved off toward the snarl of double-parked cars in the parking lot.

Once the kids had settled down, cleaned their desks, stacked up the textbooks in the cupboards, despite his effort to drag out the process as long as possible, Cece's sub, Mr. Blaine, found that only forty minutes had passed. He went to the cupboard containing indoor games, as the kids broke out again in a wildfire of whispering.

Jamal raised his hand.

"What is it, Jamal?" Mr. Blaine asked, voice just on the edge.

"May some of us go to the computer lab?"

The teacher's face cleared. "Of course. If it's open. But if it isn't, they'll just send you back, won't they?" he added, talking mostly to himself as he rummaged through one of Miss Robin's boxes.

The lab was open, and already a lot of upper-grade kids were there, but Jamal found a computer free and was soon joined by ShaNissa and Aisling.

"Watch," he said.

He punched up one of the caves where the teenagers liked to run AMs. Sixth graders were usually into that, but not the younger kids, who mostly found the sexual innuendo of the big teens incomprehensible and kind of boring. Now if they made fart jokes, well, *that* was funny!

Jamal easily got past the firewall the lab teacher had put on the comps to steer the kids to the school sites, turned the sound way down (the caves usually blasted loud music if you let them), and punched in the URL of one he knew Jamal liked.

In silence the three kids watched Superteacher dancing in the middle of the cave, pausing once in a while to push her glasses up her nose (that made them all giggle) and then put back her head, wisps of hair flying out of her bun, and say, "Tell the Taelons that we believe in truth, justice, and the American way!"

ShaNissa rocked silently back and forth, her face squinched in her effort to keep laughter inside. Aisling kept sidling glances at the big kids, glances that were so apprehensive and guilty seeming that, had any of the big kids had anything but scorn for the younger ones, they would have been instantly suspicious.

But no one paid them the least attention. Most were playing games, though across the room, through all the semidamped whizzes and whooshes and pops of the games, Jamal was pretty sure he caught an echo of Superteacher . . . and the American way!

Jamal grinned, and the two girls grinned back.

"It's her," Aisling breathed. "It's wonderful." She lost her smile. "But I don't understand how it can really help our Miss Robin."

Jamal turned round in the chair to face them. Intense dark eyes met ShaNissa's dark eyes and then Aisling's hazel ones. "If I tell you, you have to keep it secret. *Really* secret. Not your mom or dad, not your best friend across the street who doesn't go here, not a cousin."

Two nods.

Jamal nodded once, then punched in the URL for the Taelon site. In silence the three kids stared at the update about Miss Robin having been seen in Atlanta that morning, and in a low whisper, speaking so fast that the others had difficulty following, he told them what Tarek had told him. Or at least tried, for he didn't actually understand it all either, but they all got the gist—

"Can I help you students with anything?"

Three faces jerked around, and there was the lab teacher.

Jamal sidled a look back, but the Taelon site was perfectly within the rules.

"Oh, we were just wondering how Miss Robin was doing—if they'd say," Aisling chirped in a sugary voice.

The teacher frowned. "Aren't you fourth graders from her class?"

Three nods.

"Oh, well, then, of course you want to know. But you won't find much news there." A sour glance at the Taelon site. "I'm afraid no one really knows right now, children."

The bell rang. Phew!

"Do you remember how to properly shut down the machine?" the teacher asked.

"Yes ma'am."

She moved away. In relief, Jamal put the firewall back up, wiped the log of his actions, parked the machine, and waited until the terminal had gone cold and dark.

Then they left for recess. Like the teachers, the kids endured the crawl of time until they'd completed their officially mandated hours of classroom time, and the last bell released them. They picked up their report cards and headed home to start the summer.

Three fourth graders—now fifth graders—went straight to their rooms to log on. Jamal just wanted to go out and play, but the two girls had spent the day thinking of things to script onto Superteacher and make her more *real*.

TWENTY-ONE

Summer rain pattered across the windshield of the auto parked down a street in St. Louis, Missouri.

Suzanne Verda, sitting in the shotgun seat staring out, imagined the hot, humid air being washed clean—not that any molecules of that cleanliness made it inside the car, whose oxygen had been used up (she was sure) hours ago.

Suddenly desperate, she rolled down the window and stuck her head out, breathing in deeply of the wet night air. After the wretched stench of the car, the rainy wind was sweet and pure and almost made her feel drunk.

"Whatcha doin'?"

The rasping voice of her partner seared her nerves, but she didn't react. Just raised a hand to screen her eyes from the rain and pretended to peer at the apartment they'd been watching for the past seven and a half hours.

"See somethin'?"

"I thought I did," she said, figuring that the poisonous reek of cigarettes, the salt-oil stench of the fast food her partner loved to consume in barrel-sized quantities while on a stake-out, the stale coffee, and his intestinal contributions as a result of his disgusting diet had all been swept out and replaced by real oxygen.

For the moment.

"Hey, Suzy. It's cold. I get sick if I get cold."

She rolled the window back up—leaving the usual hairline crack—and said, "I was certain I saw a movement in the window. But it must have been a reflection from the lightning."

Her partner took his newest cigarette out of his mouth. Suzanne looked away from the slobbery end, her stomach crawling. He observed, "Yer wet. Lucky you don't catch cold easy, like I do." He smiled and patted her knee. Bile rose in her throat. "But that's what I call playin' heads-up ball, and so I'll tell Jamie when we get off shift. No tellin' how soon we'll get better assignments."

Never, you moron, she thought, but she just nodded and smiled. She knew better, after four years of "apprenticeship" with the Ganneck Detective Agency. Not because she wasn't good. Oh, the problem was just the opposite. She was too good.

But she was also one of too many good officers from countless municipal police forces who had found themselves out of a job after the Taelons came in and took over. They just weren't needed, not as they were. Many had submitted to CVIs and shifted to the Volunteers. Not her. No way.

She was luckier than some who'd felt the same. Though James Ganneck, the agency's director, made her baby-sit his disgusting slug of a brother—who of course took all the credit for their successes—at least she had a regular paycheck.

James knew who really did all the work. She knew that he knew, and she also knew that he would never do anything about a promotion unless Pig Boy came with the job and increased pay. Ma Ganneck, whose now dead husband had started the agency, and who still controlled it with an iron grip, made certain of that.

Pig Boy sat back amid another wave of flatulence, chuckled, and made his usual joke, "Good food, Ay-rab style." Paul Ganneck had this philosophy (whether you wanted to hear it or not, ten minutes in his company and he'd breathe it all over you) that you were never a bigot if you were just cracking jokes. Jokes about Arabs and Japanese and Italians and Catholics and women, oh, and don't forget anyone with any color of skin darker than his couch potato pallor, were A-Okay as long as they were just jokes, see?

A corresponding wave of hatred corroded her insides, and she took a surreptitious glance at the dash clock. Half an hour of this torture to go.

Meanwhile Pig Boy flicked the channels on the TV set just below the dash. Suzanne used his movement to crack the window a tad more.

She turned her attention to the stakeout. At least, she thought for the hundred thousandth time, she'd learned the business. She knew it well enough now to bide her time until she could break away for good. But for a woman to set up in business meant she had to come with a heavy-duty rep, and she was always on the watch for just that chance.

Pig Boy lit another cigarette and flicked to another channel.

". . . and the Taelon embassy reports that a landslide of reports have come in on the fugitives," the anchorwoman was saying. "Anomalies in the reports have caused a crackdown in security at all public ID portals."

Wonder what's behind that, Suzanne thought as she kept her gaze on the target apartment. Beside her, Pig Boy nearly obliterated the sound of the TV by opening another crackling bag of flavored chips. The heavy smell of fake BBQ sauce joined the smoke haze as the anchorwoman cheerily went on, "According to our spokesperson, there have been nearly six hundred sightings of the fugitives in the greater Los Angeles area during the past forty-eight hours, yet this morning the Mystery Window on the Taelon site—and the Taelons still disavow knowledge of it—reported Cecilia Robin having been located in Atlanta, Georgia . . ."

"They must be nightclubbin'," Pig Boy said, chortling. "You wouldn't think a colored boy or a pruned-up old teacher—everybody knows they don't even know what sex is—would have it in 'em, wouldja?"

You obviously wouldn't, you bigoted cretin. God, let me get a break and get away from this creep.

". . . meanwhile the sighting reports have come in from as far away as Seattle and Arizona."

Pig Boy sat up. "Arizona! Think they're comin' this way?"

"Relax," Suzanne said with forced calm. "That's just the nut quotient. I'm sure those people also seen them with little green men."

"Either that or tall blue ones," Pig Boy retorted.

An actual semblance of wit? Suzanne thought. Maybe it was that brief breath of real oxygen.

Paul opened his global and poked in the code for HQ. "Hey, Craig, you followin' that stuff about those fugitives in Aye-Zee?" he asked.

Craig's voice came out clearly. "Oh, yeah, nothin' else to do. We've been cruising in on SecNet. Somebody thought he saw that Marcuse guy in Kingman, of all places. Probably some peyotehead."

"Kingman." Paul farted. "Nobody goes there."

No, Suzanne thought. You don't say nobody goes there, you ask *why* anyone would go there, you imbecile. But then he'd never actually do the legwork on a case himself, not when he had a free car and the biggest expense account in the agency (and some of the others were actually stupid enough to envy Suzanne over that expense account!) and absolutely nothing to do but sit, smoke, eat, fart, and watch TV. Oh, and ask Suzanne out on dates, which she would agree to only after Satan and God reunited the cosmos, and even then she'd find a loophole.

Kingman. What was there, besides lightning?

Roads . . . trains . . .

Train.

Suzanne had memorized the stops on the *Southwest Chief* years ago. Part of the job, she'd thought.

Paul was still boring Craig's ear off. Keeping her voice as idle as possible, she said, "Ask when the peyotehead's call was logged."

Paul gave her a squinty look out of his fat-framed pig eyes. The shame was, he wasn't stupid, he just refused to use his brain—unless he knew there was something in it for him, something he could steal, wheedle, or threaten without any further effort on his part.

"Why? You know sumpin'?"

"What would I know, sitting here with you, watching that idiot's apartment for three days straight?"

Craig, who obviously had heard, said, "Logged long about two-thirty A.M. this morn."

Vegas to Kingman . . . definitely within the realm of possibility. And wasn't 2:30 when the train was due to pull out?

Suzanne frowned out at the quiet apartment, barely visible through the sheets of rain. Two-thirty . . . and the train usually hit Kansas City about eight A.M., if it was on time.

She'd be off duty in half an hour. Of course it was a long shot, but she'd stored the image of the fugitives in her global, as she had with every single target of every single nationwide search for the past four years. You never knew where or when the break would come—you just had to be ready to jump.

She wouldn't have to be on duty again until four P.M. Her time until then was her own. She could grab a little shut-eye, find Mike and Lynette—the two best newcomers—see if they wanted in. Take the ID to the Kansas City portal at seven, scout around, and be waiting for that train by eight.

". . . eh?"

She realized Pig Boy had been talking to her and was now frowning in suspicion.

The thought flitted through her head that if she did strike it right, she'd be working for the Taelons.

Yeah, and the alternative is?

Pig Boy farted again, long and slow.

"I got a headache," she said. "Need my z's. Thank goodness we're almost off. Did you ask me something?"

"I said, You think them peyoteheads is onto sumpin'?"

"Yeah," she said and watched him grin with anticipation. "Peyote."

TWENTY-TWO

Liam woke with a headache. He would have attributed it to the thunder outside except for the tightness around his eyes and the feeling of mental fatigue accompanying it. Simple physical cause—barometer dropping, smog, humidity, sinus pressure—would be easy to assume, but instinct dictated that to do so would be a mistake.

He sat on the edge of his bed, hands on knees, and frowned down at the carpet. As time progressed he felt increasingly comfortable in this human body. He *was* human. Being human meant accepting all its limitations; the memory of his shaqarava—the lethal spurt of energy he could release through his palms—was buried more deeply by the day. Some of the Kimeric language now took effort to evoke, whereas he could remember not so long ago when it blazed through his mind, cometlike, when he forced himself to stumble over each spoken word in human language.

But something happened last night, something extrahuman, of importance. He knew that he had to recover it, that it was important.

How? He could not sleep any longer; he was already late for the schedule he'd set himself. There would be no time alone now, he had to go straight to Augur's lair for the meeting.

In the shower he forced himself to relax and turned his face into the hot, stinging spray. The warm needles of water acted like tiny acupressures on his face. With his eyes closed he sent his mind back, back, trying to recall his dream sequence.

Dreams. Each symbol had import, but one had to find it.

The dream he recalled most easily was a frequent one, wherein he stood at the vast window of some shadowy space vessel gazing out at the eternity of stars.

Bleep-bleep.

But the firmament was not still. It moved, on its concentric courses, though the metaphor became one of weaving: warp and weft. Yes . . . and the shuttle flying back and forth, drawing a glimmering thread through—

Bleep-bleep!

Damn! He realized it was his global, and as he'd blocked all but very few codes, it had to be important. He slammed the water off and stepped out, streaming wet, got his global, and snapped it open.

"Ah, yes." Renee's brows lifted. "A late morning, I see."

She did not like to be kept waiting. Well, no one did. Nor was it a matter of arrogance, but because they all lived in a precarious interlocking series of crises.

"I'm sorry," he said. "I'll be there as soon as I can."

Renee closed the connection.

When he stepped out of the elevator into Augur's lair, two female faces looked up. He smelled coffee, and underneath it fresh pastry. The remains of a breakfast lay on Augur's antique table.

"There're about two sips of coffee left," Dr. Julianne Belman said, waving a hand. "We split your share of the croissants."

"Sandoval is shifting me to New Haven today. I'm due in two hours."

Renee leaned back in her chair, soignee and graceful as always. "And so you stayed up far too late juggling Da'an's latest requirements and trying to find Augur, right?"

It was her way of accepting his apology. "To be precise," he said, sitting down at right angles to the women, "I was digging through the reports of the chase. Nothing worthwhile. Tate is lurking in Las Vegas interrogating locals, but when I checked the Taelon site just before I got here it stated that the woman, at least, is now several states away."

"So they split up?" Renee asked.

"I don't know. No communication at all." Liam rubbed his temples.

What was it he was supposed to realize? There was some connection, some underlying meaning, that hovered just beyond his vision.

"Well, that's frustrating," Julianne said. "I called for this meeting to find out what happened to that poor schoolteacher. I've been feeling bad ever since I scared her off. Though I have to add that the fact that she's stayed out of Sandoval's multifarious tentacles so far makes me think she's a lot less innocent than she'd seemed."

"Unless that's Augur's doing."

Julianne pursed her lips. "Do you really believe our Augur would stay with her, no profit, no gain? She's not even remotely his type."

"He can be surprisingly gallant," Renee said, laughing a little.

Julianne pointed a finger. "*You* inspire gallantry. Is a little chalk-dusted pouter pigeon of a schoolmarm going to inspire gallantry? In Augur?"

"Well I hope so," Renee said, finishing her coffee. "I have to confess I will be disappointed in him if he dove underground and dumped her flat. But I guess I wouldn't be surprised."

Liam sighed, slamming his hands on the table. His palms under which the shaqarava once lay now itched. Why? Why? "We all need to get to work," he muttered, fighting for a semblance of civility.

Julianne gave him a wry look but forbore saying anything. Instead she got to her feet. "Well, keep in touch."

"What are you doing back on this coast?" Liam asked, sensing that he was still out of tune with the others, that communication was still awry in some important way. "I thought you'd be out west for a while."

Julianne felt his effort. "I thought so too," she said with a laugh. "But we obedient medicos are told to jump, and we just ask, 'How high?' We're being mobilized, it seems, to beef up the medical staff at various Volunteer sites. A couple weeks of training before something or other around the tenth of July."

"Oh. Oh!" Renee half rose, then sank back into her chair. "Duh. I hate not seeing the obvious."

"What's that?" Julianne put her hands on her hips.

Renee sighed. "A friend mentioned in casual chat that the Volunteer training camp out in Colorado is being expanded. I assumed it was a local matter and forgot about it. But you just reminded me of Zo'or's new program for college grads."

Julianne's brows lifted. "I was about to observe that our Taelon friends seem to be confident that they'll get a lot of volunteers for their Volunteers. A *lot*."

They regarded one another in silence.

Renee shook her head. "No. No way could they try to make it mandatory. Public opinion is too dicey as it is."

Liam rubbed his temples again. "Julianne, you could answer a lot of these questions by finding out through insider channels if preparations are being made in Taelon labs for implant manufacture of some sort—any sort—on a very large scale. Can you do that?"

"I *will* do that," Julianne promised in a grim voice.

The women's voices receded to the background of Liam's mind, the words incomprehensible, as he wandered around the room and then stopped before Augur's complicated computer setup.

He ran his fingers lightly back and forth, back and forth, along the edge of the desk below the keyboard, as he stared down and down and down—

Search. Fugitives. Laser strike. The fact that he could not, after hours of wasted effort, get the intruder's window off the Taelon site—and for some reason the Taelons had not done it either. Distrust . . .

Distrust. There was a key. Most of the Synod did not really care what humans thought of the Taelons; their focus was outward, bracing against the Jaridian threat. Zo'or and Da'an cared, for different reasons, but they had already demonstrated that they did not always trust each other.

Then of course there were the humans who dealt directly with the Taelons, so many of whom had been forced into difficult double positions. The mystery window on the Taelon site had caused an intensification of dissension among all the various alignments of power. Liam thought of his close call with Augur. Lethally close.

"That's it."

"What's it?" murmured a voice at his shoulder.

Liam spun around, the impulse to fight gone as fast as it had sparked. Renee fell back a step, startled. Liam was so easygoing, so . . . so austere in some ways, that whenever he switched into action mode it was quite startling.

He said, "That window is going to be impossible to eradicate. It's Taelon biotech. Just as we can't do anything to the Taelons' hardware—they grow it and keep it in their control—so we can't get at this either. Someone somewhere got hold of Taelon biotech and knows how to use it."

"Zo'or."

"He'd be our first suspect, but I don't think we ought to stop there."

Renee sighed. "I don't even know where to begin, then."

Liam's eyes went sightless again. "I think I do. But not yet. First I've got to find Augur."

Renee nodded. "Or he has to find you."

Augur was thinking the same thing.

He'd switched places with Cece in the sleeper car, but, tired as he was, he slept only three hours, waking with the dawn over the flat Kansas countryside with its mesmerizing rows and rows of crops. What a *clean* state Kansas was, he thought, staring moodily out the window as the land rolled by. Even the poor sections of small towns, built up against the railway, had ordered yards and scrubbed walls with no graffiti. To him that suggested castle-wall thicknesses of social constraint and corresponding lack of freedom.

No matter. He was not going to live in Kansas.

Liam. He had to find a way to get to Liam, find out what was going on in the circles of command.

First to get to Illinois. He had some old connections there. Well, he had them almost everywhere, at least in major cities. I'm an urban creature, he thought, staring at the farmland. It seemed alien to him, as remote as another planet. He could not imagine living here in this flat country, exposed to the sky, to your neighbors (for you saw very few fences between houses). Dawn was usually something he saw on retiring, for night was his time, and the time of those he understood best, the time when emotions might be sharper but that just brought out the adrenaline rushes that fueled one's best efforts. The virtual hunt, the run against unseen foes, chase and be chased, all at light speed along electronic highways under the forgiving cloak of darkness, that's what he understood.

He drew in a deep breath, then went down to the shower, following which he put back on his African activist outfit—the bright colored djellaba and skullcap that he'd lifted from a brother's luggage. Help me, and one day I'll help you, he said mentally when he made his pinches. The clothes—if he didn't lose them—would be handed off to a needy man somewhere, but for now it was Augur's way of hiding in plain sight. The Amtrak worker had retired back in New Mexico: too many of the crew, on seeing him, wanted to strike up talk, idle chat, flirtations. He'd fended them off as best he could; connection, any kind of human connection, was too much risk.

He went in to the diner for breakfast and ended up sitting with some tourists from Germany. He formed for their edification a Senegalese persona, complete with thick accent, which kept questions to a minimum.

Someone behind them murmured something about how they'd just crossed the border into Missouri.

Good. One more state to go.

TWENTY-THREE

Under a cloudy Kansas City sky, in a doughnut shop just down the street from the train station, the three detectives from Ganneck Agency—having just discovered that they were twenty minutes early for the train, as they'd hoped to be—bought some java and pastry, and sat down in a little corner booth for a final planning session.

Suzanne Verda dropped in the hard seat and faced the two recruits she'd chosen for this run. Mike Cowrie, short, squat, built like a bull and about as strong, perched on the plastic seat that appeared to have been designed for undernourished ten-year-olds and regarded her steadily from under his browridge. People looked at Mike, that heavy brow, the crewcut, the tats on both arms, and wrote him off as muscle instead of brains. Their mistake.

Lynette Flieger was fresh out of college and very earnest. James Ganneck had told Suzanne that Lynette's family were heavily into the Taelon Church, the very idea of which made Suzanne queasy. Lynette was twenty-three, long-faced, plain, smart, kept her mouth shut. She'd never, so far as Suzanne was aware, mentioned the Taelons at all around their coworkers.

"It's just us three," Suzanne said, to get things going. She figured they had to be as tired as she, but thank heaven for those ID portals, at least. They'd had a chance to grab a little shut-eye before getting themselves to the St. Louis ID portal. "So we're gonna have to be on the ball."

"What makes you think they took the train?" Mike asked, then gulped down half his coffee at one slug.

"Absence of any other data to the contrary."

The two considered these words. Not exactly promising, but sometimes, they'd been told, long shots were the best shots, because nobody expected them to work.

Mike said, "The woman was reported in Atlanta yesterday morning."

"And this morning in New Zealand," Suzanne added, nodding once. "Did you check the site? I did. Twenty-four hours and seven minutes after the previous posting putting her in Atlanta. No corroborating details. That suggests to me that whoever is running that fugitive window on the Taelon site is getting data from electronic comms, rather than visual reports. Could be that's how the Taelons work. I don't know."

Sidled looks at Lynette. She did not react.

"But we're humans, and we rely on visuals when we can. So if we put together visuals with these Taelon site reports, then Kingman– Las Vegas makes the most sense."

Mike said, "We rule out Seattle and Atlanta and New Zealand, then?"

"Lacking visual corroboration, yes. The fact that no arrests have been made makes this data suspicious. We saw these ID portals are all locked down so tight a flea can't get through without a retinal scan. I think someone has tampered with the woman's ID and is logging on to cover her tracks. Easy enough for the Resistance to do; no doubt it's SOP for them. And so we'll just go on our info."

"What if we find the train full of feds?"

"We still look. If they tag us, we go along nice and cooperative. Who knows what might come of it, jobwise? But I don't think we'll get a sniff of them. SecNet has shifted almost entirely to ID portals these days. Airports. Planes, scoutcraft. Cars. I'll bet they've forgotten all about trains. Hell, I would have too, except one night I happened to be sitting on a very boring stakeout and decided to memorize train schedules."

Mike shrugged, looking impressed. Lynette looked somber.

"We still don't know that they're together," Mike offered.

Suzanne paused to sip her coffee, which was too hot. Burned her lip. But it gave her time to bite back a nasty retort. Mike's tone wasn't combative. Had she spent too much time around Pig Boy and was ready for a fight? Or was it because she was desperate for a success—and the chance to leave Pig Boy sitting in his stenchmobile with a new victim?

"We have no evidence they are separate. So let's assume that they are together. Or at least, both on the train."

Mike shrugged. "So what's our plan?"

"We get on here and just stroll through. It's a major stop, and though there's a chance they might get off here, I don't think so. Still, we'll watch the detraining passengers before we get on. So that prevents us from doing the sweep the careful way, but we need to just walk through first, anyway. Get a feel for who is where, how many people, what patterns we see. Mentally mark any suspicious people, which will narrow us down a little for our subsequent sweeps. We have seven stops after this one, until we reach Chicago. If they're on this thing, we'll find them."

They nodded.

"Got your rolls of tape?"

Both patted pockets.

"We'll keep talk on globals to a minimum, but in case, let's use the Sunday picnic talk." They nodded again; Ganneck newcomers all memorized the easy verbal codes meant to deflect any casual listeners to global conversations, at least long enough to get out of range.

Suzanne opened her briefcase. "Here's a blowup of the picture on the screen, as promised."

Of course they'd all loaded the photos from the Taelon

site onto their globals, but those small screens made details difficult to make out.

In silence they all studied the enlargement, passing it from one to another. "Obviously we don't have much to go on with respect to the man. He'll have lost the tinted glasses, and probably the ponytail and mustache. He could be wearing anything—including an Amtrak worker's uniform, which is what the Kingman report placed him in."

"Did they establish whether the guy was a bona fide?" Mike asked.

"No. Seems whoever called in the report didn't get a name, only a visual, and when he addressed his suspect, the suspect excused himself and said he was on the way to the men's room. Never came back."

Mike grunted. Lynette nodded slowly.

"As for the woman, she is supposedly a schoolteacher, not a professional, so we'll stick with the usuals."

Lynette nodded again, swept her blunt fingers over the picture, stopping at Miss Robin's feet. "So we look for these shoes, right?"

"It's the hardest thing to replace on the run, if you have no credit and little money," Suzanne said, smiling. "They'll change their hair, put moles on their faces, add sunglasses or ditch them, buy radically different clothes—but keep their shoes. Never give 'em a second thought. And shoes that fit are just about impossible to steal."

Mike shrugged, Lynette nodded once. They were recruits, but that was one of the basic lessons.

"So let's go."

Down the street, the train slowed as it pulled into the station, then stopped. Cece peered out at the old structure, marveling in silence at the remains of its former grandeur. Other bits of it looked spooky. Obviously land prices out here were vastly different than in Southern California, where nothing unused was left standing long. Money-hungry developers were always ready to swoop down and build for maximum dollar in minimum space.

She watched people hauling bags off the overhead storage or digging under seats and then remembered, with an unpleasant start, that she was supposed to be hiding in the rest room. It had been three hours since the last stop at Lawrence, Kansas. Too little sleep had her nodding at the job.

So she got up and took her place in the line of people going down the windy little stairs to the lower level, wandering mentally over the landscape both past and present.

How vivid history became when you could see where it had happened, she thought. How clearly she could see the Santa Fe Trail and the wagon trains lumbering slowly westward along the very route the train took. Winslow, Arizona, still had a Harvey House standing; you could see it from the train and imagine what it must have been like for young women—girls, really—coming west to take up waitressing there, in hopes of . . . what? Husbands, obviously, but not always. Adventure? A new life in places where they were still inventing the rules, as opposed to back east, still hedged about with Victorian social constraints?

She reached the luggage racks, squeezed past the passengers yanking at big bags, and stepped to the little corridor along which were the rest rooms. Her former rest room was occupied. Phooey. She looked around and realized they all were occupied.

What now? Should she wait? But they were opening the car doors, and she saw people standing in a crowd out there, staring in. The whole idea was *not* to attract attention.

So she wound her way back through all the people in the aisle, murmuring, "Excuse me," over and over, and retreated to her seat. Maybe if she just made herself small and kept her face to the window, so all anyone saw was the scarf?

She did just that, her heart beating quickly. What would she say if police did like Augur said, and came through, checking IDs and asking questions? She made and remade plans, knowing with a kind of sick certainty that nothing she said was really going to work.

Below, the oncoming passengers waited in semicircles around the doors as the detraining people climbed down, pulling bags behind them. The smokers formed up in a semicircle on the sun-baked platform, puffing away as relatives waved good-bye and friends slowly turned away.

Cece, watching, felt sad. Why? She frowned down at her lap. Stress, that's it, she thought. Stress. Here I am, isolated from everyone I know and love, on the run from the law, and I don't even know why.

The memory of the laser strike caused her neck to tighten and her shoulders to hunch. Then she became conscious of her posture and wondered with a sort of unhappy hilarity that almost made her giddy if she *looked* guilty.

Consciously she forced herself to relax, and in a sudden impulse, she kicked off her shoes and curled her legs underneath her, in her favorite reading position. Ordinarily she never did it in public, for it didn't seem appropriate to her age and image as a teacher, but here, who would know those things?

So she tucked her shoes neatly under her seat, placing her folded plastic bag in front of them, and again turned her face to the window just as the train began to move.

And not ten seconds after that, Lynette Flieger came through the connecting door and walked slowly down the aisle.

TWENTY-FOUR

Lynette used the movement of the train as an excuse to walk more slowly. She reached for the backs of the seats to steady herself, and each time she said, "Pardon me," she looked at the people in the seats.

She really expected to find the man rather than the woman. That Cecilia Robin looked just like every other woman her age: short, out of shape, dowdy clothes, glasses. There were at least twelve women right in this car who fit the parameters.

So Lynette looked obediently at the shoes. Walking shoes, sandals, tennies, loafers. That one in 23 didn't even have any shoes apparent—she was sitting on her feet. Lynette paused briefly. How old was that one, anyway? She couldn't see the face, and the hair was covered by a scarf. Sitting on her feet like that was something kids did, but that hand was not a kid's hand, and the woman was pretty dumpy, as far as Lynette could judge. Well, she'd mentally mark that one, too, for when she came back through.

Lynette moved on, careful, observant, not permitting herself to hope that she would be the one to make the pinch. Whatever these people had done didn't matter to her. If they were outside of the law, then they joined the screaming, howling mob of selfish abusers, like her dad, people who thought themselves above the law. Thought they were justified in taking out their rotten tempers on everyone around them.

Lynette loved the Taelons for their peace and for their

strength. If they had to put a CVI in every single criminal in order to make him or her leave law-abiding people alone to live their lives, well, she'd stand right by their sides and hold the needles.

Determined, dead serious, young, strong, and focused, she made her way slowly through her assigned cars and then slipped down into one of the handicapped rest rooms and pulled out her global.

She pushed the toilet flush button, and under its sound punched in Suzanne's code. Suzanne appeared, standing near the car window it looked like, with city flashing by. "Lynette?"

"A lot of possibles for the woman in fourteen-fourteen, one in the lounge car, none in my others. No possibles for the man."

Suzanne's eyes went unfocused: She'd split her screen. "Mike?"

"One possible for the man in the last car, two possibles for the woman in the observation car."

"See where they go, mark their seats. Lynette, do your tape sweeps at the next stop. I'm staying here in the sleepers until I can scan them all. There are more of them than I'd thought, and not all of them have the curtains open."

Lynette flushed the toilet again. "Got it."

She ended the com, washed her hands, and walked upstairs to take up her station near the connecting door between the two cars with her possibles.

Augur's good spirits vanished along with Kansas City. He hated this sense of helplessness. Was it that making him uneasy, or was it the fact that he couldn't communicate with anyone he knew?

Liam. I've got to get to Liam.

Damn, the train was slow. He brooded out the window at the inoffensive jumble of streets, intersections, houses, and felt the restless urge to go wandering. Then repressed it. No. He'd stick to the plan.

Looked out and up. Storm brewing.
The look of the sky matched his mood.

Cece's mood stayed buoyant. How she loved the train! She could understand why it was full of people. Unlike airports, where people just wanted to get where they were going as fast as possible, there was little tension here. Instead there seemed to be an unspoken consensus among the train passengers to enjoy the ride, even if the train was a little late, or if the track got rough, or the dining car emptied too slowly because people lingered over their meals. They all had plenty of time. A rare, luxurious feeling.

Cece stared out at the slanting streets and the mostly white, flat-sided houses, bare of decoration, with their tall, narrow windows. Were these plain buildings designed to withstand extremes of weather? Probably. Or probably it was leftover pioneer spirit. What would they think of Southern California houses, most of them low and sprawling, none of them with these intriguing basement windows peeking out above the ground line? California house design was practical for quakes, but there the practicality ended: Houses were, as often as not, tricked out with false roofs and fancy shutters that would never shut, window boxes, and other decorative bric-a-brac, evidence of weather that was unchangeably balmy.

The houses through Arizona and New Mexico had been more like California houses, except for the surprisingly frequent adobe structures. At first Cece had thought them all old, until she saw some being built. The idea of it caused a spurt of amusement: Fourth graders made little adobe houses as part of their history unit, and she taught them earnestly about how the adobe warded cold in winter and heat in summer. It appeared it was really true, if people still used adobe even now!

The overlay of history continued to fascinate her. Modern visuals vanished in her mind, there to be replaced by Union and Confederate soldiers scrambling over the rocky cliffs and kicking up red-colored mud in the westernmost battle of the Civil War; pioneers making their way across the flat plains under the ever-changing summer skies; Native Americans riding free, until the land-hungry whites forced them into smaller and smaller spaces.

Cece winced at that part of history. She never hid it from her children, for she felt strongly that human beings learn from their mistakes. If they don't know about mistakes, they might perpetrate them again. But it did not make for pleasant lessons, and the children's faces when she talked about broken treaties and differences between the people's attitudes toward the land invariably turned sober and even sad. Children, healthy happy children, had an innate sense of justice. After the first impassioned exclamations about time machines and sending superheroes back to fix things, she told them that retroactive justice was impossible but future justice wasn't. She always exhorted them to remember, always remember, so that when they were adults, and voted on what might end up being a similar situation, they could do the right thing.

As she sat there and the miles flashed by, she mentally revamped many of her old lessons, based on what she saw.

And completely unknown to her, Lynette passed by three or four times, patient, vigilant, expectant.

When the train attendant announced La Plata, Cece sighed, unfolded herself, pulled out her shoes, and got up. This time she would make certain she did her duty.

She got downstairs just before Lynette came through the connecting doors into her car again and frowned at her empty seat. Who was it that sat there?

Well, she'd find out.

She was beginning to get a sense of who was where.

But first the train was stopping. Now to tape the bathroom doors.

TWENTY-FIVE

Augur wished he hadn't drunk that third cup of coffee at breakfast.

Ready to damn the world, he got up and listened at the door, automatic habit. His hand reached for the latch—and paused as he felt more than heard quiet footsteps outside his compartment.

The person passed, and he slid the door just enough to mark whoever it was, make sure he or she was gone. A woman: tall, short brown hair, blue polo shirt, and khaki slacks. She had a global in one pocket. Nothing out of the ordinary, but Augur had been on the run too long, and very ordinary people with no distinguishing characteristics whatsoever to him always conjured up cops trying to pass as civilians.

He wished, suddenly, that he could see that global. One glance would clear it up: Police and feds had access to models not sold on the open market. Of course there was always the other market, the one he used . . .

She was gone, around the corner up to the luxury compartments. Good.

The train was slowing. He hoped Cece remembered to hide. He slipped out and moved swiftly up to the little toilet directly opposite the coffee station. After he washed his hands he listened at the door, and his finger had just slid the latch from Occupied to Free when he heard the murmur of a voice. High: woman's voice.

He paused, hoping the woman wasn't about to try this toilet. Surprise!

She stopped—his hearing, acute when his adrenaline was up, sharpened—and clinks and whooshes at the coffee station mixed with her voice as she said, "Then wait for your RSVPs. I still have several to invite."

And the distinctive click-and-slide of a global closing.

Innocuous enough. Isn't it? Of course an innocuous conversation could be coded terms for not-so-innocuous cause; he'd employed them himself, both spoken and online. On the other hand, one could start seeing spies in every person carrying a global and hear codes in every scrap of chat.

At least she was moving on.

Relieved, Augur eased the door the tiniest crack and saw that same woman, now retreating up the car in the other direction. She glanced either side at the compartments as she walked. Including his, which he'd left with the curtains closed. That didn't mean anything necessarily either—a lot of people did the same thing. So, in fact, had Augur.

As soon as she vanished through the connecting door to the next sleeper, he made it to his compartment in six steps and shut himself in.

Wedged himself in comfortably, adjusted the curtains to a hairline crack through which he could see a segment of the corridor without him being easily seen. And waited.

Outside, large drops of rain spattered in streaks along the windows.

With the train so still Cece heard someone press lightly against the rest room door. She assumed it was someone who had sealegs after all the rocking; she certainly felt that odd sensation of rocking even though they were still.

Outside, Lynette finished her taping—with many looks over her shoulder to make certain no one saw her, and many pauses when people appeared, dropped off luggage, or slipped in and out of rest rooms. She noted who came out and who was still in (five still occupied), then ran upstairs to move to the next car and perform her task all over again.

In the sleepers, Suzanne made her circuit again, each time picking up some item to give her a reason to be moving around.

Augur saw her pass twice, once with coffee, once with one of the freebie train magazines. He saw two other people pass twice and wondered if maybe some of these people were trying to get some exercise after a long ride. He knew he needed it.

But with those others, he heard compartment doors slide shut. Frowned.

The train began to move.

Lynette hurried back to 1414, where she had the most suspects. Now four doors occupied, three of them still with the little piece of tape she'd placed along each door down at the floor level undisturbed. On all the others it had been broken.

She took up station near the windowed door that gave access to the car, to wait for them to come out—

"Hey, babe."

The heavy smell of stale beer made her hold her breath.

Her stomach squinched tight. A hand gripped her shoulder as the train lurched, and a man grinned down at her. Thirty, bad teeth, zit scars, about six feet and maybe 225, T-shirt, jeans, hiking boots.

Her brain made the rapid assessment as her body sent off zings of alarm. The man backed her into the corner, still smiling genially. "Hey. Where ya goin'?"

"Chicago," she said.

A rest room door snicked open.

"Me too!" Another waft of stale beer. "But we got hours, babe. Hey. Upstairs, two of us, me 'n' my buddy Thomas, we got us a party goin', since yesterday. Nonstop. Wanna join?"

She saw a man walk by: old, white, dressed in a suit and tie.

The drunk glanced speculatively down the rest room corridor, then back at her. She realized she looked like someone hanging around.

Who would hang around *rest rooms*? Did she look suspicious to him, or like she was hanging about to make pickups?

She said, with barely controlled violence, "Excuse me."

Went into the rest room just vacated. Fumed while she counted to thirty—and heard all three locks in the other toilets slide back. Heard three doors shut and moments later three locks engage.

Pressed the flush mechanism, washed her hands, went out.

An old lady was waiting to go in. The drunk was still there; she got past him before the old lady lurched into the toilet she'd just vacated.

"Hey, waitaminnit, babe—"

Bounded up four steps at a time. Got to the top of the stairs, hoping to see who had been below. Not one but *all three* were middle-aged women!

Lynette glanced back and forth—*of course* they had dispersed in two directions. Saw the one with the scarf just as she sat down. She might not even be middle-aged, just a little dumpy.

That big one with the dyed black hair. Glasses? Yes. Lynette followed more slowly. And there was the third, just sitting down next to a middle-aged man. Glance. The man—white, fiftyish—just had to be her spouse. They had a picnic basket between them and began talking in low voices.

Back to the one with the black hair. Lynette cruised by, glancing down at her footgear: sandals. Of course that was no guarantee of anything. Lynette kept on moving to check the other car and to find a bit of privacy in order to report to Suzanne.

. . .

"We have an hour to Fort Madison. Let's work as a team, sweep the lounge and observation cars."

Suzanne felt intense frustration. It was supposed to be easier than this. She still had about nine sleeping compartments whose occupants she had not yet seen. But then the train had been moving only an hour or two. Some of them were probably deep in blameless sleep.

The one that bugged her most was the single luxury compartment. Those were built for families, or rich folks. They had their own toilet and shower. Two could easily hide in there the entire journey and even have their meals sent in. She was considering whether to approach the attendant when Mike and Lynette both reported no luck so far.

They withdrew to the lounge and observation cars and cruised back and forth, until they'd ruled out all the people there.

By then it was 11:20. Ten more minutes until Fort Madison.

"Back to our stations," she murmured as they passed in single file through the connection.

Augur saw the woman with the global pass by yet again, this time empty-handed. He decided it was time to take a stroll and find out where her compartment was.

TWENTY-SIX

Was the entire world filled with stocky, middle-aged women?

Lynette leaned against a wall and struggled against anger. Deep breaths. The Taelons taught that anger was destructive, corrosive to body and mind. Peace. Rational thought. That was the way to accomplish goals.

Middle-aged, after all, was really kind of misleading. It could fit anyone from, say, thirty-five—especially if she was overweight and so her face sagged or her body looked dumpy—to sixty, if the woman was well preserved. Maybe even older. Well, looked at that way, it covered an awful lot of the female population.

Four of them had come into the lounge, either new passengers or from other parts of the train; Lynette saw the conductor take the last tickets from one. That meant by the time she'd finished the rest room sweep and got upstairs he'd already been through car 1414.

Well, they were going to stop soon. She would stand *right here* in car 1414 and see who went down to the rest rooms. Nothing would budge her—

"There y'are!"

The aroma of stale beer announced the creep from before.

She whirled around, backing away from a groping hand.

"Shy? Hey, a beer will fix that right up. C'mon. You look lonely, standin' around all by yourself. We been watchin', Tom 'n' me. You lookin' for someone to party with? Why not us?" He pointed up to the front of the car, just beyond the scarf woman, whom Lynette still hadn't seen from the front yet.

"Excuse me."

She turned around, slowing only a little when she passed the woman with the dyed hair. The woman was talking on a global!

Lynette paused, pretending to fuss with her shoe.

"Say, babe, I'm tryin' to talk to ya—"

Was that Arabic she heard? Was it a code?

"Hey, sweetie, playin' hard to get? Well I can play hard too—"

Lynette stalked through to the next car, ready to turn around and paste the jerk if he touched her again. Her head pounded, her blood thumped through her body. Peace. Peace! Argh, it was almost impossible to reach one's harmonic balance point when one was tired, and—

She saw that all the rest rooms were empty. She locked herself into the handicapped one, took a shuddering breath, and coded her global.

"Yes?" Suzanne said. Almost snapped.

"I'm having trouble." Lynette closed her eyes, fought to still her voice. "This drunken jerk keeps trying to pick up on me, and I'm afraid to say anything and blow my cover—"

At her end, Suzanne compressed her lips and fought exasperation. Didn't that kid know *anything*? Well, Lynette was new, and she did work hard. And she obviously hadn't encountered many scumbags in her life.

Suzanne split her screen and tabbed Mike's ID. Flushed. Reported the situation as briefly as possible, ending with, "Will you cover her?"

"On my way. Nothing looks good here anyway."

Flush. "Lynette. Mike's on his way. He'll do this sweep, and I'll come through from the other direction. You go up and sweep the sleepers, focusing on the luxury cabins. Number fifteen is the one I'm trying to scan." Flush. "In fact, why don't you knock and ask for the Andersons, or something, and see who's in it? You'll never go back through there again, so it won't look suspicious."

It was a perfectly good assignment, but Lynette closed her eyes, feeling hot tears squeeze out. Tears of defeat and humiliation, because Mike was being sent to do her job. Rationality defeated by the centuries of conditioning declaring that the victim—if she's female—is at fault.

They all closed off communication.

And when Suzanne came out of the rest room, where she'd gone when she got Lynette's call, Augur stepped into an empty compartment full of people's stuff and slid the door closed.

The woman passed by, hands empty. Augur knew she'd been on the global, because he'd heard the low murmur of her voice in the can, despite three flushes. Either she was sick as a dog, or some kind of snoop. For whom?

She walked on, not looking back—a good agent wouldn't—and he slipped after, mentally spotting cover here and there. Not much, either.

The attendant came through to announce Fort Madison, and the train began to slow.

Cece had been watching the increasing rain slant down like a gray-silver curtain over the crops. The rows of green and gold looked like seas, all bending before the driving rain. How beautiful it was!

But, oh. It was time to go hide in the ladies' again. *How* she wished she had a book!

She was just stepping off the bottom stair when Mike started down behind her; she had slid home the lock when he got to the rest room area.

He bent and started taping the doors.

No, I have to check myself, Suzanne thought. The nagging urge to oversee Mike's sweep was doing its best to convince her the impulse was thoroughness and not paranoia.

Lynette's problem with the drunken lothario was a reminder of the fact that these two she'd brought were raw recruits, despite their brains and willingness to work.

So she kept right on going into the coach area.

Augur, behind, felt his sense of alarm spike when the woman did not go all the way through 1414, but turned at the stair and went down. This didn't seem a casual walk, but a goal. And 1414 was Cece's car—though she was not in her seat. He mentally awarded her points for remembering the rest room hides.

As rain buffeted the still cars, he risked being seen and slipped down behind, stopping in the steep turn and peering down at an oblique angle. He could just see the mystery woman in the acute angle formed by the stairs and the hallway past the baggage storage area, talking to a big bruiser. Both she and the bruiser looked at the restrooms, and Augur frowned, puzzled. What the hell? Were they just waiting their turn, or what? The woman began to pivot, and Augur retreated fast, shaking open a newspaper he'd scored along the way. He plunked down into an empty seat, holding up the paper, and heard the deliberate tread of the woman as she passed by, going back in the direction of the next coach car down.

Well, damn. What did that mean? Meanwhile, he was back here, far from his hidey-hole, and Cece would be out in half a minute.

The train started to roll.

Augur stayed put, and moments later the bruiser came up, moving slowly toward the front of the car, staring at the seats as he went.

Augur got up, slipped down the stairs before the guy could get to the front and look back. He hoped the people around weren't watching what he knew would seem odd behavior, but he also knew that to pause and check would be sure to garner notice.

Three people stood in line waiting for heads. A man came out of one. Rest room etiquette is definite: You don't meet someone's eyes. Augur, who was last in line and perforce partially blocking the passageway, glanced floorward as the man muttered a pardon and pushed past—and what Augur saw sent white-hot fear through him.

At the bottom of every door there were tiny bits of tape.

As he watched, a door opened, tape broke, and Cece emerged.

She saw him, and her eyes widened. He half raised a hand, and she made a sharp turn and stood at the car door, staring out the window. He stood three feet away, listening to the others breathe, no one talking.

God! Would these people *ever* get done?

Snick! A woman came out, a wake of heavy-smelling lotion coming with her. *Snick.* An elderly gent emerged, and the last person in line moved into the head and shut the door, leaving Cece and Augur alone.

He thought of the heavy guy up there, waiting to see who came up the stairs, noting their seats in order to watch their movements at the next stop, and he *knew*. Not how many of them, but the main fact—

"Cecilia, we're busted."

The train was slowly beginning to pick up speed.

Instinct was fast. He unlocked the heavy car door, slid it open. "Jump," he said.

Cece stared at him, her face blanched with terror.

"It's only going to get faster."

"My stuff—"

"History," he said, stepped up, and jumped.

She was right after him.

On the upper level of the car, Mike and Suzanne waited for those last people to come up. But for a long minute or two no one appeared on the stairs, and then they heard a woman yell from down below.

No one upstairs reacted, because none of them had been looking down at the sharp angle needed to see anything.

Mike and Suzanne gazed at one another down the length

of the car, then both started forward. Then a young woman appeared at the top of the stairs, looked around wildly, and saw the attendant, who was involved in a labored conversation with a couple who did not speak English.

The young woman raced up the aisle to the attendant, spoke, jabbing her hand toward the lower level, then both raced back.

Other passengers watched this byplay and exchanged looks, some startled, some puzzled, a few alarmed. Two or three people got up to follow the pair down, and their movements of course drew more people.

The yell? It was a woman emerging from the rest room who, on seeing the car door open, panicked and shrieked for the conductor! Another passenger heard her and ran up in search of the attendant.

The attendant pushed through the gathering crowd, slammed the door shut, latched it, and reported an open door on the intercom. By then quite a crowd had gathered on the stairway, blocking Mike and Suzanne from getting all the way down. The two detectives didn't speak but listened to the crowd of passengers exclaiming and wondering and surmising and adding to the general confusion. They began to worm their way downward but were blocked at the halfway point by the accumulation of bodies.

Suzanne met Mike's eyes and was about to signal him to retreat back upstairs again, when a very old man appeared in the doorway of the handicapped section, just below where Mike was standing. The man chewed his cheek for a moment or two, then he announced in a thin, quavering voice, "Coupla bums hitchin' a ride jumped off, 'swhat I saw."

None of the talkers paid him the least attention. The attendant, surrounded by expostulating passengers, didn't hear him: He was trying to ascertain if anyone was missing or had fallen out. He couldn't be heard past the pelting of questions about train safety and wind sucking you out like on planes and how often did the doors just come open?

The old man shrugged, shuffled back inside, and sat down.

Mike looked up at Suzanne, who leaned over from the first level and mouthed the words, "Go get Lynette."

Mike was gone in three vaulting steps.

Suzanne eased down through the space made by Mike's massive body and stepped into the handicapped section. She spotted the old man sitting there next to the window and walked up, smiling. "Excuse me, sir. Did you say you saw someone jump off the train?"

The man turned his head, looked her up and down, chewed his lip some more. He was not in a good mood. That young man in the uniform had ignored him, just as most young men ignored an old fellow these days.

"What's it to you?" he finally asked.

"Well, I'm undercover. My job is train safety. I need to investigate whether the door was faulty. Someone might have fallen out."

It was pretty lame, but the old man didn't seem to care. He shrugged one shoulder, then shook his head. "Can't say." He chewed his cheek a while longer, and Suzanne waited. Finally he added, "Two of 'em. Didn't see th'other one that clear, outside o' blue clothes. One was a skinhead. Maybe from down Mexico way. Mighta been drifters. Was lots of drifters, back in the thirties. Dust Bowl days. Jumped off trains alla time, when they saw the conductor. Had no tickets."

The old woman sitting behind leaned forward. She was very old indeed. In a high, quavering voice, she said, "He was young, the Mexican."

"Maybe lookin' for work up here? No work down south?" the old man ruminated, his mood changing. "I remember back in the thirties, there was no work for anyone, and hundreds o' bums rode the trains. . . ."

Suzanne realized that the man was about to launch into personal history, which was more interesting to him than his brief glimpse of supposed bums jumping off the train, so she thanked him and retreated back upstairs. He sat back in disgust at modern manners.

Suzanne met the other two between the cars, balancing with difficulty on the covered connectors. Holding both doors shut, Suzanne said, "See if any of your possibles are missing, then report back."

They dispersed, checked, and were back again in five minutes.

Lynette said, "We have three new ones in my cars, one of whom fits the woman's description, and one missing."

"A missing possible?"

"Yes. I never got a good look at her face, but I think she was middle-aged. Short and out of shape."

"Which seat?"

Lynette frowned, then nodded. "Twenty-three."

"Stay here. I'll reconnoiter."

Suzanne walked out and proceeded down the corridor, then slowed, putting her hands out, as she scanned the empty seats along the twenties.

When she reached 23, she saw a bag tucked under the seat, and with deliberate self-assurance sank into the seat next to it. Reached down, pulled out the bag.

Keeping it between her body and the window, she scanned the contents. Toothbrush, toothpaste, stockings, glasses case—dark glasses. A folded cloth, looked like a dress. Frowned when she saw the plain beige color.

Pulled out the folded printout of the enlargement photo of the teacher. Beige dress. Damn! How many beige dresses were there? Oh, probably thousands, especially on teachers, but still. Suzanne's heart pounded when she recalled the old man's words about a Mexican man, and the old woman adding that he'd been young. The mystery hacker's skin had been honey brown, and Suzanne could understand an older man thinking him Hispanic.

Coincidences? Maybe, but there were far too many of them adding up to a strong internal conviction that she had been right, that she'd almost had them, but that they had eluded her.

But as yet she was the only one who knew it.

She looked up and saw that the conductor was now going along the seats to see who was missing.

Thought fast. Tucked the bag next to her. When the conductor drew up, he looked down at 23, puzzled, and then at Suzanne, his expression altering to question.

"Are you looking for Mary?" She pointed at the seat, then added in a chatty tone, "She went down to the lounge to get coffee. I'm from the back car, but we got to talking over breakfast—"

"Thanks," the conductor said with a preoccupied smile and moved on.

With him safely gone, Suzanne got up and, with complete self-assurance, clasped Cece's bag. She retreated down the aisle to the connecting doors. Lynette and Mike were still there. She slid the door shut behind her, enclosing them in the tiny, shifting space, and then said, "It was them."

TWENTY-SEVEN

The world spun crazily, water filling Augur's eyes and nose. A brief glimpse of surprised faces at lower-level train windows swiftly lost as he rolled down a sharp incline and into shrubbery. It seemed to last forever, and he concentrated on keeping himself in a ball so he could shed velocity and not get hurt. At last he stopped in a thick patch of shrubbery.

Sick and dizzy, Augur forced himself to stand up. "Cecilia?"

Was the train, just barely visible now, slowing? The world spun too hard, and the rain was too blinding, to see for certain.

"Here."

"Are you all right?"

"I think so." Her voice was high as a child's, but there she was, apparently unhurt. "I—I lost my glasses at first, but I found them. But they're horribly scratched. And one lens cracked." Her hands shook.

"Come on," Augur said, in a coaxing voice. "We have to make tracks."

Cece looked around, bewildered, frightened. She nodded. "Yes. Okay."

She followed as he led the way away from the rail and down alongside a stream, into a thicket of trees. They couldn't see or hear the train.

Then Augur stopped. "Damn."

Cece hadn't said anything because she too felt sick and dizzy. Her joints had turned to water, and she was afraid she'd either throw up or faint or maybe both. It took all her strength to put one foot in front of the other, to keep Augur's slim form in sight. Rain blurred her scratched, dirty glasses, and she thought longingly of her expensive prescription dark glasses now left behind, along with her beige dress.

She now had nothing at all.

No, don't think of that.

"What's wrong? Oh." She emerged from behind Augur and stared down at the huge river stretching away toward the distant dark line of trees. "My gosh. I've never seen anything that big. It's almost like a sea."

"It might be pretty another time, but right now all I can think is that we have to get across." Augur rubbed his chin.

Cece stared at the flowing brown water. "That must be the Mississipi," she said, and despite the situation, a thrill of excitement tingled along her nerves. Here, in this very place, Mark Twain had once passed. Had he gazed once where she was standing?

"We aren't swimming that," Augur muttered. "All right. This way."

He led them back around toward the city, along an oblique angle, poor Cece following with her mouth open because it was so hard to breathe in the pounding rain, while squelching along ankle deep in mud.

The nightmare trip eased just a little when they found a highway, but Augur would not permit them to walk along it. Instead, they had to toil their way through the undergrowth a few yards off the pavement.

At last the eternity of walking, as steady as the rain, ended with Augur giving a grunt of satisfaction. "Perfect," he said.

Wearily Cece looked up and made out through the smeary fog of her lenses the round red sign of a truck stop. Huge long rectangles hulked around, recalling the night café in Kingman, which now seemed months ago.

"You wait here," he said. "We don't dare go in. Too many questions. I'm going to find us another transport, one going east."

"One without a fridge if you can," she said past chattering teeth.

"You got it," he promised.

She waited, shivering, in the pounding rain. Augur slid into the first empty truck cab he came to and reached for the manifest papers.

And while they were thus occupied, far to the east, Da'an stood in the peaceful blue chamber at the center of the embassy, while rain poured down onto the deceptively thin fabric of the ceiling, contemplating the data stream flowing ever downward in rainbow glory.

Waved it off and glanced into Liam Kincaid's office annex. The area was quiet, of course. Empty.

Soft of foot, Da'an entered. Sat down at Liam's console. Stretched out fingers in their human skin to touch the keyboard where Liam, becoming so much more human as time progressed, habitually touched.

Paused to consider time, its rapid pull here on this planet. That rapidity appeared to strengthen Liam, but then he was so very young a being, at least in his physical form. His spiritual essence? Ah, what a mystery. A complex mystery beginning with the question: Why did Ha'gel do what was done? It is given to me to discover, Da'an thought. For of course it was no accident that Liam Kincaid was bound to Da'an.

Looking down, Da'an considered the human computer construct. Liam seemed to prefer it. Why?

With rapid touches Da'an activated Liam's computer and entered the necessary code words to give free access. Oh, there were protected corners here and there, but Da'an, used to very long-term thinking, did not disturb them. Such secrets inevitably either resolved or altered, far too swiftly to be followed except by exertion of energy, which Da'an must conserve.

Underlying the decision not to investigate those secrets lay trust, of which Da'an was aware. But also with it came the awareness that Liam, like his secrets, was evolving rapidly. What would he become? No answer—yet.

So for now, certain secrets did require probing.

Da'an windowed up Liam's log on his attempt to discover who had broken into the Taelon site. What Da'an read there was no surprise. The confirmation that no human had made that trespass onto the Taelon site created a subsidiary line of thought. A Taelon, then? Or—? That was for later meditation.

Now Da'an keyed up one of Liam's customized search engines. Augur was a known quantity to Da'an—known far more than either Liam or Augur was, as yet, aware. But this teacher?

Tap, tap, in went her name, Cecilia Robin. Da'an waited and an intriguing list came up. The news stories could safely be ignored. But this connection with something called Superteacher?

Da'an tabbed that link, which apparently would lead to one of the virtual rooms where teenagers gathered for social interaction.

On the screen a female figure, recognizable as the teacher whose face had been pasted in the renegade window on the Taelon site, cavorted through animated figures of surprising variety. Da'an even saw a Taelon, though this one had physical characteristics added that were decidedly un-Taelon. In the midst of all these animated beings Superteacher danced around singing a song that appeared to be about freedom of birth.

Da'an watched for a time and then ran a search on Superteacher, subsequently discovering that she existed all over the Net, the newest fad among youths not just in America but in other countries as well. A little digging showed that inappropriate scripts—offensive scripts—attached to the teacher were swiftly killed off by nameless others, strengthening the one form that appeared almost everywhere, traceable to no single location. How many scripts had been lovingly, or gleefully, or challengingly added on, giving the animated figure almost a semblance of life?

The teacher stopped, pushed up her glasses in a gesture that Da'an knew would be instantly recognizable in the living, breathing woman, and then put her hands on her hips. "Do you believe in freedom?" she asked.

To see what would happen next, Da'an typed in *Yes*.

"Then send me to all your friends and let me dance the freedom dance. And you dance with me, you and your friends. Work together, dance together, for freedom." She whirled around and danced away.

Not a word about Resistance, or revolution, or the federation of nations that called themselves the ANA (dedicated to resistance, as if the Taelons were not aware), or the Taelons as conquerors. And it appeared that most of this work had been done by youths under the age of fifteen.

Da'an, though not human, knew what thumbing the nose meant and knew that children all over the world were thumbing their noses at the Taelons—and in such a manner that official recognition, and action, would lower the authorities in everyone's eyes.

The mind that could calculate this plot and set it in motion was admirable.

And must be found.

TWENTY-EIGHT

Sandoval gazed into his global, silent with fury.

"Who are you?" he snapped. "Why was it necessary to insist on intruding on my schedule?" He glanced up. Zo'or was nowhere in sight; Sandoval preferred to deal with certain business on one of the lower levels of the Mothership, and here he was almost within earshot of the bridge, but it couldn't be helped. This woman had bullocked her way past all three of the aides he'd placed specifically to protect him from frivolous harassment by phone, global, or E-mail.

Luckily—though it wasn't luck at all—these techs here on the Mothership were smart, sober, and implanted with CVIs, so they were totally his. He snapped his fingers at the comms technician who turned, devoid of expression, to trace the call.

"My name is Suzanne Verda. I was once a peace officer in St. Louis, though that doesn't matter right now. I think my business is important enough to warrant your attention."

The tech looked up and drew a finger across his neck, the established sign for a block on establishing GPS.

Sandoval made a "try again" motion out of view of the global's vid pickup and turned his attention back to Verda.

Verda probably carried a police model global. Technically they weren't supposed to have blocks programmed in, but a lot of them did. He could break the block fast enough if he so desired, not that he wanted even the implanted techs to know that. The less they knew, the less there might be to have to explain.

"And so I felt I had to talk to you directly," the woman finished.

"You have my attention now," Sandoval said and watched the woman blanch at the threat in his voice.

But she didn't back down. "I have a proximate location on your fugitives," she said.

"You have them?"

"No." Quick looks from side to side.

"Where are you?"

"Galesburg, Illinois," she said readily and did something to her global.

The comms tech motioned thumb up, meaning he'd gotten the location.

Sandoval moved across the floor to glance at the terminal. There in blinking green he saw a street name in Galesburg.

"Where are they?"

"Negotiation first."

"You mean the blackmail price?" His teeth showed.

Her lips tightened, but she kept her gaze steady.

Sandoval felt another wave of fury and made an effort to dismiss it. The woman looked back with unhidden desperation, and determination, but none of the smugness or slyness he expected of the dealer mentality. He could—and would—run a check on her, but he already knew what he'd find: She'd be just what she said she was.

But he didn't have to make it easy. "What's your price?"

She replied in a firm voice, "A job. My agency is adequate, but I think I can do better. But jobs in law enforcement these days are hard to come by. You're in a position to fix that, and all I ask is a chance, for me and my two partners—without a thing in our necks. I think we proved ourselves with our having tracked down your perps, and though it's true they escaped us, it was by a matter of seconds."

Sandoval didn't know the circumstances yet, but what he knew about Augur made him nod. He wasn't surprised. Of course Augur would find some hole to crawl into. He'd apparently spent a lifetime doing just that.

"Granted," he said. "As it happens we are expanding the Volunteer program, and we're hiring instructors in basic police technique. That does not require an implant, for you would not be working with Taelon tech. You can report to FBI headquarters in D.C., give them your name, and I'll set it up. If you're good, there'll be other opportunities."

"And my two assistants?"

"We'll find something for them as well." He glanced at his waiting aide and wound a finger in the air: See to it. The woman turned obediently to her keyboard. She'd find out the assistants' names, run backgrounds on them all, and turn it over to the FBI Recruitment Office.

"Then here's my report," Verda said, and Sandoval tabbed Record on his global.

He listened with only part of his attention as she spoke in a clear, concise voice. He caught the key words: train, Fort Madison, and the time. With one hand he waved up the data stream and then manipulated it to bring in a map of that area.

Verda finished her report. By then Sandoval had mentally established his perimeters and was calculating whom he could send, how many, and how quickly they could be deployed.

The woman stopped, and he glanced at the global, to see her waiting expectantly. "Would you like us to carry on with the investigation?"

"Not needed. You've done well. Take your people to D.C. and talk to the recruitment officer." Glance at his aide, who nodded. "It's all set up."

She nodded, and he closed the communication before she could think of anything else. He had her report; she herself faded from his attention as he tapped a finger against the global and studied the map.

Already an hour. Verda and her people might have been reliable on stakeouts, but they knew nothing about the hunt when the prey was someone like Augur, who was both fast and slippery.

The perimeter widened every second; logistics were going to be a bitch. This one he'd have to oversee himself. He did a fast mental triage on his schedule, then began to hand out orders.

Cece watched Augur staring moodily through the crack in the truck's door. It felt like they were riding in a moving barn. The truck sides were made of weather-warped fence slats, just strong enough to support a roof. They were reasonably dry, but most important, the rusty lock on the chain holding the door together responded to a little metal thingie Augur carried somewhere on his person.

If they had to, they could be off the truck in moments.

She tried to derive comfort from that thought. There was little enough comfort in her immediate surroundings, or in her perception of the immediate future.

Augur turned around to face her. Blue-white light lanced across his face as lightning flashed outside.

"Sandoval's going to come after us himself," he said.

Cece grimaced. "You're certain of that?"

Augur sighed, fighting for patience. He knew that nothing was her fault, but he felt responsibility for her like a weight around his neck.

"We can be certain that at least two unidentified agents were after us, because I saw them. I saw the tape, which is a cheap, easy, and old method used by police and investigators of various sorts. Now, they could be working for anyone, but I'm going to assume the worst: that if they weren't Sandoval's bloodhounds, they'll have gone straight to Sandoval with the evidence because they'll want a piece of the action."

"You don't think it's possible that they were on our side?"

"If they were on our side, they would have tried to make contact in some other way than by trapping us."

Cece nodded. "All right. So what does it mean?"

"It means that Sandoval is quite capable of forming an outer perimeter by multiplying maximum speed by how long since we jumped off that train—and our investigators know that to the minute—forming an arc that, for our purposes, extends roughly from Cedar Rapids, Iowa, to Peoria and south to Springfield."

Cece nodded, remembering when Augur had chosen this truck that its next stop was supposed to be Peoria.

"I take it our plans have changed," she said.

"We can be sure there's a roadblock waiting somewhere ahead. We might have to jump for it again." He gestured with graceful irony at the doors.

"Not at seventy miles per hour I'm not," Cece stated.

"This thing can't get up to seventy," Augur retorted. "I'll bet we're barely doing fifty, though it sounds—and feels—like a hundred. But no, a fall even from fifty miles an hour is not going to do us any good. What I'm hoping is that these guys are going to need to make a pit stop well before then."

Cece opened her mouth to remind Augur that the two men in the truck had gotten gas just after they'd climbed into the back, then she realized what he meant and shut her mouth. They'd both seen the two six-packs of beer the skinny man had been carrying from the diner. Drinking and driving had been Cece's first worry. Not that she knew which man was drinking and which driving, for the cab was completely separate from the wooden back part of the truck. At least they weren't swerving all over the road.

"We might not be able to wait, though," Augur said. "I hate to risk being seen, but we might have to get off at a red light in the next township. We'll keep watch for marshaling of official vehicles."

Cece nodded. She was hungry and tired, and felt nastily

grubby in this half-dried, filthy three-day-old dress, but she would not utter a complaint. What could Augur do that he wasn't already doing?

She looked around at the piled farm equipment, wishing that the men had wives who packed them picnic baskets with red-and-white checkered cloths. Of course such a thing would be stored in the cab. . . .

"Here we go."

She realized she'd drifted into a jumble of daydreams and brought her attention back. The truck clashed noisily down through the gears—bad mechanics, liquor, or both?—and slowed as it crawled around in a loop.

Augur kept his eye pressed to the crack, and Cece gripped her hands together, as the truck crossed the highway and pulled into a gas station.

Yes. Right behind the building, next to the men's room.

Both men got out, went into the rest room.

In seconds Augur had the lock unpicked—and then he froze, as two men came ambling round the corner of the building and curiously eyed the truck.

Augur cursed under his breath, holding the rickety door shut with his fingertips, as one man walked around the truck while the other went into the rest room.

Moments later the first man emerged from the rest room and said, quite clearly, "Naw, it's Chuck Van Broek. Works for Stanton Combine."

The second man spat on the old pavement full of ancient ice heaves. He shrugged, and the two retreated back around the building. Again Augur was about to open the door when the two men came out of the rest room.

Cece thought of that unlocked door, and her heart thumped heavily in her ears. But either they were too drunk to notice, or too torpid to care, for they parted and headed for the cab.

"Now."

Cece needed no further encouragement. She jumped off as silently as she could, though one thigh scraped painfully on something rusty on the back of the truck. The engine fired up. Augur flung himself out and whipped the lock onto the chain, was about to click it safely in place when the truck lurched into first gear and pulled the lock out of his fingers.

At least the lock was still on the chain, though how long that would last was anyone's guess.

"This way," Augur whispered, and they retreated in a straight line away from the station to the shrubbery beyond.

They kept to the shrubbery, winding around occasional buildings.

Finally Cece said, "I think that lock will come off."

"Safe bet," Augur said. Then his brows rose. "Evidence one should never drink and drive, eh?"

The men would certainly be blamed if their farm equipment fell out onto the road. They might even blame themselves; if they were drunk enough, they might not remember locking the chain.

Either way, Cece and Augur were out of the truck, and she was fairly certain that they'd left no evidence of their brief stay. Or had they? Had she touched anything? Left fingerprints? No, she couldn't remember touching anything, except the back of the truck when she'd hoisted herself in, but it was all rusty and gritty with mud—

Augur halted, looked up.

Cece realized then that the rain had stopped, though there were still dark clouds overhead, and the air was humid. At least a breeze blew. And through the cracks in the clouds you could see shafts of sunlight.

"That way," Augur said, pointing.

"Where are we going?" Cece asked, as they set out along a path winding between copses of oak and willow. She realized her feet hurt. Knew they were going to hurt a whole lot worse.

Augur grinned. "To the safest city in America."

"Which is?"

"Taelonville."

TWENTY-NINE

A distinctive alarm buzzed in Liam's global.

He knew what that one meant. Someone—probably Da'an—had fired up his system and had broken past the initial firewalls, back in D.C. Augur had put those alarms there himself.

"Sha'bra," Liam muttered in Taelon, not quite under his breath.

A CVI-implanted bodyguard looked up, startled.

"Never mind." Liam gestured. "I hit my shin. Go on."

The young student assigned to give Liam the tour of the buildings comprising Yale's Old Campus gave a helpless shrug and then resumed her discourse. "This statue over here is Nathan Hale. You notice he's got his hands behind him, suggesting his stance on the scaffold when he made his famous speech. He was a student over there in that brick building, Connecticut Hall, which is one of the oldest . . ."

Liam tuned her out and began calculating how soon he could break away from this tedium. His techs could do the superficial security scans, of course; in fact, on the surface, this entire gig was a no-brainer.

That did not explain why Sandoval wasn't here, right now, grilling this kid, and her bosses, in person. That would be more his style.

As soon as they reached Phelps Gate he excused himself. His staff all stood around, most of them longing for a cup of coffee, as the tour guide pointed the way to the men's room.

He shut and locked the door. Snapped open his global.

"Renee?" He breathed her name, willing her to pick up herself. Her message picture stayed in place for two, three excruciatingly long seconds and then cleared, and there she was. "Liam. Have you been on-line in the past twenty-four hours?"

"No time. Instead I've been earbanged by every official in New Haven," he said grimly. "Buried in officialdom. And I don't have the time now, either. I've got meetings scheduled back to back until midnight."

"And so you rang me because . . . ?"

"One of Augur's pet bugs just let off a squawk. Someone is messing with my system in D.C."

"Someone as in Da'an?"

"He's done it before. I don't have the time to block him, or even try to find out what he's up to. Can you interfere? At least stall him off?"

Her brows contracted, and then she smiled. "Oh, yes. After all, two can play the officialese game." Her smile turned wicked. "When you can, do a search on Superteacher. You will enjoy this one." Her screen blanked.

Liam muttered "Superteacher?" Pocketed the global and stepped back out into the foggy embrace of bureaucracy.

And it was midnight before he was free. By then he'd forgotten all about Renee's Superteacher, which meant he was, as yet, one of the few in the United States who didn't know about the new AM dancing her way through the virtual chat rooms and gathering halls of cyberspace.

It was nine P.M. in Los Angeles, and the sun had just set on another hot day when ShaNissa and Aisling both logged on to the Ghost Horse fan chat room. Lots of other kids were there, but Aisling (Star Pony) and ShaNissa (Firebolt) found one another. They keyed to private mode at once.

<FIREBOLT> Guess what! After school I came home and scripted S.T.

<STAR PONY> Me too!

<FIREBOLT> What?

<STAR PONY> I put her dancing to Gramma's favorite song, "Born Free."

ShaNissa smiled out her window, thinking of Aisling's grandmother, with whom Aisling and her mom lived. At Open House she'd come with her gray hair in beaded braids, wearing a long rainbow-tie-dyed caftan, with a shawl that she'd beaded and embroidered herself. ShaNissa thought her cool, especially after Maguire Billiger-Ledundas's skinny, prune-faced mother, Ms. Billiger-Prattgill, said nastily to the other skinny, prune-faced moms she was standing with, "Who does she think she is, Jane Fonda?" And Taylor's mom said in an even nastier voice, "Someone ought to do her a favor and tell her that even old hippies can grow up." Luckily Aisling had been showing her mom some artwork across the room and didn't hear. ShaNissa's mom had said, "Let's go look somewhere else," and ShaNissa had been glad to go. She'd never told Aisling about it, either.

Uh-oh. Type something!

<FIREBOLT> Wow! I like that song too. Guess what I did.

<STAR PONY> What?

<FIREBOLT> I put in a move. That one where she pushes her glasses over her ear and forgets she's holding chalk and it makes a mark in her hair.

Sitting in her room, which she had painted herself, Aisling giggled. She also wished she were that adept at scripting. Oh, well, she had a whole summer stretching out before her, during which she could certainly practice. But, oh, that wasn't what bugged her the most.

<STAR PONY> I want to tell Gramma. I think she'd totally love it.

Aisling sent the words and saw them write on her screen. What she wanted, very badly, was for ShaNissa to say that it would be cool to tell her. She writhed in her chair with the intensity of her mixed emotions, because she knew, as well as she knew anything, that Gramma would never tell, but still, ShaNissa was the smartest kid in the class, and if she thought the idea bit rocks, then Aisling would not tell her.

And at her house, ShaNissa hesitated. Though she was just a month short of her tenth birthday, she already knew that when girls said they wanted to do something, but didn't actually do it, it meant, May I? No, it meant, Will you still like me if I do it?

ShaNissa thought hard. She hesitated, fingers on keyboard. She did so like Aisling's gramma, and she thought it would be fun to tell her, especially since the creepy moms of those dorky girls at school who thought they were so cool would never know.

But she also knew that your feelings ought not to decide what was right. Yet she didn't want to make Aisling feel bad. So . . .

<FIREBOLT> How about waiting until Miss Robin gets back, and everything is safe? I know I'd like to tell my parents, but what if some grown-up comes and threatens to take them to jail?

Silence. Her words were there, blinking on the screen. ShaNissa counted one, two, three, four, oh, did I hurt her feelings after all?

<STAR PONY> You're right. I would hate to have those people with the things in their neck take Gramma away. We'll tell people after Miss Robin gets back.

ShaNissa sat back and sighed. Their secret was safe.

THIRTY

It was eleven at night central time.

The place, the police station in Fort Madison, which Sandoval had taken over for his command post during the search. Outside this office was a nest of cables, computers, busily keening printers, people talking on globals, or updating maps. The air smelled of EM and stale coffee.

As soon as the door shut on the hum of activity Sandoval threw down the printouts the local police chief had just handed him. He stared moodily out at a clear night, stars twinkling in the clean-washed sky.

He didn't need to read the reports. He knew that he had lost Augur and Robin in the first hour.

This despite blasting down from the Mothership in his scoutcraft and, his ears still ringing from the shock wave, using his authority to strong-arm local officials past jurisdictional bickering and the lumbering clumsiness of various departments deciding whose equipment, whose field agents, and whose communication system would cover what. Considering what they'd had to do, they'd mobilized with commendable rapidity.

But not fast enough. Despite the line-of-sight foot searches radiating out in circles from the Fort Madison rail just west of the river, despite the roadblocks and vehicle searches and the flyovers. An enormous expenditure of manpower and resources, and all a waste of time and effort: He'd seen it immediately, though he'd had to follow through, just to make certain.

He turned around, fist gripped with the urge to strike, to smash. For a moment he contemplated the intense pleasure of throttling that idiot Suzanne Verda. Throwing her and her two stooges in jail for incompetence instead of hiring them. Surprise! The price of being a fool.

Except she wasn't a fool. He knew what she was: a sober, steady worker, used to the patient sifting of clues, the long-term stakeout. He could just see it, after Augur and the teacher jumped the train. Verda and her two flunkies probably hunkered down over coffee in the Amtrak lounge car and spent the next half hour talking over their plans, confident that at least they had a definite time and exit point. Of course they'd catch up with the chase through faked cash cards, or one of the usual boneheaded mistakes that the usual criminal made. They'd never dealt with anyone like Augur—and hadn't been trained to deal with the Augurs.

Meanwhile Augur had been calculating the perimeter of danger a crucial fifteen minutes before Sandoval even heard about his presence and thus had been able to go to earth and effectively vanish.

No, he had to keep his word to Verda. She'd done her best.

So Augur had slipped through his fingers. He was here to consider his next step, because instinct insisted there was something missing. Not something in that pile of useless printouts. It was . . .

It was . . . He looked out again, westward. No. East—

Smiled. Of course. L.A.—Vegas—Kingman—Fort Madison. A vector.

He snapped open his global. "Tate."

"Hey, boss. Augur's Fort Madison train hop is now on the Taelon site."

"By now everyone in continental United States knows."

"I just thought you'd want an update."

Sandoval ignored the defensive sidestepping. He said, "You're on your way here, and you're going to take over this search."

Tate sighed. "He's long gone, boss."

"Of course he is. But you're still going to be here, directing the search, and you're going to make as much noise as possible."

Tate's face altered into what he probably thought was cleverness. Oh, *now* he was on the inside track. "So he gets overconfident and emerges somewhere else, right? Where, D.C.?"

"Probably. I'll handle that end since I have to be back there anyway. You just stick to your job here. Run everyone, including the journalists. Put some spin on the possibility of hostage situations, thievery, so on. Assure everyone that Augur's armed. Probably is, anyway."

"The whole enchilada. Got it."

No you don't, Sandoval thought, smiling as he shut the global.

But Ronald Sandoval got it. At last. Cecilia Robin had run from Carlton's place, definitely aided by Augur. That would be an easy enough Resistance call. They then showed up together in Las Vegas. Therefore, Robin had to have spilled the results of her talk with Carlton into Augur's waiting ears. Now it seemed clear what Augur was going to do about it.

Augur's being seen here with the woman meant two things: The woman was heading east to stop her little student friend, and Augur was playing knight errant.

So Sandoval had to get back to his real task, which was to make certain that nothing got in Neville Carlton's way.

It was even later when Da'an entered the embassy, soft-footed as always.

The place glowed with gentle blue light, a peaceful light that humans and Taelons alike found soothing. But humans preferred spread-spectrum lighting for work, and so Da'an moved toward that source of light to find the night crew.

Not the receptionist. He merely relayed the constant inflow of data; embassies on the other side of the world were busy with their daytime activities, and the net of shared information was effective only when constant. It was the computer tech Liam Kincaid had hired to work at long-term, difficult tasks during night, when there was the least amount of interruption, whom Da'an moved toward now.

The tech, a woman, sat squarely before her terminal. Humans' ages were difficult for Da'an to approximate, so swiftly did they age, but this one appeared to be mature in years, short and of sturdy build, her hair a bright red that accorded oddly with the calm blue surroundings. The lighting picked gold highlights out of her hair, making a glittering aura.

The gold in her hair reminded Da'an of his protracted visit from Renee Palmer. Another complex individual, so fascinating to study. Da'an had rarely spent much time in her company. She tended to speed in and out of one's presence, always forward-focused, much like Ronald Sandoval, except without that ferocious intent. Sandoval's boundless energy appeared to be fueled by anger as well as a hunger for power. Renee Palmer's motivation was more difficult to assess.

Her overall motivation. Today's motivation had been transparent to Da'an, though of course it would not do to hint of awareness. That she'd appeared so quickly after Da'an had breached Liam's computer system had been transparent enough, despite her many sensible reasons for insisting on a personal interview.

She'd then spent hours attempting—in truth, it was an admirable attempt—to subvert Da'an from pursuing the intriguing promise of the little animated figure of the fugitive teacher dancing its way across the Internet, proclaiming freedom. So Da'an had willingly cooperated, going over Doors International's security setup for not just the Yale unveiling but also for several other planned public appearances. She had initiated a discussion of the Taelons' intentions on future appearances, stressing the need for an improved public image. She had talked about patents, and tech, biotech, energy sources, and a number of other urgent, immediate, and fascinating topics, promising to be in contact later on several fronts.

Da'an had thanked her sincerely for an informative session, promised personally to seek out some necessary data and see to it that it was provided as quickly as possible—a task that had taken less than half an hour of meditation with the data stream.

Now Renee Palmer's image in memory gave way to the present and this woman sitting here, who looked up, startled.

"Your name is Kitty La Briusca, I understand?"

She swallowed, a sign of nervousness. It had to be startlement, for Da'an had just finished monitoring her work from the data stream and found nothing to which one would attribute guilt: She had merely been creating the text of a work of fiction, something about spaceships and photon weapons. Perhaps it was considered inappropriate to thus occupy oneself with personal projects while on duty, even though there were no immediate demands? Da'an dismissed the observation for later contemplation.

"Please. I have a task for you that you might find interesting, if you have a free moment?"

Smack! Her hand cleared her screen abruptly, and she turned around, relief making her face go crimson.

"But first." Da'an made gestures evocative of harmony, of inner calm. Saw her gaze lower to those silvery-peach fingers in the human skin and then rise. "How is it that a human takes as a name the noun designating a small animal?"

"It's a nickname," Kitty said.

"I see. So humans, then, prefer nicknames that denote domesticated mammals but not rodents?"

"I—I guess," Kitty said, very confused indeed.

"And yet I do not find any reference to humans with a name, or nickname, of Cow or Calf or Puppy, yet we have *kid*—the offspring of goats—so common it has become a noun indicating either boys or girls."

"It's old slang," Kitty muttered, thinking, And your point is?

"Old as in thousands of years, or merely hundreds?"

"Um, I think maybe two hundred at most. You see the slang 'flash kiddies' in some old novels from around eighteen hundred," Kitty said.

"Interesting. The word *flash* is yet another whose evolution? Devolution? It is another word that has undergone considerable change."

Kitty nodded, still guarded, but at least she'd relaxed.

Da'an pointed to the now blank terminal. "Slang and fads are a subject of fascination to me. Right now a new fad has sprung up. If you will trouble to initiate a search on Superteacher you will see the one I mean."

In silence Kitty found her way to a cave where Superteacher whirled around in the middle of a circle of whirling AMs, some crudely made, others complicated, all of them chanting "Freedom!" over and over to a vigorous beat as Superteacher recited the Preamble to the Constitution in rapper rhythm, sometimes waving chalk, pushing up her glasses, and making other intensely human gestures that conferred an amazingly real overlay on this cartoon figure.

"I want you to capture Superteacher and locate the source code," Da'an said.

Kitty worked for a minute or two, and then her screen shifted, filling with data.

Da'an stared down at it. The human symbolism was incomprehensible; it was so very primitive and to learn it so labor-intensive for what little it could accomplish.

"Can you discover who made the original figure?"

"You want an ID?"

"And a location."

"Um." Kitty took her lip between her teeth and began to work.

Da'an stood watching, interested in the process, the interface among hands, mind, and symbols on screen.

It was the kind of puzzle that Kitty enjoyed most. That was partly why she wrote science fiction mysteries in her spare time, because she loved interlocking puzzles. It was all too rare that she was given challenging tasks.

Hours passed, and the night, unobserved by both, began to fade in the east, before Kitty looked up, reached for her cup, made a distracted frown of disappointment when she realized the cup had long been empty.

"I can't break the origin's location," she said. "Superteacher was put up by a master hand, someone who was able to mirror the locational input immediately. You can regard it as traceless. But most of the accretion of scripts has all been done by less talented hands. From the look of a few of the more recent headers I teased off and decoded, by little kids."

"Children," Da'an said, as if discovering something new. "This fad has been initiated by children?"

"Well, I don't know about that, but the figure seems to have appeared first in the cybercaves, according to the ones that keep logs and archives, which is where you mostly find teenagers hanging out. And little kids who want to copy the teens."

"So you could say, then, that Superteacher is a model, or a symbol, for resistance created by children?"

Kitty looked, and was, uncomfortable. "I don't know about resistance," she said. She was a decent sort; though she liked the Taelons just fine, she did not want to see a bunch of kids slung into the cooler just for this silly thing. And you never knew who might get their knickers in a twist bad enough actually to threaten and then follow through. "Looks more like a neener neener."

"A what?"

She put her thumb to her nose and sang out, "Neener neener, I know something you don't know. Neener neener, you can't catch me!"

Da'an nodded. Smiled. "A harmless expression of independence, then."

"Yes." Kitty smiled in relief.

"Interesting. Well, I am interested in education, as you no doubt know from our various plans in development. If you could, as you say, tease out a few more headers, I would appreciate a demographic map. I have no intentions of invoking the exigencies of the law for what I perceive as a harmless prank: I merely wish to study the propagation of fads among humans, especially those so young. I have little interaction with the young."

The last sentence was softly uttered, almost plaintively, to Kitty's ears. She nodded. "All right. That I can do."

"Thank you, Kitty. I shall make certain to commend your efforts to your supervisor."

Da'an smiled in benediction and moved back up the ramp to sink once again into the data stream for meditation.

THIRTY-ONE

Cece was never quite able to recover the rest of the day or that night.

She developed a horrific migraine from the combination of her fall from the train, walking in wet clothing, lack of food, eyestrain. It at least kept her from thinking about the raw blisters her water-ruined shoes rubbed against her feet as they walked for miles and miles. Not that she spoke about it. She kept her mouth resolutely closed, her consciousness narrowed to two directives: Follow Augur, and Don't Throw Up.

She knew at one point they were in a nice new truck. She recalled worrying about her soggy clothing making mud marks on the upholstery, so clean and unused and smelling like new vehicles do. Was it a rental truck? How did they end up in that? She was beyond asking. At another point they were in a conservatory, with miniature roses growing all around, perfuming the air while overhead rain drummed on the glass ceiling.

And last they rode in a trash truck. She recalled that one, all right, because of the smell as they walked up and because the rising sun had so hurt her aching eyes. Only how did they get a ride in it? She couldn't hear, or think, past the pain haze. She could only follow directions.

Until then, Augur thought she was either angry or ignoring him.

Well, fine. He didn't have time to deal with teacher snits. "Sit down there." He pointed to the neat little bench behind the driver's seat. "I'll ride up front."

She folded down like a rag doll being dumped. Augur stared down at that blotchy-pale face, the drawn skin on her forehead. Cecilia didn't look pissed, she looked old. It was then that Augur finally figured out that Cecilia wasn't angry or ignoring him. That drawn look, those glazed eyes: She was in pain and beyond communication.

"Mind goin' on the route, brother?"

Augur looked across at the old black driver.

Augur, tired, preoccupied, had just assumed that the parked trash truck they were walking past was empty when the driver rolled down the window, looked right at him, and offered him the ride. Overwhelming exhaustion had prompted him to say yes. They were seen anyway, so what would be the harm?

"Not a bit."

The man nodded his head, not once but several times, as if to an internal rhythm, and once in a while chuckled to himself, "Hee hee hee," a high sound.

The truck roared into gear, the man rolled the windows up. Frosted windows, Augur realized. Air-conditioning tabbed on, and the rotting Dumpster stench from outside whipped away into nothingness.

The interior of the truck was worn but very clean. Various Rasta symbols hung down as decoration.

They proceeded up an alley behind a row of stores, and the driver manipulated the controls, which lifted the Dumpsters, dumped them, set them down with a crash.

After the second or third street the man tabbed the radio on, and Jimmy Cliff played, the volume turned down low. The driver moved to the beat; it was difficult to resist that beat, the pure Jamaican sound. Augur, exhausted, hungry, fell into a reverie, comparing music from faraway Senegal with Caribbean rhythms, to be interrupted by an urgent voice. Jimmy Cliff had ended, or been interrupted:

". . . and they apologize for the disruption of traffic patterns. As soon as the criminals are apprehended, we are assured that our streets will be returned to normal. Until then, all citizens are advised to carry their ID with them and to plan commutes to allow for extra time."

Augur resisted the impulse to turn it off. He glanced at the driver, who went on with his work, his movements smooth and automatic, his expression preoccupied. How old was this guy, anyway? At least sixty. Probably a year or two from retirement.

"Description of Marcuse and Robin . . ." And the announcer read off about as perfect a description of the two of them as you could get. Damn.

Augur looked at the driver again.

Nothing.

Did he hear?

Nobody spoke, not until they finished the row. Then Augur cleared his throat, his mind already buzzing with lies. "You might be wondering—"

"Ain't no one in the cab," the driver cut in, looking straight ahead, his voice old and raspy. "So nobuddy to talk wi'd."

Augur shut up.

Nods, and a couple of those high "hee hees," and suddenly the driver swung out of the alley and drove up a street, turned, then drove up another. Stopped at a red light.

Augur, looking up and down the intersection, saw that the huge boulevard they were about to cross had a full-on roadblock at the other end, where several streets bottlenecked before a freeway entrance.

Sick at heart, Augur wondered what the reward was, and if it was enough to permit an old trash man to retire early. Could he really blame the guy?

The light changed.

Through the intersection. Down a street. Past that and to the alley behind another row of stores.

One by one they Dumpster-cleared their way up that alley, while behind them scarcely a quarter of a mile away the traffic built up behind the roadblock. No words, just the radio, now playing Bob Marley.

At the end of the street, the driver said, "No one in de cab."

He was facing straight ahead.

Augur looked, saw that they were heading toward a dirt road that led under the freeway. And, just visible, was a patrol car, with a cop standing with another man, both white, young, husky, and armed. The cop had his global in hand.

Augur didn't think, just acted: swung out of the seat and crouched down beside Cece, who had her arms clasped tightly atop her knees, her head resting on her folded arms.

The truck eased down through the gears.

Came to a stop. Window rolled down. A terrible stench wafted in.

"Delivery," said the driver.

"That's old Caleb. He's the regular."

"Right. Caleb, have you seen a young black man, goatee, black clothing, ponytail, shaved crown, or a short woman aged between forty and fifty, weight around one forty, brown hair worn long, blue clothes, could be wearing glasses? They might be separate or together."

"Ain't seen nobuddy," Caleb stated, nodding.

"You wanta search Caleb's trash, officer?" the second man asked.

"Not unless they give me combat pay. Damn, what is that reek?"

"That will be the trash from behind the sushi place just over there, is my guess," the second man said, laughing.

"No one could ride in that, it'd kill 'em first."

And further conversation ended when the window rolled up again.

The truck moved into gear.

Under the freeway, slowly approaching the recycling plant. Augur, still behind the cab, could just see the sign and the top of the plant. A lot of groaning hydraulics and engine racing and clanks and clunks sounded for a short time, and then they began to move once more, the truck noticeably lighter. The plant slid away to the right and then vanished.

The truck kept moving.

It kept moving for another half an hour, until it pulled up once more, and the driver stopped, rolled down the window, and then spoke: "Big coffee, fries, burger, pie. Chocolate shake."

He paid, hauled forward, picked up his food, and then drove once more.

Next time he stopped, he said, "Here's de main crossways. From before dey put de freeways in."

Augur contemplated that and then realized that the information, offered as it was to the dashboard, was a hint that it was time to depart.

"Come on, our stop," he said to Cece.

She looked at him with a face of gritty despair and followed him out.

Augur turned, to find the food in the cardboard holder pushed to the end of the seat. "I don't have any money," Augur began.

"Take it."

Augur took it. "Thanks, brother."

His answer was that high laugh, and then the door shut, and the trash truck roared away in a cloud of exhaust mixed with vintage garbage aroma.

It was the final straw for poor Cece. She fell to her knees on the muddy dirt road and retched. Heave after heave wrenched her, until she thought she'd turn inside out. Though she had nothing in her stomach—maybe because of it—her system wrung itself out. At last she sat back, heedless of a rain puddle, eyes blinded with tears, her limbs trembling.

Augur set the food carefully on a rock and knelt down next to her.

"Cecilia?"

She had dropped her head forward, but as she lifted it her cheeks suffused with color. Her eyes opened, bleary, bruised looking, but she gave a hint of a smile. "Curiously," she said in a faint voice, "I feel a bit better. Except my mouth. I would trade anything for a toothbrush."

"I've got napkins," Augur said, relieved. "Are you sure you're better?"

"Migraines are like that. I don't get them often, but when I do, they make sounds into bees buzzing, and light is sheer torture. Oh my, I do feel wrung out. I could sleep for a century."

"Well, I hope we have to walk just a little longer. But first, we've got some food. Maybe that'll help. I know I need it."

But her stomach wasn't ready for a burger or fries. She nibbled a corner of the apple pie, grimacing at the overload of sugar, and then drank the shake. That made her feel much better. Augur poured a little of the coffee into her shake container, and she drank that while he polished off the rest of the food.

Cece's eyes became noticeably more alert. "Who was that?" she asked finally. "Did you know that man?"

"No. But if I know anything about human character, he is gloating to himself right now over having scored off the authorities, and he'll continue to gloat for a long time."

"And may he gloat in good health. Tell me, where are we, and were we in another truck?"

Augur grinned. "We passed the night driving back roads in a rental truck. Rental car agencies won't take cash anymore, but the smaller rental truck places will, because most of their business comes from people who are moving and who are in between banks and addresses and so forth."

"Oh."

"We abandoned it, hood up, beside a nice place to rest out the remainder of the storm. With a note on the seat. I imagine someone will find it and return it to the rental people within the next day or so."

"I remember roses," she said doubtfully.

"I picked that place just for you," Augur said with an elegant bow. "To wait out the worst of the storm. Then we started walking, because I knew there was going to be a roadblock. I kept us to back streets. Then our friend Caleb saw us and became our guardian angel."

"Ah."

"I scored a map off the rental truck, from which I will shortly be able to determine whether my instincts are right and that way leads to Taelonville." He pointed toward a clump of trees.

Cece sat where she was. It felt good just to sit. Soon, she knew, bodily needs would clamor for attention again. She was filthy, and tired, and her glasses were still broken, but oh, it was so good to have the headache gone. So very, very good.

Happy to be passive, she breathed in the clean smell of the rain-washed field, all strewn with wildflowers. Sage, she smelled somewhere. And what were those purple flowers on stalks?

Birdsong in the distance, and closer, the sound of crackling paper.

"Aha! Not far. Not far at all. A morning's walk, if I calculate right, and we're on the outskirts."

"But won't we be in more danger there?" Cece asked, reluctantly returning to their problems. "As I recall, Taelonville once had another name, but they voted unanimously to change it in honor of the aliens."

Augur knew a lot more about Taelonville because of Liam's experiences there, but why go into all that? "From most people," he said. "But remember the safest place for the thief to hide?"

"Under the sheriff's bed," Cece stated obediently.

"I have an old contact here who has a sheet as long as

your arm. He won't want to have his cover threatened, and he owes me a few favors."

Cece didn't like the sound of the "long sheet." "I have a friend who I think is not very far from Taelonville," she offered tentatively.

"How long have you known this friend?"

"Well, we haven't actually *met,* but we've corresponded on-line for several years about research and teaching methods for reading disorders—"

Augur fought impatience once again. "You'd trust our lives to someone you've never met?"

"And you'd trust ours to a criminal?"

"*I'm* a criminal," he returned with a sardonic look. "By most rules."

Cece sighed, aware of having somehow trespassed. How, indeed, could one quantify trust? She would be willing to swear that she could trust Phoebe with her life, just from the tone of her letters, her passionate devotion to justice—not the power of the majority, but the ephemeral justice toward which humans yearned and didn't always attain.

Trust was not always a matter of intimacy, or why did some long-married couples discover terrible secrets?

All this passed through her head, but she did not voice it. "You've been right so far," she said. "And I don't know that putting Phoebe in jeopardy would be fair to her."

"What we'll do, then, is find a comfortable place near town for you to take a rest," Augur said. "I'll go in, do my business, and come get you. How's that sound?"

"Fine," Cece said. "I confess what I need most desperately—besides a bath—is rest."

"Then let's get going. Sooner we do it, the sooner you snooze."

"All right. Let me just pick up my trash and kick some of this rainwater over my digestive juices here in the road."

Augur buried the paper products, Cece smothered her vomit with mud, and they continued on cross-country, amity restored once again.

THIRTY-TWO

"Oh, Marina," Scooby exclaimed, moving to stand before the magnificent view. "You can't imagine what this place is like."

At the other end of the phone, Marina laughed. "The hotel? The view?"

"Well, both!" Scooby exclaimed. "The view from the penthouse is incredible. It's so *green* here. I mean there are trees *everywhere,* and you don't see sprinklers constantly going."

Laughter again from the other end of the phone.

Scooby gazed out at the soft, hazy afternoon air over the great greens in the center of New Haven. "It's weird. Feels like I'm in the dead of winter, because it's so cool out, and rainy. You know, because in L.A. we *never* get rain in the summer. And L.A. is greenest in February. So my brain insists it's mid-February and not the end of June."

"Sounds heavenly."

"It is! And not a stupid, boring palm tree in sight. I never realized before how really *stupid* palm trees are. They just drop gunk all over, they don't cast any shade, and why are they all over L.A. anyway?"

Marina answered. "Probably because they don't need to be watered. Or maybe they were an early film industry publicity marker."

"Well, here they have trees like willow and maple, and they are everywhere. And huge rivers! I've never seen a *real* river before!"

Marina, a well-traveled Navy brat, laughed.

Scooby looked at the phone, which was a handsome old-fashioned model, the earpiece and speaker little bells connected by brass, with a discreet little protuberance connecting the current to the base. But there was no vid—it was a real old-fashioned phone line. They had them at school, of course, and a lot of homes still had them—they even had the ones with cords—but Scooby had, like most young people, been living exclusively with her global ever since they came out on the market.

"This thing is weird," she lamented. "I wish I could see you." She added suddenly, as her emotions veered, "I wish you were here."

Marina's voice was guarded, "I have my assignments here at home."

"I know. I just wish those hadn't changed so suddenly."

Marina paused. Asked delicately, "Are things all right with milord?"

"Well, you know—" Scooby stopped. She hated saying that. She'd hated it ever since Miss Robin had checked the unthinking habit, way back in high school, by answering in a laughing voice, "No I don't know—tell me!" The problem was, Scooby didn't really know how she felt!

"He's nice. Always. And so interesting. But kind of, I don't know, I keep feeling I've done something wrong. There are all these rules. Like I couldn't bring my global. Can't go outside without him, or one of his local friends, who never talk to me. At least he didn't say anything about the phone, though—"

"And of course we're just talking about a boyfriend," Marina put in.

"Oh! Oh. Yes." Scooby thought wildly. She hadn't remembered about bugs, or tracers, or any of that TV show spytech. But then she remembered that the penthouse had been registered in the name of some friend of Neville's, and so that person's ID would show up on the calls, wouldn't it? So, surely it was okay to just call? Not discuss the plan or anything?

Scooby suddenly felt her throat close up.

"Scoob?"

A sob, a dry one, that Scooby tried to fight down. "S-sorry, Marina. I guess I'm just tired." She sniffed, wiped her eyes, and tried to smile. "And it's stupid to be so babyish, when this place is so lovely. So quiet, and *civilized.* And the view is spectacular. This room here in the corner of the suite looks out over the Green. There really *is* a village green here, or what was once the village green. Three Churches on the Green. You can kind of see them, though all the trees obscure the view. And Yale is behind them, kind of cater-corner from me. I can make out just a bit. It's a little like an old castle!"

"It sounds great. And the hotel?"

"In-credible! Everything is so new, and so fancy and tasteful, and the people so very polite and discreet. It's weird about rich people," Scooby added in a rush. "They can just do whatever they want. Or send someone to do it for them. No hassle, no stress. You want a car? You got it. You can even say what kind and what color! You want messengers? A computer? It's there. Food delivered? And no one ever asks how much. Not like us, when you have to save for a thing forever, or agonize between buying this thing and going without that thing."

"It sounds like fun," Marina said with conviction. "So you ought to enjoy it. You deserve it."

You deserve it. The sudden reminder of what she was here for—to kill someone, even an alien—caused Scooby's insides to squirm and her throat to close again.

"Scoob? Something's wrong."

"Just me. Being chicken." Scooby fought for control and tried to laugh. "But he says my . . . tour . . . is all set up. Some super-cloak-and-dagger way inside that nobody knows about. Like some movie! I get to see it tomorrow, or maybe the next day. And at least his lordship said that if I still feel . . . that way . . . that he knows this doctor friend here, who will be able to help me. He promised me, he says this guy is amazing."

Marina, at her end, frowned out at the ducks swimming lazily in Neville's pond. It was she who Carlton had placed in charge of his house, instead of Scooby, as had been planned. And Marina had been intended for the New Haven team. "Did he say *how*?"

"No. But if he can promise, it's good enough for me."

Marina continued to frown, even when Scooby passed on and started describing the beautiful Connecticut scenery and the great restaurant they'd eaten in right after deplaning at the airport. Scooby rattled on about first class on the flight (because anti-Taelons never used portals) and dinner at the yacht club and all the historical sights she'd glimpsed so far and how Neville had promised her a full week of nothing but sightseeing. Once the "tour" was complete.

That last word seemed to choke Scooby into silence. After a pause Marina said, "It sounds great, Scoob. Look, call me again—any time—if you need to. Okay? Promise?"

"Sure," Scooby said, sounding uncertain.

"Just promise. I care about you a lot, and I know that certain things are stressful." Marina tried to be firm but not nagging.

"Okay. I care about you too. Thanks, Marina."

They rang off, and Marina prowled around the quiet living room and then out into the peaceful garden, there in beautiful Beverly Hills. "Certain things." What a euphemism. Scooby was expected to pick up a weapon when she'd never touched anything more lethal than a table knife, and she was suddenly expected to kill someone.

Why *her*? Oh, at the time it sounded convincing—that no one would suspect sweet young Scooby—but you could say that about almost anyone in the group, except maybe Che, who looked, and was, dangerous.

Che, who was here to guard Marina while she guarded the house, until the very last day, when he'd portal to his assignment and leave her here in charge of communications. What a weird change in plans it all was!

Marina prowled back inside, and sure enough, there was Che, sitting in the breakfast room. Watching out the window.

Marina went up to her room to think.

. . .

She wasn't the only one thinking hard, either. Midway across the nation, halfway along a small, scrubbed-looking side street in Taelonville, Augur lay on a roof and stared down at the freshly painted row of shops bracketing the pretty little diner called Carrie's.

He was thinking fast, and swearing under his breath.

It was so very rare for Augur to trust someone. Lili Marquette, yes, but she was gone. He would have said Liam Kincaid, except look how fast reflexes had had Augur ready to believe the worst within a minute after the laser strike. The fact that he'd been manipulated into doing so only made him angrier.

As he watched the hired muscle cruise back and forth on the street below—not very effectively disguised in their suits and ties to anyone who'd ever been around hired muscle—Augur forced his mind elsewhere.

All right. The fact was: Despite their supposed friendship, despite the fact that Cruise owed him big time, Cruise had set Augur up. Maybe the price was just too tempting, or maybe he had a congenital dislike of owing anyone. It was too fast, too easy, his "Sure, sure, money, clothes, keys to a vehicle. Easy. By, say, five? Meet me at Carrie's. Everyone goes there—no one will notice us."

Too easy, and Augur always scanned meeting sites first. Always.

And surprise! Two HUGWWAS (huge ugly guys with wrap-around sunglasses) trying to look like normal citizens as they contemplated little gift novelties, kiddie books, and women's hosiery in the shop windows at either side of Carrie's. Probably more of them inside, and out behind the building as well, to prevent a line of retreat.

So Cruise was out. Now Augur had to vanish, fast, before Cruise realized he wasn't going to show up and sicced these guys, or the feds, on his trail for whatever price that would bring.

He backed away slowly across the neatly shingled roof

and eased down the ivy clinging to the back wall of a clothing store. There, he looked down at his filthy clothes. Oh, they looked fine, but he was very aware of having worn them for a couple of rough and dirty days.

Taelonville.

He made a noise of disgust.

Cruise was going to bark anyway, so why not stir up the somnolent Taelon lovers with a crime spree? He just wouldn't tell Cece, who, he felt certain, would squawk about stolen goods, even from the enemy.

So two hours later, he found her right where he'd left her, just outside the outskirts of town, along an old buggy trail. She sat primly on a rock, her knees and ankles together, a rather sickly smile on her face, their map folded on her lap.

"Migraine again?"

She blushed. Went crimson. Shook her head.

Augur tipped his head and regarded her. "Something's wrong."

"Something that never happens to glamorous ladies on adventures," she countered. "Never mind. I take it your friend came through with all those things you have there?"

"Well, yes and no. Oh, he sang a friendly tune, but I'm afraid there must be some kind of price on our unwashed heads."

"You mean he turned us in?"

"Well, I suspect he's going to consider doing that right about now—since we haven't conveniently walked right into his trap." He proffered his bags. "I spotted a stream just over there, and while I don't know about drinking the water, at least we can use it to wash up a little. And here is a change of clothes for each of us. I hope I guessed right on your size. I picked clothes that might be practical for hiking. I also picked up a few groceries and some bottled water."

"Bless you," Cece said gratefully, taking the water first.

She got up rather cautiously, and they set out along a

windy bike trail with green grass growing at each side. The afternoon was balmy, the air clear. Danger seemed so far away, and yet, and yet.

Cece forced herself not to consider that, at least not until immediate needs were met. They reached Augur's stream and clambered down the rocky banks. He'd gotten dish towels along with his booty, two each.

By mutual agreement they parted, each using a place on opposite sides of a bend around a screening willow. Cece worked fast, scrubbing herself with the stream water as hard as she could, until her skin tingled. Augur hadn't brought soap—and she wasn't sure she would have used it anyway, for wasn't it environmentally unsafe?—so she hoped that cleanliness would come with vigorous scrubbing.

At least she felt better, even after shockingly cold rinses in the water. And—sniff, sniff—she smelled better as well. She kept one towel for her own purposes and folded the other along with her wretched old clothes. Then she stood up, deciding that Augur had a good eye. She now wore soft brushed-cotton trousers of a pale green color, with a long, loose tunic top over it, pale green and white. No hairbrush—he'd forgotten that—but she wouldn't cavil. She unpinned her hair, fingered the worst knots out, then braided it tightly and pinned it up again.

"Done?" came a soft call.

"Yes."

"Then let's bury these clothes, eat, and plan."

Together they pushed up a big boulder, and while he held it she scraped out a hasty hole, using her hands. They rolled up their old clothes and placed them in the hole. Augur gave a grunt and let the boulder fall; they both pushed up dirt against the edges, packing it tight, then washed their hands again in the stream.

She sat down on the boulder and he sat on the grass just up the bank, shaded by an aspen, as they divided the groceries he'd scored.

It was a peculiar meal, lettuce, cheese, bread, cherries.

Why no cooked food? Cece remembered that Augur hadn't exactly said that his friend had provided money to buy the clothes and food. These bags would be easy to lift from unsuspecting shoppers on their way out to the parking lot, for example. Then she dismissed the thought. What could she do?

What *could* she do?

She fought the impulse to hunch into a ball and wail. One thing at a time, that was the way to get through this experience. Eat the lettuce, the cherries, put a hunk of bread around the cheese. Eat.

"Oh. I found these on the way back," Augur said, pulling two small, hard green apples from his pocket and handing her one.

Well, one item not stolen, unless picking apples was stealing.

The apple was very hard and very sour, but Cece welcomed both sensations, for her teeth felt much cleaner after she worked her way down to the core. And when she was done, she washed her hands a third time, scattered her crumbs for birds, and then said, "So what now?"

Augur's eyes in this light were almost golden. He looked up, the edge of his cheekbones sharp; he'd lost weight and looked lean and elegant. With a kind of whoop of hilarity inside, Cece considered mentally her own mirror: short and round, frazzly hair that desperately needed shampooing, and cracked glasses. A glorious heroine!

Shaking with suppressed laughter, she waited.

Augur looked at her and smiled. He did not misinterpret her expression of self-mockery. He shrugged and opened his hands. "I have to admit that, at least for now, I am fresh out of ideas."

She said tentatively, "Do you think we might try my friend Phoebe?"

"Why not?"

The sudden agreement almost made her dizzy, it was so unexpected. For years she had been absolute despot in her classroom, then she'd been pitchforked into this adventure, knowing all along that she was a burden, a useless one. She'd felt rather like a kid again, the slow one on the field, the one who always got social cues just a little late.

Now it appeared to be her turn to find a way out.

"Well, while you were gone I amused myself with studying the map. I looked up her hamlet, and it seems to lie that way. Not far, really. We might get there just after dark, judging by our walk this morning, and measuring by pinkie joints. Though I'm probably way off. Inevitably."

Augur nodded. "Lead on."

"Oh, dear." She shook her head and laughed.

Augur cast a look over at her. "You don't trust your own abilities, do you?" Augur observed.

"Not in these circumstances," she said, thrusting her hands into the pockets of her new trousers. "In my own circumstances, a classroom, yes I do. I guess that may seem contradictory."

"Go on," he said. "We've got nothing to do but talk and walk—unless we see helos overhead, at which time we'll go back to running and hiding."

Cece sighed, her smile crooked. "Being short and built like a pouter pigeon, and having a sister who's tall and thin and naturally good at sports, made me into a physical coward, I guess."

"Coward?" Augur asked, looking surprised.

"Aren't I? I have always hated competitive sports and felt afraid of physical threat. At a young age I got used to using wits instead. Brains, I mean. Not wit." She put her head to one side, smiling slightly.

"Wit being cruel?" Augur asked. "Humor with a knife edge?"

You are acute, aren't you? she thought and then shrugged. "Yes. Wit usually cuts someone. I like laughter that all can share. Maybe that, and my lack of physical prowess, is why I became a teacher. Is this boring?"

He saw the defensive quirk to her brows and realized

that she wasn't boring him. He really did find her interesting. "No. Tell me more. About choosing to be a teacher."

Cece laughed very softly. "All right, then. Good grades was something I did excel at getting. But I discovered that no one liked you for being the smartest—until I realized ways to make other kids see things that the teacher wasn't getting across. Some teachers couldn't, and some just wouldn't. Made the classroom a power struggle, not a place where questions were safe to ask, no matter what the question. Becoming a teacher arose out of that. It seemed the most natural thing in the world. You don't need glamour or sports trophies to be a teacher. You do need to know how people learn, you need to know how to listen, and most of all you need patience. And humor."

"That," he said, "describes a very rare teacher. And ought not to."

"Oh, I think there are more good ones than we know. And that's just it, we *don't* know. The good ones appear to be the default; we really hear about teachers only when they do something terrible, something out of character for a teacher." She tipped her head back. "I once memorized the end of George Eliot's great novel *Middlemarch,* because it so beautifully sums up the life of those unknown, unfamous good teachers."

And she quoted, in a light, pleasing voice—Augur realized that her voice was the most attractive thing about her—" 'The effect of her being on those around her was incalculably diffusive: for the growing good of the world is partly dependent on unhistoric acts; and that things are not so ill with you and me as they might have been, is half owing to the number who lived faithfully a hidden life, and rest in unvisited tombs.' "

Augur thought of the brothers in the monastery, high in Senegal, and shook his head. If only life were so simple!

"Do you have any experiences to share?" Her voice, again, was tentative.

"Oh, plenty of them," Augur said, smiling. "But they would all be fictional."

"I'm sorry if I seemed to be prying."

"Let's talk about books instead," he said. "How often have I met anyone who's read any Eliot at all? Shall we compare favorites?"

The atmosphere between them, which altered so easily, for they were both as sensitive as creatures with antennae, had become companionable, and in this way they whiled the time as they walked eastward, both unaware that the search that Tate was scrupulously running had shifted safely to the north, to give them time to get away.

THIRTY-THREE

Liam smelled the ozone with his hindbrain first.

He had stretched out on the hotel bed, arms crossed behind his head as he stared at the ceiling and permitted his mind to drift; the first awareness of a radical alteration in atmosphere gave him perhaps a nanosecond of warning. At once he was up and moving toward the bureau, on which he'd left his weapon, then he saw the fiery blue torus of someone punching through interdimensional space. A blue square appeared, a woman's silhouette stepped through, and the temporary ID portal—illegal as hell—collapsed into an angular twist of interconnecting rods.

"That was dangerous," he said as Renee picked up the fast-cooling rods.

"These are dangerous times," was the predictably cool reply.

Renee folded the rods together with quick, assured movements, fitted them into a slim case, then slung it across her back by a strap, evoking in the semidarkness Robin Hood and his quiver of arrows.

Then she cocked her head to one side. The pale light coming in through the window sidelit her expression of appreciative humor as she regarded him. Liam realized he was dressed only in a pair of trousers.

Laughing, he finished crossing to the bureau and picked up his shirt.

"So what brings you here?" he asked, keeping his voice devoid of innuendo. "Besides—" He waved toward the collapsed portal.

A smile highlighted her voice. "Is there coffee anywhere?"

By which he understood that she didn't trust the room. Well, he didn't either, come to think of it. Though so far he'd not had any conversations in it that couldn't be held in Sandoval's office. He'd been in it too seldom, for much too scanty amounts of sleep.

He pulled on socks and shoes, picked up the key card, and they left, Liam buttoning his shirt as they walked.

They kept silent as they descended the New Haven Hotel's elevator and then walked out into the warm night. Brief drifts of cloud overhead obscured and revealed the stars, celestial hide-and-seek.

They walked up George Street. "The Alley Cat Café's around the block," he offered.

"Farther."

So they were watching for tails, were they? What kind of news did she have to share? Something, he hoped, about Augur.

She walked with her gaze down, hands in the pockets of her expensive linen summer jacket. The portal carrier was a tripod sling; Liam realized she had a camera—at least a camera case—also slung over her shoulder.

He kept silent until they reached Chapel, which was crowded with all kinds of stores and emporia. They walked on, Liam monitoring their turns. He let her pick the place. He, in his turn, used reflections in store and car windows to check behind. Nothing.

Renee settled on a tiny bar. They moved all the way to the back, sitting in the last booth before the rest rooms and back exit. The walls of the booth were satisfyingly high, the lighting a candle in a red bowl, the ambience cozy. A cocktail waitress appeared, took their order, vanished.

"Look at this first," she said and handed him a palm. "I thought you might welcome a clean system. In case you hadn't brought one of your own."

Liam nodded appreciatively. No need to explain that he hadn't had the chance to get one—he'd been bustled directly from the Sandoval's briefing to the ID portal, and thence here.

He took the slim wallet-sized square, quickly unfolding the keyboard and flipping up the screen. He flicked it on, sat with his back in the corner so that the screen couldn't be seen, and in silence observed the automatic log-on that Renee had programmed in. He touched the single bookmark, and the screen windowed up one of the music-punctuated meet-and-greet spots frequented by teens. As he watched, Superteacher danced in.

Their drinks appeared. Renee handed the woman a couple of bills, said, "Thanks," and the waitress went away.

"What am I seeing?" Liam asked.

"You are seeing the woman Augur rescued, and is apparently still with, turned into an icon. Apparently by kids," Renee murmured. "And it's not just this cave. She's all over the Net, where kids hang out. That's what's drawn Da'an's interest. I did my level best to deflect him, but no go. He's fascinated."

"Intentions?"

"According to Zeelah, who is friends with Kitty, he wants to find the designer but not to bust him or her. He says."

Zeelah: Doors International's plant in the embassy staff. How many of those quiet, efficient workers downstairs were secretly reporting to someone or other? Most, probably.

Liam smiled at the thought, logged off, folded up the computer, slid it into his shirt pocket. "Thanks," he said, and she opened a hand in acknowledgment. "It's possible that Da'an might even be speaking the truth. He does research all kinds of things, and when he finds out what he wants, doesn't act. Or doesn't immediately act. Since we can't stop him, we'll have to let it slide for now. What else?"

"The Taelon site yesterday put Augur and Cecilia Robin at Fort Madison, Iowa, in the morning. Massive manhunt. Sandoval himself in charge."

Liam whistled softly. "I spent the day surrounded by his handpicked flunkies and not a word about any of that."

"Well, today the search parameters shifted north of Taelonville."

"Taelonville? Illinois?"

"The very same." She nodded. "Apparently to be continued tomorrow."

"And?"

"I went on SecNet from Augur's lair right before I came to you and checked the logs. Sandoval handed off command to Tate today. And some stooge in Taelonville reported personal contact with Augur at noon. Tried to set up a trap, but Augur slipped out. The woman wasn't mentioned."

Liam sat back, fingering his drink. "Stooge?"

"I checked the files on him and came up with a fairly nasty record."

"Ah. A double cross, then?"

"Probably. But as of ten minutes ago, Tate did not have them."

"Point to Augur," Liam said, impressed. "Is that all?"

Renee's eyes reflected the candle flame, two bright golden pinpoints in huge black pupils. "No."

Liam had been enjoying the report. The enjoyment vanished like fireflies drenched by rain. "And?"

"And Julianne contacted me. As she promised, she investigated the medical side of the new 'educational opportunity.' She said that the sources are labyrinthine in the extreme, but apparently huge orders for a new sort of implant were okayed a month or two ago."

"Any of your labs?"

"No. Not a one. Labs in out-of-the-way places with up-to-date tech and personnel. All guarded." Renee sipped her drink, then said, "Supposedly these new implants are the latest thing: removable microchips. The idea being to cut down on expensive training time, particularly with complicated, dangerous tech. Instant expertise."

"Who is programming these chips? Humans or Taelons?"

"Julianne didn't know. But she said what can be programmed by a legit outfit can easily be replaced by programming not so legit."

"The key feature being, say, complete obedience instead of expertise."

"We all know that Zo'or has tried to manipulate the human will in half a dozen ways. That we know about. What we might not know are other labs located in just these sorts of out-of-the-way locales. Anyway, trying to find out more data was my last search while I was in Augur's lair. I got down quite a number of levels before I found areas with Zo'or's protective seals all over, doubled with Sandoval's. And those in turn are protected by enough bitbombs and suspicious code probably hiding savage viruses that I dared not probe any further. I'm afraid that Augur's the only one who can excavate that stuff."

Liam pressed his thumbs into his eyesockets. Sparks zapped across his inner vision; he wished he could rub away the pressure, but that was internal. Too many fronts.

"All right," he said. "That will have to wait."

"So what's going on here?"

"Nothing."

"Come again?"

Liam gave a soundless laugh, and Renee rejoiced to see

the tautness leave his face, even for a moment.

"Utter and total cooperation." Liam made a grand gesture. "It's as if Sandoval is here looking over their shoulders. His people are eager to communicate with me, are constantly appearing in order to brief me fully on every aspect of logistics, personnel, communication, timing, monitoring of local potential problems, interfacing with journalists, and anything else you can name. Right down to the catering for the banquet afterward, who will deliver it, and how it will be served."

"Sounds . . . weird."

"It is weird," Liam said. "Just before you showed up so dazzlingly I'd closed the door on the last of them and was enjoying being alone."

"Ah. Pardon me."

"I'd rather enjoy—" Liam stopped and shook his head.

I'd rather enjoy you, Renee thought and smiled. She was about to say something but refrained. Fair was fair. He was under too much pressure to be teased, and her own sense of honor prevented her from flirting seriously. But, oh, it would be so easy. So very easy, she thought, looking at the curve of his lips, the long lashes framing his light eyes.

"Well, if we're done trading gossip," she said, pausing to dash off the rest of her drink, "you had better get back to your beauty sleep. I've got an executive breakfast at eight."

"Would you misconstrue if I assured you you don't need beauty sleep?" Liam murmured as they left the booth.

"Gallantry, Major Kincaid? Surely not," she rejoined, laughing.

"Just playing the part." Liam held out his arm. "In case there are any spies."

"Confusing the enemy?"

He saluted. "Confusion to the enemy."

They linked arms. Both felt, and banished, the spark of physical awareness; it was a pleasure to be considered another time, another place.

Anticipation was sweet, but for now, companionship was sweeter.

They strolled back through the soft summer night toward Liam's hotel. In Liam's room, Renee assembled her portal and vanished.

Just about that time, in southern Illinois, Augur and Cece walked up a quiet street in misting rain. Thunder grumbled in the distance, far north toward the lakes, but here the moisture was soft and clean.

"Here it is," Cece said, looking at the house numbers. How many times had she written this number on envelopes and seen it on Phoebe's return address when Phoebe mailed things to her?

She paused, though her feet hurt and her back ached, and she was desperately hungry, for they had not dared to get food since their picnic outside of Taelonville.

The small house was neat, with a garden across the front. Pretty lace curtains hung in the front windows. Lights glowed upstairs but not down.

"She's not in bed yet is my guess," Augur murmured. "But she will be soon. Either we try it now or sack out on her flower beds."

"Let's not be seen in the front," Cece murmured back.

Augur had been about to suggest the same thing but forbore. This was Cece's contact and her plan. He only nodded.

So they trod up the little flagged path to the kitchen door, and Cece knocked. At first quietly, and then a couple quick, loud raps.

In the distance a dog barked once or twice, but otherwise there was no noise. Through the little window in the door they saw lights come on in the distance, and then closer.

The door opened, and Augur and Cece both stared up at the big woman standing there. Augur met eyes much darker than his own and recognized in that intelligent gaze not just someone descended from Africa but also an emigre like himself.

Cece looked up at that smooth dark skin, the clear Bantu

bone structure, and thought wistfully that at age ninety Phoebe would be as beautiful as she was now.

"Cecilia?" Phoebe asked, her accent slow and musical. She opened the door wider. "Welcome, and be at peace."

THIRTY-FOUR

Augur watched Phoebe lead Cecilia away. Phoebe. Cecilia. One African, one Caucasian of mixed background. Both Anglo names, Augur thought, testimony to Western imperial legacy. Just as his own real name testified.

Augur shrugged away the thought. There were immediate problems to attend to, and even Augur couldn't reprogram history.

He heard Cece's high voice, tired, embarrassed, saying something about feminine needs, followed by Phoebe's low laugh and her promise that everything was right here for the asking.

The woman might be a fellow African, but that didn't mean squat. Especially after that long speculative look she'd given him, right after they'd stepped inside her kitchen.

"Of course I recognize you," Phoebe had said, smiling. "Your picture is all over the news these days—and all over the Net."

"The Net?" Cecilia looked dismayed. "Oh, dear."

"But that's for later," Phoebe had said, leading Cece away and giving Augur that look again as she added, "Take a seat. I'll be right back."

Augur could have vanished, of course, right then. Cruise had tried to sell him out, but there were other fringies he knew. Though if there really was a price on his and Cece's heads, just how high was it? Fringies were pragmatic, most of them. He could just envision certain old business associates giving him an apologetic shrug and a "What could I do? I need to pay for my Net time" as they turned him in. Were any of them friends, of the sort Cece believed this Phoebe to be? No. Augur didn't like the implications of friendship—the obligations, the expectations. And wouldn't former "friends" sell you too, only not for money—that was practical—but pretending to some sort of ideal?

Ah, forget it. Fact was, he knew the woman didn't trust him, but as yet he sensed no danger. And he was tired, his head ached, his body clamored for rest. So he stayed put, staring down at the grain in Phoebe Wingate's kitchen table, until he became aware of footsteps.

Phoebe sat down across from Augur and settled her forearms squarely on her table. Despite the old chenille bathrobe, and the edge of a flowered flannel nightie showing at neck and wrist, she was a figure both imposing and dignified.

And intelligent. "She's enjoying a nice hot bath right now. So I think our first question," she said in her low, slow voice, her gaze direct, "is this: What are you intending to do with Cecilia Robin?"

Here it is, he thought. I was right. "I'm not intending to do anything 'with' her. She's on a self-appointed mission of mercy, and I'm just going along to see that she gets there."

Phoebe Wingate drummed her fingers on the table. "Make no mistake. I admire Cece. From our correspondence I've learned that she's a devoted teacher, and from the awards she'd earned—which she herself never mentions—I know she's a fine one. But in street smarts she ain't got brain one, as some of my worldwise sixth graders would say. She's got no street smarts, and she's got no politics."

"True."

"I've had some time to think, since that trash first showed

up on the Taelon Internet site. Those crimes she's accused of—Net tampering, false identities, false cash cards, and the rest—she's just not capable of. That must mean they're yours."

Augur spread his hands. "Think what you like."

"I don't want to think what I like, I want to know the truth, which is why you and I are here talking, instead of me getting my rest while you are hauled off to the blue boys' version of the slammer." Her accent intensified, her cadence singsong. "Talk, my young friend. Tell me why someone had to shoot a laser at Cece, who won't even squash a spider, and what puts the two of you together?"

"How much do you really want to hear?"

Phoebe's mouth was wide, her smile generous, her teeth strong and white. "Let's just say that I obey the laws, but I don't appreciate someone—whether from here or from another planet—superseding our laws and enforcing their own views with big guns."

Resistance. All but admitted. Augur met that direct gaze. Nodded once and said, "She won't go back to L.A. Even if there was somewhere for her to go. There's serious trouble ahead, and she thinks she's responsible."

Phoebe sighed and got to her feet. "Of course she does."

Somehow, just now, the interrogation had altered to discussion. "You like hot cocoa?"

Augur repressed a laugh. "I don't think I've ever had it."

"Well, you'll have some now. Hot milk calms the body, the chocolate the spirit. You both need sleep, I can see it in your faces, but a little preliminary planning means I can get some things done while you rest."

Augur, instantly alarmed, began to frame an objection, but Phoebe forestalled him. She waved the milk carton in his direction. "We're talking supplies, maybe a route. There are a lot of us, many of whom she knows. What she doesn't know is how many of us are connected not just in the teaching nets but also by Resistance contacts."

"Ah." She'd said the word out loud first.

Phoebe's eyes narrowed. "My guess is that you're adept

enough at playing on whatever side nets you the most profit. But for whatever reason, you're doing right by Cece. She had a lot to say in your favor, as I was showing her around upstairs, or we would not be having this conversation."

More intimidation? Augur felt impatience tighten his guts.

Phoebe spooned fine powdered chocolate into a pan and began to stir. "All right," she said over her shoulder. "This is not a classroom and I am not your teacher. But we're talking about human lives here, not games. If I am not mistaken you see life largely as a game. Cece doesn't. She still thinks that this mess with the Taelons will get resolved and in September she'll be right back in her classroom, pinning up new bulletin boards. She has no idea her career has been destroyed, and she'll never teach in any classroom in California again. Maybe nowhere. She's become too notorious."

Augur frowned. "Notorious?"

"Oh, so you don't know about Superteacher?"

"What's that?"

Phoebe nodded, still slowly stirring. "I can see you've been out of touch. Well, well."

Augur hesitated, then thought wryly, may as well get it over with. "May I use your computer?"

"I'll show you both when Cecilia comes downstairs. She'd better know about it before she proceeds."

Augur moved restlessly on his chair. "Can you get a message up the Resistance chain of command?"

Phoebe frowned, considering. "Probably, but I don't know how soon. Most of the new cell leaders are young singles—people with no dependents who could be used against them. Ours here has been incommunicado while on a business trip. And the recent reorganization limits my knowledge of who or how many are above him on the chain."

Augur repressed a sigh. He dared not speak Liam's name, head of the Resistance as he was; his double role was far too precarious. How the hell to get a message to him?

Cece appeared then, looking ten years younger than she had that afternoon. "Oh, thank you," she said to Phoebe, her cracked glasses winking and gleaming in the cheery kitchen light. "That felt wonderful. Though ohh, I didn't think feet could hurt so much."

Phoebe nodded. "You think your feet are tough from standing at the chalkboard all day."

"I wonder how many miles we walked? At least I had good shoes. Once good shoes. Leather does not like water, I learned to my cost." She sighed. "Thanks to your daughter for the clothing loan." She pointed down at the pale pink chenille bathrobe she wore.

Phoebe chuckled. "Just as well my girl is going to be a big one, like her mother."

"How old is she now?" Cece said. "Eleven—no, twelve, isn't she now?"

Augur, watching Cece covertly, decided that some of her appeal was that she didn't ask the question to be polite, she really was interested in this unknown kid. And the formidable Phoebe responded just like a proud mom.

"Twelve just a month ago. Off to summer camp, which makes your visit a whole lot easier. My son stayed in Berkeley, hoping to get a job and take a couple courses. So that frees up two beds for you both."

"Is your husband traveling?"

"Yes. He'll be back tomorrow, but if you're still here, there's no problem. Thomas is about as communicative as a mountain."

Augur, looking appreciatively at Phoebe, could imagine the type of man she'd find attractive as a mate.

"I can brag on my kids all day tomorrow," Phoebe added. "Two things before you get some sleep. One, hot cocoa, my sleep-inducing standby."

"Yum," Cece said. "Mine too!" And she accepted a mug with gratitude.

Augur also took his, nodding a polite thank-you, and took a tentative sip. He probably hadn't drunk milk in twenty years. But this tasted good. Not too sweet, not too hot, not the least cloying. It really did feel good going down inside his exhausted frame.

"Here's the other thing. I hope it'll amuse you, but you ought to know about it before you proceed," Phoebe said, leading the way through a dining room into a study.

This room had wall-to-wall books. Not elegant first editions, as comprised most of Augur's library, but all kinds of books, most of them well worn. On one wall was literature; he recognized most of the titles.

Phoebe, meanwhile, fired up her system and in a few quick movements logged on to a cybercave. And there she was, Superteacher, dancing away.

Cece gave a tiny gasp. Augur whistled softly under his breath, tribute to a fellow artiste. I've got to pursue that, Augur thought, and his tired mind began spinning along several tracks: who might have done it, why, how, and how could it be used?

"Oh, dear," Cece said, face as pink as her borrowed robe. "Who? How?"

"Nobody knows," Phoebe said. "But there she is, doing new things every day. Sprang up not long after you vanished. Kids all over the place have been adding on songs and bits of poetry, all kinds of things, either about freedom or independence. It's a thumb of the nose at the Taelons, of course, but obviously by kids, and harmless."

"What have the Taelons done about it?"

"Not a blessed thing," Phoebe said. "I expect they consider it all beneath their notice. Come on, you two. Cecilia, you take my daughter's room, and you, young man—"

"Augur."

"Augur." Phoebe pronounced it with irony but not unfriendly irony. "You can bunk in my son's room."

THIRTY-FIVE

Da'an waited patiently until Kitty paused her work and went off for her break. Moving with swift assurance, Da'an used Liam's override to invade her system. Kitty was, as requested, still industriously working on the massive accumulation of scripts that Superteacher had accrued and was accruing every day.

Da'an tabbed through screens of names and log-on locations, at last giving a soft exclamation in Taelon. Two or three quick codes, and that screen shifted to the data stream for further exploration.

When Kitty returned to her desk, her system was just as she'd left it.

And the next day, while Cece and Augur faced the prospect of a day of rest, everyone else was quite busy.

Especially the luckless individuals who'd drawn duty under Tate's enthusiastic direction. Rain swept out of the northwest, making the roadblock and house-to-house searchers thoroughly miserable. Tate just grinned and ordered them to keep on looking to the north, to the west, to the south—everywhere but to the east.

Liam spent another long day being taken from site to site around New Haven so that he could personally inspect the security preparations and sign off on the status reports. But as he did he used his global to monitor SecNet and check on Tate's progress. Not that he contacted Tate. Instead, he tapped in on the constant stream of reports by underlings and twice windowed up maps of the area.

Renee Palmer spent a long day dealing with business matters, but in between all her chores she exerted herself to find out just exactly what Doors International was providing in this new educational program about to be unveiled. And what they were getting for their money and resources.

What she saw made her frown in puzzlement and growing suspicion.

She set aside several high-priority tasks and began to do some digging.

Sandoval sat in a café with iced coffee before him and watched the front window of a very elegant restaurant where Neville Carlton sat with two other men, talking. The front window of a restaurant! A typical combination of incompetence and arrogance.

From time to time Sandoval switched his global from real time monitoring of Carlton's spy mike to the SecNet, making certain that none of Liam's busy team had gotten whiff of Carlton's plans. No, at Sandoval's own direction they were far too busy hounding New Haven's underworld element, small as it was. No one thought to scan certain wealthy and respectable Yale grads who had also been part of Yale's most elite secret society.

Sandoval sat back and smiled.

THIRTY-SIX

When Augur woke up, he heard a man's voice.

Alarm ripped him out of bed and halfway into his clothes before he realized that impossibly deep voice was not growling but laughing.

So since he was awake anyway, he veered to the bathroom and took another shower. He'd showered before sleeping, so this one was just because he could. It felt great.

Phoebe had said to help himself to the unknown son's wardrobe. Augur found in the closet the sort of clothing you'd expect to find from a hip guy of twenty-two. From the sizing, it seemed he was a little taller than Augur, but slim of build—a miracle, considering the rest of the family.

It would have been a rich private joke if the man belonging to that deep rumble of a voice had been five-three and weighed in at one twenty, but one glance at the massive frame in the big chair at the dining table banished that.

"Good morning, Augur," Phoebe said. "Thomas, my husband."

Augur put his hand into the huge paw, waited for his own to be crushed, but Thomas Abrantes had never been one to use his size and strength against others. After a firm shake, a keen, assessing look from eyes even darker than his wife's, Thomas retired into his newspaper.

Augur sat down, helped himself to a piece of toast and coffee, and waited for a planning session to begin. There wasn't one. The two women talked about their classes the year before, changes in curricula, good books, good teaching, bad teaching, new ways of dealing with reading disabilities, the current topics of interest on their common listservs, and then back to teaching again.

When they finally rose, Phoebe said, "Now you amuse yourselves here. Sleep again if you like. I'll do some shopping. Oh. Cece, do you know your eyeglass prescription?"

"Yes, but won't you have to get an ophthalmologist's okay? I don't dare contact my own doctor."

"You leave that to me." Phoebe smiled faintly.

"And my prescription is very expensive," Cece added, turning crimson. "I don't have any money at all—"

"You can pay me back when all this foolery is over. Just go rest, or curl up with a book. I'll be back later." Phoebe's dark gaze rested reflectively on Augur, and then she was gone.

Thomas got to his feet, gave them both a courteous nod, and vanished, his step quiet despite his size.

Cece, relieved to have her worries recede even for a few hours, happily perused the shelves in Phoebe's office and was soon buried in one of John McPhee's geographical tours de force as she mentally retraced her travels.

Augur picked up the newspaper, glanced at it, put it down. Prowled around and then finally gave up. He wanted. No, he *needed* to get on-line, even though he knew better than to risk any kind of contact with his usual sources.

So he walked upstairs. The son had taken his equipment with him, but there was a computer in the daughter's pretty blue room. Augur sat down in the pastel blue chair and fired up the system. Using the child's ID, he logged on and surfed the Internet, at first visiting Phoebe's daughter's sites and then branching out—as a kid might—to some of the caves.

He found Superteacher there. Watched the animated figure go through her gyrations, as he brooded moodily. How he wanted to send a message—but he was certain that Liam's system was compromised as well, or at least the unknown cracker had watchdog code all over looking for signs of Augur, no matter how deeply buried. He couldn't risk writing something with this limited system and having it blow up at the other end and bring Sandoval and his minions down on this family.

So he shut the system down.

He walked outside in Phoebe's garden, fresh from the rain, but did not see a single one of the blooming plants as he paced back and forth, back and forth, his mind freed along well-traveled electronic paths.

His thoughts kept coming back to Superteacher. What did Renee and Liam make of that? They had no idea, probably. But surely they'd seen it—

Seen it.

Back and forth, now at a quicker pace. He was almost on to something. Exhaustion fugue had slowed his thoughts; he was impatient with his own mind. Superteacher—the need to communicate with Liam—Superteacher—Yale and Zo'or—Neville Carlton—it all rammed around in his mind like supercharged particles.

The air became balmy. Augur felt the warmth of the summer sun on the back of his neck and retreated to sit on the porch. He looked out over the garden for the first time and became aware of the sounds of the suburbs, the shearing noise of a lawn mower, the excited barking of a dog. Children's voices. A neighbor, with windows open to let in the fresh air, letting out, just ever so faintly, the melodic strains of Delibes's *Lakme*.

Music.

Music . . . was that the covalency, then?

Augur shut his eyes. Music. Superteacher, music vids. Kids and their AMs, slapping together animated figures with popular music. Some of them had Superteacher dancing to popular—

Ahhhhh!

He dashed inside and up the stairs back to the daughter's room. Fired up her computer again, logged on, captured Superteacher. Now . . . how to get Liam's attention?

Augur sat back, his eyes half closed, ranging with his

mind back and forth through history and literature. What would get Liam's attention?

And then he laughed.

John Dryden's poem "A Song for St. Cecilia's Day, 1687."

Mentally Augur reviewed the verses, memorized so long ago. He settled on a portion of the Grand Chorus.

> As from the pow'r of sacred lays
> The spheres began to move,
> And sung the great Creator's praise
> To all the bless'd above;
> So when the last and dreadful hour
> This crumbling pageant shall devour,
> The Trumpet shall be heard on high,
> The dead shall live, the living die,
> And Music shall untune the sky.

Think Liam would find it?

Damn straight.

Humming a counterpoint to the melody line from the Delibes still drifting in through the open window, he began to type.

The sun moved, unnoticed, steadily to the west. In Washington, D.C., it had set when Kitty reported for her night shift.

She went straight to Da'an, her expression wary, as she said, "I finished the project up at home."

She held out a disk, and at Da'an's gesture inserted it into a waiting machine. A neat table windowed up, listing date, location, ID, and a basic description of the scripts to date added to Superteacher.

Da'an tabbed down, nodded, said, "Quite interesting. It does appear to be a popular pastime, does it not?"

Kitty put her hands behind her back. "Cross-country," she ventured. "And in other places as well."

"Fascinating. Thank you."

"Is that all you wanted?"

"Yes," Da'an said, tone and face benign, gestures tranquil. "I am always eager to learn about humans, including their diversions."

"Then I can take this disk back?" Kitty asked, her relief unmistakable.

"You may indeed. I do not require the information."

She smiled, deleted the file, popped out the disk, and returned to her desk, so relieved that she hadn't gotten a bunch of kids into hot water (for she'd regretted agreeing to the project the more intensely the longer she worked on it) that she didn't mind having spent all that time for what amounted to a few seconds of Da'an's interest.

"Besides," as she said to Zeelah over the global some hours later, not noticing that Da'an was missing from the embassy entirely, "it really was an interesting puzzle, and I do like puzzles. Still, I erased the disk, and when I get home, I'll erase the stuff off my system, just in case Taelons change their minds as much as we humans do."

But Da'an's mind was quite focused.

While Kitty was on her way back to her desk, Da'an sent an already prepared E-mail, using Liam's embassy ID. And while the night staff settled in for a routine evening, their XT ambassador used the embassy ID portal to transfer to Los Angeles.

In Southern California the sun was still bright, the afternoon endless. Louise Pinochet sat at her computer. Since she had no one to interrupt her, she had worked steadily until she finished up her year's report for the district.

With a great sense of satisfaction, she tabbed Send, thinking, And so another year vanishes. She sat back and looked into the next couple of weeks, trying to decide how she might spend them, before the preparations for another school year began to wind her back into routine.

At times like this she missed her spouse the worst. With him she would have traveled; without him, what was the point? She'd tried once and ended up repressing the urge all day, every time she saw something wonderful, or funny, or curious, to say, "Did you see . . . ?" or "What do you think . . . ?" And at night alone in a strange room she'd spent far too long crying.

Her thoughts poofed away when her E-mail signal chimed.

E-mail? No one was in the district office now, she was quite sure of that. Who else would it be?

Later she'd wonder if the sense of tension tightening her neck was a real premonition or just the odd hour for E-mail. When she pulled up her E-mail, there was a letter purportedly from Major Liam Kincaid, Companion Protector to Da'an, North American Companion.

"Damn," she muttered under her breath.

The letter was brief. It requested an interview ASAP.

She hit the Reply button, wondering if whoever was at the other end was waiting, and typed, School is over, and I am quite busy with my private schedule—knowing it was petulant.

She shrugged, appended her sig, sent it, and seconds later there was the incoming mail ding.

Major Kincaid wanted to meet her within an hour. His business, it seemed, would take only five minutes of her time.

Two, three, five excuses all streamed through her mind, to be banished. This guy had the power to do pretty much what he wanted. If she dug in her heels he could send his Volunteer bullyboys to pluck her right out of her house and bundle her off to God knew what, and no one would lift a finger to stop them.

Well, then how about a last resistance?

She typed, Meet me at my school at nine. And she added the address, sending the letter without signing it.

One minute, two, three, five went by. Twenty minutes later she realized she was still sitting there staring at a blinking cursor, her hands clenched together, and got to her feet. No help for it now.

She'd wear her most intimidating power suit.

The rays of the westering sun danced in a trail of molten gold from the horizon to the softly purling waves. The colors of the ocean were amazing, silvers and golds and reds mixing with the azure.

Da'an looked out with mild pleasure, making a note to visit such sites again. Time, however, was fleeting.

Making a sign to the driver of the limo to move on, Da'an sat back.

The sun sank swiftly, becoming a red crescent on the horizon before the limo turned inland from Pacific Coast Highway and sped toward the school where Louise Pinochet waited.

Only one car was at the school. The front building was lit. Everything else was dark. Da'an looked about at the small-sized equipment in the playground, noted the smudges of handprints on corridors and poles, all about three feet off the ground, before following the Volunteer guards into the lit building.

There a human woman waited, unsmiling. When she saw Da'an, her expression altered to startlement.

"You will await me here," Da'an said to the guards, who nodded and took up their stances, one at the front door and one finding the back exit elsewhere.

In silence Louise Pinochet led the way to her office. She waited for Da'an to precede her, then shut the door. Somewhat helplessly she indicated the guest chair, which Da'an took.

She retreated behind her desk and said, knowing she sounded totally ineffectual, "Well?"

Da'an said, "First I must apologize for the deception. I did not want to risk publicizing my presence any more than I think you wished this interview to be widely known."

Louise just nodded.

Da'an continued. "I am doing some research into the learning processes of human children."

That pacifistic statement gave Louise a vector for her own opening shot. "And your researches have nothing to do with Cecilia Robin?"

"On the contrary, they concern her directly."

"Please explain."

Da'an's hands opened, graceful, pale peach, as fluid as water. Louise found it difficult to look away from them and forced herself to meet those wide cerulean blue eyes. "You have seen the animated figure Superteacher?"

"Yes."

"I want," Da'an said, "to meet the original designer."

"I can't help you," Louise stated, feeling considerable relief.

"I believe you can." Da'an's contradiction was gentle. "You see, I have made a study of the accretions. The original design is too well hidden to be traced, at least as yet. There are reasons why I wish to pursue this . . . question . . . in my own manner."

Louise bit her lip against asking for Da'an's reasons. She knew she wouldn't hear the truth, only what this alien wanted her to hear.

Da'an paused to consider her, then continued. "I studied the demographic breakdown on the first day of the Superteacher AM's appearance. Two of the scripts originated with individuals whose registered addresses are local. Neither of these names appear to be adults, for the names do not show up in voting registries or tax records."

Louise compressed her lips.

"It seems to me," Da'an went on gently, "that those with the most vested interest in . . . dissuading searches for Cecilia Robin would be those who know her. The animated figure has become popular in its own right, so much so that what I suspect might be its original purpose has been all but hidden."

"Purpose?" Louise asked, when the silence became protracted.

"To provide random log-ons, using Cecilia Robin's own ID. This random log-on, in turn, I believe threw off the electronic search being conducted through our Taelon site. A search, I might add, being conducted without our sanction."

"It's certainly convenient to your cause," she pointed out—the closest she could come to saying, "Tell it to the Marines."

"Yet it isn't, not at all," Da'an said, hands gesturing. "It makes us appear to be ineffectual."

"Then why don't you take that window down?"

"That is more difficult than it seems," Da'an countered. "Not impossible, I am told, though as yet I know comparatively little about how your Internet is constructed. And as yet I believe that more is to be learned by patient observation."

Louise frowned. The words sounded peaceful, all right, but . . .

With difficulty, she forced her mind back to the matter at hand. "And so you interrupted my evening because?"

"Because I wish to interview these two individuals. I suspect they are in fact students at your school. Maybe even students acquainted with Cecilia Robin."

"Names?"

"English being idiosyncratic in its pronunciations, I have printed them here," Da'an said and held out a slip of paper.

Louise looked down, saw ID numerals, which she skipped, and next to each a name: Aisling Goldstein and ShaNissa Bolt.

Both girls in fourth grade. Louise knew, by each October, every child's name in the school. She hedged now, staring down, trying to think. Finally she looked up.

"You could just as easily get this information from the district."

"Yes. I am aware," was the imperturbable reply. "But would not such an enquiry cause considerable . . . interest?"

"What does that matter to you?"

"I wish, as far as I can, to conduct my research as quietly as possible," Da'an replied. "The reasons for this privacy may not now be discussed, but I can assure you that they do not threaten these children in any way. Whereas I suspect that the inevitable publicity, were I to demand my information more publicly, would."

Warning—or threat? Louise said, "So what do you want from me?"

"Their addresses. Or better yet, access to them for an interview. Here, if you like. Visiting their homes would, I feel certain, entail just that same unwished for publicity."

You got that right.

Louise thought furiously.

As yet I believe that more is to be learned by patient observation. Yes, and what then? That was, if you looked at it right, a threat, too.

The power was all in this alien's pale pink hands. Oh, he sat there looking so benign, but there were those armed guards outside the room, with their little microphone things, and no doubt if Da'an spoke two words to them they could bring one of those insectlike faster-than-light craft smashing the atmosphere directly overhead, or send squads of armed thugs thundering through the school and neighborhood.

Or maybe he could just blast her with some kind of energy bolt without even moving from his seat.

Yeah, this situation was rotten with threat. So she'd keep what control she could.

"All right. But I contact the parents. And I'm present for the interviews."

"Granted."

"And those will be here, in my office, without any of your needle-waving medical people or guards threatening them."

"None of that would be necessary, but if you wish assurance, please, be assured."

"And no publicity."

"We are agreed, then?"

Louise forced herself to say yes.

THIRTY-SEVEN

Liam dropped onto the hotel bed without even bothering to turn the covers down. The room air-conditioning whispered, and for a moment he just lay there, feeling the cool, filtered air move over him.

What a long, dreary, frustrating day. Not that anyone had been insubordinate or recalcitrant. Far from it. But as each day passed, Liam's conviction increased: He did not need to be here. He was not in command, he was only a figurehead steward. Someone else had laid out the complicated security measures, and his part appeared to be merely to stand around and watch it all come together.

Testament to Sandoval's authority and his expertise, but why did Liam need to be there? Tate could have as easily baby-sat this show, or even someone with less authority.

But Tate was out there in the field, conducting searches, which raised a new set of questions.

Liam frowned. Questions but no answers. That summed up his life at the moment.

He sat up, rubbed the blear out of his eyes, and snapped open the laptop that Renee had given him. It logged straight on to a virtual cave, just where he'd left it. He knew that Superteacher was somehow a part of all these mysteries. Instinct—he trusted instinct—prompted him to believe that if he could solve the mystery of Superteacher, he'd have the key to the rest. The timing was just too coincidental not to be related.

So he watched the interactions. Superteacher was still at the center of the virtual space, though all around other figures whirled, danced, and interacted, all to the beat of the music programmed by the cave's deejay.

Superteacher. It was so very much the sort of thing Augur would have done. The extravagance of the gesture—the time involved in its making, just to score off the authorities—that was so like Augur, Liam thought, watching. But of course Augur couldn't have done it, for if he had, he would have communicated. No, some bright adolescent had fashioned that figure, someone who was willing to risk the heavy hand of authority just to make that gesture.

And that, too, was so like Augur! Was that the key to adolescence, then, the willingness to blow off future consequences in order to make the perfect score now? The humorous expression of independence?

Liam found the concept of adolescence fascinating, the way that people always were fascinated by what they never had. No, Augur's insouciant independence evoked adolescence but not with the thoughtless selfishness of some teens—at least in Liam's limited experience. Augur could, and did, think out the consequences of his actions, though the ethical bargains he made were often obscure. But they were not unaware.

Liam frowned down at the screen and realized that the Superteacher had begun another cycle of gyrations. He realized that a new accretion had caught at his hindbrain, and there it was again: Superteacher brought her hands together, and in them appeared a silver ball. She looked down at it, her glasses rimmed for a moment with reddish fire, then she threw it up and it vanished, and another script whirled her into another combination.

Silver ball. Silver ball, or maybe a crystal?

As in *augury.*

Aware that he could be reaching for a connection that simply didn't exist, Liam switched to another cave, one of the ones that did not have preprogrammed music. Instead, the AMs could cavort to music Napstered off the Net. Here the competition was different: Kids ruthlessly stripped off boring song sets and added their own vids.

Superteacher sang and danced her way through five or six songs, two of them new, and then she stopped, and as a brilliant cascade of harpsichord music surrounded her, stars formed and exploded like fireworks. In the midst of this technically impressive animated display the Superteacher began to recite poetry. Her glasses glinted with a reddish tinge, reflecting the fireworks around.

This one would last, Liam thought. It was a tour de force of animation style. He frowned as the tinny voice recited; some of the words were lost under the music. He turned up the volume a tad.

"... the dead shall live, the living die,
And Music shall untune the sky!"

She threw her hands wide, and then the next vid took over. Liam looked down, saw that he'd logged the session, and clicked off the connection.

He backspaced to the beginning of the poetry session and watched closely. Crystal, reddish glasses. All those could signify Augur. They could. But why this form? It made no sense, really, for Augur to be on the run and then suddenly reappear just long enough to play with AMs—

Unless it wasn't play.

Liam tabbed it back and watched again, listening, this time, with all his attention.

The harpsichord music, and certain words, did not change in pitch or tone. Liam felt the force of memory and surrendered willingly. For a short time he did not see the dark hotel room, or the lit screen with the animated figure declaiming Dryden's poem: He saw Augur sitting in the lair, ruminating on encryption methods and how to hide in plain sight, relying on the Taelon unfamiliarity with human culture.

"Steganography," he had said. "A lot of work, but impossible to find. You use one of the big MP3 sites to put a message up, hidden in the music, and they'll never find you, even if they have pattern-seeking tech—"

Never find you.

That's it, Liam thought, his nerves tingling. This is Augur. I have to decode the message! But for that he'd need access to his own system.

Renee.

He pulled out his global, tabbed her code.

Waited. And waited. And waited, ignoring the prompt for leaving a message. Where the hell was she?

She was, at that moment, standing with Julianne Belman in the unlit corridor of a medical facility several stories underground.

They stood side by side in silence, staring in at the neatly lined up boxes of implants. Thousands of them, all the very newest model: not CVIs, which were being phased out as no longer effective, but the newest wrinkle, the CNI, Cyber-Neural Implant, hitherto implantable only in embryos.

Now, it seemed, they'd found a way to get them into people outside the womb, and further, they could insert various programs directly into the brainstem of the implanted individual. Julianne explained in a few terse statements, keeping meditech jargon to a minimum. "And this is just for Texas," she finished, as if Renee had said something.

Maybe she had. Renee stared, sickened. Now the anomalies she'd been seeing in the program reports began to add up.

"Where are we, anyway?" she asked, facing the older woman.

"This used to be some sort of arsenal, cleared out after the last war," Julianne said. "The military were induced to turn it over to Zo'or for storage purposes. The labs are down farther under us," she added, pointing at her feet.

"It's got to be for the program volunteers," Renee murmured. "I wonder how they're going to sell the idea?"

"Well, the insertion might be painless. Big improvement on the nightmarish needle in the neck," Julianne said grimly. "I don't know. Since I'm not supposed to be here, or know about this stuff, I can't exactly ask questions about procedure."

"Shall we blow it all up?"

Both women turned, remembering their contact with the local Resistance. Tracy May Kerrighan stared back, deceptively innocent with her bouncy blond curls and cheerleader face and figure. Tracy May was deadly in five forms of martial arts and could fieldstrip, clean, and arm just about any weapon in sixty seconds, blindfolded. A woman after my own heart, thought Renee, looking at that snub nose and those perfect rosebud lips.

"No," Julianne said. "We're not going to tip our hand, not until we get all the facts. This stuff isn't hurting anyone sitting here. And this is only a part of the whole."

Tracy May nodded once. "Right. You give us the word, this place is history. Ah already mapped out mah logistics." She pointed with her weapon back over her shoulder. "In that case, we better be movin' alawng."

Renee loved her accent, too.

"Patrol will be by in a minnit, or purt near."

Julianne nodded to Renee, who flicked her ID portal into its square and then activated the power source. All three felt rather than heard the weird hum of intense power pulled from beyond the four dimensions they knew, then the blue torus appeared, and one by one they stepped through into Renee's office.

Renee reprogrammed the portal, sent Tracy May home;

Tracy May hit the Return control, and the portal reappeared.

Julianne sat down in one of Renee's tasteful, expensive chairs while Renee disassembled her portal and stashed it. Julianne sniffed the air, wondering just what that Taelon tech did to Earth oxygen, but then the efficient climate-control system whisked away the tincture of electrical discharge, replacing it with cool, scrubbed air.

Julianne said, with some satisfaction, "One of these days my good friend Doctor Geoffrey will learn never to tell me that something is none of my business."

Renee laughed. Geoffrey, moving up in Zo'or's private medical staff, had once worked for Doors. She'd been glad when the arrogant jerk quit, saving her the bother of firing him and having to furnish a severance package. "What he'll learn first is just how valuable human beings are to Zo'or," she said, "when he winds up on the street unemployed, or else on a lab gurney with something wired into his own brain."

"Sooner the better." Julianne leaned forward. "I'm tired and hear my pillow calling me. Let's put together what we've got."

Renee said, "What it looks like is that this program to be launched in a few days is expected to net thousands. Maybe more. There've been legal codicils added to our end of things. Each one appears inoffensive, no more than 'numbers adjustments,' but when you sit down and put them all together, you realize that the project is big. Very big."

"So might we say that Zo'or is somehow going to make this program mandatory and not voluntary?"

"It would look like that, but how? The laws—"

"We can leave out Congress. They sit up and beg when he gives President Thompson a biscuit to hold out. Even Hubble Urick can't get him to budge if he thinks Zo'or might frown in his direction. No, something else is going on, you can bet on it."

"I don't see how Zo'or could get away with it. His credibility has to be about zero." Renee sighed. "I wish Liam were here. He's the best we've got at figuring out how the Taelons think."

"Anyone seen Zo'or at all?"

"No. But he stays on the Mothership, so that's not surprising."

"Huh." Julianne got to her feet. "Sandoval?"

"No sign. Maybe he's on the Mothership as well. Liam did say that he got this assignment because Zo'or had him on something else."

"That's bad news. Wonder if we can find out what?"

"If we poke into the data stream, perhaps, but without Augur here, I hate to risk using his link. I can't cover us if they find us in real time. Don't know enough."

"Um." Julianne pursed her lips. "Well, that's that. Let me know if you do find out anything. I have to get back across town and into my alibi, as well as my bed."

"Want a quick transfer?" Renee indicated the portable ID.

"I hate those blasted things." Julianne let herself out the door.

Tired, her mind battling on several fronts, Renee closed down her system and activated Augur's internal security device. Then she activated the external security and left, waving to the desk monitor on her way out.

When she got home she thought longingly of her Jacuzzi, looked at the time, and winced. She hadn't had a full night of sleep in two weeks, and felt it, from her scalp to her heels.

She opted for a fast shower, then refreshed but still weary, padded into her room . . . and saw her message relay glowing green.

She hesitated. She'd programmed it to relay only first-priority messages; everything else could sit in her global.

Sighing, she pressed the button and heard Liam's voice: "We've got to talk."

THIRTY-EIGHT

Tarek groaned.

"Wake *up*."

Shot a fist out to bat away whatever it was yanking him out of this great dream—

"Tarek, it's the *Taelons*."

Taelons? Nobody wanted Taelons in his dream—

"Tar-*ek*!"

The high squeaking voice broke through the vision of endless summer and mile-long, perfectly breaking waves. Tarek rolled over and opened his eyes. Annoyance stung him the moment he recognized his brother. "You better have a good reason to be in here in the middle of the night—"

"It's *almost noon*!" Jamal retorted. "Wow, you are the laziest slob I ever saw in my whole life."

Tarek reached, tried to make a grab, but Jamal danced away. "Never mind! Never mind! Tarek, this is serious."

"It's gonna be serious noogies on that empty skull of yours—"

"Tarek, stop it. The *Taelons* are *here*."

"What?" Tarek stopped midlunge, the words blitzing the urge to take out the shattering of the perfect dream from his brother's worthless hide. "What's that? Taelons? Here?" Tarek realized his mouth felt like the bottom of a hamster cage. "Ugh."

Jamal followed him into the bathroom. "Well, not here as in at our house, but they're at school. Or one of 'em, anyway. And he wants to see ShaNissa and Aisling!"

ShaNissa? Aisling? Weren't those brats in the kid's class—oh, damn. Oh, hell. "Superteacher," he whispered.

Jamal slammed the bathroom door shut. "Quiet!" he squeaked.

"Are you boys fighting again?" The shout came faintly from below.

Jamal yanked the door open.

"No, Mom," both boys called.

Jamal shut the door with desperate care.

Tarek glared down at his brother. "Talk fast."

"Well, I've been trying to," Jamal muttered. "Okay, here goes. A little while ago Mrs. Pinochet called Aisling's mom and ShaNissa's parents. For an 'interview,' she said. About education. To stay very quiet, because the Taelons are doing research, and it's not ready for TV yet, or some hogwash like that—"

"Bottom line."

"Okay, okay. The girls both wrote scripts onto Superteacher."

Tarek smacked his hands up onto his face. Not even the scratch of whiskers—new ones—dissuaded his agony. Much. "Those stupid little buttheads! I told you—"

"It wasn't my fault!" Jamal had the door open, ready for a quick escape. He lowered his voice. "They promise they won't tell."

"Oh, won't they," Tarek muttered, visions of jail driving away all memory of twenty-foot waves and the perfect ride. "That little blond one looked like the biggest weenie ever born. You cross your eyes at her and she'll squeal her whole life's story."

Jamal sighed. "I offered to go with 'em. For, like, moral support—"

"Oh, yeah, and look totally guilty." Tarek snarled, "Why did I let you little brats talk me into that idiocy?"

Because you wanted to score off us and the grown-ups, Jamal thought. Though he was barely ten, he'd already learned that the right answer sometimes is better kept inside your head.

So he said, "Well, ShaNissa said she'd call soon's she gets home."

"If she gets home," Tarek muttered.

ShaNissa was wondering if she even wanted to go home. Nobody talked in the car on the way to school. She could feel how upset her parents were, though they didn't say anything. The whole ride was done in silence, ShaNissa sitting in the backseat listening to the engine, the tires on the road, and noises from outside, while inside the car she could hear her mom and dad breathing, and she felt her stomach acting like a pile of snakes.

It was a relief to see Aisling just getting out of her grandmother's car, when they pulled into the school lot. Poor Aisling! But her grandmother looked tough enough for ten Taelons, ShaNissa thought hopefully, viewing that determined face.

Mrs. Pinochet was waiting at the door to the office. The adults all said hello, and then Aisling's gramma added, "I think I want to scope some things out with Mr. Blue Boy first. No one busts my granddaughter for playing around on the computer like every other kid in the country, not without going through me."

"Please. Come inside," the principal said, indicating the inner office.

She didn't raise her voice like the gramma did, but somehow she sounded like the Principal, and the grown-ups walked quietly into her office. ShaNissa and Aisling sat down side by side on the waiting bench outside the office and held hands. Each was relieved to find the other's hand sweaty too.

"Gramma says I don't have to say anything," Aisling whispered. Her face was blanched and pinched looking. "But what if the Taelon tries to stick a needle into my neck to make me talk?"

"If we see any needles at all, we'll yell for help. How's that?" ShaNissa asked.

"But what can the grown-ups do? They don't have those gun things." Aisling pointed at the armed Volunteer standing just outside the outer office door.

"Well, we can run. We don't have to stand there and take it, not when we know we didn't do anything wrong."

"Didn't we?"

"Not that a million others haven't, if you mean the AM—"

"Girls?"

They looked up, startled. Mrs. Pinochet looked out of her office at them. "Come inside."

They walked in together, each terrified, each trying to be a support to the other while glad she was there. All the grown-ups sat in a row, but the girls' eyes went straight to the glowing blue figure near the door.

"This is Companion Da'an," the principal said, "who wishes to ask you some questions. Your parents, ShaNissa, and your mother and grandmother, Aisling, will stay right here with you."

ShaNissa drew in a deep breath. Aisling felt her insides quiver.

Da'an said, "Do not be afraid, children."

They both stared back, one stony pair of dark eyes and one pair of light eyes already brimming with tears.

Da'an could see at once that his words had had no effect whatsoever. "I am only here to discover, if I can, who provided you with your mascot, the, ah, Superteacher, who I understand is based on your Miss Robin."

"Superteacher was already on the Net when I saw her," ShaNissa stated.

Aisling nodded, jerky quick nods. ShaNissa was telling the truth, without telling all the truth. Could she do the same? She couldn't think fast enough! A tear streaked down to her jaw.

"I admire the cleverness and invention of this person. If the designer is young, I wish to make certain that she, or he, will have the very best training offered," Da'an went on. "A special scholarship."

Neither girl answered.

"Can you tell me how you found Superteacher?"

Oh. That one was easy enough. ShaNissa felt her insides ease just a little, and she looked to her parents. Her mother nodded just slightly.

"I got home from school," ShaNissa said. "It was the last day. I was worried about Miss Robin, because nobody would tell us where she was, or what happened, or why the bad gu—the police, and them, were after her."

"You apprehend your authorities to be villains?" Da'an asked.

ShaNissa bit her lip. Beside her, Aisling hiccoughed on a sob.

"I guess so," ShaNissa said. "You hear people whispering about other people being taken away and creepy needles put in their necks and then they turn into zombies. Only bad guys do that. 'Specially if they can take away people like Miss Robin, who never did anything wrong, ever."

"It's true," Aisling whispered. She sobbed again and wiped her eyes with her fingers. A hot tear splashed on ShaNissa's hand.

"Please continue." Da'an gestured.

"I did a search on her name and found Superteacher. So I decided to add on a script of my own."

"So did I," Aisling spoke up, now giving a defiant sniff. "I did it for Miss Robin. I didn't know it was against the law."

"There is no law against scripting AMs," Da'an said. "At least, as far as I am aware."

ShaNissa burst out, "So why don't we have Miss Robin back? Somebody said you tried to kill her with a laser, and you got bad guys chasing her."

"We have people trying to find her, it is true, but not because she is in trouble with the law. That laser was not initiated by us," Da'an said. "It could have been done by real criminals, people who obey no laws, either human or Taelon, but use force to get what they want."

"Why would anyone want to hurt Miss Robin?" Aisling asked.

"That is what we wish to discover," Da'an said. "Our initial contact with her was to consider her for a possible educational television program in development."

"She'd go on TV?" Aisling exclaimed.

"Teaching Taelons?" ShaNissa asked.

"No. Teaching humans. A new kind of school program, developed by humans, I might add."

"So you want to study Miss Robin's methods?" That was Mrs. Pinochet, speaking for the first time.

Everyone looked at her, then back at Da'an.

"Yes. Do you consider that prospect threatening?" the alien asked.

"I don't know what to think," Mrs. Pinochet replied. "But I know that the whip handle is in your hands. Not ours."

Da'an considered the row of humans, the polite faces of the adults belied by the tension in their bodies, the two terrified children. Their terror was manifest; their motivations, their awareness of truth, of the metamorphosis of truth, were impossible to gauge. The adults' distrust was obvious and unspoken only because, as the principal had said, they perceived that the power of possible retribution lay with Da'an. They did not see that their emotions, their emotion-driven reactions, made them far more volatile than Taelons, and thus more dangerous.

Something to consider. Meanwhile: Human children, Da'an realized, were too alien to read.

"I thank you," Da'an said, "for the informative interview. It appears my innovative young designer is not here, so I must seek elsewhere. Talent is sometimes hard to find but always a pleasure to train."

No one answered.

Two hours later, ShaNissa crouched in the backyard, whispering over the global to Jamal, who'd locked himself in the bathroom.

Five minutes after, Jamal relayed ShaNissa's story to Tarek, who dazzled himself for the rest of the day with the bait Da'an had so skillfully set.

THIRTY-NINE

Three days to go.

Those seventy-two hours increased the pressure on everyone.

"Steganography," Renee repeated, frowning at Liam.

"Augur explained it to me as a method of hiding code in music. The key notes are those that do not change in pitch or tone."

They were in Augur's lair, the atmosphere cool, still, unchanging, giving no hint of the ferociously humid heat on the street. It had the effect of making the place seem timeless. That sense might have been soothing had not both Liam and Renee been tired, hurried, and stressed.

As Liam downloaded Superteacher's "St. Cecilia's Day" performance into Augur's computer, he said, "I portaled to the embassy. Da'an's AWOL. So I used the tracking device the ANA gave me. He's in California. Probably looking futilely for Cecilia Robin."

"Is this good or bad?"

"Good because I didn't have to use any of my carefully thought up reasons for being here." Liam hesitated, hands just above the keyboard. "What did Augur tell me next? . . . Ah."

Renee watched him type. "What did you tell your staff in New Haven?"

"Nothing." A brief grin. "Pulled rank."

"You'll have to give them a reason when you return, you know."

"Of course. Half a dozen of 'em probably broke their necks reporting to Sandoval soon as I stepped through the portal. But that might flush him out, give us a clue about what he's really up to." He glanced up as the computer screen rippled through its decoding program.

"You want my portable portal?"

"Might be a good idea," Liam said. "I certainly can't get one of my own, not surrounded by Sandoval's goons. Ah."

The screen showed letters highlighted in a bold font:

NEVILLE CARLTON PLOT TO ASSASSINATE ZO'OR AT YALE.
WE ARE ON WAY TO STOP IT.

"They're heading for New Haven," Liam exclaimed.

"Right to your arms." Renee sat down, set aside her expensive handbag, and opened the discreetly labeled jewelry store bag she'd also brought.

"What've you got there?" Liam asked, temporarily distracted.

"Judging from the way my life has been going lately, this is as close to a social occasion as I'm going to get—and probably the only time for a meal. So I stopped on the way at my favorite deli." As she spoke she produced two brown-wrapped packages and then two tightly sealed coffees.

"You are brilliant," Liam said, unwrapping one of the sandwiches. The aroma of fresh bread smote him amidships, and he realized he was starving—and that he had not yet eaten. "Brilliant." That one was said around a wolf-sized bite.

"So I'm sometimes told," Renee returned, looking quite amused.

Liam inhaled about half the sandwich, vaguely aware that he was not doing justice to the taste, and then with one hand began working the keys. "I ought to go back to the embassy and get on the data stream," he muttered. "Faster. Except if Da'an is back—"

"Or if Zo'or is watching, or Sandoval, or one of the Synod—"

"Right. Ah!"

SecNet flashed on-screen. Liam typed in the name NEVILLE CARLTON and was asked for his access code. He carved his way through various levels of firewalls, sometimes using his own codes and other times letting Augur's computer activate its own mysterious cryptographic skeleton keys.

"Here we are!"

Side by side they stood, munching their sandwiches, as they read Sandoval's report on his interview with Neville Carlton. Not that it was very long.

"Strange." Liam frowned. "Nothing about Cecilia Robin, not a word."

Renee read Sandoval's words again, out loud. " 'Carlton's group is comprised of students. Broke Resistance ties after Siege; now they are best characterized as anti-Taelon. On investigation it appears no one in Carlton's group has the expertise to hack into military sites. The equipment in Carlton's home was standard computer hardware, no Taelon tech.' " She looked up.

"How could he get all that in one quick visit?" Liam asked and glanced again at the times reported on the interview. "He was there a total of only eight minutes."

"Sounds like he already knows this Carlton. Or of him," Renee said.

"Let's do a fast contrast."

Liam brought up the other L.A. interviews directly after the laser strike. He remembered checking this information before. Nothing had changed; several people had been brought into FBI headquarters and extensively questioned. Sandoval had reserved half a dozen names to be interviewed personally. All those interviews before Carlton's had lasted at least an hour. Carlton's eight minutes had been last.

"Then there have to be other files on Carlton," Renee pointed out.

Liam was already digging. After a time he sat back and lifted his hands. "Nothing. And apparently no attempts by Sandoval to order investigations."

"That's not Sandoval," Renee said. "Not unless he's hiding something."

Liam whistled softly under his breath as he typed. "Let's take another look at that search . . ." he muttered, but not to Renee.

She gazed down at his dark hair falling unnoticed on his brow, the narrowed eyes, and felt an unexpected moment of intimacy. Curious, as he was no longer aware of her at all. And yet here they were together, sharing the little picnic she'd so hastily contrived.

Moments. Unexpected moments. How strange life was—

"Sandoval knows they're coming," Liam stated.

Danger tightened Renee's neck. "What?"

"Look at Tate's route." Liam indicated the screen, which now showed a map. "Augur's heading east. They nearly pinpointed Augur and sent out the search in a circle from here. Next day, a report of them in Taelonville—and the search shifted to an arc. Not a circle."

"Leaving them to run east," Renee murmured. She felt sick inside. "What can that mean?"

Liam frowned. "There are actually two questions."

"Which are?"

"How far is Sandoval planning to let this supposed plot of Carlton's run, if he does know about it?"

"And?"

"And why didn't he brief me when he put me in charge of the Yale security setup—damn!" He slammed his hand down. "Computer! Get me out."

"Yes, Liam," came the breathy voice of Augur's latest femme fatale AI.

And the screen froze. Renee saw down in one corner a red light winking. "Sandoval?" She pointed.

"Yes. Trolling the system. My guess is he's going to be

trolling for me real soon. And I have a few questions for him."

Renee paused in picking up their trash. "You're really going to ask those questions?"

"Not all of them," Liam said, crossing his arms and looking quite dangerous, especially when he smiled. "But I will find answers."

How, he wasn't sure. His mind made and discarded plans as he headed out, in order to portal back to New Haven.

Renee stayed long enough to close up Augur's lair and then started back to Doors International.

And while both were on the move, Sandoval stood beside Zo'or reading the data stream. What they'd just discovered had put both in a fury.

After a protracted time, during which all the techs watched in subdued silence, Zo'or said to Sandoval, "We have just three days. This invader is now your first priority."

"Very well," Sandoval said, thinking, Just where the hell is Kincaid?

It was time to get down to the embassy and find out himself.

While he took the lift from the bridge to the portal in the security section of the Mothership, and while both Renee and Liam inched through afternoon D.C. traffic, to the northeast a wide summer weather pattern swirled with deadly force.

Scooby stared out of the window of Neville's limo at purple lightning branching with shocking suddenness across the green-gray sky. Though the car was too well insulated for the sound of thunder to smash at their ears, its air system could not remove the heightened ozone from the atmosphere. Flight or fight, instinct clamored. The driver confined himself to white knuckles as wind and fast sheets of rain buffeted the windshield.

In the backseat, Neville brooded about all the extra police and government people he'd seen. Including—especially—those Taelon-altered thugs, once human, but no more, in his view. As yet none of them had harassed him, but he'd been on the streets only once, to walk Scooby's final route himself.

Today was to be Scooby's first trial run. He glanced over, saw her trembling, her face blanched, her eyes wide and frightened as she stared out at the sky.

What a twit. Until the teacher came along he'd intended this assassination to be done by someone with brains and coolness—Marina Aguilara—but really, it was better this way. Scooby would screw up. Of course. But she'd make a perfect target for the bullyboys with Taelon traitortech in their necks, a perfect martyr to the cause.

And then he, himself, would have the intense pleasure of nailing Zo'or while the flunkies swarmed around Scooby.

Perfect plan.

Almost perfect. He took another look at her. He'd wanted her to be terrified to the last, as a little lesson to that bitch of a teacher out there somewhere, but that feeling had faded. Too dangerous. Terrified people couldn't be trusted. No, if Templeton couldn't brainwash her into sticking to her purpose within the next three days, then he'd have her drugged to the eyebrows.

Scooby, sitting beside him and trying not to shake, looked out as they turned the corner from Chapel onto High and splashed under an old archway to pull up in front of a windowless, unmarked stone building.

Lightning flared.

On the other side of the weather front, Liam entered the embassy's front door just seconds after Sandoval stepped through the portal.

Liam dashed upstairs, to find Sandoval standing at his computer, looking down at the system. Sandoval glanced up, cool, immaculate in his elegant suit; he appeared to control everything within the range of his dark, speculative gaze, including the weather.

Sandoval said, "Why don't you answer your global?"

Liam pointed at it on the desk. "Left it here."

"Where were you?"

"Out to lunch."

Liam expected more questions, but Sandoval just picked up his global, hefted it, turned it upside down. From his coat pocket he drew a thin rectangle. Liam caught the brief glow of the Taelon building material called bioslurry, and then a faint hum emitted as the tool zapped the global with a spurt of data.

"What's that?" Liam asked.

"Call it an upgrade. We're going to need it," Sandoval added, dropping the global onto Liam's hand and sliding the tool into his jacket pocket. He leaned against Liam's desk. "Someone has gotten the new codes to all our military sats."

"Again? How?"

Sandoval lifted one shoulder in a shrug. "If I knew that I'd be closer to knowing who. And why." He smiled, just slightly. "I shall be working on that, while you return to your duties. If Da'an requires a Protector we can furnish him from staff. But you are to return to New Haven. You are, you will remember, at T minus seventy-two hours. Make that seventy."

"I haven't forgotten." Liam picked up the global.

Sandoval indicated it. "Carry it with you. The new tech, among other things, will enable me to always find you."

He stepped into the portal and zapped away in a flash of light.

Liam stayed where he was, cursing softly. He was still there when one of the secretaries came in, looking annoyed. Behind her was Renee.

"She insisted—" the secretary began, indicating Renee.

"It's all right," Liam said, and the secretary withdrew, giving them both a single covert glance.

Renee waited until the woman was out of earshot, then said, "Someone got into my office. The portable portal is gone."

Liam gripped the global, then dropped it into his pocket.

"I have to return to New Haven. When can you get there?"

"I'm scheduled to leave tomorrow. After all, I have Doors's security to oversee," she said, smiling. "I figured a couple days would do it."

"Leave today. Someone has tapped the military sats again. Things," he added, "have gotten a whole lot worse."

"So . . ." Typical. Anyone else might have panicked and would have been justified in so doing. Renee looked both cool and ironic. "You want me to do what?"

"Find out what you can about Neville Carlton. And his plot. Because if I'm right, Sandoval won't let me anywhere near that data."

"What about Augur?"

"I don't know." Liam looked beyond the cool blue virtual glass at the fierce sunlight baking D.C. "He's got three days to get to New Haven. At this point I'm going to have to rely on him to find us."

FORTY

Augur was at first bemused, and then fascinated, not just by Phoebe Wingate's network but also by Cecilia Robin's acceptance, without any apparent suspicions or reserves, of the network's help.

Did Cece know that most of them were in the Resistance? Augur didn't think so, and he forbore asking. He already knew her views on the Resistance and saw no reason to jack up tension by pressing the issue.

Not that danger dogged their steps. They had only two close calls, and those were not nearly as harrowing as the escape from the train.

Word obviously ran ahead; they were given the next contact name and meeting place by each person they met. And so they traveled from Illinois east, sheltered and conveyed by artists, one musician, and a great many teachers. Resistance, yes, but these were not military folk, and they did not carry weapons, or have access to black market tech. The meeting places were in coffee shops, post offices, once a communal strawberry patch in Ohio, where they helped their unnamed hosts pick their crop while on the highway a mile north a sudden roadblock kept traffic backed up for half a day.

They helped serve food at a tented wedding reception (Cece got to wear the cook's hat this time); they worked for an entire day cleaning litter pans at an all-volunteer, no-kill animal shelter, while a sudden police search went on through the streets beyond. Augur perched on a rock, alternately watching a narrow view of intersection between two slats of the fence and playing with half a dozen seven-week-old kittens.

Those were their only close calls. When they reached Poughkeepsie on the morning of July 2, both of them sheared off when they saw the armed and implanted Volunteer standing behind the ticket seller, doing a visual head-to-heels on everyone who plunked down money. But their host, an elderly teacher who'd been retired ten years (but was quite active on Cece's teacher listserv) got through the line, no problem, while Cece hid in the rest room and Augur stood at a community bulletin board, gazing at a flyer for a local theater group as if he really was mesmerized by the prospect of *The Dead Don't Talk: A Tragedy in Five Acts*.

Their little old lady safely wended her way back and provided them with tickets for the commuter train to New York.

Hitherto no one had asked their plans, or had held any political talks. Dinner conversations had all centered around local activities, children, teaching, books, movies, listserves, the vagaries of district supervisors. Cece talked, happy, confident, and Augur listened.

Now this last conductor on their underground railroad leaned forward, pale myopic eyes earnest, and murmured, "Is there some way I can help?"

Augur's sense of alarm flared at once.

Cece stared into that gentle, earnest face and guessed at what really lay behind the question. "No," she said in a low voice. "We have to save a life, but we're the only ones who can do it."

Augur watched the old woman's expression smooth in relief, and he saw what Cece had perceived: not suspicion, but the worry of a good person who did not want to believe evil of others.

The old woman murmured, "New York?"

"No. New Haven," Cece whispered.

Augur winced. The price of working with amateurs!

The old woman leaned close to Cece and murmured, "Go in at night. Use the Farmington Canal." She then turned away, her cane tapping.

Cece and Augur exchanged looks. By now they could read one another fairly well. They'd talk when they reached their next destination, one of the small towns north of New York; she'd already forgotten the name, but it was on the ticket. She had only to find a seat and read her book and try not to fiddle with the scarf that she'd taken to wearing to hide her hair.

How would she find Scooby? What would she say?

Later. One thing at a time, wasn't that what she taught the children? You complete one task at a time. First she must get to New Haven's center. Then she would plan what to do next.

In silence they filed into the train with thousands of commuters, one sitting in front, and one finding a seat in back.

Cece pulled a novel from the pocket of the denim trousers Phoebe had bought her and buried herself in the fictional world of the nineteenth century.

Augur opened the *New York Times,* but he didn't read the words. Questions chased around in circles through his mind: Had Liam gotten the message? Where was he? If only his fringie pal Street paid the least attention to kids on the Net, and had seen Superteacher, she would have tagged the steganography in seconds, and he'd find her riding into New Haven, backpack full of strictly illegal tech, the twenty-first-century cavalry to the rescue. But he knew she wouldn't, not without clues, and he had not been able to provide any clues. If she were even looking for him (and that would depend on her mood), she'd probably be back in Chicago.

He sighed and shut his eyes.

In California, Da'an walked slowly through Cecilia Robin's house.

Outside was no scoutcraft, no phalanx of implanted storm troopers, just a discreet car and a low-ranking Protector deliberately selected for his lack of initiative.

No doubt the storm troopers and their commanders had already tramped through here, not long after that laser strike, on Sandoval's orders. But of course they would have discovered nothing of use to them.

Since that day the house had been locked up. Da'an, experienced in the opening of long-forgotten archives, reflected how in this, too, Earth managed to convey great antiquity in a relatively short measure of time. The air in the house was still and redolent of dust, as if it had been unused for centuries. Yet not even a month had passed.

The living room was much like living rooms in most of middle-class America. Da'an had visited some and had seen more on the Internet. This one varied only in the fact that the stuffed chairs and couch did not face a television set, as obtained in the homes of most humans. Here, the television was in a corner, looking neglected. Bookshelves lined three walls, and the couch and chairs formed a square, evoking the salon square of the recent Western European Enlightenment. And would that not be a part of her particular heritage, if he gauged racial characteristics aright? Cecilia Robin might very well fit the Enlightenment ideal, Da'an thought, moving on.

The kitchen was a small square, tidy except for a little pile of breakfast dishes in the sink. Tea had dried to dust in the bottom of the cup. The refrigerator hummed; LED lights on the microwave glowed the time.

The next room was a bathroom. Da'an passed by. Human biology was familiar but of little interest, unlike the following chamber: a study!

Da'an sat in the worn armchair before the desk. Examined the organized clutter. Looked past pens, pencils of several colors, stacks of what appeared to be childish writing. Yes. Ah, so the teacher of children spoke during the day, commanded these evidences of learning in written form, and then spent the evening looking at each one? No, there would be no tech that could do that for her, Da'an thought. But if so, where were the teacher's free hours from such tediousness?

The childish papers looked alike to Da'an's eyes. The scrawled glyphs, amended by distorted efforts at representational drawings. What did Cecilia Robin see when she evaluated these? It appeared that she approved, for in blue and green pencil a fine cursive hand had written, many times, *Good work, Ashley!* and *Excellent, Tomas,* though Da'an did not think any of it approached even competence.

Was it hypocrisy? Or were human standards so low? What was missing here, besides the inescapable fact that human young and Taelon young had nothing whatever in common, except perhaps a tendency to haste and ill-contained emotional reaction?

Da'an activated the computer and waited a long time as the obviously outdated machine slowly brought itself to functional status. The screen offered choices, including checking E-mail. Though it was exceedingly unlikely that this would provide any clues (far too many had had access to her ID, which had been the most basic type), still Da'an tabbed that choice and sat back to watch.

It took time, but Da'an was patient. At last the machine declared that 273 E-mails waited. Da'an glanced at the old-fashioned telephone, and yes, it too blinked, indicating messages waiting.

Da'an took a couple of minutes to scan the beginnings of both E-mail and phone messages, to find no surprises: person after person expressing concern, offering help, demanding to know what had happened.

Da'an rewound the telephone messages, restored them as new, then excavated the computer files, reading rapidly as, unnoticed, a sweetly chiming clock tolled off one hour, two, three.

Kilobytes later, Da'an looked up and glanced through Cecilia Robin's back window at her garden. There were nodding roses and other bright blossoms. But was this not California, where rain seldom fell except in the winter months? Da'an realized that some neighbor had quietly crossed the invisible boundary the authorities had placed around this house and had poured water on all those plants to keep them alive. Interesting, the symbolism here. Interesting.

And so was this written expression of a complex mind.

Da'an's eyes returned to one of Cecilia's many reports and letters. *We have to remember that children learn the most during play. We did, too. I know that's why I remember so much of my childhood as happy, because what I did was fun. If we bring that sense of fun to the classroom—in other words, if it's fun for us—won't it be fun for the kids?*

Human young learned through play? Da'an contemplated the concept of play but found it as elusive as the facial expressions and scarcely controlled gestures of the two little girls, Aisling and ShaNissa.

Something of vital importance underlay these observations, but what?

Da'an glanced again outside and realized that the light had changed. The Taelon brought out a crystal and stored the information from this little computer—it took only seconds—into it for later meditation.

Meditation would be a priority, Da'an decided, as was waiting for the Superteacher artist to take the offered bait. Perhaps human youth was still an anomaly, but Da'an felt confident of certain things: that the target was young, and human youths were impetuous and eager for prestige.

If so, it would not be long before the unknown artist found a way to communicate. Da'an trusted that Zo'or would be too busy to demand the youth be handed over directly; Da'an wished, very much, to interview this promising person and discover what made some humans attain brilliance before the inevitable pressure of the Synod to harness the youth with one of Zo'or's new CNIs took him away.

There remained one further matter to investigate now, while Liam was involved elsewhere and did not have time to continually check that Taelon tracking device the ANA had so obligingly provided him.

For this journey, a much-used public portal.

Da'an closed Cecilia Robin's front door with care, climbed into the car, and said, "Orange County Airport."

FORTY-ONE

While Cece and Augur's commuter train rolled down the eastern shore of the Hudson (Cece forgetting her book to watch the spectacular scenery unfold), not far to the east, a limo pulled up in front of the row of government buildings along Church Street, overlooking the green. Nobody looked twice at limos in the vicinity of City Hall, the federal courthouse all bracketed by prestigious banks—that is, no one but the driver of a battered Toyota that also pulled in two cars behind, engine running, of course, because the driver of a Toyota was sure to get a ticket in the No Parking zone.

The driver tapped his earpiece and murmured into his pin mike, "Blake here. They've reached the fed building."

Sandoval, sitting comfortably five blocks away at the York Street Café, smiled at the vision of Neville Carlton and his student flunky walking right up past Liam Kincaid, busy in the fed office. Neither knew about the other, just the way Sandoval liked it.

"Stay there," Sandoval said, and he leaned forward, sipped from his iced coffee, then tabbed his global, switching the sound to the wiring at the base of his skull. The CVI did have its uses—when you knew how to program it. Carlton's irritating drawl spoke right into his head: "Are you sure you don't want something to eat first? Templeton can wait."

And, more distant, the high, vapid voice of Karen Geneva (Scooby—what a stupid name for an adult), "No, I'll be okay. Really, it was just a headache—bad dream last night—I already feel better."

"Tell Templeton about it," came the response, superficially soothing but so condescending Sandoval wondered why the girl didn't hear his contempt and slap him silly. Was she as stupid as she sounded? Or was it just fear?

While he amused himself with an inward debate, John Blake, Sandoval's trusted tail, watched with sour pleasure as the tall, slim Carlton emerged from the limo, freshly shampooed ponytail hanging down his back, pissant little mustache and beard. How Blake hated rich people! Carlton turned around and helped the girl out. Now, that was more like it. Why was it California girls all had those long legs? Was there some kind of genetic design thing going on there? And that long brown hair, right down to that cute little ass. Hoo-ee. But she sure had crappy taste in men.

Blake settled back. He didn't care why Sandoval had a tail on this Carlton. He just wanted to be there when Sandoval sent in the goon squad to bust Mr. Rich Boy. Hah. That was the cool thing about these Taelons, really: If the Taelons wanted to fry your ass, even the thousand-bucks-an-hour lawyers of the rich weren't gonna get your buns off the barbeque.

Unaware of their visual and audial audience, Neville and Scooby got into the quiet, air-conditioned elevator and rode upward. Scooby stared up at Neville, her emotions veering like a seagull on a shore breeze. All of a sudden, these past few days, he'd paid her so much attention, said all these nice things about her. The crush she'd never acknowledged had bloomed into romance—all in her head, of course. But at twenty, aren't most of our romances mostly inside our head, anchored onto the briefest smiles or gestures from the Beloved Object?

He smiled at her now. "Well, Dr. Templeton will help," he said.

"Oh, sure," Scooby replied, more eagerly than she felt.

When they reached their floor, they trod down expensive carpet that made their steps soundless, past suites with expensive wood doors, to the one with the tastefully engraved brass plaque that said, very discreetly, E. J. Templeton, M.D. Though Neville walked beside her with his usual long stride, Scooby still felt as if she ought to tiptoe.

Neville opened the door for her, something that always made Scooby feel sort of awkward, and there was that perfectly groomed receptionist person.

"The doctor is waiting," she said. Not to Scooby—she never looked at Scooby—but to Neville.

"Thank you, Marla," Neville said, like they were cousins or something.

Scooby scooted past, sending a covert glance down at Marla's computer. What were those manicured purple nails always typing at? Scooby felt a strong wish to peek and almost giggled, but she managed to suppress it. Neville hated nervous giggles.

Through the hall, and past doors that Scooby had never seen opened. What was behind them? Scooby couldn't imagine a shrink having people lined up waiting, sitting on steel tables in hospital gowns, like a regular M.D.

The urge to snicker again. What was wrong with her? She knew what was wrong with her. In three days she was expected to kill someone.

She bit her lip and straightened her shoulders as Neville opened the door to where Dr. Templeton waited.

Scooby had to admit that she liked this room. It reminded her of Neville's house—expensive books on the walls, smelling like some kind of prince's library, with all the leather binding and gilt titles, and the beautiful Persian rug, and that slender telescope on the tripod by the window. Did Dr. Templeton work at night and watch the stars down south there, over Long Island Sound?

She had no idea that Dr. Templeton watched pretty women down in the square and in fact had been doing that before they came in. There was a blonde walking around down there, a gorgeous blonde who knew how to dress, the sort of woman with the taste to go into New York just for fittings.

Reluctantly E. J.—short for Evelyn Jasper, but only his fellow Bonesmen had heard those names spoken aloud since E. J. was four years old—thrust that blonde out of his mind. Art appreciation was over for the afternoon. Back to work.

"You seem tense," Dr. Templeton said to Scooby, after greeting them.

Scooby gulped in air, staring helplessly at the man. He did *seem* so kindly, with his curly light brown hair and his little gold-framed glasses, like he was a very young Santa Claus, except he'd always send Neville these *looks*. And Neville would send them back.

Scooby glanced defensively over her shoulder. Neville's

eyes shifted to her, but there was this faint smile at the corners of his mouth—really, such a handsome mouth, if only he'd kiss her, just once, and she thought he almost would, a couple times—and she knew they'd exchanged looks again.

Would he kiss her if she shot Zo'or? Was that it? Was she going to, like, prove she was worthy of a leader, or something? Only why didn't they tell her, or was she supposed to figure it out? Was that what leaders did, figure things out, instead of take orders?

"What happens after?" she blurted and realized she was staring at Neville. She whirled back to face the doctor, her face *burning*. Argh!

"You will be famous," Templeton said.

"You will be famous not just today, but in history," Neville said. "We've talked about it many times."

"But if it doesn't work? I don't mean here. You're here to make sure it's all right. You know Yale, and what to do," she said. "But what about in London, and Zurich, and Rio de Janeiro, and Moscow, and the other ones? What if something happens to our people there, and they can't do it?"

"That will not be your problem," Templeton said.

Glance.

"Yes it will, if the Taelons are not dead. That means they'll still be in power, and we'll be criminals," Scooby said, wringing her hands.

"And the Resistance will hide us," Neville said. "We'll be covert heroes, Robin Hood figures, to everyone who wants to get rid of the Taelons. And maybe other countries will rise and rid themselves of the overlords, like we did. We Americans set the example," he finished.

It was a measure of Scooby's romantic nature to hear his arrogance as heroic. She nodded, convinced.

Templeton gestured toward one of the comfortable wingback chairs and smiled at her. The chairs were close together, a tête-à-tête meant to induce intimacy and confidence. "Now, remember what I told you. To be familiar with every aspect of the plan is to be secure. The greatest fear is of the unknown, correct?"

"Yes," Scooby said.

"And if you know the plan by heart, it is known, correct?"

A numb nod.

"So let's begin. Zo'or is evil. Zo'or is an alien bent on domination. He does not even remotely care about human beings. Are we agreed?"

Scooby nodded vehemently. The nightmares she'd endured the past couple of nights had been the direct result of the nasty vids they'd shown her, stuff smuggled from government archives, of kryss farms, and biosurrogates, and other ugly experiments, the goon squad attacks, the wholesale slaughter of Resistance leaders, the wiping out of cities, all of it caused by Zo'or.

"So getting rid of this evil blight on human beings is a moral act."

"Yes." Her hands writhed, but yes, she was convinced. It was a moral act, it *was*.

"Just as moral as getting rid of Hitler would have been. If he'd been assassinated in 1939, how many lives would have been saved?"

"Millions," she said.

Templeton smiled with approval. "Yes. Millions. And Zo'or is even more hostile, even more mad, because he is not and never was human."

Scooby nodded, and so it went, for another twenty minutes. Question, answer, praise, over and over, until her heartbeat calmed a little, until she felt that yes, she could do it. Yes, she would do it.

Still . . . still . . .

When they left the office, Neville felt the resistance in her step.

He didn't speak until they were in the elevator. Then he said, "Are you feeling stronger?"

She turned her face up to his, eyes pleading. "You'll be with me afterward, won't you? If you are, it'll be okay."

He saw what was required and complied. Bent down to kiss the trembling lips, then breathed into her hair, "Yes. Right by your side."

As the elevator sped silently downward, he slid an arm around her, then kissed her again, more deeply.

When they emerged, neither looked right or left; Scooby was too dazzled by Neville, and Neville was trying to decide whether it might be better after all for him to kill Zo'or—what exquisite pleasure—or to stick with Scooby as hit woman.

As they clambered into the limo (with Blake sighing as he set aside his sandwich and revved up the Toyota), upstairs Templeton finished making certain that the session had not recorded and returned to his telescope. But a quick scan disappointed him. The blonde—who was, of course, Renee Palmer—was nowhere in sight.

Of course, because Templeton was a connoisseur of both beauty and expensive grooming, and Renee turned heads both male and female when she strolled out along the walkways on New Haven's historic green.

Not that she had been thinking about admiring glances.

Just before Scooby's appointment with Templeton, Renee walked out onto the green straight from Yale, after a frustrating morning. Her stated purpose of overseeing Doors's security setup was a boondoggle; she had a highly paid security team that could do its job quite well without her breathing over everyone's shoulders and that was interfacing with Liam Kincaid in his role as chief of operations. She had spent the morning instead charming the Yale administration staff, using her prestige as a Doors executive and her considerable personal skills to get not just a private tour and a pep talk on Yale's most promising seniors (suitable for hiring at executive level at Doors) but also a glimpse into past stellar Yalies.

For that she evoked the friendly Harvard-Yale rivalry; mentioning her Harvard background in the right way enabled her, after some judicious flattery, to see more of the records than most people would be permitted, but somehow the context was discreet, intimate, rather the same tactic Templeton, on the other side of the green, planned to use against Scooby.

Only she used it to plumb the records for one Neville Carlton IV. And what she saw was completely useless. As she stared at long-dead addresses, she thought, What am I doing here? What did I think to find?

More likely she might find something at UCLA, where he'd begun his doctorate program three years before—but even then, what was she likely to find in his transcripts or confidential records? Member: Resistance. Contacts: X,Y, and Z. Yeah, right.

And yet . . . and yet . . . There was something, she sensed it, but she couldn't quite see it.

So she took a walk to try to clear her head. Sometimes, especially when she'd been under stress for so long she couldn't remember when it began, she found that to think about anything but the problem at hand produced better answers than intense focus.

While Templeton was expertly leading Scooby into a fog of moral ambiguity and Neville sat, bored, within arrow shot, Renee took several trips up and down the green, her eyes and ears taking in the well-kept grass, the soft summer air, the birds singing, the people strolling about, her brain not registering any of it.

And just about the time Templeton was seeing Carlton and Scooby out of his office, Renee stopped before the summer theater and put a hand to her forehead. She thought:

Fact: Augur is on the way to stop Carlton's assassination plot.

Surmise: Sandoval knows.

Surmise: Zo'or knows.

Fact: Zo'or is going to be here anyway.

Fact: stockpiled all over the country are stacks of CNIs, waiting to be implanted in volunteers—

Volunteers. Flash memory: the State of Siege.

She whirled around and began walking. Stopped at a signal while the limo passed by, and while Templeton up in the big expensive suite got his chance back at his glass, alas, the lovely blonde in the linen jacket and trousers had just crossed Church Street out of sight.

On the corner, she paused and activated her locator device. Sandoval had inserted Taelon tech locators on all his forces' globals; Liam had matched the frequency for Renee. What was sauce for the gander could be sauce for the goose.

She expected him to be in the federal buildings, but instead he was two and a half blocks to the north. So she turned left, set out on a brisk walk, checking messages on her global as she did and making a few calls.

She found him sitting in a charming little place called Koffee? She opened the door and breathed in the heavenly scent of fresh-ground coffee.

"Ah," he said, betraying no surprise. "Iced or hot?"

"Iced," she replied, as if this had been a planned rendezvous. The sky was cloudy, the air humid.

A couple minutes later they sat at a tiny table next to a wall of glass, overlooking a little courtyard. Renee looked out as she stabbed her straw through the shaved ice. There appeared to be some sort of art center nearby. A girl sat directly below, sketchpad on her lap, her fingers deft as she captured the profile of a very handsome boy at another table. Another artist shaded, with butterfly surety, touches of light on a drawing of one of the blooming trees set around the court.

Art. It was always there, on the periphery of the endless power tug-of-war, just like the sun and weather, the birds and flowers. She felt a sudden urge to throw her global in the disposal and walk out, and sit among the artists, and for a time glory in the prospect of her biggest problem being something like tracing Paul Klee's influence on the current art deco revival, while listening to the somnolent buzzing of the bees.

But she'd never do it. Once you've tasted command, can you ever give it up? Cincinnatus did. And Charles V. But they were old.

She drew a deep breath and looked up, to meet Liam's steady blue gaze.

"It does look nice out there, doesn't it?" he said. "Shall we?"

She realized that the little table just next to them had a single occupant. A couple might be safe, for they'd be involved in one another, but the single person was too apt to listen idly to surrounding chat.

They walked out, to find that the artists had been joined by musicians and a cluster of skinny young teens in ballet toggery. All of them were oblivious to Renee and Liam strolling along, iced coffee in hand.

"You found something?" Liam said.

"No, but I think I realized something. In fact, it's so obvious now that I am feeling stupid."

Liam started to make a gesture of denial, and Renee laughed. "Never mind. You don't have to tell me what we both know: that between the two of us we've probably gotten ten hours' sleep in two weeks, yada yada. My humbleness will not last long, I assure you. I found nothing interesting in Carlton's files, and I believe I saw everything."

"So?"

She flicked her hair off her forehead and watched his eyes watch her hand. "So I looked at the television crew beginning to set up their equipment—you know the unveiling will be on national television at the least—and I thought about all the clues we've assembled so far."

"Ah." Liam turned his head, his gaze now distant.

"You saw it too? Zo'or is threatened by a wild-eyed graduate student, you Companion Protectors either leap forward and save his life, or you're not fast enough. Either way, the student is the villain, the Protectors and the Taelons the heroes, and Zo'or can use the emotional fallout to ram through his 'program' and make it mandatory."

Liam's jaw was grim. "Mandatory for every college kid in the country. Every one of them fitted with a CNI and trained to lawful obedience."

"No more riots, no more demonstrations, no more crime, no more drunken youths plowing up the roads—"

Liam shook his head. "There are a lot of people who won't even need the faked-up assassination attempt to go for that."

"What a chilling idea," Renee whispered. "And the sad thing is, we humans would be doing it to ourselves: handing over the next generation to the aliens, in return for peace and order."

Liam frowned, his gaze still distant.

Renee said, "So you should probably know that as soon as I located you, I put in a call for Julianne."

Liam shifted his gaze away. Looked at her. "Resistance contacts?"

"She can find out where all those medical facilities are. Tell them what we think. And the Tracy Mays of the Resistance can wire them for July Fourth fireworks, soon as we give the signal."

"Do it." Liam nodded. "All at once. Nobody has to know what was really there—except Zo'or. Maybe he'll take it as a warning."

"Not if he's dead, and Sandoval is in charge," Renee said.

Liam slung his half-finished drink into a trash can and moved away, as if to leave the horror of that image behind. Renee followed, surprised and then puzzled when she realized he was intent on something.

He kept walking across the courtyard to look at the art garden. It was a pretty garden, sloping gently, green, peaceful. Renee looked at it and back up at Liam's face, for his expression made it clear he did not see a garden here.

He stared down at that sloping grass and then up the other side. Turned his head. The slope slanted to the southeast, just a few yards. Liam shut out the present and focused on the topography.

"It's a canal," he murmured. "Some kind of old canal."

"And so?" Renee asked, amused.

"I'm not sure." Liam glanced at her, a distracted glance that did not really see her. "But I need to check it out. Fast, before my supposed lunch hour is over, and I have to get back to Sandoval's waiting goons."

Renee sipped her coffee. "Well, I'm not clambering about fences and alleys in this suit, if that's what you intend to do."

Liam gave his head a quick shake. "No. Listen, I'll meet you later. Or rather, you meet me later."

Renee shrugged and gave him a casual flick of the hand.

FORTY-TWO

The sun was just setting when Augur climbed down the rocky, grass-and-weed-choked pathway to the little cliff overlooking the Hudson River, where Cecilia sat, staring out at the softly flowing water.

Augur paused for a moment, contemplating Cecilia's unromantic figure. He was thrown back in memory to their first night together, when he'd seen her standing on the barren cliff overlooking I-15, grieving over her laser-blasted life.

Was she weeping again? It wasn't as if she hadn't the right, but that kind of thing—the profound loss resultant upon one first experiencing just how indifferent the universe really is to moral justice or rightness—was nothing he could address. Certainly couldn't fix.

But the face that turned his way when he deliberately rustled through grass and leaves was dry and thoughtful, not creased in sorrow. "It's so very beautiful," she said, indicating the river. "And so quiet! The ocean is always hissing or booming, never so soundless."

Augur spared a glance at the Hudson and waited for an appropriate moment to get down to business.

Cece smiled a little. "Do I sound like a schoolmarm chattering away?"

Augur snorted a laugh. "Nope."

"Then have a sit. Just for a minute or so. The peace here is as exquisite, as precious as the beauty. We will be back to danger soon enough, unless I miss my guess."

"No, you're right."

Augur hitched up his elegant trousers. Cece, watching, felt a spurt of laughter at how Augur managed, somehow, always to be elegant. Even on an adventure. Where had he gotten those?

No, that was one of those questions she did not ask. And maybe it was merely a sign of her eroding ethics, rather than one of perspective, but at least she could be certain that *those* slacks had not come from anyone poor or needy.

Augur, meanwhile, perched on the rock she'd spent the past couple of hours on, and she stood, glad to be standing, her hands in the pockets of her denim trousers. The fact that Phoebe had bought them two sizes big also gave her a private laugh, one of rueful self-mockery. Or wait. Hadn't Phoebe asked her size? Yes, she had!

Cece looked down, bemused at the thought of having somehow dropped two sizes. Well, with all that walking, and the scanted meals, it was quite possible. For a moment she entertained herself with an inner vision of a svelte outline, but reality, as always, asserted itself with its usual humorous promptitude. It was more probable that she looked exactly the same; furthermore, when she got home, she'd soon fit right back into her old clothes. Her metabolism was permanently set on pouter pigeon, not sylph, and anyway, she was too wise to believe that she would eat salad and carrots for the rest of her life and give up the occasional cheese Danish on a hot Monday morning with the prospect of a long faculty meeting louring at the other end of the schoolday. If the question comes down to someone else's standard for looks, she thought, or for the little joys of life, I will always opt for the joy. If this is weakness, so be it.

Joy. I will always reach for the joy, she thought, looking out at the gray-blue river reflecting the clouds in the sky and the green banks lined with willows and poplars, trees so rare and exotic at home. She loved her life as a teacher, and she wanted so very badly to get back to it, to bring all her insights home, and review them, and discuss them, and to find ways to make history come even more alive, now that she had walked ground that familiar figures had walked and had seen places their eyes had seen.

Looking aside, she realized that she'd fallen into a reverie, and Augur sat there quietly, waiting for her unraveling attention to knit itself back into its usual sleeve of care.

"What did Benedict Arnold really *feel* when he so very nearly sold out West Point?" she asked. "Major André must have ridden along this very path, thinking he'd soon be a hero. And Arnold was thinking the same thing."

"Each deceiving the Americans."

"Yet there's a moral difference." Cece waved in the direction of West Point. "André dressed as a civilian, but his was the act of loyalty. Arnold's wasn't. Or was it? I can't help wondering, as I stand here looking where their eyes once looked, if the traitor hasn't first been betrayed?"

"Arnold did seem a pragmatist, from what I've read," Augur commented wryly. "Hopped the fence back and forth. Indicted for embezzlement."

"A charge that Washington quashed," Cece replied. "Arnold was a pirate, or as near as one can be without a fast ship with raked masts and the black flag flying as ensign." She sighed. "I tried to make history vivid, but I spoke from the spectator's view and not from within the people involved. Being here makes the people real, and I realize I don't know enough to see through their eyes."

"Would you really want to?" Augur asked, tossing a rock on his hand.

"I don't know," Cece admitted. "Oh, Washington had his foibles. I certainly heard about those in college, when revisionism was the fashion. But my context is a class of innocent faces. And I don't mean innocent in the carnal sense."

Augur grinned inwardly at the quaint term.

"I mean that each group of children, given the blessing of good homes with food and comfort, and trust, and love, trusts the world to be just and moral. And we teachers are really spending our time eroding that trust of theirs, in preparation for reality." She kicked the rock with her scuffed shoe. "How can I fix that? We try to fix the children's lives, but maybe we ought to be fixing the world."

"Both need fixing, to that I can attest," Augur said. "If you're asking me—"

"By all means!"

"—then here's my answer to you: each to the task to which he or she is best suited. You keep on doing what you are doing. It has value, though the result might not be immediately measurable."

Cece nodded solemnly, her glasses winking in the fading twilight. Then she said in a tentative voice, "It seems that you had little trust in your young years." Almost at once her shoulders came up, and she shook her head. "I trespassed and promised I wouldn't. Forgive me."

Augur thought about all the memories of her own young years that she had shared so freely and waved a hand as if pushing the matter aside. "Nothing to forgive. But we had better get back to our danger."

"Yes," she said briskly, though the twilight did not hide her blush.

"I scouted out the local library, as I said I would," Augur began. "Got us a map of New Haven. Also got us a weather report. And bus lines. It looks like bad weather is heading in by tomorrow. What I suggest is that we spend tomorrow making our way by circuitous methods over to the north side of New Haven. We can ride buses. Take one bus to

Yale Bowl, walk to West River Sanctuary. Maybe take a bus from there to Edgewood, or Beaver Pond, and then to Science Park Volunteer Training Facility."

"Urk," Cece said. "Oh. Of course. Tours by families considering enrolling a youth, right?"

"Of course. They're not going to expect to see *us,* and I'm sure that stop-searches are not part of their PR tactics. We can ride in on separate buses, meet at their south entrance at a given time, and if the predicted rain hits, we hike down your friend's Farmington Canal—which is on the maps—and into New Haven."

Cece nodded. "All right, it sounds good."

Augur saw her bracing up her courage. He never would have picked this woman of forty-odd to share a cross-country trek with; she had a schoolmarmish attitude toward excess property, she would be totally useless as backup in action, and she was an avowed coward. But she also had the most generous heart he had probably ever met.

"By the way," he said, just for the pleasure of deliberately trusting someone. Ah, what a rare luxury. "My name is Marcus Devereaux."

Cece's glasses twinkled, reflecting the emerging stars peeping from the clouds. "Pleased to meet you," she said, pretending to flourish a cape. "Call me Superteacher!"

They laughed and thought no more of the computer AM, for they had more pressing matters, such as finding dinner and a place to spend the night. Superteacher was, however, very much on the mind of at least one person: Tarek Curan, her creator.

He prowled the Internet that night, gathering info on all the best graphic arts schools in the country, gloating over the ones that cost the most. Would the Taelons really pay for everything? What an incredible score that would be, a full scholarship—especially for those bozos at the high school who gave him crappy grades and called him a slacker.

And what a score it would be for certain people who thought they were better designers, better systems crackers, better everything.

It'd be a score, but would they really *do* it?

He sat back, frowning. A lot of people thought the Taelons were all alike. They certainly looked alike, but then they were actually wearing costumes, weren't they? Human-shaped tech skins? Then there was that Commonality business. If there really was a mind pool they all dipped into, well, that sure argued for being alike.

And yet the more he dug around, the more evidence turned up that Zo'or, the one up in the Mothership, was pretty harsh. But Da'an, the one the brats met, seemed to have a better rep. Da'an had actually done some good things for people. If he could get a message just to Da'an, say, would that scholarship thing really happen?

Tarek tapped his fingers on his keyboard, hit his log-on. Killed it. Hit it again.

FORTY-THREE

Location blocks were still possible, Liam discovered when Sandoval summoned him via global.

"Thirty-six hours until the unveiling," Sandoval said by way of greeting.

As if we weren't both aware of that, Liam thought sourly. Here it comes, wait for it—

"The installation is scheduled in half an hour. I want you there personally overseeing it. I do not want any risk of sabotage."

Nothing that you haven't planned, Liam thought.

"Right," he said aloud, raising a hand to cancel the connection.

Sandoval got there first.

Did Sandoval ever see even a glimpse of himself in Liam, the way Liam saw glimpses of himself in those dark, appraising eyes? I'll probably never know, he thought as he pocketed the global. Kill me, yes. Confide in me, never. The dead don't talk, except in dreams.

Liam looked around the hotel room and slapped his pockets, hitting the tracking device that the ANA had given him to keep tabs on Da'an's movements. Was there time? He'd better make the time.

So he tabbed it, saw running lights, and heard a hiss. He frowned and tabbed it again. The tiny screen showed snow, rather than the LED display of a location.

Is he in a portal, then? Liam thought and made a mental note to check later. He walked out, his mind reverting back to Sandoval. Maybe the dead spoke in some people's dreams, but did they in those of Ronald Sandoval? If so, the voices of the hordes whose lives he'd summarily ended would clamor loud enough to drive him to madness.

Was he mad? What was the definition of madness? Was it as mutable as the definition of art?

Liam laughed at himself as he rode the elevator down and then set out on foot. The walk was only a couple of blocks, during which he could get time to think and to assess the atmosphere. Above, patchy clouds scudded slowly across a starlit sky, harbingers of rain. The air certainly felt so; soft, not cool. Humid.

He breathed the air, watching traffic along College Street as he walked north. Nothing untoward—if you discounted the occasional Volunteer cruising along on intersecting sentry perimeters.

Those increased in number when he crossed Crown. At the corner of Chapel and College, the sentries were no longer even remotely covert. They were stationed at each corner, in full gear and constant communication.

As he crossed the street he met alert pairs of eyes and nodded acknowledgment. On to Phelps Gate, arching in the midst of Victorian-styled medieval buildings. Through the gate—you could easily envision horses and carriages riding through not so long ago—and in. Another fifty feet, and he stepped around the taped-off site where the statue was to be set, dug, squared off, and ready. He noted that the landscapers had already relaid the sidewalk to circle the spot.

One of Sandoval's aides came running around the huge statue of an old professor, sitting there in his academic robe, book in hand. Liam looked at the statue, then turned his head toward Nathan Hale, still standing off to the left. No longer would these two be left serenely facing the grassy quad; instead they'd be looking at something they'd probably never conceived in their lives, a being from another planet . . . another sun!

An alien conqueror. Hale, in particular, would have hated that, Liam thought. He checked again, mentally measuring off the spaces, and thought, They're going to form the court for this Taelon.

Symbolism. Well, no help for it now.

The aide reached him then. "Delivery truck just behind Dwight Chapel, there, sir," she said, pointing behind her. "Waiting for your personal inspection."

"Can't you bring it around to the gate? Much closer." Liam gestured behind him at the archway built through the classical studies building.

"Too big. Won't make it through."

He grunted an affirmative. The impressive rectangle of buildings were lit like daylight inside and out, as was the path-crossed grassy quadrangle in the middle. Sentries patrolled, always in one another's field of vision. All orderly, all exactly as it should be. So why did he have to inspect? To keep him busy, of course.

Obligingly he went through the motions. The gauntleted workers used a sling to bring out the statue, which had been laid on its side in a flatbed, and eased it onto an air-cushion float. The thing—whatever it was—was well wrapped and padded, probably unnecessarily, Liam thought. As unnecessary as his presence, but it satisfied someone's sense of propriety. Or had the Taelons caused their gift to be sculpted in human materials—marble or granite? Cast in bronze, maybe? It didn't sound like either Da'an's or Zo'or's style.

Liam realized he was curious. So was everyone else, apparently; when he looked around again, there appeared to be a sudden increase in personnel.

Warning flared in the back of his mind, until he scanned more closely and recognized staff people and off-duty Volunteers. Even college staff, all with their newly issued ID tags, worn in silent compliance with the draconian regs that Liam knew were going to be useless in the long run. One or two of these people, Liam suspected, were Resistance, though he'd made no sign and neither had they. Everyone wanted an advance peek at the Taelons' gift before tomorrow, partisanship notwithstanding.

In silence—save for softly spoken commands by the overseer—the shrouded statue was winched upright and then settled into the waiting earth. Matter-of-fact laborers applied quick-drying cement around the perimeter, after which workers set about unfastening and pulling down the padding while others readied the big sailcloth veil, which would be tented down until the ceremony.

The base was freed first. Liam drew in a slow breath when he saw the graceful Taelon glyphs, and then, without warning, the rest of the shrouding came off. A sigh, almost a moan, soughed through the crowd.

The statue had been made of some variation on virtual glass, this one resembling crystal. Liam gazed in silence at the tall replica of Ma'el, the smoothly cast medieval robes, one foot stepping forward, the hands outstretched in the Taelon gesture for peace. He looked last at the benevolent face. Light passed through it, cool and blue and complicated with refractions. During the day, Liam realized, refracted light would blaze through this statue, here golden, there with laser-brightness, and when the sun was at certain angles, rainbow scintillants would paint the old buildings with brilliance, both beautiful and symbolic of the Taelon hidden core of energy.

Liam's gaze returned to the Taelon script.

"What's it say?" someone asked in a subdued voice.

Liam did not want to speak, but inwardly he translated: Knowledge brings peace, and peace brings harmony.

Only the word wasn't quite harmony, which carried musical overtones in English. In Taelon it connotated reunification, reunion . . . *commonality*.

He frowned, feeling the skin along the backs of his arms go rough.

"Oh, I'm sure we'll be listening to an hour-long speech about whatever it means," someone else said. "C'mon, let's get some shut-eye. Tomorrow will be hell on wheels."

The veil descended then, shutting out the ice-blue luminosity in Ma'el's face and robes and hands, and as the tent pegs were driven into the grass, and guards took up position around the statue, people began to drift off in ones and twos and threes.

Harmony. Commonality.

Evolution.

Liam thought about the artifact that had at so great a cost been brought from Ma'el's crypt, and Zo'or still waiting to open it in conjunction with Liam, for Ma'el had deliberately designed it to be opened only by Taelon and human together. Ma'el, he knew, had truly wanted harmony; Zo'or only wanted power.

Liam walked away, fighting against the chill of implied threat.

Morning came as a relief from a night of tossing, checking the global, prowling the hotel room, and then trying (with minimum success) to sleep again. At dawn, Liam gave up. He showered, shaved, dressed, and went down in search of breakfast—to find Frank Tate loitering in the lobby.

"Yo, Kincaid," Tate said with false cheer.

Liam fought against any sign of the repugnance the sight of Tate's ugly mug gave him. Reasonably sure that Tate's loathing for him was mutually enthusiastic, he said, "What brings you to New Haven?"

"Sandoval, who else?" Tate said. At least he didn't try to hide it. "He spent the night chasing phantoms. Thinks said phantoms might be related to tomorrow's shindig. Wants me by your side—two pairs of eyes better than one—so you see me, guilty as charged." He tapped his chest.

"Phantoms?"

Tate gave a shrug, rucking up his London Fog. "Someone, or something, has been ram jetting around with a stolen portal. Military sites appear to be the destination of choice. That and the stolen codes have got Ronny boy hotter than"— Tate looked up, saw a waiting aide, a female one, and hastily finished—"fireworks on July Fourth. Hello, miss. You look fresh as a daisy this summer morn. What *is* the weather back here, anyway?"

"Hot and humid." Despite his dislike for Sandoval's minion, and the prospect of a full day with the guy glued to his side, Liam snorted a laugh. "You might as well get rid of the trench coat now."

"Roger that," Tate said breezily. "I'll just drop it behind the counter." He continued to keep up a constant chatter of false bonhomie as they crossed the lobby and approached the desk clerk. Great, Liam thought, watching the coat go behind the counter in the baggage-holding area. A subtle signal I've got him on my back the entire day.

A day that already promised to be an endless drag of pointless chores anyway. Maybe that was to the good. Liam decided he'd play right along with the game, include Tate in every task—the more boring the better—so the guy would be glad to find any excuse to take a break later at night, when Liam had to be alone.

Besides, at this point, he'd done everything he could.

The rest was up to Renee.

He knew it.

She knew it.

The thought was like a vise gripping her skull all day, as she toured every single building on the perimeter of the Old Campus. With her was an old intelligence vet from before the SI war, her chief of security, who knew everything there was to know about secret passages and unlikely approach or escape routes. He walked beside her in silence, asking questions occasionally; Renee exerted as much charm as she could contrive, to inspire trust and encourage revealing comments.

She came up with absolutely nothing. The occasional mention of her "old Yalie friend" Neville Carlton brought no recognition whatsoever, not one furtive look, or snap of the fingers, or even a vague memory. By the end of a day that Renee was certain she'd long remember for its excruciating tedium, she had found out exactly nothing.

When she got to the Omni Hotel, there was one thought on her mind: a bath. And then a much-needed rest. She was actually trying to decide what scent to drop into the tub—just a single drop of a favorite perfume, a lovely touch she'd learned from her mother—when she passed through the heavy glass doors.

And all thoughts of the bath, the perfume, and rest vanished into the night when she recognized Julianne Belman crossing the lobby.

"How about a nightcap?" Julianne asked with false cheer. She looked impossibly cool and collected in a fine blue linen pants suit.

"Don't I wish," Renee replied under her breath as they passed into the elevator. How long would it be before she could get rid of these clothes and sink into that bath?

Four other people got in with them—tourists all, reminiscing about the Yale of their day—which prevented conversation. When they reached the third floor Julianne took Renee's arm and marched her out into the hall. Three doors down, she knocked. The door opened a crack, and then wider.

"Tracy May," Renee exclaimed, now thoroughly dismayed, as she and Julianne passed inside. "What's happened?"

Tracy May did not answer. She shut and locked the door, then slapped some kind of high-tech device on the lock mechanism.

Renee turned around to see the beds shoved against either wall, and in the middle of the floor a portable portal set up. She barely had time to brace herself when Tracy May gave her a rueful grin, activated the mechanism, and the familiar blue-purple torus glowed with ferocious power, filling the filtered air with the smell of ozone.

They stepped through—and Renee found herself in what had to be a bunker, who knew where. Fluorescent lights glowed in the low ceiling, and a heavy-duty AC system whooshed out frigid air.

Renee looked around the people gathered there, smelled the heavy ozone that even the industrial-strength air system couldn't banish, and realized the portal had been humming for a protracted time.

What she faced was a convocation of Resistance cell heads.

"They don't believe me," Julianne stated.

"No," an old man spoke up, his tone mild. "It's not disbelief but caution that brings us together now. If we blow up these medical facilities, we're going to bring down reprisals, just like the State of Siege."

"And we will be taking lives," a woman stated.

Tracy May stood with her back to a steel door, arms folded. "That's what bothers me too. I don't give a damn 'bout the villains who designed those dag-blasted CNIs. I mean the night shift Volunteers, most o' whom are just kids fresh out o' the program. Assigned to what's supposed to be easy—a medical facility. They got no idee what's down b'low."

"We need more reassurance than a hunch," said a man at the other end of the table.

Renee drew a deep breath. "All I can give you are a few facts, and the rest is logic." And she told them about

Neville Carlton, the plot, and the fact that Sandoval almost certainly knew about it, finishing, "Few facts, as you see. But it adds up too tightly: We see an assassination, or an attempted assassination, by a graduate student, and before we know it Zo'or and Sandoval—who are first-rate manipulators—get their program made mandatory. Oh, we won't hear about the CNIs until they're already in and functioning. If they function. We don't even know how far these things have been tested. But we know this much: Zo'or could care less about the cost in human lives, and Sandoval will do anything, anything at all, for domination."

Silence. Exchanged looks.

"An entire country hotwired after one guy pulls a gun on a Taelon?" someone new spoke up.

"Remember the State of Siege," Renee said, trying not to give in to her own emotions, her own hatred of the Taelons. "Remember how many we lost that time, because we didn't believe Sandoval would take it that far?"

The old gentleman said, "But that was a different matter; the reaction, so close after the election, was widespread. What you're giving us is a single incident, and we all know that today's shocking isolated incident, however shocking, is tomorrow's history. And you do not have proof."

"No." She hated saying it, but lying would be worse. "No, we don't. But we've been right before."

"And wrong," a woman said gently.

"But you've seen the stuff."

"We've seen," the old man said, "what we were told was 'the stuff.' "

"And I'm sure you're right about the CNIs," the first woman said, "but we can't believe a single incident is going to trigger a countrywide crackdown and widespread zombieizing of our kids."

"Why the increase in staff, then?" Renee said, fighting not to get angry. To tell them that their very caution—lack of vision—was what madmen like Sandoval and Zo'or counted on, because *their* vision was limitless, when it came to using force to attain their desires. "And all the supplies?"

"That's the single real item in your favor. Against which we have to balance the fact that we know we'd be killing innocent people." The old man nodded once. "We'll need more proof before we can agree to widespread bombing and the inevitable fallout that will result."

Proof in twenty-four hours? Sure.

Renee sighed. "All right, so you don't act. Just remember this: The Resistance will be blamed anyway. You all know it."

The looks this time were more thoughtful.

Still, nobody spoke as Tracy May reversed the location poles, and Renee and Julianne stepped back through into the hotel room. The portal winked out of existence a moment later, leaving a whirl of metallic-smelling displaced air.

Renee sank down on one of the beds as Julianne moved to the bureau. The clink of glasses followed.

"Damn, those portals make me sick," Renee muttered, rubbing her temples.

"No they don't. Exhaustion does. When was the last time you slept a whole night?" Julianne asked, coming over with two glasses.

"I can't remember," Renee said.

Julianne grinned, pressed a glass into Renee's hand, and hefted the other. "Ordinarily I do not prescribe alcohol as a relaxant, but there are times when a body needs a good slug of Scotch. Preferably single malt," she added. "Drink up."

Renee loathed Scotch, single malt or otherwise, but she wasn't going to repudiate a kindly meant gesture. So she swallowed it in two quick gulps.

"My! You got any sailors in your genetic makeup, my dear?" Julianne asked with an admiring quirk to her brows.

Renee grinned and then felt the world swoop. "Uhn. What's—?" Her tongue had turned to cotton.

"Just something to guarantee one full four-hour cycle," Julianne said. "That is my real prescription. Curse me now, but I guarantee you'll wake up feeling a whole lot chirpier."

Renee tried to work herself up to a pungent remark, but it seemed easier to lie back and study the ceiling, whoo, look at that light, and wasn't it . . . wasn't it . . .

Julianne smiled in satisfaction as Renee's breathing became deep and regular. She briskly bent, pulled off Renee's shoes, set them down, took the empty glass from the slack fingers, and cast the coverlet over her.

And tiptoed out.

While upstairs, outside Renee's room, a patient figure waited, looking with increasing desperation at a watch. Each time a Doors International employee emerged from the elevators—for Doors had reserved the whole wing on this floor—she had to duck out of sight.

An hour, two hours passed, and at last the figure in the shadows gave up with a sigh.

FORTY-FOUR

Upstairs in the Omni penthouse, with cynical deliberation, Neville Carlton put on a romantic dinner for Scooby. Not that *he* put it on. His exertions with respect to actual preparation began and ended with a session on the house phone, following which waiters appeared with silver covered trays, hovering silently about the table like black-and-white giant moths to whisk away any dirty dish and replace it with a new, beautifully prepared enticement.

What he did was make it into a romantic tête-à-tête, watching Scooby for cues and then smilingly supplying them. Let her design the dream. He'd act it out.

So he was quite annoyed when his global bleeped.

"Should I ignore that?" he said, tapping his fingers on the snow-white linen-and-lace tablecloth. "I thought I made myself quite clear: We were not to be disturbed."

"It might be an emergency."

Carlton did not misread the sudden terror in her face, or the way her disgustingly chewed and ragged nails flew up to her mouth. Despite all his unceasing labor, fear was not far below the surface in this stupid girl.

"I'm sure it's not," he said, and as she looked unconvinced, "but since the mood is broken anyway, why don't I reassure us both?" He snapped it open. "Yes? Ah. Marina. A problem at home?"

Marina Aguilara stared back at him from the vid screen. He did not recognize the background, but then he had so many cream-colored walls at home. "I just wanted to talk to Scoob. Is that a problem?" she asked.

Neville regarded those intelligent, unreadable dark eyes. Was this challenge, all of a sudden? Were his troops getting restless?

"Why, no," he said in a soothing voice. "Here she is, sitting at the other end of the table."

And, with a courtly bow, he handed the global to Scooby.

"Marina?" Scooby half whispered, even though Neville was right there.

"Just wanted to check on you, kiddo."

"Oh, Marina, you're such a good friend. But I'm okay. Really. Neville has been so—so supportive." Scooby blushed, then hurried into speech. "We're having this incredible dinner. To celebrate. Candlelight and everything. The most heavenly food."

"Good. So you're really okay with things?"

"Sure," Scooby said, her voice breathless and squeaky. She cleared her throat. "Sure. It's going to be great. You'll see. I hope you'll be watching TV."

"Oh, I'll be watching," Marina said, with a faint emphasis. "Bye."

Scooby handed the global back.

Neville bent down to kiss her brow. Then he poured her more wine. "Now, where were we?" he asked, smiling.

Two blocks away, as Neville poured the wine and then raised it in a toast, Liam Kincaid walked into the New Haven with Tate by his side.

Liam was furious. Tate, it seemed, was unshakable. Was he going to be stuck with the guy all night?

As if reading his mind, Tate said, with unconvincing apology, "By the way, I forgot to tell you: It seems that the entire town is packed to the rafters. Not a cot in the smallest fleabag to be had. And Ronny Boy didn't assign me quarters. You have two beds, right? Can I bunk in with you?"

Liam longed to lie, but he knew if he did, Sandoval would know in seconds after he shut his door, and there'd promptly be a more overt shadow put on him.

As he walked down the lobby, the manager looked up. "Excuse me, sir," he said as Liam and Tate drew nigh. "Major Kincaid, I believe?"

"Yes," Liam said. "Is there a message for me?"

"Not a message. Mail," the man said, with the faint air of apology of the well bred who is conscious of committing a possible faux pas. After all, who left actual mail these days? What was wrong with messages? He vanished into a back room behind the counter, then reappeared with an envelope.

"Thanks," Liam said, and at Tate's avid gaze, he forbore looking but stuffed it into his pocket. "This way."

No way around it. They rode up the elevator, Tate filling Liam's silence with running talk about sports. When they reached the room, Liam claimed the bathroom first, and once the door was locked, he set his shoulders to it for added security and opened the envelope.

Not even the low murmur of a voice (obviously Tate reporting in on his global) drew his attention when he saw the contents: a little paper, and two tickets to some sort of play.

Setting the tickets down, he looked at the folded paper. "It might put you to sleep, but what the hey. Support the local arts."

It was signed "JB."

Put you to sleep? Liam picked up the tickets. They were ordinary tickets, dated two days from now. Why would Julianne Belman buy tickets, write this note, and drop these off—knowing that most likely at least six people had scanned the envelope, and half of them probably opened it outright?

Doctor Julianne Belman.

Liam brought the tickets to his face, sniffed them, and felt the weirdish brush of a cottony sensation behind his eyes.

Well, I'll be damned, he thought. Did she mean this for me or someone else? Right now, who cares? He looked at the clock. There might be hope yet.

He flushed the toilet, washed his hands, picked up the envelope, note, and tickets, and went out. Forcing his tone to be more friendly, he rubbed his hands and said, "Well, what say we order some dinner?"

"Sounds like a plan," Tate said, looking surprised.

"But first a brew?" Liam bent down to open the refrigerator. He laid the note and the tickets on the top, then went to the bathroom, where the glasses were still sitting upside down, protected by their little paper covers. "What a long day. I'll be glad when it's over, Zo'or's safely back on the Mothership, and we are out of here." In the mirror he saw Tate step over to the refrigerator, glance down at note and tickets, then back away, a faint puzzlement between his brows.

Liam popped the top of the beer, poured it into two glasses, and then came out. "Even Steven," he said. "Here's to tomorrow."

"Here's to time off," Tate corrected, hoisting his glass. He drank, smacked his lips, said, "It does go down good."

"It does," Liam said. "Here. I'll get another. Companion Services can afford it. Why don't you see what room service has to offer?"

He fetched another beer, collected Tate's empty glass, and popped the top. And while Tate studied the menu with unfeigned eagerness—it had been a long day, and Liam didn't remember eating—he poured two more glasses, and then, turning his back, picked up the tickets, dunked them into Tate's glass, pulled them out, grabbed the glass, and set it down beside Tate.

The man didn't even look at the glass. "I don't care what the doc says," he muttered. "After a day like today—a week like this has been—a man really needs a good steak."

"Make that two," Liam said.

Tate grabbed the beer, drank it, picked up the phone. "Room service!" Cleared his throat. Frowned. Looked up and then keeled over, the phone dropping out of his hand.

Liam grabbed the receiver.

"What? Sir, is something wrong?" said the voice at the other end.

"Nope. Dropped the menu," Liam said in as fair an approximation of Tate's voice as he could manage. "We can't decide. I'll call back."

He hung up and stretched Tate out on the bed, then patted his own pockets; he carried all his tech toys on him, rather than leave them in the room for Sandoval's spies to nab. Remembering the palm in his pocket, he grabbed his rainproof windbreaker, zipped it up, and was out and running down the stairs in half a minute. He reached the service door and slipped out, just as the first drops of rain began falling.

Two hours later he sloshed to a stop. He'd been debating going back. This was only a hunch, and the longer he stayed out following it, the more he risked discovery. Just how long would Julianne's happy juice keep Tate snoring? At least Tate had just reported in, so the likelihood of Sandoval calling for a status report was minimal—if nothing blipped on his radar.

He stopped, staring into the darkness. Sheets of rain reflected, faint silver, from the cemetery to the west. He realized he'd heard a sound, so faint that it registered neurally before mentally.

He brought out his infrared scanner, clicking it on just as he heard a soft whisper: "Liam."

Two figures lit on screen.

Liam pitched his voice low. "Augur?"

Splash, splash, splash! There they were. Liam snapped on his flashlight, keeping the beam low. Light reflected off the rims of Augur's specs, which glowed faintly—he too had been reading infrared, then—and on his piratical grin.

"You can't imagine how good it is to see you," Augur said.

"Likewise." Liam turned to the shorter figure. He did not shine the light directly into her face, but past her shoulder; in the reflected glow he caught a glimpse of a round face, untidy hair straggling out of a blue scarf, and a wide, querying gaze behind thick glasses. "Miss Robin?"

"Call me Cece." She smothered a laugh of relief.

And Augur said, "It was too easy."

"Of course it was," Liam said, snapping off the flashlight. "I found this old canal two days ago and didn't set up sentries. Sandoval hasn't either, because he too thought it the most obvious way in."

"You mean we've been set up?"

"Not you. Neville Carlton. We think. Come on, let's get back, and I can fill you in on what we know and what we've guessed."

"So Sandoval hasn't nailed Carlton, then?"

"Not even close. In fact I think he's busy making certain no one catches up with him, and won't, right until he pulls the trigger."

"But he's not going to pull the trigger," Augur said.

"What?"

A quick exchange of looks, just barely perceptible in the

weak reflection of distant streetlights. Augur nodded to Cece, who deferred with a quick gesture.

Augur said, "This is our own theory, but we're pretty certain that Carlton has set up one of his students to make the actual hit. That's why we're here—to stop them both."

Liam whistled under his breath. "I've got to let Renee know. She's trying to track down Carlton, since Sandoval has me hedged in tighter than a pig in a bottle."

A smothered snicker from Cecilia Robin, and Augur said, his tone changing, "A pig in a bottle?"

"Got it from Julianne. She's been on my mind this evening. Having given me the means to slip the leash—the bottle—to make this meeting."

"Ah, Julianne," Augur said and stumbled over an unseen rock. "Ow! Damn it. Well, that promises plenty of fireworks. Have you figured out who shot at us, and why?"

"No. But it seems to be related. Everything seems to be related, but as yet we have only half the puzzle. What we know: Carlton shoots Zo'or, or tries, Sandoval closes in, and this new educational program that had been set up by Doors and the Taelons and some other big business to provide scholarships to smart kids after a couple years as Volunteers becomes a mandatory requirement for all youths, complete with brand-new implants, these ones far more effective, supposedly. The big glitch here is how even Sandoval can turn an isolated incident with a single fanatic into a national crackdown."

"But it's not isolated," Augur said. "It's worldwide. He's got kids in at least twelve embassies, maybe more. The signal for them to assassinate their Taelons is the televised unveiling here."

Liam frowned at the haze of light glowing over New Haven. Most of that was Old Campus, still lit up like an operating room, still supposedly secure. "And Sandoval knows it. How?" He faced Augur.

"I don't know. You should know that—you can get on SecNet. What sort of investigation did he do on Carlton? There has to have been something, after that laser hit."

"Nothing. He talked to the guy for five minutes. Didn't even bring up the Resistance—" Liam stopped, a new set of possibilities correlating in his mind.

And not just in his. Augur gazed at him, eyes wide. "He's wired!"

"What?" That was Cece, her voice tentative. "I'm sorry to be dense, but if I am to help, I must understand what you are saying."

Augur turned to her. "Sandoval's done it before. Gets nanobots into someone's system, or plants a pickup neurally. Vid only recently. Audio he's done before."

Cece wiped her hair back. "I've heard rumors about that," she said, "but I didn't know if I believed it. Yet the rumors were connected with portals—unexplained disappearances and so forth. From what Scooby told me, I gathered that Carlton's group tries to avoid using any kind of Taelon technology. And that includes portals. Though I don't know how long that was in force."

"My question is, how would he have known to wire the guy?" Liam asked. "He wasn't on a single heads-up list. Not even on lower-level possible Resistance member watch lists."

"Something's missing," Augur said, kicking at a weed in his way.

"Several somethings," Liam pointed out. "Here's another wrinkle. If Sandoval wasn't lying to me, whoever shot at you and cracked the Taelon site to post your on-line ID log-ons just scored the new codes on the military sats."

Augur shook his head in admiration. "I hope I get to meet this guy before he gets toasted. Or lady," he amended, with a courtly bow in Cece's direction. "Well, new things to think about. At least we can think in comfort soon, I trust, since Sandoval wants us to walk into a trap?"

"Right about Sandoval, but wrong about comfort. Every alum who can hobble to a portal, plus papparazzi and diplomats from around the world, is here. There isn't a bed to be had in the city."

"Then we sit up all night. Somewhere dry. With a pot of

coffee. Is there good coffee here?" Augur finished on a plaintive note.

"Very good coffee. Remember, this is a university town," Liam said.

"So where can we plan in relative comfort?"

"You plan." Liam squinted around. They had been walking fast—Augur and Cecilia stumbling often and smothering exclamations. He spotted the spire of St. Mary's Church. "We're almost there. I've got to get back and wake up with Tate in a drunken stupor."

"Sounds appetizing," Augur drawled. "Spare me the details. What do you suggest?"

"That you stay far away from Carlton. If we're right, then Sandoval knows exactly where he is at all times and so has tails all over the guy—with orders to grab you two on sight."

"Makes sense. But sitting around on my hands isn't my style."

"Yes, but I know what is. If Sandoval hasn't found his laser-shooting bogey, then my guess is he'll be desperate. The coincidence of the sat codes being scammed and the coming worldwide assassination attempt is too risky to ignore. If I can get him to lift the security control firewalls, can you get in and cut the cyberspook's access to the military sites?"

"Easy. If I have a computer," Augur said.

Liam unzipped his jacket and pulled out the palm. "You have one now."

"It'll take me some time to hack into my own system at home, cover my butt, and then get through to SecNet here. At least it'll be temporary stuff, and if Sandoval is running true to form, he oversaw it all himself, also temporary stuff, with maybe two people cleared for access."

"You guess right."

Augur's elegant wire frames gleamed in the light. "Ah, yes."

"But he'll have corresponding bitbombs all over it as well."

Augur laughed softly. "Remember my motto: *Pulchrior quam upt morier.*"

Cece gave a small gasp.

Both men turned to her. Augur said, "Is it my vanity or my declensions?"

"What did you mean to say?"

"That I'm too pretty to die."

Cece laughed, a quick soft sound, unexpectedly sweet. In the street lights, Liam could see that the lines in her rainwashed face were carved by laughter and good humor.

She said, tentative again, "Well, it's been years since I really dug into my Latin, but I think it means, 'I'm pretty, therefore I should die.' "

Silence.

"I hope that's not prophetic," Augur finally said in his customary drawl. "Very inconvenient, death, and rather hard to cure."

"Then take a rain check," Liam said, knowing that any hint of admonishment would only irritate Augur. "Or should that be a sun check? Do you have a map?"

"We both do."

"Good. Then let's cut up here, behind this fence. We'll be quiet so no dogs bark. Prospect Avenue is on the other side."

"Ah." Augur had, of course, already memorized the map.

"What ought I to do?" Cece asked. "I still intend to talk to Scooby if I can."

"And I won't dissuade you," Liam said. "But we don't know where they are. Renee Palmer, one of our associates, will, I hope. And she'll contact me, probably in person, since I suspect that Sandoval has a tap on my global as well as a locate. He knows I work with Renee, but at this point any sort of contact will be highly suspect."

"And so I should do what?"

"Go on down to . . . York and Broadway. Lots of little food places and bookstores. Don't stay in any one too long. Renee will find you. Keep that scarf on. She can orient on it."

Cece nodded. "What does she look like?"

"A blonde dream." Augur kissed his fingers. "But cold." He sighed.

Liam saw Cece laugh and nod. "Will you be all right?" he asked her.

"With the prospect of bookstores and of getting off my blistered feet? I will be fine."

"Do you have any money?"

She shook her head. "Oh, dear—I forgot—"

Liam pulled out his wallet. "Here. On Companion Services."

She took the bills he held out but gave him another of those querying looks. It wasn't a judgmental look. Curiosity and kindness were the foremost expressions in her eyes. Liam, looking down, felt a pang of unexpected emotion and a sudden, vivid memory of Siobhan Beckett—his mother—dying in his arms. Would she ever have looked at him this way?

"Are they tender with their young?" she asked. "The Taelons, I mean."

The question paralleled his thoughts so closely it sent his mind reeling. He realized that he was staring, that the silence was longer than the question warranted, as she added in haste, "Forgive me. It's just that you're around them so much, and I'd hardly have the opportunity to ask any other Protector, should I meet one. It's the curse of a teacher: curiosity. Some would say terminal nosiness," she finished contritely.

"It's all right," Liam said. "I just had to think. I spend a lot of time around them, but they are not physical beings, so I would have to conjecture that no, tenderness is not a familiar concept. At least as we define it. And yet I know they are protective of their unborn young."

Cece murmured, "Thank you." Giving no further clue to her thoughts.

The three parted soon after.

Liam shifted his mind back to Sandoval. He reached the

hotel room, and Tate was still snoring. Working fast, Liam pulled the rest of the beers out of the refrigerator, emptied them into the sink. Then he dropped the cans all over the floor of the room, stretched out on the bed in his clothes, and went to sleep.

Tate would probably waken first; let him conjecture what he would about their wild drunken evening.

FORTY-FIVE

July 4th. Morning.

In a way it was kind of cool, this idea of catching a fireball with a fishhook. Tarek had decided he'd just scope out that offer, sort of. But he'd be cagey, oh yes. He'd put up a new AM in a cave—written on his generator—write to Da'an from the library letting him know it was there, and if Da'an wanted to contact him, well, let the Taelon script a message on. Tarek would find it.

He'd about finished designing the AM when he realized how late it was. His brothers had already eaten breakfast and raced outside yelling like usual when Tarek woke up.

He was just starting downstairs when he heard voices from the kitchen. Mom and Dad alone.

"So shall I turn on the Taelon thing? It's almost noon back there. Isn't it supposed to start at noon?"

And his dad: "The hell with it."

His mother's laugh. "It concerns you, though, doesn't it?"

Whoa. Time to listen in.

Tarek eased his butt down onto the stair and leaned forward. Any farther, and the stairs—off-kilter since the last quake—would creak, giving him away.

"Does it?" Dad snapped back, in his now-hear-this voice.

Mom sighed. "Look, dear. It's you who said that this offer down at the new Volunteer Training Center is twice what you've been making. Plenty of perks. I thought you wanted it, despite the long commute to Newport."

"Yeah. Hold my nose and take their money. But that was until I talked with Lassiter. I changed my mind. The whole thing stinks."

"What? A spread-spectrum youth program? Scholarships? We'd have more kids in college than ever before. I just wonder if the universities will have time to gear up for the influx," Mom said.

This was beginning to sound boring, and Tarek almost got up to retreat when Dad said, "But it's not checkups they want us for. It's prepping."

Silence.

Mom. "You sure?"

Dad must have nodded, because she said, "Prepping for what?"

"Well, that's what we can't find out. Most think it's just catch-up on vaccines, blood tests, and the like, but I don't know. I don't know. I don't like the sound of that. Why not be up front? Sure, those of us at the outer office are to do routine screening, but the facility is set up with more lab space than we'd use for that. And Lassiter said that Doris told him they're bringing in their own doctors to run those labs."

"Labs?"

"Yeah. Labs."

Silence again.

Then Mom said, "So, what? You're not taking it? Staying at the clinic, at half the pay, with all the politics?"

"Yes." Dad was doing the or-else tone now. "Yes, I am. Taelons' money might be like everyone else's, but their motives aren't. They just aren't. Bottom line is, they're aliens, and we still don't really know what they want with us, do we?"

Good question, Dad. *Labs!* Tarek got up and soft-footed back to his room.

He shut his door and looked at his system. Didn't wipe the AM. No, too much work went into that. So he sat down and turned on the TV.

All over the country a lot of people turned on their televisions. More, perhaps, than might have. What was going on? Something was going on. That strange search for the schoolteacher, who later showed up on the kids' sites. All this rumor about high school grads and free rides through college, Taelon style. What exactly did "Taelon style" mean?

Taelon style was certainly in evidence as Zo'or's scoutcraft arced in gently over Yale campus, founded in 1701 when the only aliens known to the founders were the native peoples they arrogantly, and inaccurately, termed Indians.

Taelon tech was at its best when seen moving, framed by an honor guard of matte-black, slim-line police helos. The scoutcraft set down on the green opposite the Three Churches, and Liam was there to motion his teams into position as Zo'or emerged, tall, silvery-blue, the focus of all eyes.

As he watched Yale's president lead the procession of official grandees forward for the greetings, he rubbed his sore chin and reviewed the morning. He had to admit to a small spurt of sympathy for Frank Tate, who'd woken up with what was obviously a headache and an appallingly dry mouth. Liam at least had clean clothes to put on after the fastest shower and shave of his life, but Frank perforce had to climb back into his grubby duds from the day before; he'd meant to send out his clothes to be cleaned overnight, and how many beers did they down anyway?

Liam only shook his head as they raced for the elevator. At least they managed to get some coffee and egg sandwiches before bolting out of the hotel, through the traffic-clogged streets—it was faster to walk—and to the federal building that housed their command post. They ate while stopped at red lights, arriving to find everyone running around crazily.

Liam had one moment alone with Sandoval; despite the crowd, the sheer force of his personality kept his minions at a discreet distance as he faced Liam, his eyes like red cinders.

"Find anything?" Liam asked, knowing from that grim face what the answer was going to be.

"Do I look like I found anything?"

Liam said, with care, "There might be a way. No—not from me."

"Ah yes. The mysterious Augur. You have dealt with him before."

"Everyone has. It's the nature of his business."

"Where is he?"

"I don't know," Liam said. Truthfully. "But if you lift the security firewalls he'll do what he has to do."

"No."

"The horse is already gone from the barn."

"One horse. I don't want the Resistance in there stealing the rest."

Liam shrugged. "Suit yourself. But you should know this: Rumor says that there is a plan not just for Zo'or's assassination, but for Taelons all over the world."

Sandoval's expression did not alter at all. "And if there were?"

"Either way, the assassins make their hits, or they don't—if those sats are aimed right, they take out your people as well as theirs."

Sandoval's jaw tightened.

"Then world power is up for grabs, eh? Who do you

think will come out on top? Federov, the richest terrorist on Earth?" Liam turned away before Sandoval could answer.

He got himself down to the green, and while he was reviewing his morning's work so far, he watched Joshua Doors emerge behind one of the state senators, which reminded him of Renee.

Where was she?

Renee woke up late, to find Julianne waiting with a ready breakfast and fresh coffee. "I spent the entire morning trying to find your Carlton, my dear. Dead out of luck. Wherever he is, he didn't use his own name."

"I know that," Renee said tiredly. "The only thing I can hope for is that Carlton is going to try to slip through the crowd behind Phelps Gate. There'll be a million people there. We'll have to trust Liam's and Sandoval's troops to get him, if mine don't. Though to tell you the absolute truth, I don't give a damn if they shoot Zo'or to kingdom come."

"Neither do I," Julianne said, laughing. "I take it you feel better?"

"Lean and mean," Renee said wryly, tucking in to the breakfast.

After that, Julianne went out to do some scouting on her own, and Renee retreated up to her room to the shower.

She was just getting into her most damn-your-eyes power suit when a soft rustling sound caused her to turn around. Silence. Finished buttoning her tailored shirt—and heard it again.

Someone scratching at the door!

She went to her purse, unclipped a slim but quite lethal energy weapon, then stood at the wall, not behind the door. Opened the door a crack—to see a tiny Hispanic woman waiting outside.

"Miss Palmer, I have to talk to you. It's about Carlton," the woman said.

Instinct? Go with it. Renee held the door open. "And you are . . . ?"

"Marina Aguilara." Marina looked relieved when the door was safely shut. "You were asking about Neville at the campus yesterday."

"So I was."

Marina sat down on the edge of the bed, looking very tired indeed, as if she'd been up all night.

"Here, kid, have some java," Renee said, pointing to the covered carafe she'd brought from Julianne's room.

Marina poured it into a mug—her hands shook—and Renee said, "I'll make some more. This hotel room stuff may not be designer, but it'll do the job."

"Thank you." Marina drank, then held the mug in both hands. "I am—was—a member of Neville Carlton's group. Make no mistake. I hate the Taelons, more than anything in the world."

"Oh, so do I," Renee said, with all the force of repeated betrayals. Brother. Roommate. Her own health, for a frightening time.

Marina's expression eased a little, from grim to earnest. "I don't like what Neville is forcing Scooby to do. That's the problem, he's using force, I think just out of spite. Because Scoob's teacher friend turned him down flat and almost got some of his people on her side. All in about five minutes."

"Wait, wait. Who is this Scooby?"

"My friend. Who is supposed to do the actual killing."

"Oh, Lord. This is bad," Renee breathed, sinking down onto the other bed. "This is very bad. Tell me from the beginning, as fast as you can, because Zo'or is already *here*. And the actual unveiling is going to happen in about an hour."

Marina gulped down more coffee and told Renee everything. When she was done, Renee got up and paced back and forth. "Okay. There are clues here. What was that again about cloaks and daggers?"

Marina repeated, scrupulously careful to point out that her memory might not be exact, what Scooby had said during that first phone call.

"A 'cloak-and-dagger tour.' That might be route, right?"

Marina nodded. "Something no one knows about."

"I found out yesterday that there are tunnels directly under the Old Campus, but those are filled with security squads. It can't be—"

What was it she'd seen in those files?

Cloak-and-dagger . . .

She snapped her fingers. "Skull and Bones. Ugh! Why didn't I see that before!"

"What's Skull and Bones?" Marina asked doubtfully.

"It's one of the oldest Old Boy networks in the country—and for ages the most powerful. Oh yes, oh yes, and Sandoval would just hate that, wouldn't he? If he could get a renegade Bonesman to pull a stupid stunt, he could blow them wide open."

Marina smiled a little. "Lost, but still tracking."

"Never mind. We're gonna have to run, because I think I know where our cloak-and-dagger route is, but how to find the door, and the key, is anyone's guess. But first—" She grabbed her global and was about to tab Liam's code when she hesitated. She knew Sandoval had doctored it; was he also monitoring Liam's calls?

Probably, but he couldn't have the time right now to listen unless the call triggered alarms. Thinking rapidly, she hit the code.

Liam came on immediately, sky in the background. He was on the green, then. "Renee Palmer here," she said formally. "Listen, there's a woman demanding escort, instead of the CEO we'd expected."

"I got the same message, but I don't have enough personnel for escort duty," Liam said. "You'll have to send a Doors driver." And a window bloomed in the corner, showing the corner of Yale and Broadway. Within that a tiny marker blinked. Liam had already signed off; she touched the marker, which evolved into an animated drawing of a blue scarf floating down. It winked out as she watched it.

"Scooby is at Yale and Broadway," Renee said as she tabbed her global again. Then she frowned. "Julianne? Are you there? I hope you check your messages: We got our proof. This plot's worldwide—" She gave a brief rundown on Neville's plan, then smacked her global shut.

"Let's go." Renee grabbed her purse, threw in her weapon and global while Marina gulped down the last of her coffee.

The two women dashed for the elevator.

FORTY-SIX

Neville Carlton caught hold of Scooby's hands, looking from one to the other. He'd admonished her gently about the nail-biting, but it was clear from the inflamed fingertips and ragged, bloodstained cuticles that she'd been doing it anyway, probably sitting alone in the dark.

She hung her head, looking like a guilty schoolgirl.

It's my fault, Neville thought. She should have been at my house, cheering us on TV, as I'd planned all along, and Marina ought to be here with her cool brain and her fiery hatred of the Taelons.

But Marina wasn't. Scooby was here, and the damn holier-than-thou teacher who'd tried to make a fool of him was probably sitting in some Taelon prison with a tube in her brain and would never even know what was about to happen. Well, live and learn.

"My dear Scooby," Neville said, smiling at her. "It's time. We both have to take our places, in order to make history and free America."

"Okay," she whispered. Her eyes puddled, and she dashed her cheek against her shoulder. "Sorry. I know I'm being a baby."

"You're being normal. You're here because you're loyal,

and because you're an ordinary citizen, not a warrior. The time has come for ordinary people to rise, just as they did in 1776."

She nodded, a jerky, almost convulsive movement.

"I want you to take Dr. Templeton's pills."

"No drugs." She looked up quickly.

"They're not *drug* drugs. Not like the crap sold on streets. Remember, Dr. Templeton is a doctor, my dear. What he gave me is a simple medical prescription. Nothing harmful or addictive. It just eases that part of your brain that sends worry into overdrive."

"I don't want to turn into a zombie."

"You're almost a zombie now," he said with mild rebuke, but easing it with a kiss on her palms. "From terror. Needless terror."

If I'm to kill someone, I have to know the cost, she thought, but she couldn't say those words aloud. Just stared at him helplessly while he smiled down into her eyes and stroked her hands and face, and at last she gave in, because otherwise she was afraid she'd throw up, or faint, and someone would find her right there on the street, with that pistol thing in her pocket.

Neville watched her swallow the tabs. He made her drink the entire glass of water, ostensibly to make it easier on her stomach, but he was hoping they'd dissolve faster. Get into her bloodstream, stop that rabbit-in-the-headlights look of terror.

They worked. At least her breathing eased, and some of the strain left her face, strain that he'd gotten so used to, she'd begun to age before his eyes and he hadn't realized it. Now she looked like herself, a kid, again. A stab of remorse lanced through his mind, which he banished. All right, so it was a mistake. But she'd soon be dead and beyond pain.

"Come on," he said finally, fighting to conceal his impatience. "It's twelve-thirty. We want that extra margin of ten minutes, right?"

She nodded, wiped her hands down the sides of the

pretty new slacks that Neville had bought for her, and slid the weapon inside the deep pocket of her new linen jacket. The H&K was a heavy weapon, so she jammed her fist into the other pocket to balance it.

"Ready?"

"Hold my hand?" she pleaded.

"Right until we have to part," he promised.

And hand in hand they went down to the Omni lobby, looking like a pair of young lovers, as Neville had intended. How many Volunteers did they pass, professionals who didn't give them a second glance? Every one of them caused him to gloat inside. Damn, he was good.

Hand in hand they walked out and up Temple to Chapel. It was tough getting past the crowds heading toward the Vanderbilt entrance to the Old Campus, but not as thick as those visible on the green, surrounding the Taelon, who was apparently just heading west toward Phelps.

"We'd better pick up our pace," he murmured.

Scooby obediently walked faster, following in his wake as he threaded through the knots of tourists. And at the corner of High Street he kissed her a last time, then said, "I'll be watching you," and smiled.

She gave him a pathetic smile, straightened her shoulders, then crossed High. He watched her until she was swallowed by the crowd milling about under the Fine Arts archway.

Then he joined the throngs shuffling toward Vanderbilt, and inside, past the weapons scanners. He smiled, held out his hands, was waved on through. Incompetent scanners, just as he'd counted on. Where did they get them, from airport discards? Proof—as if he'd needed it—that Companion Services was peopled by idiots.

He was already fetching parts from his various pockets and fitting them together as he followed the crowd inside past Connecticut Hall toward Nathan Hale on his pedestal. It was by Nathan that Neville had decided to take up his post. Within the shadow of a national hero, before the philosophy studies classrooms—Nathan Hale's old dorm—was where he'd watch history being made.

"There," Renee said, feeling desperate. "That is the bluest scarf I ever saw."

Marina looked and then again shook her head. "But that's not Scooby. Too short, and too old."

Renee could scream. She could *feel* the seconds ticking away. By now Zo'or had to be inside the campus, being taken from room to room, for a tour that was to last exactly half an hour. Half an hour, and they still hadn't found this benighted girl.

The woman in the blue scarf was seated in a booth drinking a latte and reading something literary. She didn't look like someone about to commit a murder. Renee sighed and was going to turn away when the woman looked up, then her lips parted.

Renee stared. Did she know this woman? No. Yes. No?

"Renee?"

Marina stared, looking ready to fight or flee. Fight, probably, from the jut of her jaw.

"Renee?" the woman said again and smiled. "We have a couple mutual friends."

"Oh, my God," Renee breathed. And to Marina, in her softest whisper, "It's Cecilia Robin. Isn't it?"

Marina stared, her eyes narrowed. "I'm not sure. She seems familiar. But the glasses are different, and she's skinnier than I remembered. And her hair is all hidden."

"Well, let's see. She certainly knows who I am."

This conversation took place in the fastest of whispers, then Renee and Marina looked around guiltily at the other patrons (who ignored them) and dropped down across from Cecilia as if drawn by magnets.

Cecilia leaned forward. "I'm Cece. Liam said that you'd take me to Scooby."

Renee rubbed her forehead, trying to get this sidestep

into perspective. "Come on," she said. "We're going to have to run."

Liam watched Zo'or vanish inside Phelps Gate and turn left for the beginning of the official tour. At least Zo'or's company manners were acceptable, he thought.

He felt a presence at his side and turned his head. Instead of Tate, there was Ronald Sandoval.

In the sunlight, Sandoval's pallor and the marks under his eyes were shocking. He's running close to the edge, Liam thought. Don't push him.

Yet.

"Half an hour," Liam said.

Sandoval's lip curled. "Everything is proceeding according to plan."

So Carlton must be in place. And Scooby?

"What about the sats?"

"That is . . . still pending." Sandoval spoke with obvious reluctance. Then he recovered fast. "But we do not gain our positions of command without developing a sense of timing."

"Or a sense of how good your team is," Liam said. "I know mine can do the job. Can yours?"

"Do your job, Major." Sandoval walked away, subvocalizing into his pin mike.

Liam motioned for his inner perimeter team to sweep and move, and the outer team closed in smoothly behind.

Time to get to Old Campus.

Luckily the three women had only a very short block to run, poor Cece struggling silently to keep up with the other two.

"Look," Renee said, pointing down High Street from the corner of Elm. "The guards are funneling everyone away from the art buildings now. Skull and Bones is right next to the art gallery."

"Is there a back way?" Marina asked as she looked around.

A sentry stood on the opposite corner. He wasn't watching them—yet.

"Either of you have a camera?" Renee asked.

"I do," Marina said, surprising the other two.

"Start flashing it around. Here, Cecilia, you take this and make like a journalist. Keep your head down." She handed Cece her palm.

They started walking south on High, Marina aiming her digital camera around without actually shooting anything. Before they made it fifty feet a Volunteer came out from somewhere, and while the one on the corner watched, she approached with firm and deliberate step.

"Excuse me," she said. "This area is out of bounds for tourists. Just for another hour."

"I'm Renee Palmer, executive at Doors International," Renee said, showing her ID. "You can check with my security team, if you like. They're working directly under Liam Kincaid, Companion Protector and CIC."

The Volunteer hesitated.

"All we're doing is some background on the college for an interview," Renee said. "Go ahead, clear it with Major Kincaid."

The Volunteer spoke into her pin mike. Her gaze went abstract, then she raised a hand, and the sentry on the corner fell back a step. "You've got the go-ahead," she said. "But Major Kincaid said I was to tell you fifteen minutes tops."

"We'll try to be out in ten," Renee said, smiling. "Thank you!"

The Volunteer nodded, gaze sliding past Cece, who busily tapped away at the palm pilot with the stylus. She walked away, and the three started down High Street, just as the Harkness Tower carillon began pealing the half hour.

"How did you do that?" Renee looked over at the teacher. "*I* almost didn't notice you, and the guard never glanced. Good acting, or experience?"

"Acting," Cecilia said, pushing her glasses up on her nose. Renee recognized the same exact gesture from Superteacher's antics on the Net and was charmed. "Augur taught me. He said that the expected isn't noticed."

Augur. The faint, slightly self-conscious pronunciation caused Renee to think in amazement, If I didn't know better, I'd swear he told this woman his real name.

But no one spoke as they made their way rapidly down the empty street, slowing when they drew near the decorative late-Victorian Jonathan Edwards College. The next building was a stone structure, mostly square. But it had no windows, nor did it have a sign.

"This is it," Renee said. "Has to be."

They stood there, staring in dismay at the door—was that steel? iron?—that was so obviously locked.

"Somehow I don't think knocking is going to bring a butler to invite us in," Renee drawled.

"I'll try it." Marina's clipped tones reminded them that time was passing fast.

"I'll look this way, and you that," Renee said to Cece, pointing.

Cece eased around the south side of the building, saw only stone. She kept glancing back at the two guards at the archway just beyond the next building, but they were facing outward, toward the adjacent street.

She slipped around to the front again, to find Renee beckoning.

Marina joined them. "Nothing. Everything locked tight."

"There's no way into the crypt itself," Renee said, "but there seems to be a tower that belongs to it." She pointed down the north side. Marina and Cece looked, puzzled; the only signs indicated some sort of sculpture garden.

"This way," Renee said, beckoning.

They walked down the stone pathway, looking up at two round towers that appeared to be joined to one building, and adjacent to the Skull and Bones crypt. A high fence connected the towers to the Bones building, surmounted by barbed wire.

But below, the door in the wall stood slightly ajar.

"The question is, is this the sculpture garden or Bones territory?" Renee asked, hands on hips.

"We have to find out. Fast," Marina said.

"Then in we go," Cece muttered, bracing herself as she eased the door open. Somewhere in there poor Scooby waited, probably all alone.

They slipped in. No one was around. The flagged pathway was mossy; it led down the back of the Bones crypt on one side, and a stone wall framed the other. To their right was an arched doorway leading into the nearest tower.

"Up here, I think," Renee said, reaching into her handbag and closing her fingers on her weapon.

They circled up the stone steps, around and around, until they came out onto a landing that gave onto what appeared to be a private garden. Grass, flowers along more stone fencing, and at the other end a stone bench all marked a peaceful scene.

"This must be the art garden after all," Marina said, sighing. "Come on—"

"Oh, no it's not," Cece exclaimed in a low voice, pointing behind them. In silence they looked at the huge stone fresco of two skeletal figures facing one another. It extended up the wall between the two towers. At the feet of the skeletons was a stone baptismal font.

"Is that supposed to be scary?" Marina asked, head tipped.

"It's common nineteenth-century secret society stuff," Cece said, smiling. "You know, religious symbolism mixed with occult or death symbols."

"Is it supposed to impress? I'm not impressed," Marina declared.

"I think the denizens would be more angry that Cece called it 'common,' " Renee observed with an ironic smile.

"Well, this is definitely Bones territory. Come on, we've got maybe eight minutes left."

They ran back inside and raced up the stone steps to the next level, around and around, until they came out on another landing. The dirty windows at the left would have looked out over the garden if they had not been blanked with some sort of paint. At their feet the stone flooring was adrift with ashes and a few feathers from what had to be bird nests from higher up in the tower, which was open to the sky.

The room between the two towers appeared bare except for the ashes. They stared into the space beyond, which was set into the second tower, the only furnishings a wooden table and a chair. On the table sat a half-burned white candle. Puzzled, wary, the three women proceeded inside and looked around. Marina smothered a giggle when she saw the brown and red paint splashes on the curved walls.

"Is that supposed to be blood?"

"Oh, it probably looks real enough at night, candlelit, to a lot of imaginative twenty-year-olds," Cece said, trying to keep her voice from trembling.

"A lot of powerful men have come through here, fiddling with candles and paint stains and ashes and all the rest," Renee observed, looking around. "Still powerful and still secret. How Sandoval would just hate it all!"

"That would explain Liam's hypothesis about him having some kind of internal wire," Cece murmured, looking around.

The other two stared at her.

"So Neville has been set up, is that what you are saying?" Marina asked, her face blanching.

"From the gitgo, as my friend Tracy May would say," Renee answered. "It's *just* like Sandoval. And it means that everyone with your Neville has also been set up."

Marina looked grim. "Then Scooby will get killed!"

"Not if we act *now*." Cece sighed, her insides cramping

with fear and anxiety. "But it does seem to be a dead end, doesn't it? Maybe we have to go out again and search the tower below here." She pointed down at her feet, saw her fingers shaking, and quickly put them behind her.

"What's that?" Renee pointed at the wall behind the chair. They stared in silence at a niche, some twelve feet high or so, bricked in.

"No entrance or exit, not with those bricks," Marina declared.

"Oh, no?" Renee edged around the table and stood directly before the niche, examining it with narrowed eyes. "If this place is full of secret society hugger-mugger, then it stands to reason there will be at least one secret passageway."

Marina murmured, "Cloak-and-dagger. That's what Scoob said."

All three crowded in and began pressing, pushing, tapping at the bricks. No one ever did discover who actually activated the mechanism, but suddenly a crack appeared between brick and stone, and when Renee pushed, the brickwork swung inward, a heavy door. Below was blackness.

"Flashlight," she said, reaching into her bag.

"You always carry a flashlight?" Cece asked, intrigued at the unexpected qualities of this elegant woman whom Augur and Liam both obviously admired.

"When I carry this," Renee said, holding up her weapon. "Now, the question is, do we all go, or ought I to retreat and find Liam?"

"I'm going down," Cece said. "This is why I came."

"And I will go to help you. I know Scooby," Marina stated. "And Neville." Her voice went tight.

Renee nodded. "All right, then. Scooby might be intimidated by three, especially if the third is a stranger. I think at this point I can be better employed with delaying tactics, if I have to."

She smiled as reassuringly as she could, thinking, I will

watch, delay if I can, but this I promise: If Sandoval hurts one of you, I am going to kill him myself, and he will look into my eyes before I do it.

Out loud she said only, "Ladies, good luck and goodbye. We are almost out of time."

FORTY-SEVEN

Augur plumped up the cushion and shoved it up higher on the wall, then turned around again. He sat cross-legged on the floor in the dusty, quiet philosophy section of a used-book store, reflecting on how one experienced gratitude for the most unexpected things.

In this case, he was grateful to Liam for being so methodical. It would have been grim indeed had the palm battery run out on him, but no, the green light still glowed above the keyboard, and the little battery icon showed that it was slightly more than half full of charge.

Enough to get him past whatever was going to be happening in the next . . . what, quarter hour? Longer, if there were repercussions.

Or shorter, if he'd underestimated the extent of Sandoval's animosity, or his resources.

Augur frowned down at the screen. In one tiny window a Ping-Pong ball ricocheted back and forth. That icon represented the hasty program he'd cobbled together first thing, mirroring the computer's log-on back-and-forth to sites all over the world. It wouldn't fool a sophisticated search program for long; Sandoval could have someone vectoring in right now, even though the other tiny window reflected Sandoval's cybercommands. Sandoval could easily speak commands to his tech detectives, especially if he suspected that Augur had hacked into his virtual command center.

But Augur was a gambler by nature, so he sat there, programs in readiness, fingers resting lightly on the keypads, whistling Siegfried's Funeral March under his breath. He watched the main window, which showed the Taelons' cerulean blue Web site front page.

Come on, Liam . . .

"Do it."

Liam turned away from the window and stared into Sandoval's angry black eyes. He knew what such a concession would cost—and he knew the likely consequences. Even if Augur did manage to deflect the mystery cracker, Sandoval would not be grateful. He would just get more angry, and as soon as Augur's traces showed anywhere in virtual space, Sandoval would have his unseen computer jockeys exerting every nerve to close in for Sandoval-style retribution.

He tapped on his global, which bleeped as a squirt went out. Not E-mail. It was an update to the Taelon site. Mentally he saw his signal appear, a brief starfall; he thought, I hope you were watching, Augur. Physically he turned back to the window, which was set in Phelps's second floor, overlooking the festivities below.

He could see Zo'or standing there on the podium adjacent to the statue. Saw all his own security personnel in place, and Renee's, and Sandoval's. What he couldn't see was where the key people were hidden.

The rustle and murmur of the crowd increased slightly, but it was not loud, certainly not loud enough to drown out the sweet sound of the Harkness carillon, now working its way through "The Battle Hymn of the Republic."

He sent his thoughts out.

Cecilia? Renee?

He wished they could hear.

. . .

But of course they couldn't. Even if they had developed a sudden psychic affinity, they would have been far too busy to use it. Renee was at that moment trying to make her way through the tightly packed crowd that backed right up into the greensward between Dwight Chapel and the Lanman Wright building, alternately using charm and her ID as warranted.

Cece and Marina chased Renee's slender flash beam down the tunnel that cut under High Street, skirted the English building and McClellan Hall. The tunnel was dark and dank, but it was not full of spiderwebs or dripping moss; both women realized that this tunnel saw traffic at least occasionally.

Ahead of them, Scooby walked like an automaton, for no one had seen fit to give her a flashlight. The men who had shown her this route before had always had their own lights, the first time with a lantern, the second with a flash. Did they all think the other would give me a light, she thought as she felt her way along the walls, the heavy weapon in her pocket whapping against her side at every other step.

Don't be scared, was her other thought, until she realized she wasn't scared. It was kind of funny, really. She'd had to creep down the spiral stairs in the second tower like a gnome, but after that she remembered the tunnel, which was straight enough, and just walked along cautiously, running one hand along the wall.

It was the silence that was so odd, she thought. That and the fact that she couldn't see how far ahead she had to go, or how far she'd come. It was kind of like walking into eternity, wasn't it? As the Taelon soon would. Yes, that was appropriate. That was right. She could hardly wait to tell Neville about her thought. Wouldn't he be impressed? Wouldn't he think she was wise? Was it wise?

Her mind ran on, far outspeeding her careful steps, for

she knew that eventually she would encounter the stair that led up to the basement at Connecticut Hall. Ran and ran, but funny, wasn't it, she really didn't have any *feelings* anymore. Kind of a relief, come to think of it, only would she not be happy when it was over?

When at last she encountered the stairs, she thought, This is it. And—weird—her knees buckled, and she sat down there in the dark, listening to her heart's frantic syncopation.

And there she sat, suddenly unable to think at all, though voices called in her head. Oh, God, was she going crazy? Only she didn't feel bad about that either, because didn't only crazy people shoot—no. No. Remember the Revolution.

"Scooby? Scooby?"

It was a voice! A real one!

"Scooby?"

It was Marina! Why was she here? Oh, no, did Neville not trust her after all?

"Karen?"

"Miss Robin," Scooby whispered, dismay overcoming even the cotton batting of Templeton's prescription courage. Scooby was going to shoot someone! What would Miss Robin think?

"I have to do it," she moaned and got to her feet and forced herself up the stairs.

"I heard her," Marina declared. "Wasn't that her? Scooby! Wait!"

"She's got to be terrified," Cece panted.

"Or drugged," Marina added grimly, as they bustled down the laundry room. And, in a few terse words, she told Cece what Scooby had said on that first conversation.

Cece thought hard and fast. "Let's let her see us first."

Marina gave a nod, and together the two raced up the last fifty yards of the tunnel, to the stairway. Up those, and through—

Cece fell over a box, and Marina almost fell over her.

The weak yellow light seemed unnaturally bright after the pencil beam of Renee's flash.

"What? Where are we?" Cece sat up, glasses askew.

"Storeroom. Come on."

Marina led the way past old bedding, trunks, and lumber. Through the next door, to find themselves in a long room lined with washers and dryers.

And, at the other end, a brown-haired figure, looking like a ghost, was just vanishing through a door.

"Scooby!" Marina screamed.

FORTY-EIGHT

From the window in Phelps Hall, Liam watched as a young woman in cream-colored linen, with flying streams of brown hair, propelled herself from the front door of Connecticut Hall, then stumbled to a stop.

A moment later, just three feet away from where Liam was standing, Sandoval clapped his hands to his ears and backed up a couple steps, wincing. Liam whirled around, saw the earphoned staff members blinking, and one laughing.

"Wagner?" She rubbed her jaw. "What's that supposed to mean?"

Liam leaned over and tabbed one's computer to speaker mode, and the room filled with the sound of Siegfried's Funeral March.

From outside the open window came Zo'or's voice; the human speeches were over, and at last it was his turn. The blend of Gothic grief and Zo'or's slightly metallic voice proclaiming, "Let this gift symbolize peace," whipsawed through Liam's consciousness, making the universe, for the space of a heartbeat, seem unreal.

"What's it *mean*?" someone demanded in a plaintive voice.

"Turn it off!"

"It's Kincaid's—it's the contract cracker he hired," Sandoval snapped. "Who wouldn't be necessary if you weren't incompetent." Silence. "Vector on him."

He turned on Liam then, as if daring him to speak. To move.

No one spoke. Each tech busied himself or herself at a keyboard, and for the space of two or three seconds the only sound was the ticking of keys, until the faint sizzle of air, the rush of incipient sound made them look up again. A purple torus forced its way into space and time, causing Sandoval to step swiftly backward.

As everyone stared in amazement, a portable portal appeared, and Da'an stepped through. "I require your presence on a matter concerning Taelon safety," the Taelon said to Liam.

"But I—" Liam fought his protest into silence. He had to protect Augur! That was the promise!

"Now," Da'an said with gentle command, as behind, Sandoval watched.

The portal hummed behind the Taelon. Liam sighed, thrust his global into his pocket, and followed Da'an through.

The portal snapped off, leaving the smell of electrified air. They faced one another, alone in the embassy.

"Da'an. I don't often ask for favors," Liam said, driven to desperation. "I have to return."

"I shall go in your stead," Da'an murmured, silvery-blue eyes utterly unreadable. "And when you are finished, you may return. The coordinates are programmed in, under the Taelon glyph for renewal."

"Why now? Why me?" Liam demanded, not even trying to hide his antagonism. "I just hope it will save as many lives as my absence in New Haven is likely to lose."

"I shall go to New Haven in your stead," Da'an stated, indicating the embassy portal. "Your friend Augur has successfully taken control back of the military satellites, which has temporarily defeated . . . our adversary. It is for you to see that our adversary's work is terminated."

Liam stared at the Taelon, whose hands floated through the gestures for sublime awareness and the anticipation of eternity.

"You knew," he said, voice raw. "You knew all along who it was."

"Not all along. Only since we established that it was stolen Taelon technology that was the medium for the intrusions."

Thought moved again, rapid—desperately rapid—through Liam's mind.

"It *was* a Jaridian!" Liam felt tension grip the back of his neck.

"It is," Da'an corrected. "And you know I cannot be in his presence. It is a physical impossibility. Make haste." The last two words were uttered as a request, and then Da'an stepped through the embassy portal.

Da'an reappeared in the portal set up temporarily for the visiting Taelons and for the Companion Service, in an office off the Phelps Gate. For a short time nobody noticed Da'an's presence, for their attention was all on Zo'or outside.

"Many misunderstandings have arisen between our species, engendering regret. Distrust."

Silence had fallen over the listeners, for here was the most powerful Taelon of them all, so rarely seen by humans.

Even Scooby stumbled to a stop, there on the grass just before Connecticut Hall, while inside Cece and Marina spent precious seconds getting lost in a building they had never been inside before. While they opened and shut doors, trying to find Scooby, Scooby herself listened to the amplified voice and blinked in the blinding sunlight, so painful after the tunnel's dark. Her eyes teared, making

Zo'or into a blue-silver smear. But she could hear that voice, talking about distrust.

"I regret it as strongly as do you, this distrust, this misunderstanding. And so I am here today, on a mission of peace."

False peace. Wasn't it? It's not peace when those in power force you to obey through threat, is it? All the terrible vids of what Taelons had done . . .

"The statue is a gift, a symbol for the Synod's intention to eradicate misunderstanding."

"Here! This is the front door," Marina yelled.

Cece felt her glasses slipping down her sweaty nose and jammed them up, leaving a smear across the lenses. Her clothes were damp with sweat now, her legs rubbery as she fumbled through the door after Marina.

"There she is!"

"Scooby!"

"Just as you humans believe that the key to eradicating ignorance is education, so do we Taelons believe."

"Oh, no!" Marina breathed.

Unseen by anyone as yet but the two women, and Sandoval in the Phelps window—which he would not share with anyone else—and Neville Carlton, who watched from just yards away, Scooby raised her weapon with shaking hands.

Neville smiled.

Sandoval smiled, relieved that Da'an had so handily appeared and saved him the task of getting rid of Kincaid.

"Education—"

"KAREN!" That was Cece.

Scooby's entire body jerked. She looked around wildly, then forced her attention back to Zo'or, once more raising the weapon.

"She's got a gun!" someone screamed, and people nearby backed into others, tried to escape, or dropped down flat on the grass, leaving a wide swath between Scooby and the dais on which the officials stood with Zo'or.

"Hell! That kid's waving around a forty-five," Liam's handpicked Companion Protector said, squinting.

"What is a 'forty-five'?" asked a lady on the podium.

"It's an H&K UPS45 Tactical Pistol," the Protector said, gaze on the girl. "It means a blind man can hit a target, as long as he keeps finger on the trigger. I suggest you all take cover."

And he stepped to Zo'or's side.

"Keep your distance, human," Zo'or ordered.

The Protector said into his pin mike, "Kincaid?" And on hearing no answer, looked up at the second-story Phelps window, where only Sandoval was visible.

"Down! Down!" the woman on the dais screamed, throwing herself to the floor, and panic vectored out through people in waves.

Perimeter security people began closing in, finding their way blocked by panicky people. Others looked up to Sandoval for orders, but he stood unmoving in the window as the seconds ticked by.

Carlton, seeing an efficient armed pair coming up from Vanderbilt, said in a sharp voice, "She's shot someone! Over there!"

He pointed behind him. People around him reacted in terror, sending more shockwaves through the crowd; bodies shoved this way and that, all trying to force themselves to a path of safety, causing a trampling jam-up. Within three heartbeats the mob effectively hemmed in the two guards. Carlton watched, there in Nathan Hale's shadow, laughing inside.

At key points all around the square, journalists swung cameras away from Zo'or toward the girl standing there, alone on the trampled grass, weapon held tightly in a trembling two-hand grip.

Cece didn't see any of that. Her eyes, her whole attention, were focused on the white-faced young woman before her.

"Karen. Darling Karen, my favorite Karen. Scooby," she said in a low, soothing voice, advancing slowly.

"Stay back, Miss Robin," Scooby cried, jerking around to look.

The weapon jerked as well, her fingers tightened convulsively—and a spray of bullets zapped above the heads of the crowd, glancing off the side of Phelps just below Sandoval. The sound echoed as the rest of the crowd dropped flat, like scythed grass.

Guards, given a clear field, raised weapons, waited for the order to fire, or for the girl to fire again—

Except what was that? That short woman in the dirty scarf, she was right in their own line of fire!

"No, Scooby," Cece said, trying for calm, though her voice shook as she circled slowly around the terrified young woman. "I know you won't hurt me. I know it because I trust you, I have always trusted you. Bright spirit, kind heart, best of all my children, I trust you never to hurt me."

Scooby's mouth worked, but otherwise she stood, weapon still gripped in two hands. "I have to do it," she whispered, in agony.

"No. You have to do nothing but live," Cece said. "Anything else is choice. Begin with faith." And she stopped, taking up a stance directly in the line of fire between Scooby and the dais, on which everyone but Zo'or had crouched down.

"Please put the weapon down," Cece said, hands open.

"I can't. I can't," Scooby cried, tears now making a bright ribbon down her blanched cheeks. Her eyes were stark with fear. "I promised N—I promised. Someone who loves me."

"I love you," Cece said, stretching out her hands. "And I am here by your side to show you that I love you. If anyone else loves you as much as I do, where is that person? Not by your side."

"Damn it to hell," Sandoval snarled under his breath, as the journalists' vids clearly picked up the voices and broadcast them all over the world.

"That's Miss Robin," Jamal said, and his parents were

silent. Upstairs, Tarek brooded, thinking, How close I came. Geez.

"Let's talk about peace," Cece said.

From across the courtyard, Renee Palmer spoke urgently into her global to her team leader: "Surround them. Get in between them and Sandoval's people. We don't want an accident."

"Close in," said Tate, on the command channel. "Sandoval?"

Sandoval did not answer. His eyes flicked from Zo'or, who stood alone on the dais, to the girl, and then back again as another Taelon emerged from directly below, through the archway. Da'an! Where did *he* come from?

"The peace guaranteed by the Constitution," Cece said. "You remember, that we all agree to follow the same laws."

"But the Taelons don't. They *kill* people. I have to stop them!"

"By more killing?" Cece asked.

And in London, Neville's lieutenant Che watched on a wrist vid, muttering, "What the hell?"

In Bombay, Liana, also watching on her wrist vid, fingered the weapon in her pocket as she stood outside the embassy there, and thought, Scooby? What are *you* doing in New Haven?

In Rio and Tokyo and Johannesburg and Moscow, Neville's handpicked team all saw what was going on and eased back into crowds, waiting. Watching, not knowing that they too were being watched, and not just by Sandoval's coverts.

"They are evil," Scooby cried, the desperate cry of someone whose will fights against her spirit.

"Do you then judge for us all?" Cece replied. "On whose authority?"

Scooby gulped on a sob. "Miss Robin, I thought you'd believe in me."

"I do, child. I do. With all my heart. I believe you will do right. And now that means to listen. Did that Taelon over there say anything about war, or killing?" She pointed back toward Zo'or. "Is it possible that today was meant to begin a time of trust?"

Scooby shook her head, crying openly now. "I—I don't know."

Beside the silent Zo'or, the Protector said again, "Kincaid?" and looked up to Sandoval for clues, for Major Kincaid's orders had been specific: No violence initiated by us.

"Then why not listen? If we want them to show us good faith, well, someone has to begin, so why not you and I?"

Slowly—just a millimeter, two—Scooby's hands began to come down.

Sandoval's fist struck the windowsill. He tabbed the channel used by the Protectors. "Take her d—"

A hand appeared, reaching past Sandoval's ear and pressed over his pin mike, then twisted the fragile wire. "I suggest not."

He snapped around, glaring at the handsome older woman who stood there, arms now folded. "Who the *hell* are you?"

"I," she said, "am Doctor Julianne Belman. You might remember me working with the Taelons during that plague a couple years back? Investigating Dr. Whitfield's death, when we first opened the portals? As a result, the American Medical Association recently made me liaison officer in your new education program." She smiled, a shark smile, as she flicked the ID clipped onto her linen jacket. "To give official advice. And I am advising you not to raise a weapon on that child, because nothing has happened yet, has it? And wouldn't our side look really, *really* bad shooting down a kid in cold blood?"

Outside the weapon in Scooby's hands shook so hard that Cece lifted it from her hands.

And Zo'or, ever the master manipulator, met Da'an's gaze. Challenge met, answered; on another plane, Taelons listened to the unvoiced struggle between these two.

Zo'or said, knowing that everyone could hear, "You shall begin our era of peace. And education. Please come join me." Held out a hand in a gesture of peace.

Cece sighed, looked around for cues, but the people who were just getting up from prone positions were all too angry, or puzzled, or terrified, or curious, to offer her any advice.

So she took Scooby's trembling arm, and they paced the last few yards to the dais and clambered up beside the Taelon.

"Here, I'll take care of that," a kindly voice murmured in her ear.

Cece was scarcely aware of the Companion Protector removing the weapon from her hand, engaging the safety. Her arms stretched around Scooby, who wept silently into her shoulder, but she did not have attention yet for Scooby, either. She gazed up at Zo'or, eyes narrowed attentively; veteran of so many administrative and district political grandstands, she suspected that she, too, was about to become part of the Taelon's political grandstand just as surely as she stood here on the physical one.

I hope you like the smell of human sweat, she thought.

FORTY-NINE

The smell of burning smote Liam's nose before he saw the Jaridian standing in a room bare except for a data stream, a high window showing a night sky beyond. No clue to where he was.

"Da'an sent me," he said, feeling his way.

The Jaridian stood there for a long moment, big, rough-hided, eyes glowing with cherry brilliance. He stared at Liam, then wiped the data stream free. Behind Liam the portable portal hummed; his sensitive ears, highly attuned to sound, recognized it as Renee's.

"Yes," the Jaridian replied. Took a step.

Liam felt charged particles in the air, and heat wafted against his face. The heat was from the Jaridian. He's dying, Liam realized.

"I was sent on a sabotage mission, or so I thought," the Jaridian said. "But Vorjak was subtle."

"I will agree to that," Liam said.

A lift of the furrowed chin. "You did know Vorjak, then."

"Yes." Liam gestured. "We . . . spent some time together, on his first mission. And later I saw him again. Before the end."

The Jaridian flexed his great hands. "He died well?"

"The death of a leader."

An intake of breath that sounded like a firestorm beginning.

"Time presses," Liam said. "Why did you try to destroy Augur?"

"That was my original mission. To locate the most powerful random particle . . . you would say—"

"A maverick. I get it. You were to find someone in a position of power between the human and Taelon species, take him out, and see that blame went both ways. Engender more distrust from within."

"So it was," the Jaridian stated, voice like a monster's growl. "Yet what I found was that there were many such random particles. Further, that some of you were not what you seemed."

"Ah." And yet your mission was quite successful, Liam thought.

"You, in particular. But Da'an also. He found me days ago. Yet he never struck against me. Not even when I took the new laser sat codes. I took the portal from Renee Palmer's office. To make myself faster. As I felt my time diminish. I changed my objective, to find out the truth."

"The truth," Liam said, "is mutable."

"No. Truth is immutable. But as yet none of us, of all three races, see it. . . ." The Jaridian threw his head back. Cracks appeared all over him, glowing with furnace heat, and he uttered a primitive cry of agony.

The being was dying yet remained here in the oxygen-rich atmosphere, obviously determined to communicate until the very end.

Liam said, "What can I do?"

"Send me—out there. Vacuum will . . . give me peace."

Liam stepped to the controls, tapping fast. A glimpse out the window showed the stars too sharp and clear, the darkness too black, for any atmosphere: They were somewhere in space. Probably on the space station.

There was plenty of vacuum to choose from. Finished, he stepped back.

"Da'an . . . Da'an is the exception . . . Sent that. In. My." The Jaridian's voice harshened as he fought to speak. "Last . . ."

His body rippled, contracting, and heat seared Liam's face, almost taking off his eyebrows and lashes. His clothing smoked.

The Jaridian plunged through the portal; a blast of heat whooshed inside the room. Liam closed his eyes and felt something deep within him flex. Warded the hammer of energy until it dissipated.

The portal, though, was clearly unstable. Liam assessed the strobe effect running up the arms and hit the Taelon tab that Da'an had indicated. Thrust himself through—and the interdimensional portal collapsed inward, and vanished just after depositing Liam safely in New Haven.

Sandoval whirled around and gazed at Liam, who was limned for a dazzling moment in fire.

The techs watched in a stunned silence, the smell of burning strong.

Sandoval felt a thrill of—could it be fear? No. He said, "Da'an is below."

Liam left.

". . . and now," Augur said, whistling to the music still surging through SecNet. "The Ride of the Valkyries—appropriate, eh?"

He sensed Sandoval's attention splintering, for his last set of commands was still unfinished on the part of the unseen techs.

And so Augur triggered his last program, and another burst of steganography peppered the triumph song of the hero-bearing war women, this one shorting out the new location tech in the globals.

Augur watched the bar widen at the bottom of the screen. Four, three, two, one—it took!

All right, strike now, while *something* is keeping Ronny Boy at bay—

And then the screen vanished, bounced back, jiggling. A cursor demanded Augur's ID. The firewalls were back up. That meant the tech jockeys would be riding his tail in seconds. Augur logged off fast, folded the palm, and leaned his head back, laughing softly to himself.

A good day's work, eh?

But what was going on over there at the Old Yale Campus green?

At that moment, after a benevolent gesture of invitation from Zo'or, Cecilia Robin pushed her glasses up her nose once again and then took firm hold of the silken ropes binding the sailcloth veil.

She tugged. The white canvas slipped free, belling slightly in the wind, and the multitude drew in a deep breath as sunlight kissed blue crystal and threw itself back in brilliant shards of light.

"Ooooh!" A sigh soughed through the crowd.

"Ma'el was the first Taelon here, centuries ago," Zo'or said. "The gift Ma'el gave was knowledge. Wisdom. And Ma'el's last behest was a directive to humans and Taelons to find harmony and understanding between our species. Our gift to you is this replica of Ma'el, as a reminder of our vow to fulfill Ma'el's mandate."

He nodded, made the gesture for universal peace, stepping back.

The Protector turned his head, saw Liam Kincaid emerge from the gate. In relief he too stepped back, deferring to his superior officer. A protest against having received no instructions, there at the crucial moment, formed in the back of his mind, but when he saw the wide blue eyes, smelled the singed clothing, sensed what in a normal human would have been lethal levels of adrenaline, he decided that he didn't need to know why the boss had been off-line. Obviously it hadn't been to down a quick beer.

Da'an studied Liam, to find the appraising pale blue gaze hit with impact palpable in the realm of the mind. A distant whisper murmured through the Synod, but that could wait.

"We need to talk," Liam said in a low voice.

Da'an heard his grim tone, but nodded, gesturing in the mode of one accepting an invitation. "We shall soon be at the embassy again, and in a cooler clime. I am fatigued. So are you."

In other words: Don't say what you will later come to regret.

The delicate balance between the two of them, trust and distrust, loyalty to one another and to their own kind, required a daily—sometimes hourly—mental dance.

Zo'or passed them. "Where is Sandoval? I want that girl arrested."

Da'an murmured, "Major Kincaid will see to it."

Liam nodded. Of course. The action was over: now the time for the cleanup, the reports, the endless repercussions. "This way, ladies," he said to Scooby, who turned in renewed terror to Cece, who sent an inquiring glance to Liam.

He gave her just the smallest hint of a nod, and Cece stated in a loud voice, "It'll be all right, Scooby. You will have a hearing. Remember what I said about the law. You pulled a weapon on someone, which is against the law. But you had reasons, which will be heard. And I will not leave your side until they are."

As she spoke, Liam's people closed in around them,

leading them in one direction, while the Taelons walked toward the gate and the portal there.

Liam fell in behind, after sending one last glance at the statue of Ma'el, gleaming clean and blue in the mellow summer sun.

On the other side of the quadrangle Renee stood as people streamed past, most talking in excitement about what they'd seen, or thought they'd seen. "The teacher had a gun!" "No, she didn't. It was the Taelon who had the gun." "No, didn't you see the kid? She killed a bunch of people over thataway before the teacher came out—"

She sighed, leaning back against the granite wall at the side of Dwight Chapel. Her own weapon was back in her pocket, hidden. Her hands were cramped from the protracted stillness with which she'd kept Sandoval in her sights. If he had issued that order to fire . . .

She straightened up a moment later when she recognized the elegant figure coming toward her with purposeful stride.

"Julianne," she murmured. "Did you get the message?"

"Oh, yes. And so I got a ringside seat, right there with dear Ronald."

"What?"

Julianne rubbed her hands. "Oh, the look on his face when he first saw me is something I shall treasure beyond the grave. How very, very pissed he was! And not a damn thing he could do, either."

"All right. Spill it."

Julianne looked around, but no one paid them any heed; the knots of people were too involved in their own conversations. "Soon as I heard your message I spent the rest of the hour calling in favors. Many people owe me," she added with evident satisfaction. "And so I became, in that hour, the new liaison with Zo'or's 'program.' And, using that, I got hold of every M.D. connected with every training site in the country and told 'em just what that big shipment of supplies that required guards consisted of."

"All Resistance?"

"No. I think some of them even knew damn well what was in those boxes. But threatened with total exposure through the AMA, they expressed a quite proper horror, and a little more pressure took care of the problem in a way that our friends who objected to explosives found acceptable."

Renee laughed in sheer joy. "You mean it's all gone?"

"All of it. Contamination leaks, fire-sprinkler floods, fires— mysterious disasters hit every one, alas, destroying all those supplies, forcing the program into hiatus. And the nasties in charge had to stand by and fume, because they couldn't do a thing. Not and risk investigators swarming around to find out just what had been lost."

"Perfect." Renee laughed again. "Julianne, it's brilliant."

"Ran the charges down in two globals," Julianne finished smugly.

Renee glanced back one more time at the emptying quadrangle and the lovely blue statue, still sending shards of light in every direction. "What about the teacher and the girl? Are they all right?"

"Liam has them in hand. At Da'an's direction," Julianne said. "My guess is, they'll put 'em through enough red tape to appease Zo'or at least officially, and then—" She fluttered her fingers outward.

"And Augur?"

"No one's seen him."

"Which means everything is fine." Renee sighed. "Almost fine. I suppose it's too much to hope that that slimy Neville Carlton got caught."

Julianne shook her head, because of course she couldn't see or hear the crowd on the other side of the quad, over near Nathan Hale, where a disappointed, no a *seriously pissed* Neville Carlton watched helplessly while Scooby and Cecilia Robin were escorted safely behind an alive, and equally safe, Zo'or toward Phelps Gate.

He turned away in disgust—to find himself face to face with Marina Aguilara—with two big, husky Volunteers on either side of her.

"That's the one," she said, pointing a finger right at his nose. "That's the one who gave that girl the gun. His name is Neville Carlton the Fourth," she added in a loud voice, as people gathered around, staring, exclaiming. "And he didn't even have the guts to do it himself!"

The two Volunteers closed in on the loudly protesting Carlton and muscled him away.

A third—undercover Resistance—who stood just behind Marina Aguilara murmured into his pin mike, "Shall I arrest this girl, too?"

"Look the other way," Liam responded.

The Volunteer busily began dispersing the crowd, into which Marina vanished.

On the other side of the campus, Julianne Belman was saying, "I have a magnum of very fine champagne in my room, brought for good luck. Perfectly good champagne, *not* doctored," Julianne added at Renee's wry look. "What say we toast a very long and nasty day?"

"Lead me to it," Renee said.

FIFTY

As the hours stretched into days, and the days weeks, Neville Carlton, sitting alone in his steel cell somewhere far below the ground, had plenty of time to think.

He worked his way from disbelief to outrage, and thence to the amazing, astonishing, terrifying conviction that—for the first time in his life—he couldn't lie or buy his way out of trouble. The family lawyers did not show up, apologetic, with a waiting limo and cash cards and promises of lawsuits to come. Fellow Bonesmen did not arrive either, including E.J. Templeton. No one came, no one at all. Did his group even know where he was? Or had Marina gone back to L.A. and told them a lot of lies?

The only person who spoke to him was Liam Kincaid, Companion Protector to Da'an, as he was pushed into this damn cell. "You can cool your heels here until we assemble the evidence against you," Kincaid had said.

"My lawyer! I demand my rights," Neville had exclaimed.

"You can explain it to Ronald Sandoval," was the chilling reply. "When he has time for you." And then the slam of the door.

Since then he'd been alone here, the bland meals delivered through a dumbwaiter, a television showing only the news that the Taelons wanted you to hear. Sitting there on that thin mattress, in his stale-smelling clothes (at first he refused to put on the green prison garb they shoved through with the food, until he could no longer stand himself), he watched the news smooth over the events at Yale, until within scarcely twenty-four hours it seemed nothing had ever happened outside of Zo'or's successful unveiling of that blue statue and his launching some damn program for college students.

And then nothing but the endless smiling promises of peace and prosperity, Taelon style.

Carlton's shock and fear were slowly giving way to a kind of numb despair when the routine was quite suddenly broken: With his breakfast appeared his street clothes from July Fourth, now clean and pressed. Half an hour later armed Volunteers appeared, and one motioned for him to come out.

The fear came back then, hard. Neville had never been this afraid in his life, as he followed the huge figures into an elevator up to what he knew would be a very bad time, beginning with Ronald Sandoval.

But instead they emerged into a little room, where he saw, to his utter astonishment, a familiar person. Not Sandoval, or even Templeton, but an older woman of Japanese descent—Professor Chie Edo. She was his faculty adviser at UCLA. What was *she* doing here? She signed something, then looked up, unsmiling, her dark eyes cold.

"Come along, Neville," she said. "You've been released."

"Professor Edo!" he began. "What? My lawyers—"

"I have a cab," she cut in.

In silence he followed, out into the sunlight. Oh, how good it was to see sun again! But hard on that joy came the old familiar reactions, outrage foremost.

He contained himself during the short cab ride through streets he did not recognize (where were they, anyway?) until they reached a public portal built into a little park. Professor Edo paid the cab and motioned him out. They stood on the sidewalk.

"You're lucky," she said without any kind of greeting. "Very lucky. That child you apparently suborned refused to implicate you, so there are no charges, except for carrying a concealed weapon. That's the cause of your academic probation. But we all know what you were doing, and there is no excuse whatsoever for doing it through that girl. Tell me, would you have showed the same loyalty to her?"

Neville opened his mouth to speak, but she forestalled him.

"Never mind—I wouldn't believe anything you'd say anyway." She faced him. "We're going back to L.A., where you can speak to the academic—"

"I don't use Taelon tech," he began.

"Suit yourself," the professor said in a cold, flat voice. "Then I'll give you your messages here. You are on academic probation, Mr. Carlton. You may go to the graduate office to find out what that means, but basically it comes to this: You do anything, anything at all, to bring negative attention to the university, and you will be dismissed."

"But I—"

She waved a hand. "Save it. Get back to Los Angeles however you like. You've got the wherewithal. But contemplate this." Her voice lowered, as people streamed around them. "The Taelons have won." Edo's face was bleak. "Get it through your head: They are in control, and there's nothing we can do. So we have to make the best of it, and that means you mind your own business and don't bring their attention onto innocent people." She began to turn away.

"Just a moment, please," Neville began. "Where are we? New Haven?"

"We're in Washington, D.C.," the professor stated. "Oh, speaking of New Haven, don't bother trying to contact your New Haven friend. He's far too busy with his own problems."

"But all Templeton did was register rooms at the hotel. That's not illegal—"

"It's not illegal, but he got the Taelons' attention," Edo stated. "That's all it takes." And, as Neville listened with growing dismay, she said, "They can do what they want, when they want, Neville. Including search and seizure. An investigation of his offices on July Fourth appears to have turned up evidence of insurance fraud, tax fraud, illegal distribution of drugs—you name it. Mr. E. J. Templeton—I leave off the title 'Doctor' advisedly—apparently had a very flexible sense of ethics. And he is going to be in trouble for a long, long time. With human authorites, such as the AMA and the IRS. The Taelons don't even have to bother with him."

She turned her back and joined the line at the portal, leaving him standing there alone, glaring after her, and thinking, Just what you'd expect from sheep. Well, I'll show you leadership. I'll show everyone.

He never spared Scooby or Cecilia a thought. The reverse was not true.

Between July Fourth and that same day Cece's life became an endless series of interrogations, interviews, and painful sessions with poor Scooby, who was at first devastated by the complete lack of any communication attempts by Neville Carlton. Liam Kincaid kept his implied word, and the two were not separated. So they spent their nights in this military hotel-cum-jail who knows where and their days sitting in rooms painted industrial pea-soup green, waiting for this or that official.

The same day that Neville Carlton was released, the officials appeared to lose interest in Scooby. They were shown to a little room with windows, through which they could see a street, traffic, and people—a glimpse of normal life again.

Dr. Julianne Belman appeared, smiling, to say, "You've been released into my custody, Karen. And my prescription for you is a nice long rest before classes at UCLA begin again in September. Or if you want a transfer, that can be arranged as well. You don't have to decide now."

"Oh, thank you," Scooby said, turning to Cece and holding out her arms.

"Stay in contact," Cece said, hugging the thin young woman. "I can't help it—I'll worry about you."

Scooby shrugged and smiled crookedly. "When my folks split up, Mom kept telling me men were after only one thing." She gave Cece a sour smile. "Neville wanted one thing, but not my body. He wanted my fingers on that gun, instead of his. And I was dummy enough to fall for his act, so it's not like it's totally his fault." A tremulous smile. "I'll be okay. Thanks to you. For everything," she added huskily.

They hugged again, and then Julianne and Scooby were gone.

But that door did not open for Cece, not yet. Liam Kincaid came in, looking apologetic. "There's a last interview, I'm afraid, that can't be avoided. And one other. But then you will be able to go."

She'd seen him rarely since the Fourth, but she'd felt the effect of his protective umbrella. "All right," she said, bracing inwardly.

He took her through a portal, down a hall somewhere, then smiled, opened a door, said, "I'll be back when you're done," loud enough for the person inside to hear.

She stepped in and immediately recognized Ronald Sandoval.

FIFTY-ONE

She was vaguely aware that this was not just another pea-green interview room, bare except for desk and chairs and computer. Instead she found herself in a high-tech office, the desk a beautiful teak one that exemplified both wealth and power.

Ronald Sandoval stood at a window—was that *outer space* out there?—with his hands in his pockets. At the sound of Liam's voice he turned around to regard Cece in silence.

She felt vague surprise that he was shorter than she'd expected, and slender, but elegantly built as well as elegantly dressed. The long coat shoved aside by those fine hands probably cost more than she made in a month; his dark, curling hair was beautifully barbered.

Dark eyes met hers with the force of a blow to the heart.

Her mouth went dry. She straightened up, breathing deep. She would *not* speak first.

"Cecilia Robin," Ronald Sandoval said. "I have been reviewing this pile of . . . fiction." He picked up a sheaf of papers, then dropped them onto the desk, his manner expressive of contempt. "You maintain that you crossed the country by yourself, miraculously evading search, unhelped by anyone, unrecognized by everyone."

"I'm sorry you don't believe me," Cece stated. "But then I find it difficult to believe that some mysterious alien shot at me when I tried to be law-abiding and contact the authorities, after Carlton made his offer."

"Nevertheless it is true."

"Yet no one can show me this alien. Or provide me with

proof," she said, knowing from long experience in the faculty trenches that if you went on the warpath, Admin would backpedal in order to deal with your questions and have no time to try to force its politics on you.

"When you attain military clearance levels, say, above B-five," Sandoval stated, "we can resume this portion of our conversation."

So much for staying on the attack.

"And we will meet again," he added. "In case you did not take my meaning. If I, in turn, discover any proof that you were aided and abetted."

"Leaving us nothing to say to one another."

"On the contrary. There is much you could tell me," he retorted, unsmiling. "Much. But—for now—you are under Da'an's protection. It could be that he will discover that data with his own methods, which can be less pleasant than mine. The main point is that you are out of my hands. But not out of my sight."

She drew another breath and managed not to say anything. The door opened again, and Liam said, "Miss Robin? Da'an is expecting you for an interview."

She felt the urge to back out, as courtiers once did to Louis XIV, but forced herself to turn around. Her shoulder blades crawled, but at least she did not have to see that merciless dark gaze anymore.

Liam shut the door. "Really bad?" he asked, with quiet sympathy. "Or only medium bad?"

She tried to smile, hoped it looked competent, without any idea how pathetic were the pensive line of her brow and the tired lines by her mouth.

"This won't be bad, I promise."

Back through the portal, to terra firma. Cece found herself in a building with smooth walls, curving vine-shaped forms, a bluish tone to the cold, fresh air being circulated by a silent system.

"We are in the Washington embassy, Miss Robin," Liam said.

By Liam's formality she knew that they might be overheard, and so she suppressed her questions, thinking, I admire you, and I'm glad you're on the side of the angels, but what is the cost of living a lie among enemies? And you all do it.

Liam led her through into a spacious chamber whose shape and flooring were strange but not displeasingly so. How much of what she saw was unspoken compromise with the ideals of human art? Just as the "skins" the Taelons wore were pleasing to the eye, when they could just as easily have chosen shapes and sizes that terrified or threatened.

Glowing glyphs and images flickered through the air; they painted the face of a Taelon and vanished, like music, into the beyond.

"Do not," Liam murmured almost under his breath, "expect the predictable."

No time to answer, not that she could have thought of one. As Liam and Cece came nearer, Da'an became aware of them and waved away the data stream display.

Liam withdrew to a desk partially shrouded behind what seemed to be willow leaves without the tree trunk, leaving Cece standing alone facing the Taelon and wondering what being interrogated by an alien would really be like. Sandoval had hinted fairly strongly that she could expect nastiness.

Da'an regarded her for a few seconds, saw the braced shoulders, the lifted chin, the hands clasped together in a deceptively meek pose . . . but also the fingers that gripped hard.

Da'an said, "I have read your writings."

Cece whipped up a hand to shove her glasses against her nose, as if she could get Da'an into better focus. "My writings? I wrote nothing down for anyone here," she stated.

"I do not refer to your interviews."

Was that a smile? If so, was it a real smile, or something the alien did with its face to make her think it was smiling?

Then she realized what was meant and felt indignation send heat up her neck into her cheeks. "Oh. Of course.

You must have had your bullyboys snooping all over my house looking for Resistance flyers and contraband weapons after that Jaridian tried to fry me," she said. "Did you like the E-mail letters to my parents about their health problems?"

"I can understand your anger," Da'an replied, smooth, gentle. Non-confrontative. "And I did not read any of the obviously personal missives. I did read that which you wrote for other eyes to read, your Internet postings to educators, administrators, librarians. Parents of school-age young."

Cece drew in a deep breath.

"I read them, and admired them, even when I failed to comprehend. You know that our program is to go forward?"

"Which program?"

"The one I originally designed and presented to the investors. College-bound youth become Volunteers for two years and get four years of college stipend at the study institute of their choice."

"And what happens to the Volunteers?"

"No invasive physical measures, if that is your implication," Da'an responded. "Zo'or and I, you must understand from the outset, have the same goal: the safety of our species. You freely proliferating humans do not even remotely comprehend the . . . spiritual cost, say, of the knowledge that your species will die, and soon, unless you yourself take extraordinary measures. But I do not mean to discourse at length on a topic that can interest you so little."

Cece forced herself to breathe again.

"Time is a relative measure," the soothing voice went on. "We perceive it differently. Zo'or perceives the necessity for control, sometimes without gauging the consequences. I prefer compromise, but that comes only of understanding."

"I will agree with that," Cece said.

"I thought you might. Now, to the matters that concern you. In that spirit of cooperation, I want to use the resources that had been stockpiled against the . . . false start, let us term it . . . so summarily ended."

He doesn't mean the CNI, she thought. Those were destroyed.

"I would like to use the excess funding to further the cause of education. There is a growing movement toward home schooling in this country. My original proposition for you still holds, despite the unfortunate circumstances that prevented our meeting for so long."

"Some sort of television show, that's what rumor said."

"Rumor, for once, is correct. The idea is to form a network for home-schooling families who wish to participate. They would be connected by computer, global, modem—the usual technology, which has nothing to do with us Taelons—and the fulcrum would be you, teaching a class of children, on television. Using your own methods. Teaching what you wish to teach. Furnishing a standard, one might say, that can be refined over time."

"By whom?" Cece asked.

"You. As director. Though you certainly may hire consultants."

"What do you get out of it?"

"I watch," Da'an said, "and learn."

"And what, attempt to shape our children to your own ends? I'm sorry to sound rude," Cece said, "but I have to speak the truth. And to demand it: What would have happened to me, had I stayed at school that day and permitted myself to be taken to your interview?"

"We would have held essentially the same conversation we are holding now."

"Why me? Why so covert? It would have made better sense had you advertised for teachers and held open auditions."

"But how much time would have been wasted sorting through the ineligible? Za'el's mission was to sift records in Southern California districts looking for a certain type of instructor. Southern California because television studio equipment is immediately available there. Besides the obvious qualifications, we wanted someone who was reasonably young but not younger than the parents of the children selected, for that presents problems in your culture. Single, because the job would probably entail many more hours than a family person could give."

Cece stared up into those blue eyes, blue as the sky and about as blank of human emotion. The aspect is benign, she thought, but how real is that?

"And the CVI that was rumored to come with the job?"

"There rumor is wrong. A misunderstanding, I believe in retrospect. I should not have stated my intention of observing the proceedings in order to learn about the human education process. Erroneous assumptions appear to have been made about my methods of observation."

It was so reasonable, so convincing . . . except did the Resistance really misunderstand so swiftly? And why not a teacher from anywhere? Obviously the Taelons could put their portals up without much material effort, if they so chose. A teacher from Alaska could step through a portal in his or her front room and arrive right on the studio lot.

The business about a single teacher, now, was scary. Wouldn't it be much easier to put one of their brain control things into someone without a spouse or children to notice the difference?

There was no clue in that peachy-silver face.

Cece bit her lip. You said you'd speak the truth, she told herself. So do it.

"I guess it comes down to this: I don't trust you. I haven't had cause to trust you. I still see you Taelons holding the power over us and using us for your own ends. I can't make myself a part of it. I just can't."

"Very well," Da'an said. "What do you wish to do?"

"Go home." She didn't believe it would happen, so she said it as a challenge. "Go home and put my life together again."

"Taelons," Da'an murmured, "have never believed in the

'full circle' metaphor for time. Time does not, from our observation, repeat itself. But that is an observation and in no wise any threat from me. Go, then, when you wish. Major Kincaid will see to the logistics."

Da'an nodded once and then waved a hand to reinstate the data stream. Cece looked at the Taelon's back and felt herself forgotten.

It was not true. Da'an's mind had accelerated past Cece into the probable future. Not just hers. Da'an expected to communicate with Cece again, and before too long. No, the future included all those children, specifically the one brilliant mind that had eluded him. Da'an strongly suspected that the unknown youth was also still thinking about the Taelons and what they could offer. . . . So how to provide a stronger lure?

Da'an smiled. Patience and care brought the surest rewards.

Between this youth and Cecilia Robin, surely the Taelons would obtain the key to human potential. . . .

Meanwhile Cece found Liam waiting. He indicated the hallway.

Surprised—amazed—Cece followed. He did not lead her to the portal, though. Instead, they proceeded down the ramp, past embassy staff all busy at their jobs.

No portal here, either. They walked through the front entrance. At once ferocious heat and humidity smacked her in the face like a boiled towel. Liam did not seem to react, so Cece said nothing. Just followed him into a cab, which dropped them a street away from a quiet church. By then her pretty cotton-print dress was damp.

Cece was beyond reaction now, she felt, as they walked inside the cool church, which smelled faintly of incense. She just followed, glad to be out of the punishing summer sun, into an elevator. And then there was a drop. A very, very long drop.

At the end, she felt apprehension for the first time and

sent a questioning look at Liam. She was quite transparent; he smiled reassuringly, and then the doors opened.

"Surprise!"

"Augur!"

Cece laughed in delight, then caught sight of a soignee blonde woman behind him. "Oh, Renee, I'm so glad to see you. I wanted to thank you in person for the lovely clothes you sent over for Scooby and me!"

Renee laughed. "Liam faithfully reported your thanks. I'm just glad everything fit and that it suited you. Being kept in those cells incommunicado must have been a somewhat maddening experience."

"Not maddening. Difficult, but bearable. Only frightening at the last."

"Oh, you met Sandoval?" Augur perched on the edge of what Cece realized was a very costly antique table. A fine one that had probably once belonged to some emperor.

"Yes." She braced for questions, but no one asked. Of course they would know Sandoval's style, and threats, well enough to surmise what had happened.

Augur said, "We have a rather choice luncheon spread out here, if I do say so myself—"

"Yes, you have," Renee pointed out. "Several times."

"—but," Augur went on, with a fine disregard for interruptions, "I first wanted to thank you, in person, for keeping my name out of your reports."

"Well, I think they knew I wasn't alone," Cece said. "But I figured, since Sandoval went right along with poor Scooby's pretense of being alone, well, I could lie too. And so I did. And I *enjoyed* lying. So if I've been corrupted, well, so be it." She frowned. "I just loathe the thought that Neville Carlton was permitted to walk away without retribution."

"But he wasn't," Liam said, sitting down beside Renee. "He cooled his heels in the ugliest cell I could find, with no company at all. Sandoval wouldn't touch him—and we couldn't. So I gave him a good stretch of boredom in which to consider things."

Cece winced. "Oh, yes. I completely forgot about the possibility that he has some sort of bug inside. Audio bug, I mean."

"He does," Renee said, pouring out a very fine wine for each. "Not that we have direct proof, but the way that Sandoval lost interest was fairly good evidence."

"And so, what? He returns to UCLA?"

"And his studies—if he wants. Academic probation. And most of his group is gone. Marina Aguilara also walked away—I saw to that," Liam said. "And she had quite a tale to tell the kids back home. His house is pretty much empty now. Except for a couple of the real crazy ones."

"But Sandoval will be hearing their plans, right?"

"Not just theirs. My guess is," Renee said with cool irony, "that Carlton will not like being big frog in a reduced pond, so he'll probably try to regenerate his Resistance contacts."

"And our people in Los Angeles know that he's wired." Augur handed Cece a fine porcelain plate. "And so they will smile, welcome him back, and give him all the group hugs he wants—and then they will feed him lots of juicy disinformation, which Sandoval will in turn hear. Please, help yourself."

Cece happily studied the platters of fresh vegetables with delicate sauces, the perfectly prepared fillets of sole, the fruit compote, and sighed. "Where to begin? Problems should always be this difficult."

Cece's mouth was soon full of fresh croissant, and for a time there were no other sounds besides the clink of silver on plates and the murmurs of "Please pass the . . ." and "Thank you."

The conversation ranged out into general talk. Nothing upsetting, nothing controversial. Cece knew it was because she had so resolutely refused to have anything to do with the Resistance. She respected these people. Had come to trust them. But the methods they used in their shared cause were not her methods.

And they understood. Liam and Renee had little in common with Cece beyond mutual goodwill, but Renee was as adept as Cece at the art of pleasant conversation, of making certain there were no awkward pauses or subjects. And so the lunch came to an end.

Liam and Renee fell into a conversation at one end of the cavernous room, over something on one of Augur's computers. Augur remained, his aspect serious.

"I don't know what to say that isn't trite," Cece said, "except that I hope we will see one another again, when there is no dread or danger. You know where I live."

Augur smiled. "Which is, I suppose, your way of encouraging me to stop my shadow life."

Cece shook her head. "I make no judgment. I haven't the right. But possibly, just possibly, you might be happier, someday, finding a place and people among whom you can be yourself."

"I am always myself," Augur retorted but without heat.

"A delightful self," Cece responded, deciding she'd played teacher long enough. "Remember to come visit me."

"I will."

Liam showed her into the elevator, then handed her some folded bills. "Here's money for transportation from your local portal to your home. Is there anything more we can do?"

She smiled. "All I want is my own house, my slippers, my roses, and in a month's time, after the blisters on my feet heal, my own classroom again."

"Remember that we're here." Liam led her across the street to the Mall and to the public portal. He set up the coordinates for her, held out his hand. She shook it and stepped up, pushing up her glasses.

"Hey," a kid's voice chirped from just a few feet away. "Are you Superteacher? Mom! That's Superteacher!"

The ID transfer seized her, shut out the voices, and deposited her in Orange County, California.

EPILOGUE

Of course that wasn't the end.

In fairy tales, in adventures on big and little screen, the heroes get to live happily ever after, but alas, it seldom works that way for real people.

With the word *Superteacher* echoing in her ears, when Cece emerged from the portal closest to her house she felt uneasy, as if people might point and stare. So she tied her blue scarf on again and took a cab home, then realized she'd lost her keys long ago. So she walked around to the back and saw her bathroom window open its usual inch. Forced it open. Shimmied in, scraping her hips painfully on the sill. Plopped down and wandered into the kitchen to find a sour smell. Butter and milk had spoiled in her fridge. Once that was cleaned up, she walked into the living room and winced when she saw the huge pile of mail on the floor. Most of it, of course, was junk, but near the top was a notice of her car having been impounded.

She turned her back on that mess and retreated to her study, to stare at her computer. What awaited her there? She logged on to find more than fifteen hundred E-mails waiting. She scanned the subject headers on the first twenty, growing steadily more appalled and then depressed.

Not one from anyone she cared about. Offers of various kinds, weird rants, threats, scams, and spam was all she found. On impulse she deleted the entire list and shut down the system, feeling she might never start it up again.

She looked with apprehension at the blinking light on her old-fashioned phone machine. With a reluctant gesture she pressed the button, to hear an upset call from her mother, another from her sister, a third from her brother.

Two more from them—progressively more upset—and she deleted all the calls, too.

So she sat there with her chin in her hands, then reached for the phone and dialed Louise Pinochet.

"Hello?"

"It's Cecilia. I'm back."

"Oh, my Lord."

Cece's throat closed up without warning.

"How are you?" Louise asked, her voice sounding both kind and cautious. "Are you all right?"

"Yes," Cece squeaked and then uttered a watery laugh. "At least I thought I was until I got home."

"I paid a boy across the street to water your plants and pick up your paper. Did he do it?"

Cece wiped her eyes and looked out back, smiling through her tears. "Faithfully. I'll pay you back—"

"Never mind that. Are you . . ." Hesitation.

Cece, now mindful of tapped rooms and lines and even persons, said, "I haven't even called my family yet. I don't think I'm ready for hours of hysterics until I convince them I'm really alive. I feel guilty, but—listen, can we get together?"

"The family can wait a few more hours. Meet me at school. We'll go somewhere for a bite."

"At least an hour—I'll have to take a bus." Cece tried to laugh and failed.

An hour later the two women sat at a café on the Huntington Beach Pier. Cece had changed into one of her summer caftans and did her hair up under a print scarf. That and her extra pair of sunglasses seemed to be enough to avoid stares. No one on the bus had looked twice.

Having eaten Augur's wonderful lunch, she was not hungry. Louise was too tense and upset to eat, though she claimed she'd just had a sandwich. So they settled for iced coffee, as seagulls cried overhead, admonishing those strange humans below to drop! more! food!

The rollers swept on, gray-green, smelling wonderfully

of brine, of *home*. Surfers sat out, waiting for a good set, as they had ever since Cece was small.

The world had not completely changed.

She drew a deep, steadying breath and turned her head to find Louise's watchful gaze. Winced. "There can't be bad news. Can there? Did the Taelons do anything to the children in my class?"

"Nothing. Besides an interview. That Da'an came and spoke with ShaNissa and Aisling. Seemed to think one of them might be a budding genius, the one behind Superteacher."

"Good grief! Those poor girls must have been scared to death!"

"Oh, they were, and I hope the fellow felt guilty. If aliens *feel* guilt. Do they?"

Cece sighed. "I don't know. I was around them for only the briefest time."

Louise's mouth corners turned sardonic. "You did look suspiciously matey with Zo'or there, on TV."

"I was zonked half out of my mind with lack of sleep and fear."

"So was it just hyperbole, that about peace?"

"I don't know. What I can tell you is my part. Oh, that day was so horrible."

"Is the young woman all right?"

"Yes. I—she—"

"Start at the beginning," Louise said, laughing. "You know you're going to have to get it all out of your system."

And so Cece did. It took several hours, until the sun began its slow summer slide toward the ocean, lighting up its golden pathway on the sea. They drank another iced coffee, and then had a malt, while Cece told Louise everything. Everything, except Augur's real name, and she made up names for Liam, Renee, and Dr. Belman as well, just in case. Not because she didn't trust Louise Pinochet, but because she wanted to spare her what might become an unwanted burden, if Sandoval did make good his threat.

She talked about Augur at length, until Louise assembled

a fairly accurate portrait of the mysterious cracker who had been the real focus of so much covert back-and-forthing.

"... and appropriately enough, it was at his place that everything ended today. Suddenly. No warning. I thought they would keep me there on some pretext—never spoken—for *months*. But no. Lee walked me out, and we went to Augur's place—which he will change soon, he said, he never keeps one long—and then I came on alone."

"Augur sounds like a brilliant young man."

"That's the word. Brilliant. His mind is like a crystal filled with lights, complex, refracted. Wonderful. But oh, so complex. And I learned much from him."

"Indeed. Sounds like he might have learned a little from you, too."

"I don't know. We can never assume that, can we? We do our best, year after year. We take our students and help shape them and hope that something of what we say will stick." She sat back and sighed. "I feel less horrid now and will feel even better when I get back into my classroom. Never thought I'd miss making name tags and bulletin boards and numbering textbooks, but that all sounds so blessedly . . . normal now."

"Normal." Louise looked out at the blue waters stippled with fire touches from the setting sun.

"What's wrong?" Cece leaned forward, half laughing. "Oh, surely I'm not *fired*."

Louise's brows snapped together. "No. But let me tell you, some want just that. However, I told the district that if they interfere with my employees without just cause, then they can find a new butt for my office chair."

"Did it scare them?" Cece asked, feeling apprehension return.

"Damn straight it did," Louise said, a trace of her childhood New Orleans accent coming back. "Damn straight. They know I'm good, and if I walked, that school would go up like a rocket. As it was, they had nothing against you but notoriety."

"You mean a few seconds on TV that day was that big a

deal?" Cece looked, and was, surprised. "To tell the truth, I didn't think many people watched silly stuff like statue unveilings. I know I wouldn't have."

"You forget. Anything the Taelons do is interesting, because they hold the controls. And those who didn't watch soon saw the clip played over and over on the news, every channel, often with as subversive a commentary as the newspeople dared. Feeling ran quite high, not against the little misguided Charlotte Corday, but against the Taelons for all those guards who were drawing a bead on you. Because the newshounds showed it, you can be sure."

Charlotte Corday: the young woman during the French Revolution who had claimed, right until her beheading, that she had stabbed Marat on her own.

"Meanwhile, your Superteacher went a little wild on the Net over the next few days. Teenagers, mostly, I suspect, and other troublemakers. ISPs wiped her out after a week, when it really got out of hand."

"Out of hand?"

"You don't want to know. And it had nothing to do with you. Your name and face were just conveniently there for people to hide behind who wanted to make various kinds of mischief."

Cece scrunched up her shoulders. "I hope that's the worst of it."

"Nope," Louise said. "Listen. Do you want to wait on all this trash? Remember, you have your job as long as I have mine. Make no mistake about that. I think you're a great teacher—one of the best I've ever seen—and you did nothing wrong. You ran away from a laser beam and stopped a misguided kid from murder. Those are not, last I heard, federal crimes."

Cece wavered, then sighed. "Better give it all to me, or I'll just sit up all night and wonder. Wait. It's parents, isn't it."

Nod. "Of course! And district people, and self-appointed spokespeople for this or that watchdog group. People who use the old saw about where there's smoke there's got to be fire to blame the victim. They've always been around, and probably will be until the Taelons do turn us into high-tech zombies."

"You do sound peeved."

"That's because I've had a peevish few weeks. Never mind. It's quieted down of late, and you're safely back, and we'll go on from here."

Cece began to see why Liam—and Da'an, give credit where it was due—had kept her for the remainder of July. It hadn't been to find out anything, it had been for her own protection.

"Has most of the noise died down, then?" Cece asked.

"Most of it," Louise agreed.

Cece turned her head and watched the last red rim of the sun sink, leaving a clear sky full of stars, deepening in blue toward the east. Blue, the color of Taelons.

She wiped her hand across her face. "Just as well I have a full month, then. I'll need it, to get caught up and to be forgotten. I just want to get back to my teaching. And the way the world usually works, by September I should be ancient history, right?"

Not, she should have realized, when it comes to kids.

Logic usually goes right out the window when human beings feel the first bright fire of attraction, and then again when they have children. There is, at times, nothing so profound as the instinct to protect and conversely nothing so self-righteous as the parent who has made a protective decision based on emotional reaction.

"This is the fourth one this week," Cece said, coming into Louise's office the week before school was to start.

A paper fluttered down onto the desk. They both looked down, saw the marker-written block letters: "No Taelon-lover will teach my kid's." Unsigned, of course.

"Fine awareness of the correct use of apostrophes," Louise commented. "Why is it that the bullies are the most uneducated?"

"Educated bullies are twice as scary," Cece said, rubbing

her temples. She'd been doing that a lot. Headaches had become a regular part of her day. "That one was on my windshield."

The last two had been stuck into her box at school, and one—the scariest—had been thrust under her front door.

"Only four?" Louise commented, brows arching.

"You mean you've been getting them too?"

"Fifteen this week. Only mine are mailed. To the district, and apparently the newspaper, though as yet they seem reluctant to do anything about it."

Cece stared out the window. "Da'an said, before I left, that they don't believe in 'full circle.' I wonder if—no. That's paranoia."

"Da'an isn't behind this covert lynch mob," Louise said, "if that's what you were thinking. No, this is pure human stupidity. I also have the support letters." She leaned over and touched a file. "Three times thicker."

"But it's not going to work, is it?"

Louise shook her head. "I'll back you as much as I can, but only you can decide that question."

Cece stared into a bleak future: parents standing around the campus, arguing for and against her. Not because of her teaching, but because she'd gotten herself tangled up in blue . . . Because she'd become notorious.

Tears began to burn her eyelids, but she clenched her jaw. "I was blind, I think. Augur tried to warn me. Lee, too. Before I left Illinois my friend Phoebe Wingate offered to find me a job out her way, an offer I'd thought odd at the time. But they all saw this coming. I didn't."

"Maybe they've had more experience with the nasty side of human motivation than you," Louise said. "Is that so bad a thing?"

"No." Cece got to her feet. "No." Realized she wasn't going to make it, that she was going to weep like a child. "Listen—can you get Mr. Blaine back as a sub? One thing I have learned this summer is that the kids really liked him."

"He's ready to step in. If you really want to resign."

"Maybe I can come back in a year or two." Cece wiped

her eyes. "I'm sorry. Self-pity is the most ridiculous of human reactions."

"I see devotion, and care, and betrayal, not self-pity. But I don't want to see your gifts sacrificed on the altar of stupidity. So I suggest you reconsider that offer."

"Da'an's TV show?" Cece was so surprised the tears stopped. "You can't be serious!"

"Why not? You're too famous for them to try something sneaky: Use that notoriety for your protection. Meanwhile, you make your standards clear. You set the curriculum, not them. You pick the kids for the TV classroom. Everything on the up and up. And the minute that changes, you threaten to walk. You can squawk for help, and I can name fifty people who would be at your side fast."

Cece opened her mouth, then closed it. Then said, tentatively, "Are you hinting around that you are part of the Resistance?"

Louise gave her a smile more affectionate than sardonic. "Well, I married into the military. Maybe it's a fault of our type." She sat back. "I'd gotten out just before the State of Siege; our numbers were high then, and I didn't always agree with the leaders at the time. Recently I found my way back." She shrugged, and Cece realized that the mockery in her smile was against self, not Cece. "If I'd stayed, I might have recognized Augur's companion, that first morning when we stood outside your classroom, and saved you a whole lot of grief. In short, I think I'm needed."

"Needed," Cece repeated, responding to the time-tested word that hauled teachers back from the brink of the grave. "Needed. Maybe it's me who is at fault. I talk about safety, but I'm not the one watching over others' safety, am I?"

"You decide. Not me. Meanwhile, if you do take that job, you'll be raking in a paycheck that would make a college president weep with envy. That would give you a certain measure of influence. And, best of all, your wonderful teaching would be available to more people than you could ever reach in a classroom."

Cece sighed. "But I—the students—would be lab rats for the Taelons."

"No. Rats aren't aware of their observers. You'd be lab humans, and you would be observing the observers. Learning."

Cece rubbed her forehead.

"Go home. Think. But remember this: Liberty means choices. You have always taught that. In work, in play. Especially in play, with the little ones. Will the Taelons ever see that? In your own way, right under their noses, you can continue to show the way to liberty, because this I'm sure about: Children are utterly alien to the Taelons, at least as alien as the Taelons are to us."

"Yes." Cece made a face. "It all makes sense. Leaving me to E-mail Da'an and eat crow. And wouldn't I look stupid if they've already picked someone else?"

Louise smiled. Cece opened her mouth, then realized that she was now on her own; she had to take responsibility for the rest of her life. It was not Louise's problem.

"Thanks," she said, and they shook hands.

A week later, there she was, walking into her new office overlooking the quake-safe towers all along Wilshire Boulevard, the endless sun shining down on darkened windows.

Cool, filtered air whispered on her cheek. Everything in here was new. Bugged? Of course. Cece turned around to face her new staff. She felt the impulse to fire them all, but of course she couldn't do that, not just on the off chance (oh, on chance, we know it's an on chance!) that they were handpicked by Da'an, and their first loyalty would be to the Taelons. They still were human beings, with lives of their own, so until she had proof, she would smile and talk about education and not trust them much past her next breath.

They left her with the new computer, and she sat down, touched a control. It was the newest model, of course. Almost seemed to have a mind of its own. She turned around and looked out at L.A.'s brownish, hazy sky, thinking of all the millions of lives busily going on.

She had a wonderful task ahead, but also a dangerous one. Good pay, but a staff she couldn't trust. The support of her family, but if something went bad, she couldn't ask them for help—for what could they do, except be needlessly endangered? I'm sleeping with the enemy, she thought. But it's better than guns. Isn't it?

Is it?

If only she wasn't so alone!

She turned away and caught a reflection of herself on the smooth face of her dark terminal. What stared back was not the old Cece she'd been used to, but the new one, with her hair arranged in a sophisticated French roll, her self (which somehow hadn't gained back those two sizes) in tailored shirt and slacks of the sort that Renee Palmer favored. This Cece looked ready for action.

Was she? What was false and what real? Was she really alone?

She sat down and propped her elbows on the desk (almost as nice as Sandoval's—did it come from the same maker?) and touched the keyboard. A desktop windowed up, a blinking light indicating E-mail. How the heck could she have E-mail already, unless it was just the usual load of spam that seemed inescapable?

She activated the E-mail program, and there was a letter.

Curious now, she tabbed it. Instead of a message, a rose bloomed, then burst into fireworks. Through the diminishing bits of light she saw the orangish glint of a pair of glasses, and below, in stylish script: Welcome to the cantina.

Augur!

No, she wasn't alone. They knew that knife edge, all right, had walked it for years, between loyalty and necessity. The constant compromise, the silent protection, the unending struggle until the world was truly free again—*that* was heroism.

And now she was one of them.

She smiled, pulled the keyboard toward her, and got to work.

ABOUT THE AUTHOR

Sherwood Smith is the author of the popular Crown & Court Duel young adult fantasy series and coauthor with Andre Norton of two Solar Queen novels, *Derelict for Trade* and *A Mind for Trade*. She is also the coauthor, with David Trowbridge, of the Exordium SF novels.